Prais

ON A NIGHT
OF A THOUSAND STARS

"With suspense and heartbreak, Andrea Yaryura Clark's debut novel explores the human toll of Argentina's Dirty War, whose atrocities can still upend the most cloistered and prosperous lives. *On a Night of a Thousand Stars* turns one woman's genealogical quest into a searing indictment of the complicity inherent in cultural silence."

—Jennifer Egan, *New York Times* bestselling author of *Manhattan Beach*

"This novel sheds light on a dark chapter in Argentina's history, the effects of the country's worst dictatorship, and the consequences for those left behind and those who survived."

—Greer Hendricks, *New York Times* bestselling coauthor of *The Wife Between Us*

"A powerful debut about a chapter in history that must be told."

—Janice Y.K. Lee, *New York Times* bestselling author of *The Expatriates* and *The Piano Teacher*

"In luminescent prose and exquisite detail, Andrea Yaryura Clark chronicles a family's history through the political turmoil of Argentina's Dirty War and beyond. Both heartrending and hopeful, *On a Night of a Thousand Stars* explores the strength and endurance of love and familial bonds in the face of chaos and tragedy. A deeply moving, timely, and important debut."

—Cristina Alger, *New York Times* bestselling author of *Girls Like Us*

"Andrea Yaryura Clark's deep understanding of the complexity and savagery of Argentine history brings an authority to this gripping novel, a chilling reminder of the precariousness of human rights and the extraordinary bravery of those fighting to preserve freedom for all."
—Lisa Gornick, author of *The Peacock Feast*

"In Andrea Clark's debut novel, she has accomplished the remarkable feat of rendering the political and the human story, telling a painful narrative of lives lost, Argentinian history, and the family. Brava and welcome."
—Roxana Robinson, author of *Dawson's Fall*

"A skillful debut which serves as a reminder that a country's past can never be left in the past."
—*Kirkus Reviews*

"Vividly rendered...Both heartbreaking and race-to-the-end suspenseful."
—*Library Journal*

"A compelling story of a time and place that might not be well known to American readers, as well as a heartbreaking narrative of generational trauma."
—*Booklist*

"History is reclaimed in this magnetic debut, with Clark determined to excavate the past on behalf of its sufferers."
—*Toronto Star*

"You know you're getting some good historical fiction with a title like that."
—Betches

"A rollercoaster of emotion that draws in readers with its characters and depiction of this period in history."
—ScaleitSimple

ON A NIGHT

OF A

THOUSAND

STARS

ON A NIGHT OF A THOUSAND STARS

ANDREA YARYURA CLARK

GRAND CENTRAL
PUBLISHING

NEW YORK   BOSTON

Copyright © 2022 by Andrea Yaryura Clark
Reading group guide copyright © 2022 by Andrea Yaryura Clark and Hachette Book Group, Inc.

Cover design by Sarah Wood. Cover images: embracing couple © Nicole Matthews/ Arcangel; others from Getty Images. Cover copyright © 2023 by Hachette Book Group, Inc.

Grand Central Publishing
Hachette Book Group
1290 Avenue of the Americas, New York, NY 10104
grandcentralpublishing.com
twitter.com/grandcentralpub

Originally published in hardcover and ebook by Grand Central Publishing in March 2022

First trade paperback edition: February 2023

Grand Central Publishing is a division of Hachette Book Group, Inc. The Grand Central Publishing name and logo is a trademark of Hachette Book Group, Inc.

The publisher is not responsible for websites (or their content) that are not owned by the publisher.

The Hachette Speakers Bureau provides a wide range of authors for speaking events. To find out more, go to www.hachettespeakersbureau.com or call (866) 376-6591.

Print book interior design by Jeff Stiefel.

Library of Congress Control Number: 2021041414

ISBNs: 978-1-5387-2030-1 (trade paperback), 978-1-5387-2031-8 (ebook)

Printed in the United States of America

LSC-C

Printing 1, 2022

For my mother

ON A NIGHT

OF A

THOUSAND

STARS

CHAPTER 1

July 1998

I STOOD A SHORT DISTANCE from the polo field observing my father, Santiago Larrea, gallop furiously alongside one of his rivals. Plenty of room remained in the stands at the Southampton Polo Club but, like the players' spouses and friends, I preferred the view from ground level, where I could feel the thundering of hooves, the thwack of mallet on ball, and the churn of mud and grass. Beyond the field, a vista of dense woods seemed to thin out with each passing year, as moneyed New Yorkers continued to fill all available acreage and airspace on the south fork of Long Island with enormous summer homes.

I had arrived late, and now I glanced at the scoreboard. The teams were tied. As always, Dad's team included a couple of ringers he had flown up from his home country of Argentina. Being invited to play for a season on Santiago Larrea's team in the Hamptons was an opportunity that few Argentinian players on the polo circuit could resist. Dad was admired by his fellow countrymen not only for being a top amateur polo player but also for his decades of success as an investor on Wall Street, where he was known for his ability not merely to dodge, but also to anticipate, the region's recurring crises.

The opponent tried to hook Dad's mallet, but the maneuver caused his pony to stumble, and my father pulled ahead. A teammate swiftly smacked the ball his way. My father kicked the underside of his favorite pony, Charlie, and bent to the right to begin his backswing, his torso nearly parallel to the ground. The mallet struck the ball straight through the goal posts.

Seconds later, the bell rang, indicating the end of the last chukker and the match. Dad sat back up, patting Charlie's neck as his teammates trotted in a circle around their captain, clicking their mallets high in the air.

The players on Dad's team rode to the tent at the end of the field that had been set up with folding chairs and a large white cooler of drinks. Dad dismounted and turned to my mother, who had just left her coterie of girlfriends to join him. The assembled ladies had donned their best tournament attire for the occasion, including an array of bright-colored ruffled dresses and an array of hats, from Jacquemus to bolero. Mom had opted for a long, celestial-blue summer dress and espadrilles.

"Lila, did you see that final shot?" my dad asked my mom. "Unbelievably close, but we pulled it off, didn't we, Charlie?" He stroked the pony's snout. As usual, he had saved his best pony for the crucial moments of the last chukker. The steed was dripping with sweat, and Dad handed the reins to one of the grooms.

"You played very well, my dear. You always do," Mom said, handing him a glass of iced tea. He took a long drink.

I picked up my weekend bag and entered the tent. They turned to greet me, but my mother's smile inverted slightly when she saw I was not dressed for the occasion. It was usually acceptable to attend a polo match wearing jeans and a T-shirt, but not at the big charity tournaments as on this particular weekend. Full skirts or dresses below the knee were the norm for women, while men sported khakis, button-down shirts, and blazers. I chose to ignore her frown and kissed her.

"Where have you been, darling?" Dad asked, wiping his sweaty brow with a riding glove before kissing me too. "We thought you were coming out yesterday." My father was unfazed seeing me in a pair of ripped jeans. He wouldn't have cared if I had shown up in sweatpants. He was always happy to see his only child.

I grinned up at him. "I missed my connecting train, but I caught the last chukker. You were great!" It was the summer between my junior and senior years of college, and I had been living with my friend Emily in a sublet in Park Slope, Brooklyn. Express trains to the Hamptons from Atlantic Terminal were infrequent, even at the height of the summer season.

Juan Godoy, one of Dad's players, approached us with a relaxed, bow-legged gait, the result of riding horses since before he learned how to walk.

"Paloma. You are here, finally!" Juan said with a pronounced accent, unbuckling the chinstrap on his riding helmet. His dirty blond hair lay flattened to his forehead.

"Hello, Juan," I said with a smile. "You know I only come to one of these things per season. And only for my dad."

When I first met Juan a few weeks ago at my family's home in Manhattan, he had ignored the unspoken dress code for the dinner party, showing up in a pair of slim-fitting jeans and white T-shirt under a beige linen blazer. He spent most of the evening chatting up an Argentinian actress who was in town promoting a film she'd made with the guest of honor, a well-known Spanish director. So I was surprised when, at the end of the party, Juan sought me out to ask if I would show him around Central Park. His sun-bleached hair flopped down over his honey-brown eyes, firmly centered on mine, seeming to know the answer before I uttered it.

"Well played, Juan," my father said, still beaming from their exploits on the field.

"This has been an amazing season," he said. "I can't thank you enough for the opportunity to play on your team."

"You'll be at the party tonight, yes?" my mother asked Juan.

"It would be my pleasure to spend an evening in the company of the Larrea ladies." Juan touched my shoulder lightly. "Come with me to check on the ponies?" Polo players generally bring at least eight ponies to a match. The six chukkers last only seven minutes each, but that is long enough to exhaust a pony that continuously gallops across the length of a 300-yard field.

The visiting ponies were taken to the trailers, but Dad and his team had use of the stables on the club's grounds. I picked up my bag, but Juan swiftly insisted on carrying it for me. The chivalrous gesture marked one more way in which he differed from most men I had dated up until then. I didn't see myself with him forever, and though he was in his late twenties, seven years older than I was, I doubt he did either. Yet our fling offered a reprieve from the doldrums of a summer in New York City.

"I've missed you," he said, grabbing my hand. "I was lonely at the dinner last night. And you didn't come out to watch our match earlier this week. You're my good luck charm, you know."

"But you won them without me anyway. So it seems you have plenty of good luck charms."

His scent was a pungent mixture of sweat and oiled leather from the horse saddle, sheer masculinity emanating from every pore. The thought made me want to laugh out loud. Instead, I bit my cheek, and, hand in hand, we headed to the stables.

Later that afternoon, more than a hundred guests descended on my parents' summer home, gathering for cocktails on the manicured lawn that sloped gently from the sprawling cedar-shingle structure toward the sea. Every summer, my parents hosted their friends and business acquaintances to a traditional *asado*, an Argentine barbecue, on a night after one of the major polo tournaments.

I was still in my bedroom, where I slid into a sleeveless, black linen dress as the guests arrived. My dark hair, wet from the shower, was pulled back in a messy chignon, my bangs to the side. I picked up a pair of dangling sea-glass earrings and eyed them critically. The wiring was imperfect, but they were one of my first designs and I cherished them.

I had discovered jewelry-making only a couple of years earlier, during the fall of my sophomore year at a small liberal arts college in New England. I was majoring in literature and had little experience in design or craft-making, but decided to sign up for an arts elective in an attempt to stave off the ennui of another long winter. I soon found that the creative process tamed a dull ache of apprehension I had carried inside from a small age. When a few friends began wearing my designs, my roommate Emily suggested that if I worked on the creations, she would find the customers. Emily, who was born to work in marketing, was my first true best friend, and I agreed. Not having thought much yet about what I would do after graduating from college, I fantasized about the two of us opening a boutique in New York.

I put on the earrings and steeled myself for the party. It didn't matter how often I attended one of my parents' events, I was never completely comfortable, and I realized now that I was also no longer really interested. What had once seemed a glamorous and mysterious milieu now felt like an obligation. After one final self-appraisal in the mirror, I made my way down the stairs.

When my parents had bought the beach house some fifteen years ago, my mother had lightened the rooms by installing larger windows and discarding the antique rugs. The expansive living room with its imposing fireplace now had sliding doors that opened onto a covered veranda. The most recent home improvement had entailed swapping out what Mom deemed the dull dark-brown dining room set for a natural blond wood table with cushioned wicker chairs for a more informal beach feel.

After greeting a few guests in the entrance hall, I whisked myself outside, past the blooming rhododendrons, toward the towering white tent erected on the far side of the lawn. Garlands of bistro lights crisscrossed the ceiling, and high round-top tables covered by white tablecloths were decorated with votive candles and small centerpieces of fresh flowers that my mother had ordered from a farm stand a month in advance.

Women came in short or long dresses and delicate flat sandals. Their dates wore linen or khaki pants and colorful sports coats over button-down shirts, along with sockless loafers. Guests sipped champagne and feasted on empanadas passed around on silver trays by the catering staff. These turnovers filled with meat or cheese were the teasers before the main event—a series of different cuts of beef grilled to perfection by a grill master Dad flew in from Argentina every year for the occasion.

Dad enjoyed little more than the opportunity to show off his *quincho*, a purpose-built redbrick structure adjacent to the house that contained an enormous wood-fired *parrilla*. The ritual of grilling the meats provided guests with another form of entertainment in addition to the jazz and tango band. The smell of smoldering cuts and rising smoke drew a mesmerized crowd around the quincho. Watching the maestro (as Dad called him) expertly adjust the cooking temperature of the different cuts by raising or lowering the chain-suspended grates above the natural wood coals was its own spectacle.

My parents were conversing with a small group near the stage. Dad was in an impeccable navy-blue linen jacket and a crisp white shirt. Mom, who never missed a yoga class and religiously protected her skin from the sun by donning wide-brimmed hats and oversize sunglasses, looked much younger than her forty-two years. Tonight she wore a peach-colored silk summer dress over her willowy frame. Her hair was parted down the middle, falling to her bare shoulders.

Both my parents were from Argentina. While my father, like me, had dark features common among his Spanish ancestors, my mother, a granddaughter of British settlers of the Argentine Pampas, had green eyes and blond hair. Her creamy pale skin and faint lingering British mannerisms sometimes confused people. She would briefly explain her family's background and their migration to Argentina after the turn of the century to look after the family's agricultural interests. *The European settlement is similar to what happened in the United States*, Dad might add, as enchanted listeners nodded in understanding.

I reached my parents just as a family friend took the microphone from the bandleader and clinked his glass to call for silence.

"Good evening, everyone. My name is Michael Harris. I'm an old friend and business partner of our host Santiago. Ever since he first moved to New York from Buenos Aires, I've witnessed his many successes both off and on the polo fields." He turned to my father. "I'm happy to say that tonight there's something more to celebrate than just this incredible man, his beautiful family, and his prowess with a mallet—not to mention on the dance floor!" The crowd laughed again. "The official announcement will be in two weeks, with all the appropriate pomp and circumstance, I'm sure, but as a few of you already know, Santiago has been appointed Argentina's ambassador to the United Nations." A few oohs and aahs faded into loud applause, punctuated by a quick bada-boom on the snare drum. "Congratulations, old friend, and *salud*!"

Following the announcement, well-wishers and family friends surrounded our family of three. I fielded the usual questions about my studies and summer plans until Juan rescued me.

"There you are. I've been looking for you. You look gorgeous. Someone wants to meet you." He led me toward a caramel-haired, middle-aged woman raising her hand at us.

"Hi, I'm Paloma," I said. "Nice to meet you."

"Graciela," the smiling woman began to introduce herself, but stopped short as I approached. She looked at me quizzically through tortoiseshell glasses. "Graciela de Graaf, but everyone calls me Grace," she resumed. "Such a pleasure. When Juan told me he was dating Santiago Larrea's daughter, I just had to see you with my own eyes. I knew your father in Buenos Aires, but we lost touch years ago when I moved to Holland."

"Have you seen him yet?"

"Not yet, just from afar. He's been very busy tending to his many guests," Grace said with a laugh. "Like the Santiago I remember, always surrounded by a million friends." She took a caipirinha from a passing waiter. "These are lethal but delicious."

"Let me bring you to him," I offered. "I'm sure he'll be happy to see you."

Taking Grace by the arm, I called out to my parents across the lawn. Dad squinted as we approached but then returned to his conversation with an elderly couple.

"Your parents are just as good-looking as they were twenty-five years ago," Grace remarked.

"You knew my mother too?"

"Oh, yes. Everyone knew Santiago and Lila," Grace said. "I was happy to learn they had a child."

"Really? You sound as if you were surprised."

"I don't know…I guess we didn't talk about having kids back then," she said wistfully. "We were kids ourselves."

"Papá. Mamá. Look who I just met!"

My parents greeted Grace with blank expressions.

"Santiago. It's been a long time." Grace went to kiss him hello, but something in his eyes made her stop.

"Grace Díaz," Dad pronounced slowly.

"It's de Graaf now. I've been married, divorced, and recently re-married. How's that for a good Catholic girl? Terrible, I know!" She laughed. "But I keep reminding myself that I made a much better decision the second time around. Anyway, you must meet Erik. He's here somewhere." She gestured vaguely out toward the party.

"We'd love to meet him," Dad said. He turned to my mother. "Can you believe it, Lila, after all these years? It's Grace."

"Incredible," Mom said. "How have you been?"

"This is an unexpected surprise," Dad added. "What brings you here to the Hamptons?"

"We're staying with the de Konings. My husband and Dirk are childhood friends." By my father's expression, I could tell he didn't register the name.

"You all knew each other in Buenos Aires?" I chimed in.

"Uh, yes, that's right. Grace and I studied law together at the Universidad de Buenos Aires," he said, becoming animated as he mentioned his alma mater. "My God, that building was falling apart inside even then. And the hours we spent at the library! It turned out to be a monumental waste of time, at least for me. But we had fun, didn't we?"

"Yes, we did," Grace said with a laugh.

"My goodness, it sure is good to see you again," he said, kissing her lightly on the cheek.

"I think an encounter like this deserves a toast," Mom said. She lifted her empty champagne flute and signaled to a waiter. As the waiter refreshed our glasses, Grace's husband Erik ambled over.

After Dad shared a couple of stories from their law school days that had everyone laughing, Grace turned to me and said, "Your father hasn't aged at all."

"Like many men my age, my hair is getting thinner and my waist is growing thicker," Dad said with his typical self-deprecating charm.

"You mean to say that you have a *thin* waist and *thick* hair!" Grace laughed, calling him out on his false modesty. She spoke to him in a familiar tone, and it delighted me to see the affection between him and an old friend.

He was remarkably fit and slender in middle age. His dark brown hair, brushed back with a hint of gel, had only recently started showing silver near his temples, enhancing his distinguished looks.

"He was the most handsome man in our class," Grace said to the group. My father raised his hand in protest. "No, no, Santiago, don't try to say otherwise. You were quite a catch."

As his daughter, I hadn't really been aware of my father's charisma until one night at my high school's winter festival when I overheard a couple of senior girls in my class agreeing that if they were going to have an affair with an older man, they'd go for someone like Mr. Larrea. Then they giggled at some of the other dads with bulging bellies, weak chins, and receding hairlines.

Grace continued. "The problem is you *knew* it. But I think our friend Máximo came in a close second. Wouldn't you agree, Lila?"

"Aren't most twentysomething-year-old men good-looking? You know, when you're that young?" Mom suggested casually, but her tone was slightly pitched. Dad and I knew well enough that this only happened when she was nervous. Mom gripped her champagne glass while smiling politely at their unexpected visitors.

"I see that life has been kind to you," Grace said to my father.

"It's true. I've been blessed." Dad put a protective arm around Mom.

"Not so for some others we knew."

"Those were complicated times, Grace. Anyway, now's not the time for boring old stories."

"Boring?" Grace turned to me. "Paloma, I wonder how much you know about Argentina during those years."

I glanced at my parents. Talk of Argentina's military dictatorship in the 1970s had been taboo in our family for as long as I could remember.

"Sadly, not much," I told Grace.

"Well, I think you should be aware that thanks to your father, many people were spared—"

"I said not *now*, Grace." My father's sharp tone startled her into silence. He opened his mouth to say something else but then closed it again.

Grace looked at him with a pained expression before turning on her heel and walking off.

"I didn't mean to upset her," Dad mumbled without quite looking at anyone. "She has a good memory, but that really was a long time ago." He turned to Erik. "I'm sorry if I was abrupt."

"Not at all. I should be the one to apologize for her," Erik said. "Sometimes she likes to talk about the old days in Argentina, especially if she's had a drink or two. She's been an expat for years now, so I think she was excited to see an old friend from university. I'm sure you understand."

"Of course. No need to apologize, please."

As soon as Erik left, Mom turned to Dad.

"She still has eyes for you, that's clear enough," my mother said. She was long accustomed, if not resigned, to the effect her husband had on women.

I hadn't given much thought to my father's life as a bachelor, but Grace's remarks made me wonder: What had he been like as a young man?

"Grace is stuck in the past," Dad said. "It happened to some people...they haven't been able to move on. I did. That's all."

"But she said people's lives were spared because of you," I said. "What did she mean by that?"

It was not often that I was on the receiving end of one of my father's withering looks—a look he'd bestow on a housekeeper when a shirt had not been pressed properly or when the coffee was not prepared to his liking. But when he spoke next, his tone was gentle.

"Ancient history, sweetheart," he said.

My parents then turned with wide smiles to a group of approaching guests, signaling the end of the discussion. I wandered around the edge of the lawn to the front side of the house, where cars lined the driveway. I glimpsed Grace and Erik in the back seat of a sedan. The rear window rolled down.

"Paloma." Grace smiled at me. "I really enjoyed meeting you."

"Me too. I'm sorry about my father. I hardly ever see him like that. I don't know what came over him."

Grace took a moment before answering. "When you get to be my age, you tend to focus on chance encounters that, at the time, seemed like nothing of consequence but later turned out to be defining moments."

"I don't follow."

Erik murmured into Grace's ear.

"My husband's right. I'm not making much sense right now. Time to go." Grace reached her arm through the window to press my hand. "Have you heard of the Argentine writer Martín Torres?"

"No."

"You should look for his books. He's a fantastic writer. Take good care."

Before I could react, the car pulled away.

I tossed my sandals in the general direction of my closet and tugged and cursed at the fabric of my dress caught in the zipper. It finally gave way, and I pulled on a pair of sweatpants and a T-shirt. Coco, our cat, slunk into the bedroom and brushed my leg, announcing his presence. I scooped him up, his warm body like a balm on my skin.

"You're still my one and only, even if you abandoned me for Mamá."

I sat at my desk, opened my laptop, and connected the line to the phone jack, waiting impatiently for the dial-up modem to proceed through its sounds. Once logged in, I typed "Graciela de Graaf" and "Graciela Díaz" into a search engine and found zero relevant results. I changed it to "Grace" and alternated in both last names. Still no luck. Faint sounds of music, laughter, and clinking glasses floated through the open window. Then I looked up Martín Torres and dozens of entries appeared. A brief biography about the acclaimed Argentine author explained that he had lived exiled in Spain during the South American country's dictatorship but had returned to his homeland a few years after democracy was restored in 1983. I added "Santiago Larrea" to "Martín Torres" as an additional search term, and I came across his Jorge Luis Borges Award acceptance speech from 1988.

> …Among the people I want to thank this evening, I am particularly grateful to Santiago Larrea. Without him, I wouldn't be here standing in front of you. He was one of the few who, in his own way, took action…

Why had Dad never talked about Martín Torres, and what did he do that was important enough for Torres to mention him in a speech? Also, what did Grace mean when she said my dad had "spared people's lives"? Coco rubbed my leg. I stroked the fur between his shoulder blades and looked out the window. There was no longer any music. The party had ended.

CHAPTER 2

June 1973

Libertador Avenue, on any typical weekday morning, was a stream of buses and cars. Today, however, traffic was at a standstill across all five lanes in each direction. An accident? A broken traffic light? Santiago Larrea couldn't see what was going on and regretted not having walked to class. He shifted his Volkswagen Beetle down to first gear and looked mindlessly out the window at the upscale apartment towers along the boulevard to his right. His family's apartment was just beyond these high-rises, in Recoleta, the neighborhood that gave Buenos Aires its fame as the "Paris of South America." Jacaranda trees, which would burst into clusters of purple blooms in October, lined the small green parks that bordered the avenue and dotted the neighborhood.

As his car crawled toward the colonnades of the Universidad de Buenos Aires law school building on the left, Santiago noticed an unusually high number of people passing him on foot. He recognized one of the students and rolled down his window. "Are classes canceled? Is there another strike?"

"It's Perón. We're going to the Ezeiza airport to welcome him home."

General Juan Domingo Perón, the former president of Argentina, had been living in exile since being ousted in a military coup d'etat eighteen years earlier. Nonetheless, his presence still towered over the country's politics, and he retained millions of loyal followers. During his absence, instability and polarization had taken root, fueled by the rise of guerrilla groups on the left and paramilitary groups on the right. In March, Argentina conducted its first national election in a decade. Héctor José Cámpora, a stand-in candidate for Perón, narrowly prevailed, paving the way for the exiled general to return and reestablish himself on the political stage.

Santiago thanked the student and drove on, shaking his head, slightly embarrassed. He had forgotten about Perón after his late night out. He turned off the avenue and found a parking spot on a side street. The weather had turned cold with the arrival of winter in the Southern Hemisphere, but in his haste, Santiago had forgotten his jacket. He wore blue jeans and a button-down shirt under a navy V-neck sweater. With the momentary ebb of military rule and the prevailing fashion of the time, Santiago, like many Argentine men, let his hair grow out. It fell to his jaw and he wore it combed back.

At a newsstand by the Café de las Artes he noticed the same headlines across all the papers:

PERÓN RETURNS
MULTITUDES MOBILIZE TOWARD EZEIZA TO AWAIT THE LEADER OF JUSTICIALISM

Santiago picked up a copy. The photo on the cover showed a triumphant Perón outside his home in Madrid. Standing next to him was his third wife, María Estela Martínez de Perón. Familiarly known as Isabelita, she had been a cabaret dancer when Perón met her early in his exile.

Café de Las Artes was a favorite among students, mainly for its proximity to the School of Law and the School of Social Sciences. While it had none of the old charm of the city's grand historic cafés, like the Richmond or the Tortoni, it made up for it with a young and exuberant clientele. A long, oak-paneled bar ran along one side in the style of an English pub, but for the most part the students sat at crowded round tables, pushing aside the stainless-steel napkin dispensers and small bowls brimming with sugar cubes to make room for notebooks and newspapers.

Santiago spotted his friend at a table in the back corner. Her chestnut bangs grazed her tortoiseshell glasses as she sat there reading. Although her given name was Graciela, the anglicized version, Grace, had been her nickname since childhood. Her features were plain, but no one noticed, due to her quick tongue, tenacious personality, and bohemian flair. She was wearing a buttery leather jacket over beige corduroy pants and a black cashmere turtleneck.

He kissed her cheek and sat down.

"You're late," she said.

"Sorry, Grace. Traffic's a mess. You could've started reviewing without me."

"Class is canceled. There's no exam."

"Well, that's a relief," Santiago said, still feeling the effects of too little sleep and too much alcohol from the night before.

Grace stubbed out her cigarette and stood up. "Don't get too comfortable. You're coming with me."

"Where?"

"We're going to Ezeiza."

"The airport? Why? It's going to be a nightmare. A million people are expected to show up."

"Santi," Grace said, calling Santiago by his nickname. "Come on. Give me a ride! Let's embrace this historic occasion."

"But I'm not a Peronista."

"I know, I know. You're strictly a Larrea-ista," she cajoled him.

"I'm going back to bed," he said, picking up his backpack.

"No, you're not," she said and nudged his back. "We can tell our kids one day we were there at the airport the day Perón came back from exile."

After touching down in Ezeiza, Perón was planning to give a speech from a temporary stage that had been erected for the occasion in an open field ten kilometers from the airport. It was a strange setup for a major political address, but Perón wanted to speak directly to his followers as soon as he landed and didn't want anyone else dictating the logistics of his return. In a show of power against Cámpora, the seventy-seven-year-old caudillo had rejected possible alternative sites within the city that Cámpora's team had suggested, such as the Plaza de Mayo, the capital's main square, or the base of the Obelisk monument that rose up 221 feet from the middle of the widest avenue on earth, the fourteen-lane Avenida 9 de Julio.

Santiago envisioned a chaotic drive to the outskirts of the capital, but he finally agreed. "Fine. You owe me one, Grace," he said, as she nudged him toward the door.

"Don't worry, it'll be worth it," she teased him. "I'll introduce you to that cute girl you've had your eyes on in our civil procedures class."

They drove northwest out of the city, then looped back southwest onto the highway toward the airport. The road was congested in both directions. When they couldn't drive any farther, still a mile or so from the airport, they parked the car on one of the flat fields by the side of the road, and joined the throngs of people. It felt to Santiago like a pilgrimage.

The procession of two million people took on a festive tone. Students, couples, and entire families with their children were walking hand in hand, singing the Peronist anthem and taking photos of each other waving the peace sign. While living abroad, Juan Perón had taken on mythical proportions, even as his Justicialist Party had split into right- and left-wing factions. Many believed his return would bring back the good union jobs, affordable food, and other benefits that Perón was credited with bestowing on them during his two terms in office. Others, including students who had come of age during his absence, thought it would bring about a social revolution. Santiago, however, wasn't one of those students, and he suspected that neither was Grace. But she was a curious, enthusiastic type, and she enjoyed being part of something bigger than herself.

They came into view of a large podium outside the International Airport Hotel where Perón would address the gathered supporters. Behind the platform hung enormous smiling posters of Perón and his iconic second wife, Eva Duarte. Evita was a country girl and aspiring actress whose biggest role would be marrying the great caudillo and becoming the first lady of the Argentinians. A champion of workers' and women's rights, Evita died from breast cancer at the age of thirty-three. The *Descamisados*, or Shirtless Ones—the poor workers who were part of the backbone of Perón's political support—worshiped her as a saint: Santa Evita.

Perón's chartered plane from Madrid had yet to land, but the crowd was already pressing forward to be as close as possible to the stage. Santiago and Grace stayed back. It was pointless to try to advance further. As the morning wore on, Santiago's impatience changed to irritation. Grace was talking to a woman carrying her baby in a sling. He was about to tell Grace he was leaving when his restless gaze drifted over the sea of humans undulating across the flat green fields on both sides of the highway.

Suddenly, a few popping sounds drew his eyes back to the stage. Near the front, individuals were crumpling to the ground. Only then did he realize that the popping sounds were gunfire. Snipers had infiltrated the masses, and the shots seemed to be coming from all directions. He spotted men with rifles in the treetops. From the stage, men were shooting randomly into the crowd.

Santiago found himself jostled from all sides. The odors from strangers' bodies assaulted his nostrils. He felt a crush, and then a stranger's breath in his face as he stumbled to the ground. Grace had fallen too. Santiago, who knew from shooting at his family's ranch how much harder it was to target a moving animal, yelled at Grace to run.

They pushed and shoved to get away from the stage until the crowd thinned out and they were at a safe distance. Pausing to catch his breath, Santiago looked back at the scene they had just fled. Around the stage and beyond, piles of bodies remained flattened on the ground.

"What the hell is happening?" Santiago shouted.

It took barking orders from police megaphones to get Santiago and Grace, unable to tear their eyes away from the mayhem, to start running again and not stop until they reached his car. Their faces were streaked with dirt. Her pants had ripped at one knee. His sweater was soiled. Only when Santiago struggled to turn the key in the ignition did he notice how much his hands were trembling.

CHAPTER 3

August 1998

THE SUNDAY MORNING AFTER THE asado, I went for a run on the beach and met Juan and his friends for lunch before they headed back to Manhattan. My mother, ever the proper hostess, occupied herself with the houseguests until their departure, then retreated to her bedroom with one of her headaches, which seemed to come on during moments of stress or tension. My father was distant, and I took this to mean he was still annoyed with me for pressing him for more information about Grace the night before.

Since this had been our last interaction, I was surprised when my father phoned me a week later to tell me that he and Mom were planning to spend a couple weeks at the ranch in Argentina before his swearing-in ceremony, and asked me to join them. "If not for my sake, it's been ages since you visited Abuelo at the ranch," he said. In his voice I heard amends, and he called me Palomita like he used to when I was little.

I did not accept the invitation on the spot, but the opportunity intrigued me. Until the conversation with Grace, I had always believed my family, like many of the Argentine elite, had not had their lives disrupted by the dictatorship. But her words cast doubt on that account. My father's comment echoed in my head: "Some people remained stuck in the past, but I was able to move on." Move on from what, exactly? I called my father back a few minutes later to tell him I would come.

On a muggy, hazy evening two weeks later, I met my parents at JFK airport for the overnight flight to Buenos Aires.

Dad greeted me with a kiss. "Now that you've left us for Brooklyn, I feel like we never see you anymore."

I could have spent the summer in Manhattan enjoying the comforts of our family's Upper East Side apartment, but when Emily asked if I would go in with her on a summer sublet, I didn't hesitate. I had grown accustomed to the freedom that came with going away to college, and my parents' place felt less and less like home.

My mother embraced me and said how nice it would be to have us all together at the ranch. Mom usually complained about going back to Argentina, whereas I always looked forward to it. Maybe that's why I had a strong bond with my father. His decades on Wall Street had done nothing to diminish his pride in his heritage. Well before his diplomatic appointment, he had been an unofficial ambassador for Argentinian arts and culture. In contrast, my mother seemed to notice only what was wrong with the country, its corruption and endless crises, constantly comparing it to what she believed to be the superior examples of England, where her parents had recently retired, and the United States.

My family's ranch, Estancia El Pinar, was located a two-hour drive west from the suburban sprawl of the outer ring of Greater Buenos Aires, in the heart of the Humid Pampas region. This agricultural area, considered to have some of the most fertile soil in the world, encompasses nearly 250,000 square miles of flat land that spans several provinces. For a brief period of time in the early twentieth century, the region's prodigious exports of grain, oil seed, and beef placed Argentina among the top five wealthiest nations in the world, notwithstanding the chronic instability of its politics and the corruption of the governing classes. "Whatever the politicians steal during the day grows back at night," the old saying went. But after eight decades of relative stagnation, it no longer held true, even as a joke.

It had been three years since my family had last been to Argentina, and the flight turned out not to be as bad as I remembered. As soon as the airplane cabin went dark, I fell asleep, my book open on my lap. Only when the captain's voice came on, announcing the beginning of our descent into Ezeiza airport, did I finally emerge from a dull sleep.

My father had already received diplomatic credentials from the consulate in New York, and this allowed us to breeze through customs. A porter took our baggage as we exited the customs zone into the chaos of the arrivals area. People from the various kiosks promoting taxis and buses into the city noisily competed for passengers, pressing flyers into their hands and asking for their final destinations. Families, friends, and drivers holding up signs with clients' names jostled for space behind rope barriers.

"Mister Ambassador." A driver in a coat and tie stepped forward.

"Not just yet, but thank you, Daniel," Dad said with a broad smile. "Good to see you." They shook hands.

Daniel turned to my mom with a bow. "Mrs. Larrea, I hope you had a good flight."

"Thank you, Daniel. We're a little tired but glad to be here," answered my mother, looking perfectly well rested.

After Daniel instructed the porter to follow us with the luggage, we navigated around the crowds and approached a car with tinted windows illegally parked by the curb. Under the gray morning sky, the humid winter air felt refreshingly cool against my skin. The porter loaded the suitcases into the trunk while Mom arranged herself in the back seat. As my father was tipping the porter, a slim man in a dark blue suit walked up to him.

"Mr. Larrea?"

"Yes?"

"For you."

The stranger handed him a folded letter without an envelope, which my father briefly glanced at. I couldn't read what it said but saw that it had been written by hand. It didn't look like official ministry correspondence.

I got into the car with my mother. "Are you coming, Papá?"

Dad folded the note and joined us in the back seat. At his signal, Daniel shifted into gear and the car pulled away.

A few miles after leaving the airport, we passed a shantytown where children were playing soccer on a patch of dirt. A couple of mangy dogs barked and chased after the ball. Denser concentrations of dilapidated housing projects gradually replaced the brown grassy fields as we approached the city, and we soon found ourselves in the tail end of the morning rush hour. Small Fiats and Peugeots weaved in and out of their lanes with little or no respect for the painted lines. Gripping the door handle, I shut my eyes each time a car cut in front of us. My parents, unfazed, chatted with Daniel while the morning radio talk show blared from the backseat speakers.

Dad had instructed Daniel to make a stop in the city center before heading to the ranch. Paperwork was being held for him at a government office near the presidential palace. We took the steep ramp off the elevated highway onto Avenida Entre Ríos. With relative ease, we sped along the tree-lined avenue before making our way to Avenida de Mayo. I leaned my forehead against the window and peered up at the sloped gray roofs of the grand Haussmanian buildings along the stately old boulevard running down from Congress to the presidential palace.

As we emerged onto the circular Plaza de Mayo, a wide public square surrounded on all sides by government ministries, I saw a group of about three dozen older women marching slowly around the Pyramid monument in the square's center. Each one wore a white headscarf, some embroidered with a name and a date. The large placards they carried bore black-and-white photos of mostly young men and women with their names underneath: Jorge Ocampo, María Ester LaCroix, Carlos Caballero, Olga Agüero. Below some of the photos, the word *DESAPARECIDO* was written in large black letters. The women held the signs on what looked like broom handles. Many wore angry expressions while others appeared simply weary.

"The Madres de Plaza de Mayo," Daniel explained, when he noticed in the rearview mirror that I was staring at them. "Those poor mothers. They won't stop coming to the square until the government tells them what happened to their children. They're here every Thursday. It's been twenty years now."

The traffic halted, and I lowered the window to better hear their chants.

¡Queremos nuestros hijos!
¡Con vida los llevaron!
¡Con vida los queremos!

(We want our children! You took them away alive! We want them back alive!)

"Not knowing what happened to your son or daughter must be awful," I said. I knew about the Madres de Plaza de Mayo but had never seen them in person on the few visits I had ever made to the city.

When the car moved again, my father said, "Look, Paloma. My swearing-in ceremony will take place there, in the Casa Rosada." He pointed to the seat of Argentina's executive branch, a sprawling Spanish Colonial building with a pink façade known as the Pink House.

"Impressive. Looks like I'll have to take you more seriously from now on," I replied teasingly.

"It would be about time, wouldn't it?" he said, smiling.

CHAPTER 4

June 1973

TEN DAYS AFTER THE MASSACRE at the international airport, Santiago and Grace returned to class, still rattled by what they had witnessed. Following a tedious day of committing pages of cases and statutes to memory, they were glad to escape the confines of the library. It was a chilly night and raindrops were beginning to fall as they hurried north up Avenida Figueroa Alcorta toward their destination. Cracked and buckled cement in sections of the sidewalk made for an obstacle course until they finally found the awning of an elegant building to shelter them from the driving rain. Santiago stepped out into the street and hailed one of the few empty cabs.

The taxi eventually pulled over in front of a nondescript apartment building in Palermo. Lugging book bags, they climbed the stairs to the fourth floor. Laughter and music could be heard from behind one of the doors. Santiago knocked, and when no one answered, they let themselves in.

After helping Grace out of her coat, Santiago waited as she tugged her fringed suede miniskirt over her cable-knit tights. He hadn't been keen on going to a party, preferring to grab drinks and dinner somewhere quiet, but once again Grace had talked him into it, telling him that their friend Máximo, whom they hadn't seen in days, would be there. She was about to remove her glasses and hide them in her coat pocket when Santiago caught her wrist.

"Grace, you look good. Come on. Let's get a drink."

They inched their way through the room until they spotted Máximo in a corner.

Máximo Cassini, when Santiago first met him, wore his hair short and slicked down, parted to one side. Now his friend had let his wavy hair grow long and had developed a nervous habit of constantly smoothing loose strands behind his ears. Judging from his dark stubble, Santiago guessed that Máximo hadn't shaved in some time. That, combined with his aquiline nose and strong jaw, gave him an effortless allure. The black leather jacket that he wore year-round had been a wardrobe staple since the beginning of their friendship.

They had met during the first semester of law school. Santiago and Grace, already in the habit of studying together, had stopped by Café de las Artes after class for coffee. Máximo was sitting at a corner table, smoking while reading. They recognized him from one of their classes, and Grace went to his table to ask for a light. Without saying a word, Máximo rose from his chair and pulled out a book of matches. Santiago introduced himself with a firm handshake and then sat down at Máximo's table, uninvited. He ordered three cortados, and soon the three of them were comparing notes on classes and professors.

The waiters left them alone until just before closing time, when the lights dimmed and most of the chairs had been stacked upside down on the tables. They continued their conversation along Libertador Avenue until Máximo glanced at his watch and told them he had to turn back to catch his bus at Retiro station.

Máximo was from Quilmes, a working-class town south of Buenos Aires, where his father, like his father before him, was employed at the Quilmes beer plant. On a good day, bus number 22 got him home in about fifty minutes.

Before parting ways, the three promised to meet the next day at the library. Over the next few weeks, it seemed to some of their classmates that they had become inseparable.

Máximo was huddled in a corner talking to the host of the gathering, a leftist student leader named Enrique Medina. He had a slight build and wore a mustache and wire-rimmed glasses that enhanced his brainy reputation. They were talking about the massacre at Ezeiza airport. Newspapers reported ten, then thirteen, then sixteen deaths. Hundreds were injured, but exact numbers were never confirmed. In addition to undercounting the casualties, Enrique said the newspapers had also failed to report that some people had been sequestered in the airport hotel's rooms, where they had been questioned and tortured.

After Enrique finished his report and moved on to another group, Máximo went over to Santiago and Grace. Santiago put his arms around his two friends before either of them began talking.

"I think I've had my fill of politics for the day. What do you say? Time for a drink?" Santiago said.

"Sure. But when was the last time you took an interest in anything political anyway, Santi?" Máximo asked with a wry smile.

The makeshift bar was in the kitchen. A sangria pitcher sat empty on the counter. Santiago grabbed a knife and a couple of lemons. Máximo took the other knife and set about cutting an orange with enviable precision.

"You're too slow, *che*! Nobody's going to admire your cutting skills," Santiago complained.

"If you cut fruit in a sloppy way, it ends up mushy in the wine."

"Who cares?"

"Always arguing, you two. I'll show you how it's done," Grace said, grabbing an orange from Máximo's hand.

Neither man showed any interest. Their attention was now on a woman in a long black skirt and a puffy-sleeved white chiffon blouse standing nearby. Long dark curls framed her face. She was alone but appeared at ease listening to the music. Someone called out to the woman, and Santiago and Máximo followed her petite frame with their eyes as she crossed the room.

How had Santiago not noticed her before? He put down a half-cut lemon and, with his trademark devil-may-care grin, said to Máximo, "I saw her first, friend."

"She's all yours," Máximo replied with a brief shrug of his shoulders, and returned to cutting the fruit with Grace.

Holding three full glasses of wine above his head and energized by the thrill of a new potential conquest, Santiago deftly moved through the crowd to where she sat. When the woman noticed him standing in front of her, she gazed up from under dark eyelashes. Santiago felt the unusual sensation of a sharp tug in his chest. It was as though his heart were rebelling against his brain, which was mostly hardwired to conquer and move on. Bewildered, he looked to her for an answer. But she had turned back to her companion, indifferent to Santiago's inner turmoil. He would offer his heart, he thought. No, he would insist she take his heart. As she talked to her girlfriend, seemingly unaware of him, he understood his heart was no longer his.

The wineglasses, when he lowered them, brought him back. He bent down to the woman's eye level, but again he became distracted, this time by her nonchalant beauty. He searched for words until he came up with one that made sense.

"Thirsty?"

"Yes, thank you," her girlfriend replied.

His composure regained, he sat down beside them. The woman gave him a quizzical look but silently accepted the sangria.

"I would like to drink to your happiness," Santiago said, raising his glass. "Here's to...wait. I can't drink to you if I don't know your names."

The other one giggled. "I'm Florencia. I'm in your torts class, remember?"

"Oh yes, of course. How are you?" Santiago said, not having a clue who Florencia was.

He was usually distracted or daydreaming, not paying attention to his surroundings unless Máximo or Grace were in the same class, in which case, they'd be all seated together, uninterested in the others. Some students didn't attend classes, preferring to study at home or in the library, showing up only for appraisals, which were mostly in the form of oral exams held in front of a panel of professors from the department. But Santiago enjoyed the sport of academic banter and preferred the ritual of going to class and then meeting up with Máximo and Grace at the library or Café de las Artes.

The musicians started playing a Cuban folk song, which Santiago recognized as "Hasta Siempre, Comandante," and the woman, who had not given him her name, got up to join them. Santiago watched her close her eyes and open her mouth to sing the lyrics. The song was a reply in verse to Ernesto "Che" Guevara's farewell letter to Cuba, which he sent before embarking on his ill-fated journey to bring revolution to the South American continent.

Santiago prepared to follow the woman, but Florencia had moved over so that their knees touched. When he didn't respond to her advances, she understood.

"You don't have to stay with me just to be polite. It's obvious you want to be with her. Go on. Her name is Valentina."

CHAPTER 5

August 1998

Aꜰᴛᴇʀ ᴀ ꜱʜᴏʀᴛ ꜱᴛᴏᴘ ᴏᴜᴛꜱɪᴅᴇ an administrative building off
the Plaza de Mayo, we arrived at the ranch a couple of hours
later. The car drove through a gate built with heavy trunks of wood,
past the familiar wooden post that read *El Pinar* and down a packed-
dirt lane lined by a single row of pine trees. Flat fields extended
out on either side as far as the eye could see. We continued on a
gravel road and came to a stop in front of a colonial home with
whitewashed walls and a red clay roof.

A couple of barking dogs came barreling toward us, announcing
our arrival.

"At last!" My grandfather, Alfonso Larrea, smiled widely as his long-
time nurse, Karina, pushed his wheelchair out the main door.

"Come to me, Paloma!" he ordered.

"Abuelo!" I hugged him, feeling his bony shoulders through his
wool sweater.

"Papá, how have you been?" Dad took my grandfather's hand,
bending to kiss his cheek.

"It took a fancy government appointment to get you to come

visit your own father," Abuelo responded gruffly, but when Mom approached, he smiled again.

The hundred-year-old property was a hacienda-style house consisting of four wings connected by an interior garden. Far from a rustic farmhouse, El Pinar was filled with exquisite antiques and furniture, an eclectic mix of colonial and European art acquired in Argentina and on my grandparents' trips abroad.

Once we had refreshed in our rooms, we reconvened in the cavernous dining room. Standing lamps and a tiered chandelier brightened the space. When I was a kid, the chandelier was fitted with real candles, and I remember half hoping the wax would drip down on the table during one of our meals. It made for a thrilling pastime while the adults engaged in long conversations. The chandelier now flickered with electric candles. Not as dramatic, I thought, but infinitely more practical.

Lunch consisted of roasted lamb and potatoes with butter and chives, accompanied by a bottle of Mendoza malbec. I had a glass of wine and then stuck to club soda, which I sprayed into a glass from a violet-colored soda syphon. After my favorite dessert, flan with dulce de leche, was served, we moved to the living room.

A maid had left a tray with coffee and tea on a square leather coffee table. Abuelo and I settled into a game of backgammon. Mom pulled a beige merino wool wrap around her shoulders. It was a drafty room, and Dad, who had poured hot cups of tea and coffee for the group, stood up again to build a fire. My grandmother, Constanza, had died a few years earlier, and evidence of her absence was everywhere—in the burned-out lightbulbs in the chandeliers, the rips in the leather upholstery on the living room chairs, tired-looking mementos on display, and the pile of yellowed newspapers that Dad was now crumpling into the base of the fireplace.

When the kindling crackled and flames shot up the sides of the logs, he turned to my mother. "How's that?"

"Better, thank you." Her eyes had been scanning every room since our arrival, taking mental notes on what needed to be discarded, replaced, redecorated.

Checking on the fire occasionally, Dad had sat down to read one of the national newspapers.

Abuelo blew into his cupped hands and rolled double sixes. "Ha!" he said, and smiled..

I conceded defeat. "When will I ever beat you, Abuelo?"

"Play another one?" he offered.

Karina entered the room. "Don Alfonso, it would be good for you to get some fresh air before your siesta."

"Join me, Paloma?"

"Sure."

Far off, sheep and cattle grazed side by side in the field. Lustrous shoots of grass were essential to producing the world's best beef. The property was also scattered with the eye-catching *cortadera*—known in North America as pampas grass—that easily grew to over six feet. I remembered past summers when these tall golden grasses bloomed into translucent feathery tufts, beautiful to look at as they fluttered and rustled in the wind but razor-sharp to the touch. One of the ranch hands tipped his beret in our direction as he led some horses back to the stables. We reached the brick-and-adobe quincho that housed the grill next to a long picnic table with benches. The swimming pool had been covered with a tarp for the winter.

When we arrived at the pond, Abuelo asked Karina to help him out of his wheelchair. We put our arms around his waist and lifted him up. He straightened out his back until he was as tall and regal as he had once been. We gazed out across the pond to the endless open fields that stretched to the horizon, all of it Abuelo's land. It felt worlds away from New York, but it also felt like home.

"My father bought this land from a Scotsman, James Warwick," Abuelo said, making a sweeping gesture with his hand. "Poor fellow had had enough of the gauchos and their stubborn ways." He gave a mischievous grin, knowing perfectly well that it was the work of the gauchos that made the ranch thrive. "Now we have sixty thousand head of cattle and thousands of hectares of the most fertile cultivated land on earth." He looked at me lovingly. "One day, this will all be yours."

I smiled but felt a knot in my throat. Years ago, as a small child, I heard a farmhand say that El Pinar and the Larreas' other agricultural interests around the country could produce enough grain to feed the entire population of Paraguay, Argentina's impoverished neighbor to the north. What had I, Paloma, accomplished to make me worthy of such an inheritance? The immensity of such a privilege and responsibility felt overwhelming, so my response had always been never to think about it.

"Don't say that, Abuelo. You have many more years in you!"

Abuelo instructed Karina to remain with the wheelchair, and with my support, he carefully placed one foot in front of the other. We stopped in front of an enormous weeping willow.

"It's really grown!" I cried. "I remember when we planted it."

We walked around the drooping branches that created a natural canopy.

"These trees grow three meters a year in this soil. Your father and your tío Bautista didn't show much interest in the ranch once they became interested in girls." He leaned his weight against the trunk. "But there's no denying they were both born with a gift for riding horses."

I snapped off a piece of bark and took in its earthy scent. "The other night, one of Dad's friends from law school came to Mom and Dad's annual summer party in the Hamptons. I've never met any of his friends from his university days. What was he like back then?"

"Like most men at that age, he wasn't thinking with his head half the time. His mind was certainly not on his studies."

"Was it because he was involved in politics?"

He snorted. "Please. We've always maintained a neutral position when it comes to politics. For the Larrea family, business comes first."

"But was he *against* the military government?"

His smile faded. "Are you asking me if your father was a subversive?"

I decided not to press him. "No, I was just curious."

A few gauchos on horseback were herding cows toward an adjacent field. The men were a majestic sight in their berets, billowy white shirts, and loose-fitting trousers, with small kerchiefs tied around their necks and long knives tucked into their sashes. Their feet, fitted in *alpargatas*—espadrilles with soles of knotted rope—nudged the horses' undersides. They galloped in large figure eights, coaxing the cattle onward. One of the gauchos broke away and rode up to us.

"Sánchez! Hola!" I called out.

The gaucho dismounted from the horse, removed his beret, and bowed his head. Oblivious to any protocol, I hugged him. His weather-beaten face lit up, and when he smiled, his eyes narrowed into thin ovals framed by deep wrinkles. I noticed his wide leather belt decorated with silver coins. I suddenly pictured myself incorporating old coins into thick leather bracelets and made a quick mental note to sketch this idea in my notebook.

"Señorita Paloma. It's very good to see you again." His steel-gray hair was matted down from the beret, which he held with both hands. Sánchez's father had worked for *el escocés*—the Scotsman—and when my grandfather acquired the property, his family had stayed on.

"How's Josefina? And the grandchildren? They must be so grown up by now!"

"Everyone in my family is well. Thank you."

My grandfather interrupted. "Did you get that cough checked yet?"

"It's nothing, Don Alfonso. I've been drinking my wife's infusions, and I'm feeling better."

"Please tell Josefina I'll come over later to give her a hug," I said.

Sánchez nodded and, in spite of his advanced age, mounted his horse in one swift move. Watching him, I had a thought. Maybe Sánchez knew more about my dad during the 1970s and the early days of the dictatorship. They were close. After I waved goodbye, Abuelo and I walked back to his wheelchair and returned to the house in silence.

Abuelo and my parents retired to their rooms early that evening, but I was not ready to go to sleep. I ventured past the library to the empty living room, my eyes roaming over the threadbare carpets, the jagged cracks in one corner of the ceiling, the peeling paint around the doorframes. To me, the history of the house was told not just in its beautiful objects but also in the old or broken-down pieces that had yet to be replaced or had been abandoned altogether. So very different from my own mother's need to constantly switch out the old for the new.

I continued wandering through the house and ended up in the mudroom. I grabbed a lantern and went outside.

The sky was ablaze with stars. When I was little, my father would take me outside after dinner and teach me about the different constellations. The Southern Cross with its five bright stars hovered right above. When was the last time I had seen a constellation or taken the time to search for a single star above the Manhattan skyline? It had been so long since I had visited El Pinar that I had forgotten how much I loved it.

The temperature dropped slightly, and I began to feel cold. I was turning back when I noticed a light in a window of Sánchez's house.

"Señorita Paloma. Is everything all right?" Sánchez asked when he opened the door.

"Yes. I wasn't sleepy so I went out for a walk and saw that your light was on. But it's too late, isn't it? I'm sorry. I'll come back tomorrow to visit Josefina."

"Josefina went to bed, but please, come in. I was just going to prepare *mate*."

The house, though small in size, had everything to ensure comfortable living. To my right was the living room with a fireplace and sheepskin rugs. To my left, a dining room with a table for six. The kitchen, straight ahead, was small and clean, equipped with the basic necessities.

Sánchez filled a stainless-steel kettle with water from the tap. "Will you drink it bitter?"

"I prefer it sweet."

He added a sugar cube to the yerba mate tea to cut the bitter first taste of the grassy infusion. He poured in the hot water, waiting for the dried leaves and twigs to steep a bit before adding another pour. He inserted a metal straw and took a few sharp sips. I bit into a biscuit while he filled the gourd with more water. The mate filled me with a sense of comfort.

"I don't drink mate in New York. There's a grocery store in Jackson Heights where you can get yerba, but I never get around to going there," I said, handing him back the mate after the straw made a slurping sound.

"How are things in Nueva York?"

"Good. I'm about to start my last year of college."

"In the city?"

"A couple hours outside." I finished the biscuit. "Speaking of New York, when are you going to visit us?"

"I don't think this old gaucho would do very well in such a big place."

An image of him walking up and down Fifth Avenue in his South American cowboy gear made me grin. "We could use a gaucho in New York." I leaned back comfortably in my chair. "It's so nice to be here. Too bad we don't come more often," I said, handing him back the gourd.

As Sánchez tipped water from the kettle into the tea, I decided to ask him about Grace.

"I met Graciela Díaz the other day. She and Papá studied law together. She mentioned the days of the dictatorship and implied that Dad had been involved in helping people somehow."

Sánchez raised the metal straw to his mouth and took two quick sips.

"She seemed like she wanted to say more about it, but Papá didn't let her get into it. And when I asked him about it later, he blew me off too." I looked at Sánchez, but he didn't comment. "I don't know what to make of it. I also mentioned it to Abuelo today, but he seemed annoyed by my question."

Sánchez rose from his seat to reheat the water and suddenly doubled over from a bad cough. He waved me away when I stood up too.

"I remember Señorita Grace," he finally said. "She was a close friend of your father's. And then I believe she moved away. At least I never saw her again."

"She lives in the Netherlands now. That's probably when they lost touch. I wish I knew more about him during those times."

"Your father doesn't like to talk about certain things," he said, looking more serious. With his hands flat on the table, he said, "I'm going to share something with you, Paloma, but you have to promise you'll keep it to yourself."

"I promise." I playfully traced an X over my heart, but his expression was somber.

"Only God knows how much time I have left. And I think this is something you should be aware about. He's your father," he said, as if persuading himself. "Those were years of violence, but most of those kids had good hearts. They wanted a better world. What Señorita Grace told you is true. Your father did good things. He was a brave man."

I leaned forward. "How? What did he *do*?"

"He kept a safe house."

I looked at him, puzzled.

"He built a place to hide people who were being hunted down by the military. I helped him build it."

"But, Sánchez, I would think he'd be proud to have done something like that," I said. "Why would he keep it to himself?"

"I don't know, but I doubt he ever talked to anyone about it. In those days, you never knew who would betray you or who, under pressure or torture, might succumb and reveal names." He paused. "I'm fairly sure your mother never knew about it. He wanted to protect her. Your father saved a lot of lives, but there were many more people he wasn't able to help. I think it broke his heart."

"Did the writer Martín Torres ever stay here?"

Sánchez looked at me, surprised. "Yes, he did. How did you know that?"

"I didn't. It was a hunch. I came across a speech Martín Torres gave when he won an award, and he mentions Papá."

"Torres is now a professor at the University of Buenos Aires. He publishes articles in the newspapers from time to time." Sánchez paused and stood up slowly from his chair. "Now I've told you enough. Go get some rest, and please take the advice of this old man. Leave the past in the past."

CHAPTER 6

June–July 1973

THE NIGHT SANTIAGO MET VALENTINA Quintero at Enrique's party, he asked one of the musicians to play the tango "El Día Que Me Quieras" (The Day You Decide to Love Me). Emboldened by the wine, he serenaded Valentina on one knee. Máximo and Grace observed, amused, from the sidelines. Valentina's face reddened, but she let him get through the first couple of verses before vanishing behind a group of students engaged in a drink-infused argument.

The apartment was hazy with cigarette smoke and overheated from the young bodies crammed together. Someone had raised a window even though it was still raining. Santiago found Valentina talking to Florencia, who periodically scowled in his direction. Undeterred, Santiago walked over brandishing a winning smile and asked Valentina to dance. Florencia, acting like Valentina's chaperone, folded her arms and shot her friend a cautionary glance. Valentina hesitated, and before she could answer, Santiago's hand was on the small of her back. She opened her mouth to resist when his other hand gripped her waist, drawing her to him and away from her friend. His closeness, his hands on her body, all of it felt right. As if she had been waiting for his touch.

Without speaking, they moved in perfect synchronicity, both aware of the heat radiating between them. The song came to an end too soon.

Santiago said, "I can't believe I'm just laying eyes on you for the first time. Are you a first-year law student?"

"What makes you think that?" she asked with a faint smile. His face, so near, was making her light-headed.

"Oh, I don't know. I assumed because Enrique is in law school and I recognize most everyone here, but not you. Social sciences then?" The School of Social Sciences was housed in the same building as the School of Law.

"My friend, Florencia, is studying law."

"You mean the one who seems to disapprove of me, without even knowing who I am."

"That's the one. Oh, and she knows you. She was just starting to fill me in on your reputation."

"What reputation? I'm just trying to get through life in one piece." Another song came on, and he sashayed them away from probing eyes. "Are you studying? Or are you one of the lucky ones who already gets to do something more exciting?"

Valentina raised her finger to her lips. Santiago was at least a head taller, and he had to bend down to hear her. "Don't tell anyone, but I'm in the School of Architecture." She was talking into his ear, and her breath caused a stirring deep inside him.

He whispered back, "Your secret's safe with me."

Florencia popped up beside them. "Are you ready to leave?" she asked Valentina. "This is getting a bit boring. And I'd like to go to the other party before our curfew."

Valentina looked at Santiago. He pursed his lips. He felt he had jockeyed himself into a good position. No words were needed to express what their bodies were telling them, and he also knew better than to get on her friend's bad side. Valentina would decide their fate, he thought, smiling broadly at the two women.

"But we just got here. Let's stay a little longer, yes?" Valentina said, and, turning to Santiago, asked, "You must have someone you can introduce to Florencia."

"Sure. How about my friend Máximo?"

"Máximo Cassini is here?" Florencia asked. And she left the couple alone in search of Santiago's good-looking (when not brooding) friend.

Valentina and Santiago slipped out of the party without saying good-bye to their friends. Outside, the rain was slowing down to a drizzle, and he took her underneath an awning, waiting for the drops to fully subside. Neither one of them would be able to explain how it happened, but when his lips slowly traveled up her throat, the world slipped away. The wail of an ambulance, the roar of a cab without a muffler, the splash of cars driving over puddles were muted sounds. His thumbs traced her jawline as he reached her mouth, waiting. She tasted like sweet oranges. They stopped only to catch their breath. Two university students walking by suggested they get a room. This jolted them out of the universe they had discovered in each other's embrace. They detached slowly and laughed.

Santiago swung his knapsack over his shoulder and clasped her hand. "Where do you want to go?"

Florencia wasn't kidding about their midnight curfew (two a.m. on weekends), but if they walked in the direction of her student residence they could stretch out their time together.

After walking a block or two, kissing intermittently, Santiago said, "So, architecture. Tell me, how did you make that decision?"

"I think I always knew. I built my first house when I was eight."

"What?"

"For my dolls."

He kissed her again. "Are you going to be Argentina's next César Pelli?"

"Pelli's from the interior provinces, like me, and I admire him, but I'm not interested in buildings as monuments. My ambitions are simple: to build houses for the poor. I believe everyone should have a roof over their heads. Now you tell me. Why law?"

"Process of elimination?" He smiled, shrugging. "I don't have a particularly strong reason, but I enjoy most of the classes." Not wanting to get any further into a boring topic with this mesmerizing woman, he changed the subject. "About those dollhouses. Do you still have them?"

"Yes. Of course. They're in my bedroom back home."

"Will you show me?"

"My home's in Córdoba. That's about an eight-hour drive."

"I have a car," he said, gesturing back in the general direction of his neighborhood. "Should we leave now?" He was grinning, half joking, but if she said yes, he would turn them around to get the car. This woman made him feel capable of many things.

She laughed, swatting his shoulder. "I can't. I have classes tomorrow!"

Unwilling to call it a night when they were close to her residence, Valentina introduced him to La Paz, a corner café frequented by social-ists, atheists, and poets alike. It was after midnight, but the place was full. Men and women, from university students to people who looked to be of retirement age, sat around brown wooden tables, smoking cigarettes or the occasional pipe, drinking espresso or frothy glasses of beer. A few individuals sat comfortably alone, reading a book or flipping through the evening edition of one of the dailies. Two couples entered and sat behind Santiago and Valentina, dissecting the movie they had just watched at one of the palace movie theaters on Avenida Corrientes. A man and woman paused on the sidewalk to chat through an open window with another couple they knew seated at one of the tables.

After ordering coffee and whiskey for the two of them, Santiago glanced around, taking in the atmosphere, picking up snatches of conversation. Books, theater, soccer, politics.

When the waiter set down their drinks, Valentina said, "I hope you don't mind my telling you that your face is perfectly symmetrical but for your nose."

Santiago was, by all measures, considered a good-looking man, but he did have that one flaw. His nose sat very slightly askew to the right of his face. One noticed when examining him straight on, which Valentina was doing at that very moment.

Her hand reached out and he guided it to the bridge of his nose. "See how it moves back and forth?"

"Yeah."

Instead of squirming at the movement of the cartilage, Valentina was grinning. He liked her reaction and brought her hand to his mouth for a kiss.

"A few years back, I was fooling around on my horse and fell off. Got smacked right between the eyes and I've been too chicken to have it put back in place. Having my nose deliberately broken to reset it...you know? I couldn't bring myself to do it. Only one of my nostrils is fully functional."

He had never confessed this particular fear to anyone, ashamed as he was, and it dawned on him that he had shared it with a woman he hardly knew. Smiling slowly, he saw in Valentina someone with whom perhaps he could be entirely himself.

"I think your nose is perfect. You could pass for a boxer if you weren't so slender," she answered, still grinning.

"I'm sure I could fight in the lightweight category." He jokingly posed with his fists curled in front of his face, imitating Argentina's world middleweight boxing champion, Carlos Monzón. He lowered his hands and his voice, not sure he wanted the bohemian crowd to hear what he said next. "Boxing isn't actually my sport. It's polo."

Self-conscious about the fact that polo was an elite sport, sometimes referred to as the sport of kings, Santiago was usually circumspect about bringing it up in conversation. He had lived his first twenty-one years in privilege and comfort that he sometimes found embarrassing. Fortunately, however, his parents were dutiful practicing Catholics who were not given to ostentation, and they had been sure to raise him with a certain set of values. He would get a university degree and a job, and contribute to the world in a meaningful way.

From a very young age, he had been conscious of these advantages. Santiago never showed up at El Pinar in his prep school uniform, and as soon as his parents gave him permission, he would run to the stables looking for Sánchez, the farm manager, to help out with the horses. When he and the farmhands' kids went on horseback rides, he would insist on taking the most volatile or unpredictable horse. He didn't want to be shown any favoritism. When he entered the Universidad de Buenos Aires—a free, public, internationally prestigious national university in which students from all economic backgrounds enrolled—he took to keeping his personal life private.

But tonight he was not in control of his narrative. He was blissfully lost in Valentina's gaze. Her amber eyes fixed on him.

"I've played polo my whole life."

To which she simply responded, "I love horses. There were stables not far from my house. My grandmother—she's the one who really raised me. My parents work full-time—would take me after school. We'd get to see the horses being fed and groomed, or if they were riding in the park, we would buy chocolate bars at the *kiosco*, sit on a bench, and watch. They're beautiful animals. One year, she saved enough money and got me riding lessons for my birthday."

"She sounds like a wonderful grandmother."

An energy flowed between them, and Valentina was communicating things about herself she normally wouldn't divulge so readily. "She is something else, truly ahead of her time. She's the one who encouraged me to study architecture, move to the capital, and see the world before settling down." Valentina gazed out the large window at Avenida Corrientes, lively with pedestrians at this late hour. Buenos Aires was only the start of her journey, she thought.

"So I have her to thank for bringing you here," said Santiago.

"I wonder what she'd make of you." Valentina cocked her head comically. "For starters, she might be suspicious of your movie star looks."

"What?"

"She warned me about men who are too good-looking. They never seem to be satisfied with just one woman. And single women don't seem to mind dating a married man if he's beautiful." Valentina's grandfather's affair had come out into the open shortly after he died, when her grandmother received a visit from the mistress he'd been maintaining.

"Even with my nose?"

"She wouldn't care one way or the other about your nose."

"But that's not fair. You can't hold my looks against me."

Tilting her head the other way, she said, "But I think she would approve of your good manners." Long ringlets fell over her wide cheekbones, and he used this opportunity to touch her again by gently moving them off her face.

"Manners I can do. Abuelas love me," Santiago said, staring at the natural shade of her lips, a crimson red. It was all he could do to keep from kissing her.

"Do you know anyone from Córdoba?" she asked.

"Not really."

"Have you ever been?"

"No. Not yet."

"Life happens at a much slower pace over there."

"If I were with you, I'd want time to slow down."

As Valentina chatted more about her grandmother and her family, growing up an only child in a pleasant middle-class neighborhood, he dreamed about tasting her mouth again.

"I can't really hear you with all this noise," he said and shifted his seat next to hers. He lowered his eyelids. Her regional accent was like an incantation, and he found himself falling under its spell. Could she hear his heart quickening with want? When he opened his eyes, he saw she was rising to put on her coat.

"I didn't realize what time it was. I'm going to be really late now."

The sky was growing lighter. Janitors were already sweeping and splashing water on the sidewalks outside before the morning rush.

On Valentina's block, the storefronts were the typical shops of a middle-class neighborhood: a vegetable stall, a butcher, a bakery, a café, a laundry service, and a hardware store. Further up the street was a *milonga*, a tango hall frequented by mainly middle-aged neighbors, couples, and singles who were serious about practicing this intricate form of dance that originated in the port districts along the Río de la Plata in the late nineteenth century.

Valentina stopped in front of a building with a sign that read, *Residencia Estudiantil. Women Only.*

The building, gray and unassuming, had once been a large *conventillo*, a hotel for turn-of-the-century Basque and Italian immigrants. A few years ago, the building had been redesigned as a residence for students moving from Argentina's provinces to the capital city to attend university. The Universidad de Buenos Aires was among the most prestigious on the continent and attracted students from other countries as well. On her floor, Valentina's neighbors included women from Peru, Colombia, and Paraguay.

The superintendent greeted Valentina and grabbed the large ring of keys dangling from one of his back belt loops. He was also from Córdoba and tended to look the other way when Valentina returned after hours.

Valentina turned to say good night to Santiago, who said, "You're going to marry me." He didn't care if the superintendent heard. The whole neighborhood could be listening and he would still joyfully declare what was in his heart.

"But I just met you," she said, laughing at his presumptuousness.

"We have the rest of our lives to get to know each other," he said, feeling that he had known her his whole life.

"Well, getting married is not in my plans," Valentina began, but when she met his gaze, in her heart she was able to clearly glimpse a future. A frisson rippled through her. He was right. It seemed inevitable that they were meant to be together. She sensed they would experience immeasurable love but also terrible pain that would tear at them both. But then, perhaps because the vision scared her, she swiftly dismissed her premonition.

"You're mad," she said.

"Yes," he agreed. "About you."

The following day, Santiago waited at the coffeehouse across from the residence. A bouquet of dahlias from the flower stall down the street rested on the table. He had rung the bell at the residence a few hours earlier and was informed that Ms. Quintero was out for the day. He didn't know Valentina's schedule, having forgotten to ask her such mundane details the night before.

He had woken up late that morning in a state of ecstasy, remembering their night together. But the more he thought about it, the more he began to doubt himself. Did she feel the same way about him as he did about her? He dressed quickly, kissed his parents good morning and goodbye, and went out to find her. When he located her residence, he relaxed a little. He hadn't dreamed her up. The excitement of seeing her again, combined with the fear that he also might never see her again, was new to him, and this heady confusion of feelings led Santiago to forget about everything on his calendar that day. He missed his class. He missed meeting Grace at the library, and he missed lunch with his godfather, an old friend of his father's. The café offered *minutas*, quick meals like pastas or breaded cutlet sandwiches, but he had no appetite for food.

Santiago lit his tenth cigarette of the day. He wasn't usually a big smoker, but inhaling the smoke soothed his nerves. It was while smoking his eleventh cigarette that he spotted her through the café window, walking slowly, carrying her books in both arms. Her head was slightly bowed, like most pedestrians seeking to avoid dog poo or a crack on an uneven sidewalk. She was wearing the same belted brown corduroy coat and a pair of beige suede booties. She looked up then, and her chocolate-colored curls floated around her face. He ached to run his fingers through those curls.

Throwing down some pesos on the table, he started for the door, realized he'd forgotten the flowers, retraced his steps, glanced at his reflection in the window, and rushed out to meet her.

"Santiago! How did you know I'd be coming back at this hour?"

"I didn't." He wanted to say, *I've been waiting for you all day, unsure if I'd survive without seeing your beautiful face again,* but he stopped himself. The night before, he had told her he was going to marry her. He didn't want to come on too strong now. He remembered the pink dahlias in his hand and stuck them out unceremoniously. He had never bought flowers for anyone but his mother. His movements were awkward, stiff. What if she had woken up today feeling differently? What if she turned him away?

"These are for you."

"Thank you," she said, smiling, but her hands were full and she couldn't take the bouquet.

"May I?" He carried her books, and together they walked the hundred steps or so remaining to the dorm's main entrance.

"Wait for me here," she instructed him, taking the books and flowers. Male visitors were not allowed inside.

In high spirits, Santiago pulled out his cigarettes, noticing he was down to less than half a pack. When his foot crushed the smoked cigarette on the sidewalk, he wondered what could be taking her so long. As he paced, the door opened and the custodian stepped out. Santiago thought he would be asked to leave. But the squat man in his bluish-gray pants and shirt, a uniform for superintendents, merely nodded and went to chat with his pal running the kiosco next door.

The kiosco man greeted the custodian with a handshake.

"*¿Vio?*" the custodian said, looking up at the sky. "*Es un día Peronista.*"

It was an expression that Santiago recognized from the early days of Peronismo. On October 17, 1945, hundreds of thousands of protesters from working-class neighborhoods mobilized to the Plaza de Mayo to demand Perón's release after he was arrested for criticizing the establishment. This fervent demonstration of loyalty would catapult Perón to his first presidential term the following year. And October 17 would forever be celebrated by Peronists as the founding day of their movement.

The expression "un día Peronista" had since morphed into a phrase to describe a day with clear skies and mild, spring-like temperatures. It was a perfect day, Santiago silently agreed with the custodian.

At last, Valentina emerged. Pinned to the lapel of her coat was one of the dahlias.

"I put the rest in a borrowed vase. Do you like how it looks?"

"I do." He told her the pink flower contrasted beautifully with the brown coat and the color of her skin.

At this, she smiled. Then she rose to the balls of her feet and, as if it were the most natural thing in the world, she put her arms around his neck and kissed him deeply.

Their new love made them immune to the political instability around them. They spent every possible moment together. He took her to a small resort town on the Atlantic coast. Located just north of the large coastal city of Mar del Plata, the town's wooden houses were designed to blend into a pine forest by the water.

"I haven't been to the ocean in forever!" Valentina said, removing her shoes and running down the beige-colored sand. He followed her, hopping along, trying to roll up his pant legs. The water was too cold for swimming, but immersing their feet delivered a bracing jolt up through their bodies. The cries of the gulls sent Santiago's mind to summers past, and he pictured Valentina with him at his family's beach house farther north in Uruguay.

A dog appeared seemingly out of nowhere. The little white mutt with brown ears observed them as they dried their feet and slipped back into their shoes.

"He's cute. I wonder where his owner is." Valentina scanned the beach. It was empty.

"He might not have one. He looks like a stray."

The dog, hearing Santiago's voice, pricked up his ears and came over to sniff him. Santiago noticed that the mutt wasn't putting any weight on his back leg.

"He has a limp." Santiago knelt. "I wish there was something we could do for you, buddy," he said, putting out his hand. He stroked the dog's scruff and, when he'd gained his trust, examined his hind leg. "He must have broken it a long time ago. The bone reset itself unevenly. See? This leg is shorter than his other one."

"You're so good with him."

Through the dog's hair, Santiago felt his ribs. "He needs to eat."

"Let's see if he follows us, and we can get him some food," Valentina said.

They set out back toward the sandy road; there were no paved streets in the town. The salty sea air grew sweet from the pine trees. The dog, whom they started referring to as Buddy, limped up ahead, turning to see if they were still coming, occasionally returning to their side.

It was the off-season, but they found a *parrilla* restaurant willing to serve them lunch. The only other customers were a couple of older men playing chess at another table.

They ordered steak, fries, a salad of tomatoes and marinated onion, and a bottle of red wine. After they'd finished eating, Santiago took the meat remaining on a bone and wrapped it in paper napkins from the bar.

Buddy was waiting outside.

"What if he's lost?" Valentina asked as the dog wagged his tail at the sight of them.

"He's from here. I'm sure he belongs to a pack."

Santiago unfolded the napkins, revealing a chunk of meat on a bone. The bone was bigger than the mutt's face, but he easily snapped the meat in his jaws and, with a flourish as if to thank them, trotted away with an uneven gait.

They went back inside the restaurant.

After ordering dessert, Valentina commented, "You must have had lots of dogs growing up."

"A few over the years, but only at the *campo*. Never in the city. When we were little, my brother and I asked for our own puppies, but my father said a city apartment was no life for a dog."

"Are you close to your brother? You never really talk about him." Valentina had yet to meet the Larrea family. The lovers, without needing to say it out loud, wanted to stay in their own world as long as possible.

"Bautista? Of course. He's my brother. He lives in Spain, and neither one of us is great at writing letters."

"I wish I had a sibling. I would have been happy with just one, but I grew up around a lot of cousins. When I was fifteen, my mother told me that giving birth to me, she lost a lot of blood and we almost died, the two of us. I think she was trying to tell me why she was overprotective. I was going out a lot then, and she worried too much. It took a lot of convincing for my parents to agree to my moving to Buenos Aires," said Valentina.

"But you're at the best architecture school in Latin America. They must be proud of you."

"They're old-fashioned. They would have been happier if I had married my ex and stayed in Córdoba."

Pouring them each another glass of wine, Santiago asked half-jokingly, "Your ex? You mean, there were others before me?" He did and didn't want to know.

"Patricio. We grew up in the same neighborhood. He went to the all-boys school. He's studying to be an engineer." A handsome enough man with straight-as-a-board hair and expressive dark eyes, he had been a sweet and considerate boyfriend. They had been together off and on through most of high school, and it struck her that not once had he made her feel what she felt with Santiago.

"He, too, wanted me to stay in Córdoba." She shuddered lightly. "Getting married at nineteen, having kids. Not for me." She smiled then. "We only get one life, and I want to live it. I mean, *really* live it. I want to travel, visit all the architectural marvels of the world."

Taking a bite of her dessert, she asked, "What about you? Girl-friends? Florencia warned me she had seen you with different women around the school."

"They were friends. And now that I've met you, and we're together…" He didn't finish the sentence. Holding her gaze, he didn't have to.

It rained the first night of their trip, into the next day. They spent it in bed, exploring their desires in a way they hadn't been able to until then.

In the city, her dorm was out of the question. A few times they had stolen into his room after his parents had gone to sleep or to the ranch.

Once, they went to a hotel he knew that rented rooms by the hour. It had been Santiago's idea, but with her in the room, the suggestive decor all at once appeared to him as garish and demeaning. It was Valentina's first time in such an establishment. When she sat on the bed, she gasped and then laughed. The mattress was moving under her. A waterbed! When she asked him to join her, he said no, it was not worthy of her. It was beneath their love. But, rising to meet him, she changed his mind.

In the beach hotel, a chalet tucked in the woods, they did not let go of one another except to get a glass of water, use the bathroom, or go out for meals.

One night they snuck out to the deserted beach. There were no streetlights, and the sky was brilliant with countless stars and moonlight that guided them down the path. They took a blanket and towels to improvise a shelter against a sand dune by a cluster of tall shrubs. Nipping at each other, they fumbled with buttons and zippers under their coats. They giggled and hushed one another when they thought someone was approaching. After they made love, he ran his hand along her body.

"Valentina?" he asked, whispering. "Are you tired?"

"No," she whispered back.

"Do you want to go back inside?"

"I want to stay like this until morning."

They smiled at one another in the dark.

"I told you about my dreams. What about yours?" she said, resting her head on his shoulder.

"I don't know. I used to spend hours lying on the fields at El Pinar looking up at the sky, studying the constellations. I found comfort in the stars, even if I didn't have a clue about what I would do with my life. The one thing I knew for sure was that I loved horses. There was nothing my mom could say to make me get out of bed on a school morning, but at the campo, I was up at the first light of day with the other men, feeding the ponies, cleaning out the stalls, grooming my favorite horse. I would have been eleven years old at the time. We were playing a pickup polo game when one of the ponies, Zorro, snapped his hind leg. We had to put him down. I watched, and it was awful. I couldn't wrap my mind around the fact that a horse I loved would have to die because of a broken leg. And that's when I decided I would become a vet. I was going to discover a cure for broken legs. Not one other horse would ever have to die because of it."

"And what happened? What made you change your mind?"

"A few years later, when it was time to apply to university, I found out what it would take to get through veterinarian school. I didn't get any encouragement from my family either. My dad told me I'd be needed to help manage the family affairs, not cure sick animals. We had a veterinarian already, and he was a damn good one too, better than I would ever be."

"That's terrible, Santiago."

His lips brushed the top of her head. "My father's a rancher. When he married my mother, they inherited land and cattle from my grandfather. He bought El Pinar, and that's where I grew up when we weren't in the city. I expect to join him somewhere down the line. Meanwhile, studying law is a convenient way to finish my education."

"You don't sound excited."

He stroked her hair. "It hasn't been bad. I study just enough to get decent grades, and I enjoy some of the debates. But my heart is in the campo."

Valentina lifted her head and peered into his eyes. "So what I'm hearing is that you portray yourself as a man of the world, a cool urbanite. Yet at your core, what you really are is a simple country boy."

His sigh was one of contentment. She understood him. Like no one else ever had. Aroused, he kissed her, thinking he would levitate from happiness. He didn't tell her how small and insignificant he felt under the immense rural skies. But while she lay in his arms, he saw in the stars a universe of possibilities for the two of them, and he wept silent tears with a joy that seemed infinite.

CHAPTER 7

August 1998

T HE CLOCK ON MY ANTIQUE bedside table read 9:30 a.m. I forced myself to pull back the sheets and thick wool blanket. By El Pinar standards, it
was late. The tiled floor was cold under my feet, and I hurried to get dressed.
After my visit with Sánchez, I had stayed up most of the night thinking
about my father and the safe house. Why hadn't he ever mentioned it? I
wished I could talk to Grace, but I didn't have her contact information.
As I drifted off with the first rays of morning light filtering through the
shutters, I decided I would go to Buenos Aires to find Martín Torres.

I had promised Sánchez that I would keep our conversation secret,
but at the breakfast table, as I kissed my father, I couldn't imagine *not*
saying anything to him.

I kissed my mother next. "You could have taken a minute to brush
your hair, dear," Mom said, just loud enough for me to hear. My bangs
fell over my eyes, and a tangle stuck out from the back of my head.

"I overslept and didn't want to miss breakfast," I muttered.

I tried to thread my fingers through the tangle but gave up after
a couple of attempts. Since I'd left for college, my mother seemed to
delight in pointing out my flaws. As if she couldn't forgive me for moving
out. *Argentine children live at home until they marry,* my parents reminded

me up until the day they helped me move into my dorm room. I reached for the sugar bowl and knocked over a glass of freshly squeezed orange juice. The thick liquid spread over the white linen tablecloth.

"If you had asked for it instead of reaching across…," Mom said, exasperated, raising her eyes from the *Buenos Aires Herald*, the English-language daily in Argentina.

"I know. Sorry. You're right," I said, dabbing the wet spot with a napkin.

"Come here next to your abuelo." My grandfather patted the chair to his right.

I sat down beside him, determined not to let my mother's foul mood affect me.

"Did you sleep well?" Abuelo asked, pinching my cheek affectionately.

I hadn't, but I said yes, giving him a grateful smile.

I ate silently, my parents' and grandfather's heads shielded by the newspapers.

Later that day we rode horses around the property, and when we returned, tea and biscuits with apricot jam were waiting for us on the dining room table.

Roaming the property on horseback always put Dad in good spirits. We had spent the whole weekend together, and I knew he would be fine with what I said next.

"I'm going to Buenos Aires tomorrow. Juan invited me to dinner."

Juan had returned to Argentina a few days after the polo match and had told me to be in touch when I arrived. I hadn't called him yet, but I didn't want to give away my real reason for going to Buenos Aires.

"Of course, sweetheart."

"Is it all right if I spend a few days at Abuelo's apartment?"

"Absolutely," said my grandfather. "You can sleep in your father's old bedroom or the guest room, wherever you prefer. I'll let Celeste know you're coming."

"You'll bring Juan back for a visit, won't you?" Mom asked. In my mother's eyes, Juan was the perfect suitor. Whenever I mentioned his name, her mood brightened.

"I hadn't thought of bringing him out here, but I'll invite him, sure," I said, and suddenly wondered if dating Juan had been an unconscious way of seeking Mom's approval.

"Daniel will drive you in," Abuelo informed me.

"I'll take the train."

Mom pointed to the newspaper. "It says here that there might be a railroad strike."

"You have your credit cards, right?" Dad asked.

"Yes."

"Take some money too. Check in my coat. I should have some pesos in my wallet. And take dollars, in case you run out."

Dad's coat hung on a hook by the front entrance. His wallet was in the right-hand pocket. When I pulled it out, a piece of paper fell to the floor. I picked it up and unfolded it. Snail-like shapes doodled in fountain pen lined the borders. It was the note the man had handed to my father at the airport.

Welcome back, Santiago. Shall we meet at our usual café? Don't disappoint me. I'll be in touch. As I'm sure you remember, I won't take no for an answer.

The note was unsigned.

"Did you find my wallet?"

I swung around, ready to apologize. No one was there. Voices and laughter reached me from the dining room. I put the note back, calling out, "Got it! Thanks!"

CHAPTER 8

October 1973

By NOON, A FEW HUNDRED students had already installed themselves on the steps of the School of Law, beneath its classical portico
framed by fourteen Doric columns. It was an early spring day, and
songbirds, unfazed by the gathering, chirped from the treetops of the
surrounding courtyards. Perón had inaugurated the building a quarter
of a century earlier, on National Student's Day, at Evita's request. In
the ribbon-cutting speech, the caudillo had expressed his wish that
the school should impart knowledge to students of all backgrounds,
without regard to social class.

On a typical Friday afternoon, Santiago would have been on his
way to El Pinar, perhaps with a stop for a game of tennis or a drink at
the Jockey Club. But over the last four months, he had traded in these
pleasures for the chance to be with Valentina, even if it meant going
to a protest.

Much was happening in the world. The United States had signed
a peace treaty with North Vietnam. A military coup in neighboring
Chile, facilitated by the CIA, had deposed a democratically elected so-
cialist government. Cámpora's placeholder government had collapsed

in less than six months, and on September 23, in the second general election held that year, Perón had been elected president with his much younger wife, Isabelita, as his running mate. Yet the resounding victory of the Perón-Perón ticket belied the widening schism within Perón's political base that would soon rupture in violence.

The sit-in at the university that day had a peaceful aim, which was to demand the release of unlawfully imprisoned journalists, some of them alumni of the School of Social Sciences. Many writers and reporters had been arrested in recent months for criticizing Perón's decision to exclude progressives from his cabinet, which was seen as a further betrayal of his working-class base.

Máximo, Grace, Enrique, and Valentina, keen to join the sit-in, hastened their pace. Santiago, feeling out of place, remained a step behind. Since meeting Valentina, he had been spending more time with these activists than he would have liked or ever could have imagined. A tenet of the Larrea family was appearing neutral and staying above the fray when it came to Argentina's topsy-turvy politics. Unlike his older brother, Bautista, who had dropped out of business school in Barcelona and was now playing polo full-time, Santiago had a strong sense of filial duty and intended his life to follow the trajectory expected of a Larrea male. He would earn his law degree and eventually go to work for his father, learning to manage their expansive investments—land and agriculture, but also various financial interests and real estate projects. Of course he would continue to ride horses and play polo. And when he married, he would acquire more land and give his children a similar upbringing, if not better.

As they approached the school, Santiago quietly admired the curves of Valentina's body in her flared jeans and form-fitting sweater. She was as desirable to him then as when she wore the short skirts that were increasingly ubiquitous in Buenos Aires. As they surveyed the crowd looking for a space to sit, Valentina spotted Florencia, who had arrived with a separate group of friends. Valentina sensed Santiago's gaze on her and motioned for him to approach. He shook his head. For some reason, Florencia hadn't warmed to him. Valentina cocked her head, disappointed, but her eyes told him she understood. When the sit-in was over, they could escape back into their private world. The protesters were now chanting, and as Valentina found herself moving closer to the center, Santiago remained on the fringe of the crowd.

The demonstration was loud but orderly until a few police trucks arrived. A squad of federal police officers jumped out of the vehicles and lined up, toting riot gear. The students chanted with increased fervor in response. Santiago moved in to take Valentina's hand, thinking they should leave, but by the time he reached her, the police had formed a perimeter around the students. When a teenage boy was shoved into an officer, the cops, as if on cue, rushed at the protesters with their clubs. Tear gas filled the air. People scattered in all directions, many screaming, some falling down, others hopelessly fighting back.

He wasn't holding Valentina's hand anymore. They had been separated in the chaos. He couldn't stop coughing and his eyes stung, but he forced them to stay open. A man beside him collapsed and cradled his head in his hands, blood trickling between his fingers. The officers dragged several limp students into the back of an unmarked van. The air grew thick around him.

"Valentina!" Santiago shouted her name into the shadowy shapes. "Where are you?" He recognized Máximo about a hundred feet in front of him, pulling Valentina up off the ground and carrying her in his arms. *Is she hurt?* As he ran toward them, another tear gas grenade was launched in his direction. By the time he recovered, he looked to where he last saw them. They were gone.

Finally freeing himself from a melee he wanted no part of, he found them a few minutes later, sitting quietly in the Café de las Artes. Valentina was using the flimsy wax napkins to brush the gravel off her clothes. As Santiago's eyes scanned her body for bruises, Máximo told him she wasn't hurt.

"You sure you're fine?" Santiago asked her.

"I'm fine," she said, giving both men a reassuring smile before using a new napkin on her face.

"Let's go to my parents' place," Santiago said. "We'll get you cleaned up better there." She agreed, and he turned to Máximo. "Do you want to come?"

"No. I'm going to find Grace and the others. Make sure they're okay."

Santiago hugged him. "Thanks for looking out for her, my friend. I really appreciate it." Taking Valentina's hand and raising it to his mouth, he said. "I don't know how we were separated. Next time I swear I won't let go of you."

The moment they were inside his family's apartment, Santiago brought Valentina into his arms. She placed two fingers on his lips to stop him from kissing her.

"Your parents."

"They're at the ranch for the weekend."

Hearing those words, she kissed him with a passion that seemed to be fueled, in part, by the violent confrontation with the police. With their lips locked, her arms tight around him, and her feet barely touching the floor, Santiago brought her into his bedroom.

He pushed her onto his bed and made a comical gesture of jumping on top of her as she rolled away, laughing. He landed on the covers and laughed too. All the recent political unrest could not pierce their happiness. Lying on their sides facing one another, they traced each other's eyes, eyebrows, noses, and lips. As his lips moved down along her throat and chest, she let out a deep sigh, her body arching against his touch.

Afterward, he murmured into her hair, "I'm yours. You must know that by now. Let me be a part of your life, always." Santiago buried his face in her neck, overcome by the vulnerability he felt at the fullness of his confession.

"One day at a time, okay?"

Santiago had, in his mind, mapped out their future. But as they lay on the bed, their bodies entwined, he sensed she might not be ready to listen to his preview of the rest of their lives. He said nothing and lifted his face to kiss her.

On a shelf, among his books and other knickknacks, Valentina spotted a little red-and-blue wooden ship. She pulled the sheet off the bed and wrapped it around herself.

"Hey! Where are you going? Get back here." He reached out but she was too fast. With a mischievous smile, Valentina began to bob the ship up and down as if on rocky waters. Suddenly, she twisted her hand and capsized the boat, letting out little shrieks of horror.

"What are you doing, woman?"

Valentina was singing the lyrics of the theme song from *The Poseidon Adventure*, which they had seen at a cinema on Lavalle Street. Her voice was beautiful, even as she bungled the lyrics, throwing in Spanish words when she couldn't remember the English ones. She made funny faces as the boat struggled to right itself. He laughed, finding it simultaneously silly and marvelous. Unable to resist, he started singing along with her.

Giggling, she collapsed on the bed, the sheet still draped around her. He went to his desk and retrieved an object from a small box. He kissed her breasts before placing a lapis lazuli pendant across her shimmering, bronzed skin. She picked it up, tracing with her fingertip the tiny diamond chips re-creating the shape of a cross. Santiago took out a penknife from his bedside table and carved her initials, VQ, on the back of the stone. He strung the pendant with a leather cord and tied a knot. When he slipped it over her head, it rested perfectly against the hollow at the base of her throat. Her fingers grasped the stone and she brought her forehead to his.

"I love you," she said.

CHAPTER 9

August 1998

Iᴛ ʜᴀᴅ ᴏɴʟʏ ʙᴇᴇɴ ᴀ couple of hours since I arrived in the city, and I already missed the tranquility of the campo. The last time I had spent time in Buenos Aires was four years earlier, when my parents and I came in from the campo for dinner and to watch a production of *La Bohème* at the Teatro Colón. It was a Monday, my third day in Argentina, and the city was bustling and energetic in a manner that felt reminiscent of New York but was closer in appearance to a European city, with a mix of modern and Old World architecture, plazas, and numerous cafés. What made Buenos Aires visually different from New York, Paris, or Madrid—cities to which it was sometimes compared—was the unruly and slightly decaying juxtaposition of structures from all eras, from art nouveau shopping galleries to art deco apartment towers to modernist glass skyscrapers, with a few old Spanish Colonial buildings also in the mix in the older sections of the city. And then of course, there were the city's inhabitants, the sophisticated and proud Porteños.

Most Porteños I passed on the street were fashionably, if not expensively, attired. How one presented oneself to the world, even if everyone was dressed alike in the latest trend, seemed to matter in this town. Women were slim and petite and, if under the age of forty, wore their hair long. The men, many in tailored suits, were trim and of medium height. I rarely saw a man with facial hair. People walked purposefully until they bumped into someone they knew, in which case an effusive greeting and perhaps a pause to catch up over an espresso in one of the city's ubiquitous cafés would often follow. Porteños always had places to go, important meetings, classes, errands to run, but when it came to friends and family, they had all the time in the world. They were fiercely loyal, and their warmth and generosity extended to foreigners who moved to Buenos Aires for work or school. My parents had brought these traits to New York and quickly became a beloved couple among their American friends.

I made my way to the barrio of Caballito, where the School of Philosophy and Letters of the Universidad de Buenos Aires was located. Unlike many American colleges that housed different schools or departments on one main campus, the UBA buildings were scattered across the city. When I found the school, I paused to admire the graffiti adorning the building's façade. The lettering scrawled above the arched entrance— *Knowledge Good, Ignorance Evil*—reminded me of photos I had seen of spray-painted New York subway cars in the seventies. I also noticed the windows had bars, making the building look like a jailhouse.

It was a cold afternoon, but the sun shone from directly above. Students walked in and out of the building while others stood on the tree-lined sidewalk, chatting, smoking, textbooks open, comparing notes.

Inside, the school's walls were a dingy yellow. Bulletin boards were covered with advertisements and announcements for student meetings, class discussions, lectures, tutors for hire, used books for sale, and the like. After making some calls, I knew I was in the right place. But having lost track of time meandering the streets like a tourist, I worried that I may have missed him. I glanced at my watch. His class would have finished about ten minutes ago.

I peeked inside a couple of empty classrooms with desks and chairs that would not look out of place in an antiques show. An older, distinguished man with a beard walked past me. A couple of students called him by his name: Professor Torres. I followed them and waited until the students left.

"Professor."

"Yes?" He barely looked my way as he headed toward the exit.

"Do you have a moment?"

"Sorry, there's no more room in my class," he said, not breaking his stride.

I had read about Torres's affiliation with the Movida Madrileña, a countercultural movement that emerged after Generalísimo Francisco Franco, Spain's dictator for thirty-five years, died in 1975. When Torres eventually accepted a teaching position at UBA in the late 1980s, he rose to cult status among the students. His lectures had been standing room only for a decade.

"I'm not interested in enrolling," I explained when I caught up to him on the sidewalk. "Could I just have a word with you?"

"Please ask my secretary for an appointment." He held out his arm to hail a cab. "Good day, señorita."

A black-and-yellow Fiat taxi stopped, and he climbed into the back seat. My hand flew out to keep the car door from shutting.

"Wait. Please. I really need to talk to you now. I'm Santiago Larrea's daughter."

The taxi took us to the oldest café in the city, Café Tortoni. A Parisian-inspired establishment on Avenida de Mayo that retained its original beveled mirrors and stained-glass ceiling, it was legendary among the country's literati. Busts of literary greats were on display, and as we were shown to a small table by a window, the professor pointed out the table that Jorge Luis Borges had regularly occupied. As we waited for our server, he explained that city planners had initially envisioned Avenida de Mayo as a Parisian-style boulevard, but it eventually turned into an area more closely tied to Madrid, with Spanish cafés, restaurants, and theaters.

A waiter in a short tuxedo jacket approached our table, and Professor Torres motioned to me to order first. I hesitated, looking at the menu.

"*Una lágrima de café, por favor,*" Professor Torres ordered for himself—a teardrop of coffee. When I gave him a curious look, he explained, "It's the opposite of a cortado. Instead of an espresso with a shot of hot milk, the lágrima is hot milk with only a few drops of espresso."

"Sounds good. I'll have that too, please."

The professor held up two fingers to the waiter. "*Son dos lágrimas.*"

From his coat he pulled out a pack of cigarettes and offered me one before lighting one for himself. He shared a couple more historical details about the café and the neighborhood until the waiter returned with our coffees, along with a dish of bite-size cookies and two small glasses of sparkling water.

Except for the note I found in my father's coat, I told the professor everything, starting from the beginning—how I met Grace Díaz de Graaf in New York and how that encounter led to my finding out about the safe house. The professor smoked while he listened, occasionally stroking his neatly trimmed goatee.

"I met your father soon after my roommate Gonzalo was taken," he began. "They wanted me too, but I had just gone upstairs to our neighbor's."

"Why did they come for you?"

"Well, let me see…Gonzalo was a painter, and I was a student of literature." He clasped his hands under his chin. "You bring an artist and a graduate student together, and they become a fantastically dangerous pair."

"But from what I understand, the military was fighting against terrorists and insurgents who bombed public buildings or killed innocent people." Only after the words left my mouth did I realize that he and his roommate might well have been involved in such subversive activities.

"By the time of the coup in 1976, the Triple A, a clandestine group of military police and goons created under Perón, had essentially killed off all the real urban guerrilla groups. There was no one else to target, so the military went after anyone they pleased. Some were in politics. Some were activists denouncing government corruption. Some were lawyers representing families whose loved ones had been illegally detained or disappeared without a trace. Many were students who took classes that were deemed 'suspect,' like history, art, philosophy, sociology, litera-ture, or journalism. If you were gay or a Jew, you were a target. It didn't matter what you believed in or did for a living. Others were disappeared for being in the wrong place at the wrong time. What distinguished the military rule from the time of Perón's government was that by then, they had perfected the system for disappearing people." He fell quiet for a moment. "A friend of Gonzalo's put me in touch with your father. He helped me get out of the country. I lived in Madrid for the next ten years of my life and did not set foot in this country again until 1986."

As the waiter cleared our cups, the professor signaled for another lágrima. "I have a pre-ulcer condition, and the lágrima is gentler on my stomach," he told me, though I hadn't inquired.

When the waiter left, I asked, "How old were you when you had to leave Argentina?"

"Twenty-four." He extinguished the cigarette and then looked right at me. "How old are you?"

"Twenty-one."

I watched him light another cigarette and thought that the chain smoking couldn't possibly be any good for his ulcer. As if he had read my mind, he eyed the cigarette and then said with a sheepish smile, "These are harder to give up."

The waiter brought more water and the lágrima and tucked another small receipt under the sugar bowl.

The professor continued: "After the military government resigned and democratic elections were held again in 1983—we have the British to thank for defeating Argentina in the Malvinas, or the Falklands, as the English call them—Raúl Alfonsín was elected president and we were all free to return. Many decided to stay in their adopted countries. Those who came back to Argentina soon understood that living in exile had changed them in ways they hadn't foreseen. They would remain foreigners when they returned to their homeland."

One of his former students stopped by our table to say hello. When he left, I said, "Professor Torres, I have to admit that I'm having trouble reconciling the father I know with the one who risked his life for strangers."

"You don't know what people are really made of until they find themselves in extreme circumstances." He dropped a sugar cube into his coffee and stirred. "Some of us who passed through the safe house heard about a woman he had known. It was rumored that he built the safe house because of her."

"Do you know anything else about her?"

"I never learned her real name, but I remember that she was an architect. Soon after President Alfonsín took office in 1983, he asked the writer Ernesto Sabato to preside over the National Commission on the Disappearance of Persons, CONADEP. The commission eventually published *Nunca Más*"—*Never Again*—"a book of testimonies by the survivors. She might have been interviewed for the report. If she didn't survive, she may be mentioned if someone saw her at one of the detention camps. You could also try the Human Rights Center. They keep files on people who were persecuted and on most of the *desaparecidos*."

From the porcelain tray, he selected a miniature meringue. "You take away these small pleasures from an old man and what's left for him?" He let the sugary confection melt on his tongue before talking again. "Some trials were held under the new government, and it looked for a while like there would actually be repercussions for the perpetrators.

But when Carlos Menem was elected president in 1989, he needed the support of the military and granted them amnesty."

"Full amnesty? They're free to come and go as they please?" It seemed unthinkable to me.

"Correct. There were hundreds of torturers and they're still among us. They're in the secret service. Many are our police officers. Or they work as bodyguards. A few have gone into politics. Look at Aldo Rico. Pardoned for his crimes against humanity in 1989, he went on to be mayor of San Miguel, and now the governor of Buenos Aires wants to appoint him minister of police." He shook his head.

"Did you ever find out what happened to your roommate?" I asked.

"No," he replied with a sad smile.

Martín Torres didn't tell me at the time that he had never been able to write about Gonzalo. In fact, he could not bring himself to read the book *Never Again*. In this, I would later learn from others, the professor was not alone.

The professor caught the waiter's eye and signaled for the check. He put away his cigarettes as the waiter tallied the bills left under the sugar bowl. When the final sum was announced, the professor handed over a few pesos.

"I appreciate your taking the time to meet with me," I said as he put on his overcoat and took his briefcase.

He held out his hand to me. "Please thank your father for me. I never really got the chance."

Abuelo's maid had come to the apartment while I was out, leaving food in the fridge that only needed reheating. I arranged crackers, cheese, and ham on a plate, poured myself a glass of Coke, and went into the living room. Here, like at the campo, the furniture seemed to have faded with my grandmother's death. The white leather sofas had lost their luster and the plush area rugs showed signs of old stains. What remained the same was the splendid view of the Río de la Plata. The apartment was on the top floor, and one could see, beyond the shorter buildings, an endless expanse of water. Named the "River of Silver" by Portuguese and Spanish conquistadores, it was a muddy estuary between Argentina and Uruguay. That night, the river sparkled as if glitter had been sprinkled across its smooth surface.

I flipped through a stack of old vinyl albums. Boleros, jazz vocalists, Brazilian sambas—music my father had grown up with and had introduced me to in New York. I picked out an album, *Libertango* by Astor Piazzolla, and switched on the record player. The tango composer had spent his childhood in New York—"just like another Argentine kid I know," my father had often pointed out to me, smiling. On any rainy weekend day, Dad would shut himself in the library and listen to this sensuous and often melancholy Argentine music. As a child, I would sit by the closed door to hear him softly sing the melancholy lyrics and wonder what was making him so sad.

I thought about Sánchez's and Professor Torres's accounts. Dad had built the safe house for a reason. A missing woman. If that was the case, it might explain why he kept the safe house a secret from my mother.

I walked into his old bedroom. His bookshelves held a few old high school and law textbooks mixed in among classics: *Martín Fierro*, Jules Verne, Victor Hugo. I ran my fingers along the old spines. I noticed a slim book wedged between two volumes of the *Encyclopedia Britannica*. *Martín Torres* was written on the spine. I pulled it out and read the title: *Death by Exile*. On the back cover, a black-and-white photo showed a young, beardless Torres. I moved to the bed and, resting my head on a couple of pillows, opened the book.

Some photos spilled out. In the first picture, I recognized my father, probably in his early twenties. He was on a beach with a woman who had her arms around his waist. They were both smiling at each other. Windswept dark curls partially hid the woman's tanned face, and she was significantly shorter than my father. Not my mother.

The next photo showed my parents at El Pinar. Seated with them at the picnic table were a man and two women. The first woman was the same one from the beach. The second woman, in glasses, was Grace Díaz. A younger Sánchez stood behind the seated group, holding a large wooden platter piled with grilled meats.

A third picture showed the woman from the beach. This time she was standing between my dad and the man from the photo at the ranch. The three were in front of what appeared to be a university building. I flipped it over and found an inscription:

> Dear Santiago,
> All's fair in love and war.
> Your friend,
> Máximo

I returned to the first photo and reexamined it, narrowing in on the pendant around the woman's neck. It looked familiar. I went to my father's desk and rummaged through the drawers until I found what I was looking for in the bottom one: a wooden box.

One evening, when I was a child and my parents had gone out for the night, I'd snuck into my father's old bedroom and inspected his desk, coming across this box with his keepsakes. Once again now, I removed the lid and sifted through the old items: a Montblanc pen, a starched white bow tie, a stack of postcards from my uncle to my father. On the back of a postcard of the Spanish Steps in Rome, my uncle Bautista wrote how the city reminded him of Buenos Aires, except that the women were not as beautiful.

As I took the remaining cards out from the box, I spotted it: a bit of leather cord poking out from under a tarnished whiskey flask. It was the necklace from the photo, the cord frayed and discolored with age, but the stone still a profound blue. Two letters were etched on the back: *VQ.* I turned the pendant over in my hand, feeling once again like the sleuth who had first discovered this treasure trove half a lifetime ago.

CHAPTER 10

November 1973

THE SUN'S AFTERNOON LIGHT SLANTED through the kitchen window of Casa de los Niños. Located in a humble neighborhood outside the capital, it was a Catholic Charities day care center where the nuns looked after preschoolers during the day, as well as older children who came after school for a snack and activities. Unofficially, it served as a soup kitchen for adults. Parents, dropping off their youngest children before going to work, were invited to breakfast, often their one and only solid meal of the day.

Valentina and Sister Alice Duvernay, a French nun who had recently moved to Buenos Aires, were preparing snacks. Today the children would eat sliced apples and bread with a butter-and-sugar spread. When the final plate was done, Valentina removed her apron.

"Are you sure?"

"You go on now. We'll manage," Sister Alice reassured her.

The kitchen door opened, and Carmen, a Casa de los Niños volunteer who was also working toward her social work degree, came in to get more of the snacks. Valentina glanced into the large multipurpose room. The other two nuns were settling the children, sixty of them today, at the long wooden tables.

"Thank you. I'm sorry to leave early, but I promised Santiago I'd go to a gathering at his family's house." He had offered to pick her up, but he had already made a trip to the airport earlier that day to meet his brother. She would take the bus.

"Is he your boyfriend now?" Carmen asked.

"I told you we don't need anything official. It's such an antiquated notion to begin with. But I am meeting his parents and his brother," Valentina said, smiling in spite of the spike of anxiety she felt at the thought of being introduced to the Larreas all at once.

"Well, you look beautiful," said Sister Alice. The nun's arms stretched out toward Valentina's outfit, a sky-blue cotton dress that was belted at the waist. It was one of several dresses her mother had sewn for her before she moved to the capital. Her hand reached behind and unclipped a barrette, letting her hair tumble around her long, tanned face.

"Can we make you a little prettier?" Carmen extracted a lipstick from her pocket.

Valentina shook her head and grabbed her purse hanging on a hook.

"A little blush then?"

"No, thanks," Valentina replied cheerily. She didn't wear makeup. Didn't feel the need to. *Take me as I am*, her face announced to the world. It was one of the many things Santiago loved about her.

"Good luck!" Carmen said as Valentina kissed both women goodbye.

It was early evening and still hot. As she walked along the dirt road to the bus stop, small clouds of dust rose up behind her heels. Valentina thought of the distances the children traveled on foot every day for a meal. By the time they returned home, they were hungry again. Whenever she could, she accompanied the smaller ones whose parents were at work and couldn't pick them up. Seeing some of their living conditions—half-built brick walls, mud floors, tin roofs, lack of running water or electricity or both—reinforced her conviction to continue her work providing proper homes for these families.

After an hour-long bus ride, she entered Santiago's building, admiring the figures of cherubs cast into the plaster and the ornate walls embellished with motifs of fleur-de-lis. A few seconds in the lobby was enough to remind Valentina that she was once again stepping into a universe different from the one where homes were made of tin. Yet, since meeting Santiago, moving between these worlds had become almost effortless. Valentina felt light, floating like a balloon just high enough above the injustices she witnessed in her volunteer work. Her love for Santiago had expanded in all directions and renewed her sense of hope. One day, she was sure, they would live in a society where human misery would be eliminated. Communities would come together, putting their differences aside to build a better place for their children.

Waiting for the elevator, Valentina thought of the night they met at Enrique Medina's apartment. Santiago had told her he knew they were meant for one another as soon as he laid eyes on her. Every moment with him, the way he touched her, the way he made her feel, was sweetly intoxicating. She had never felt so loved by a man and sometimes wondered if she would wake up to find it had been a dream.

The elevator stopped on the Larreas' floor. Antonia, the family housekeeper, showed her inside. A man resembling Santiago, but not as tall or slim, was talking to several guests. He approached her.

"Hi, are you Valentina?"

"Yes. How did you guess?"

"My brother described you, and I can see he wasn't exaggerating." His admiring gaze told her he liked the look of her. "I'm Bautista. It's a pleasure." He turned to the men hovering around the guest of honor. "Meet some friends." They each kissed her cheek. One of them said he was Sebastián Díaz.

"Are you Grace's brother?" she asked.

"Yes. You know her?"

"I met her through Santiago."

"She's in there." Sebastián pointed to the living room. "But don't let my sister corrupt you with her recent obsession with student politics. God knows where she gets it from."

"From the university. There's been an infiltration of communists among the faculty and students," a blond man standing behind Bautista said with quiet authority.

Bautista swiveled around. He had forgotten this particular guest. "And this here is Pedro García," he said. The man gave her a slight nod as their host spoke on. "Our old classmate is in civilian clothes, but don't let that fool you. He just graduated from the naval academy."

Valentina managed to keep her voice neutral when she wished him congratulations. Pedro smiled a thank-you, and the dark mole above his lip caught her attention. He noticed and quickly raised a cocktail napkin to his mouth as if to blot out the one imperfection on his otherwise unblemished face.

"Hey! There you are, my love." Santiago had entered the foyer. He kissed her. "Have these guys been bothering you? I wouldn't trust a single one of them alone with you," he joked while casting a dubious glance at the group. The men, who had been Bautista's classmates at an elite private school and still thought of Santiago as the baby brother, laughed, raising their palms to show they had no bad intentions.

"Just getting to know your friend. She's lovely," Bautista answered. His smile was genuine.

"They've made me feel very welcome, Santiago."

"Good," he said, but he put a firm arm around her as though to protect her from other potential cads in the area.

Santiago had said it would be a small welcome gathering for his brother. By the number of people in the apartment, Valentina would have said it was a party. She glanced about the living room. The women her age were dressed in bell-bottoms, flimsy camisoles, tank tops, clogs, and platform sandals. Men, some sporting sideburns or mustaches, wore short-sleeved shirts and high-waisted jeans. The guests of his parents' generation were more formally attired, the gentlemen, unruffled by the heat, in double-breasted suits, and the ladies in fitted tops and skirts or slacks with matching shoes and sparkling jewelry. The matronly types wore their short hair brushed back and teased in the style of Isabelita, although these women would not have appreciated the comparison.

Guests were seated on white sofas arranged around a low marble coffee table on a Persian rug. Two sizable oil paintings of horseback riders in rural settings adorned one of the cream-colored walls opposite the enormous windows. The curtains pooled luxuriously on the parquet floor, drawn so that family and guests could enjoy the magnificent views of the Río de la Plata. At the other end of the living room, guests sat on soft leather chairs placed around a backgammon table.

Santiago directed her to a drop-leaf bar cart positioned next to the wall and poured each of them a glass of champagne. Grace came over and hugged Valentina.

"Where's Máximo?" asked Santiago.

"He had something going on last minute. We'll meet him at the concert," Grace said.

Santiago was cornered by some of his parents' friends, while Grace was monopolized by two girlfriends from her high school. All at once, Valentina was alone. She smiled pleasantly at no one, trying to appear at ease. A waiter offered her a cocktail-size crustless sandwich, and, grateful for something to do, she thanked him. Valentina thought of Máximo. He was close to Grace and Santiago but had on more than one occasion criticized the upper classes from which they came. Had he intentionally made other plans so as to avoid attending the gathering?

An elderly gentleman in a three-piece suit began making small talk with Valentina, asking her name and, when he heard her accent, where she was from. She had to repeat herself and wondered if his hearing aid was turned off.

Right when she was starting to regret taking off early from the day care, wondering why on earth she was at this stuffy party, she glimpsed Santiago. He was looking right at her, smiling while his eyes widened in mock alarm. His great aunts, two diminutive sisters indistinguishable from each other in their matching sweater sets, had latched onto his arms, remarking how handsome he had grown to be from the skinny young boy they remembered so well. He mouthed the words, *I have not forgotten you. Give me one more minute!*

When they were able to extricate themselves from the octogenarian set, they migrated into the dining room. From the high ceiling, a glittering chandelier hung over a large oval table laden with finger sandwiches and sweets. Santiago took her hand and led her across the room.

"Mamá, meet Valentina."

"Mrs. Larrea, how do you do?"

Constanza Larrea shifted in her seat to assess the guest. The only item of note on the woman dangled from a leather cord around her neck: a deep blue stone with glimmering diamond chips. Constanza's eyes moved imperceptibly between her son and Valentina. How close they stood side by side. As if they were familiar on an intimate level. This possibility perturbed her. Santiago didn't discuss his dalliances with his parents, and this was fine. Except for now. Constanza had the sudden urge to find out whatever happened to Mercedes, the daughter of their friend General Delgado. Why had Santiago stopped dating her? She thought Mercedes was a perfectly darling young woman.

"Please, call me Constanza." She remained seated but did tilt her cheek up for Valentina to kiss. Constanza Larrea's salon-lightened hair was brushed away from her face and swept upward in curls above her shoulders. Her white linen dress and perfume were expensive but tasteful. She was a beautiful woman who preserved her aging looks with grace. "So you're a friend of Santiago's from university?"

"That's right," Valentina said.

"We're dating, Mamá."

"Nonsense. Too young, all of you, to get serious. I wish I had waited. I should have had more fun, given a chance to some of the other suitors calling at my father's door." Constanza smiled then and looked toward an older elegant man with thick wavy hair, now gone silver, standing in a corner with other guests. "But I didn't do too badly. Have you met my husband? And my son Bautista?"

"I met Bautista when I arrived. You must be overjoyed to have him home."

"Naturally. His visits are never long enough. They never are for a mother."

"It must be hard having him away so often."

"It is," Constanza replied and regarded Valentina's face. "Where's your accent from? Are you from the interior?"

"Córdoba."

"Ah, Córdoba. I went once, when my mother's health was failing. My father took the family to a spa in the hills. I was small, and I remember it being incredibly quiet. The silence was awful. It was probably my father's or the doctor's orders for us children to be quiet around my mother. Years later, my therapist told me that I associate Córdoba with my mother's death," Constanza said, waving her manicured hand as if the depressing subject she herself had started wasn't appropriate cocktail chatter. "Anyway," she said to change the topic. "I've never been back."

"Córdoba City is lively," Valentina offered, but Santiago's mother was not listening. Her focus had moved to her husband, who was coming toward them.

"Papá, this is Valentina," said Santiago.

Alfonso paused to consider the woman before him. He then gave her a feathery kiss on the cheek.

"Son, I commend you. You're always in the company of striking young ladies," Alfonso remarked with a smile at Valentina, as if this should be taken as a compliment. A priest had joined them at Alfonso's side. "Constanza, Father Aznar wants to say hello."

Mrs. Larrea rose. "Father, thank you for gracing us with your presence," Constanza said.

The priest clasped her hands and, as if they were in a confessional, began to speak to Santiago's parents in hushed tones. Santiago and Valentina took the opportunity to drift back into the living room.

"Are you guys ready?" Grace asked. "Máximo is meeting us soon at the music venue."

"We'll be with you in a minute," Santiago said, glancing at Valentina. When Grace left, he asked, "Everything okay?"

"Not sure. I need a moment to recover."

"From what? Meeting my parents?"

"Mm-hmm."

"Why? You didn't really get to talk to my father. But my mother, she likes you."

"You think so?" Valentina couldn't shake the feeling that the opposite was true.

"She shared a personal story with you."

"A story about how much she dislikes the place I come from."

"I wouldn't say that. It's a story I hadn't heard before. And she felt she could share it with you. She must have seen in you what I see."

Valentina raised her eyebrows. "And what's that?"

His hands framed her face. "That you're a beautiful person, open and pure. You're someone people can trust."

Valentina had seen it differently. Constanza purposely, if indirectly, had let Valentina know that she didn't like her. She didn't, however, share this opinion with Santiago, because he was now kissing her.

He murmured into her ear, "You make people want to tell you their deepest secrets."

Even with his parents in the next room, his kiss excited her. She wanted more, but she broke away. "And your father? He practically compared me to a woman in his son's harem," Valentina said, making a face.

"Sorry. He was just trying to be charming. What can I say? He's of another generation. It probably wasn't the best time to meet them. But you didn't want any formal presentations, right?"

She nodded. His arms closed around her, and when he whispered, "Give them time," she knew she would.

CHAPTER 11

August 1998

THE FLUORESCENT LIGHTING AND INSTITUTIONAL green walls of the Human Rights Center reminded me of the decor of the University of Buenos Aires, and not in a good way. I hesitated outside a frosted glass door with etched lettering that read *Administrative Office.*

A woman on the phone sat at a desk behind the counter. Posters covered the office like wallpaper. The largest one was a montage of black-and-white headshots. Most of the people were in their twenties and wore serious expressions. On the wall to my left was an Amnesty International poster reading *We Can Change What They Do* in thick black letters against a canary-yellow backdrop. On the back wall, a poster announced a march to protest the appointment of Lieutenant Colonel Aldo Rico as head of the police force. The words *Human Rights Abuser* appeared below the soldier's face in war paint. Boxes sat unopened on the floor, and piles of books rested on a narrow table, lending a confined feeling to the small space.

When the woman hung up, she shuffled some papers before looking up at me.

"Can I help you?"

"Please," I said, setting down my bag and notebook on the counter. "I'm looking for information on a desaparecida."

"Are you a relative?"

"Uh, no," I stammered. "I mean, um, I'm a college student, visiting from the United States. I'm doing a research paper on the writer Martín Torres. And when I met with him the other day, he said that you might be able to help me. There's a woman he mentioned who was abducted…"

"Sorry, but we can't let just anyone have access to the files. You'll have to present us with a letter from your university explaining who you are and the purpose of your research."

The phone rang.

"I see," I said. "Thank you."

The receptionist gave me a brief smile before picking up the phone.

I left the office. How could I have thought that the staff at the center would simply hand over files to me? I had met with Professor Torres the day before, and had I been thinking clearly, I could have asked him to arrange access for me. Displeased with myself, I exited the building. Now I had plenty of time to return to the apartment and get changed for my date with Juan. But then I realized I had left my notebook behind. Preparing to apologize for bothering the receptionist again, I hurried back to the office. It was empty. I peeked out and glimpsed the woman at the other end of the corridor chatting with a colleague. She followed him into an office.

Grabbing my notebook from the counter, I noticed that the door next to the receptionist's desk had been left ajar. Curious, I walked around the counter to take a look. It was a small room full of file cabinets. Without a second thought, I stepped inside and shut the door behind me. After a few deep breaths, I peeled myself off the door. If I didn't want to get caught, I would have to work fast. The drawers were arranged alphabetically, and I opened the one labeled with the letters P and Q. *Good. This should be quick*, I told myself. *I'll be out of here before she comes back.*

I began by rifling hastily through the folders, but as my eyes landed on bits and pieces of images and words, I found myself slowing down. One photo showed a cell the size of a broom closet, with bloodstained walls. Another one depicted a young man holding a soccer ball, grinning into the camera. A young couple on their wedding day, broad smiles on their faces, excited about their future. One victim's account of her capture gave a detailed description of the different forms of torture she'd undergone, including one method known as "the submarine," in which her head was repeatedly submerged in a bathtub until she would nearly drown. Another victim described having his limbs splayed out and bound to a table and receiving currents of electricity to his underarms and testicles.

I snapped the folder shut. This visceral reaction surprised me. Up until now, I had approached the investigation as if I were writing a history paper for one of my classes. Words like *victims*, *kidnapped*, *tortured*, *exiled*, *survivors*, and *missing* had remained in the realm of the abstract. Yet, in skimming the files, I began to feel a strange connection to the stories. I paused and took a deep breath. *Don't let your imagination get the better of you. Hurry. You don't have much time.*

The file labeled Q contained fewer folders than P. I sifted through them until I came across a file that made me stop. Inside the folder was a four-by-four-inch black-and-white headshot of a woman, her profile at a three-quarters angle. A passport photo?

From my purse I pulled out my dad's photos and compared them to the one in the file. The picture from the ranch was the most helpful, because the brunette was looking right at the camera. The same thick ringlets falling around an angular face, and those eyes that projected earnestness. My hand trembled slightly as I took out the form and looked for the person's name. Valentina Quintero. VQ, like the letters etched on the back of the pendant. *It's her.*

The file revealed the following information:

Valentina Quintero, daughter of Antonio Quintero (deceased 1985) and María Elvira López de Quintero (deceased 1987). Date and place of birth: Córdoba City, Province of Córdoba, September 25, 1952. Profession: Architect. Volunteer at Casa de los Niños, a children's day care center.

Another name appeared in the file: José Rivera, the superintendent of the building where Valentina Quintero rented a studio. He was the last person to see her before her disappearance in April 1976.

CHAPTER 12

January 1974

CHRISTMAS CAME AND WENT, AND the new year announced itself by rolling over Buenos Aires with its hot, humid blanket of summer. As lethargic as the city's inhabitants were in their movements, the opposite was true for some members of the armed branch of the Communist Party who had nimbly robbed weapons from an armory. President Perón donned a military uniform for a nationally televised speech in which he criticized the governor of Buenos Aires for not coming down harder on terrorist elements and called on the nation to "annihilate this criminal terrorism as soon as possible." The governor was left with no alternative but to resign, making way for one of Perón's right-wing men to step in as governor and carry out the president's orders.

The oppressive heat and news followed Santiago on the three-hour ferry trip across the Río de la Plata but receded when he arrived on the Atlantic beaches of Punta del Este, Uruguay, where his family had a house. He rang in the New Year without Valentina, who had gone home to Córdoba when classes were over in December. Her mother, a seamstress, had a small shop and needed her daughter's help; her assistant was on maternity leave. But Valentina had asked Santiago, along with Máximo and Grace, to meet her at a popular music festival to be held in Cosquín, Córdoba Province, later in January.

One night, after dinner with Bautista and some of his friends, Santiago joined a large crew heading out to dance. Punta del Este's nightlife revolved around casinos and nightclubs, and was likened to that of Monaco or Saint-Tropez. "If you're here alone, then it means you're alone," argued a woman he recognized from law school when he politely rejected her advances. A friend of Bautista's, a tall, young German woman, told him, "Your girlfriend sounds more attractive than you. I'd like to meet her." That got a laugh out of him, but when he left the nightclub, he felt agitated.

Back at his family's beach house, in the chic neighborhood of La Barra on the north side of the resort, he lay in bed, wide awake. He missed Valentina's smile, her attentive eyes while she listened to his most intimate thoughts, her lush brown curls. The way she chewed on a pencil, jotting notes or underlining passages in the books she read. How sometimes she snorted when laughing. He loved making her laugh. He loved making love to her.

He took the ferry back to Buenos Aires the next morning and looked into flights to Córdoba City. When the travel agent informed him that the earliest available flight was at the end of the week, he decided to drive. Excited by this new plan, Santiago dialed the number she had given him from a phone booth. No one picked up the phone. What to do? She hadn't given him her home address, but she had mentioned the name of her neighborhood. He also remembered the name of her mother's shop: Quintero Costuras. Easy. Enough to go on. He would find her.

It was an eight-hour drive to Córdoba, but he made it in seven. Santiago thought he would get pulled over for speeding, and he had cash ready for the standard bribe. Driving through the foothills where the Córdoba mountains meet the Pampas plains, he wasn't stopped once. Unaware that the police force's attention had shifted from petty violations to matters of a secret and sinister nature, Santiago considered himself one lucky driver.

It was his first time in Córdoba City, and its rich Spanish architecture was evident in the cathedral, the buildings of the local university, the viceroy's palace, the fountains, and the monument to General José de San Martín, the liberator of Argentina, Chile, and Peru. Santiago stopped at a pharmacy and purchased tokens to use a pay phone. He tried again the number Valentina had given him, letting it ring a few times before hanging up. As he drove away from downtown, he was forced to ask for directions when his map failed him.

The Quinteros' neighborhood was on the western edge of the city. After he checked into the only hotel in the area, he went out to look for the shop. He walked past small houses with lovely flower boxes hanging from windows. He whistled, content to be in the neighborhood where Valentina had grown up. When he found Quintero Costuras, it was closed, even though it was only early evening. Puzzled, he shook the shuttered iron grate until he heard the sounds of someone unlocking the metal door.

"Santiago!" Valentina's eyes widened with surprise. She kissed him hurriedly and brought him inside. "I was supposed to meet you in Cosquín in two days."

"I couldn't wait," he said, and kissed her again.

The space was small but strategically arranged. By the entrance were a sofa and a chair for clients. Fashion magazines were displayed on a small rack. Two sewing machines and patterns rested on large tables. Spools of thread were organized like a rainbow and kept in long glass boxes. There was a bathroom, a kitchenette, and a back door leading to a garden. On one wall, a thick velvet curtain hung on a curved rod, allowing a client to change in private. The opposite wall was covered in a thick sheet with buttons pinned to it; their range in shape, size, and color made for a beautiful mural. Mannequins were draped in partially sewn dresses and men's suits. A large calendar hung behind a desk, with dates circled for fittings. More than a seamstress's shop, it had the feel of an artist's workshop.

"Are you alone? Where's your mom?"

"She left. My parents' friend was found dead earlier today."

"What happened?"

"He was kidnapped in front of his home a week ago. He was pushing for a raise in transportation salaries."

"And they killed him for that?"

"Probably," she said, biting her lip. "His body was dumped in a landfill. My parents left and I stayed behind to close the shop."

The people of Córdoba did not know of the police activities being plotted at the local and federal level, activities that were already playing out in the illegal detention and treatment of its citizens. Perón had accused Córdoba, an automotive manufacturing center, of being infected with Marxist infiltrators. This condemnation would lead to a historical day of violence a month later that would upend the province, with union syndicates attacked, bombs detonated in the homes of public officials, and hundreds detained, including the governor, in the first-ever police takeover of a provincial government. The abduction and brutal death of the Quinteros' family friend would be the first of many.

Valentina fluttered about as she spoke, turning off the sewing machines, straightening out the desk, folding scraps of fabric into drawers. When she was done, she asked, "Can you drive me to their house?"

"I left the car at the hotel."

"I'll take a bus then," she said, turning off the lights and opening the door for them to leave.

"Let me go with you," he said.

"I don't think it's a good idea. Where are you staying? I'll meet you there."

By the time she showed up at his hotel room, it was long after midnight, and Santiago had fallen asleep waiting for her. He was drowsy when he opened the door, but she was ready for him. They hurriedly undressed while kissing each other everywhere. The wait was over, and, getting under the sheets, they finally rested in each other's arms.

Santiago nestled his head between her breasts. "Did you miss me?" he asked.

"Very much. Couldn't you tell?"

"I was miserable without you," he said. He had never been this honest with anyone. With her, he didn't need to hold anything back, be someone he wasn't.

"I missed you and thought of you all the time too, but I've also been incredibly busy. I think my mother is hoping I'll transfer back to school here. She could use my help, especially if her employee decides to stay home with the baby."

He lifted his head up. "You wouldn't dare."

"*Tranquilo*. Of course I won't. I love Buenos Aires. I want to make my time there last as long as possible."

"And me, what about me?" he asked in a teasing tone, though it was a serious question.

"Silly. I love you more than I love Buenos Aires." They kissed and rested comfortably in silence until Santiago spoke again.

"Can I come to your house tomorrow?"

"Oh, Santi." She kissed the tip of his nose. "The timing isn't good. It's better that my parents not know about your visit. There's too much going on. You understand, no?"

Valentina had told him her parents were socially conservative when it came to their daughter, but he had expected to meet them. During his drive, he had had time to imagine their first encounter. He would arrive at their house with flowers and chocolates. A bottle of scotch for her father. They would invite him in for an asado or a tea. He would charm them and show them he was the right man for Valentina. Looking at her, he understood that she hadn't told her parents about him.

"It could be a quick visit. To introduce myself, for them to meet the man you're dating. I won't even hold your hand in their presence." He moved to the end of the narrow bed so that their bodies weren't touching. "See? I'm very capable of keeping my hands off you."

Smiling at his clownish behavior, she nevertheless said, "It's not the right time, Santiago."

His face soured.

"Stay tomorrow, and we'll go to Cosquín the day after. I'll tell them I'm going with some of my friends. But it'll be just you and me."

And Máximo and Grace and Enrique, Santiago thought.

She inched her way to him until their bodies were one. Their kiss was long, and then she got up to get dressed.

"You'll meet them next time you come to Córdoba," she said, and he nodded.

Drunk with love, it could not possibly occur to either of them that such a time would never come.

CHAPTER 13

August 1998

I WAS IN THE FILING room of the Human Rights Center, copying down Valentina Quintero's address when I heard a noise. Had the receptionist returned? As quietly as I could, I returned the folder to the file cabinet. My notebook was still in my hand when a young man stepped out from behind a cabinet. I let out a small yelp.

"I'm sorry. I didn't mean to scare you."

"It's okay," I said. Collecting myself, I added, "You almost gave me a heart attack."

"I didn't expect anyone to be in here," he said. "You surprised me too." He tilted his head. "Who are you? What are you doing in here?"

"I, um, I'm doing research. A project related to Martín Torres."

"Rosana let you in?"

"Who? Oh, you mean the receptionist? Yeah. We spoke. She was very helpful."

"Martín Torres, you said? He's one of my favorites. Up there with Paul Auster and José Donoso."

"I've been meaning to read Donoso. He's Chilean, right? And I should read Auster. Funny how he seems to have a bigger following outside of the US even though he's American."

I needed to leave before Rosana returned. He shifted his weight to one side, and I saw an opening between him and the door.

"So you're a writer?" he asked.

"Me?" I let out a short laugh. "No. No, I'm a reader, except for when it comes to, um, you know, writing a school paper, like this one on Torres. I'm majoring in English. But who knows, maybe someday?" I inched toward the door. "I bet *you* write, don't you? You look like you could be a writer." An incredibly dumb thing to say, but I was too nervous to think straight. I had to get out of there.

"Well, I'm not. I'm in graduate school. Anthropology."

"That's cool." I was almost at the door.

"It looks like you're ready to leave."

"I am."

"Let me show you out, Ms.....?"

I briefly considered giving him a false name. "Paloma."

"I'm Franco."

The receptionist was not yet back at her desk, and when we walked out into the hall, my shoulders untightened. I turned to say goodbye. Franco was about my height, and I guessed that he was probably a couple of years older than I was. He wore an old mustard-colored sweater with a hole in one elbow, brown corduroys, and a pair of beat-up red Adidas. His black wavy hair fell just below his chin and, when he pushed his round, wire-rimmed glasses back up his nose, I saw that his eyes were a marine blue.

"Where's home for you?" Franco asked.

"New York."

A few young people waved to him as they walked by and entered a conference room down the hall.

"Your Spanish is pretty good for a Yanqui."

A man with a rugby-player physique broke away from another incoming group and clapped Franco on the back.

"Che, Mateo, what's going on?" Franco asked with a grin, returning the firm pat.

"All good," Mateo said while also nodding hello to me. He wore a black T-shirt with an image of Che Guevara stretched across his massive frame.

A woman in a brown leather jacket with navy blue streaks through her hair kissed both men hello. "Meeting's starting," she told them.

Franco said he would be right there.

"You should probably go," I said when the door to the conference room closed.

"Yeah. Well, I hope you got everything you needed," Franco said.

"I did. Thank you."

"Good luck with the research."

"Thanks."

When he reached the conference room, he looked back. "I don't know if this would appeal to you but we're having a meeting. It's for HIJOS." He paused and smiled. "But I'm guessing you probably haven't heard of us all the way over in New York."

"I haven't."

"HIJOS is an acronym for *Hijos por la Identidad y la Justicia contra el Olvido y el Silencio.*" Sons and Daughters for Identity and Justice Against Oblivion and Silence. "We're children of the desaparecidos or people whose parents were political prisoners or lived in exile during the dictatorship."

I regarded him with renewed interest.

"Do you want to sit in? Maybe it could be of some use to you for your project on Torres."

I glanced at my watch. Juan was waiting for me. I really couldn't stay. But when I looked back up at Franco, I decided I would.

The room was filled with twenty people, ranging in age from eighteen to thirty years old. They sat around the oval-shaped table or in fold-up chairs against the wall. Others were perched on the windowsill or leaning against a sideboard piled with books and magazines. A few had settled themselves on the carpeted floor. Franco brought me over to the burly man in the Che T-shirt.

"Mateo, meet Paloma." Mateo kissed my hand with old-fashioned gallantry. Beside them sat a man engrossed in a graphic novel. "Julián! This is Paloma." A scrawny guy with prematurely gray hair stood to give me a quick kiss on the cheek.

A middle-aged woman in a pale-blue smock entered the room with a mate gourd and a large thermos. She flipped her frosted blond hair back as she approached a man in a ponytail and a black T-shirt with the Rolling Stones logo of Mick Jagger's mouth.

Franco explained. "Miriam works in the building. She takes care of us during our meetings." A petite black-haired woman in gray slacks and a cardigan walked to the front of the room. She put a notebook on the table and faced the group. Franco murmured, "That's Sofía. When she's not working for HIJOS, she's an accountant."

Having Franco next to me, filling me in on who was who, made me feel less conspicuous. He would put his mouth close to my ear and with each comment he made, I felt his minty breath on my cheek.

"I know some of you have to get back to work, school, or other things, so let's get started," Sofía said. The room quieted down. "And for those of you who attended the protest against Aldo Rico earlier today, a special thank-you for coming."

After some orderly applause, Sofía turned to Julián, who hadn't looked up once from his book. He reached into his backpack and extracted a large cardboard tube.

"Here it is," Julián mumbled, unrolling a large black-and-white image of a priest with bold letters underneath:

Padre Reinaldo Aznar, ASSASSIN. Turned over 23 of his parishioners to the military junta. All remain missing.

The room was silent for a respectful moment before a few members of the group spoke up with design suggestions.

"I think the part about his parishioners should be in bigger type," suggested a guy with a guitar case slung across his back.

"We should stamp ASSASSIN across his face," interjected a girl with two hoops pierced through her left nostril and eyes rimmed with thick black liner.

"Excellent ideas," said Sofía. "Julián, why don't you put together a couple of different options and we'll make our final decision then. How long do you need?"

"I could have them in a couple of days," Julián said in a near-whisper.

"Once we approve the final design, we need to get it to the printers. Mateo, how many flyers should we print?"

"We'll check in with the Abuelas and Madres. See if they're using their own materials for the *escrache*. That'll help us get our final number," Mateo replied.

I would learn that an escrache was a protest held outside the home of a political, military, or government figure found guilty of human rights abuses.

People started chattering and Sofía clapped her hands. "All right, everybody, listen up. The escrache is Sunday. You know the drill. We'll meet here at 11:00 and leave no later than 11:30. We'll march from here to the church. We should arrive just as his congregation is leaving Mass. And then we confront him. Be loud, get in his face. But as always: nonviolent. Any questions?"

"What if it rains?" asked a teenage boy in skinny jeans and a Metallica T-shirt. His name was Alejandro, and he wore an old Nikon camera around his neck. A budding photographer, I thought.

"We're not canceling even if there's a hurricane, *tonto*," replied Sofía, lightly tapping the back of his head.

He pretended to fall over, and the room erupted in laughter. It dawned on me that everyone around me had lost either one or both parents to the dictatorship. I recalled the reports I had just read and wondered if I had come across some of their parents' files. I looked at their faces, laughing or smiling. How did they manage to find humor in their lives? Filled with respect for these strangers, I nevertheless felt like an interloper. It was time to leave, but the room was crowded. I would have a hard time reaching the door without causing a disruption, which would have made me feel even more uncomfortable. So I stayed still.

Right before the meeting ended, Franco briefed the group on plans to make a presentation to an eleventh-grade class in the neighborhood of San Cristóbal. As everyone in the room already knew, high schools around the country only presented the "official" story. The assigned textbooks stopped on the date of the military coup, March 24, 1976, and picked up again only after the democratic elections of 1983. As the group discussed how to structure the presentation, Franco's voice became impassioned.

"One cannot and must not try to erase the past merely because it does not fit the present," he said, quoting Golda Meir, the former prime minister of Israel. Others responded with grave nods of agreement.

As his briefing concluded, I caught Franco's eye and signaled that I was leaving. He gestured for me to wait. I nodded and stepped to the side of the room. On a table I noticed a well-thumbed book with the words *NUNCA MÁS* stenciled in capital letters on its dark red cover. It was the compilation of survivors' testimonies that Professor Torres had mentioned. I opened it and read the first page of the prologue. Thousands of human beings had been kidnapped, tortured, and assassinated by the Armed Forces. I slowly turned the pages. The typesetting was small, the pages dense with the words bravely spoken by the few who had survived their detentions.

"Do you want to borrow it?" Franco asked, appearing beside me.

"May I? That would be great. I'll bring it back before I leave."

"Sure."

"Thanks so much for inviting me."

"No problem, but it probably didn't help much with your project, right?"

"It did! I thought it was very interesting. And this book...I think it'll be really useful too," I said, holding the *Nunca Más* report up. "Well, then..."

He looked at me with a shy smile. "Listen, some of us are going to La Academia after we're finished here. It's a bar around the corner. Pool tables, reasonably priced beer, and decent empanadas. Do you want to come?"

I said, "I'm pretty good at pool. Are you sure you want me to come?"

"Even better," he replied, his blue eyes showing a twinkle I hadn't seen yet.

"It sounds like fun, but…"

"Franco, can I talk to you for a minute?" Sofía called out.

"Yes," he said, and then turned to me. "Wait here. I'll be a minute."

"Okay," I said, but when his back was to me, I slipped out.

The atmosphere at the HIJOS meeting had been intense, and although Franco had invited me, I felt I had no business being there.

Walking down the street toward a main avenue, I began gathering my thoughts. They were a fascinating group of people, unlike any other I had ever encountered. What must it have been like to live under such circumstances, on the periphery of society, having to grow up before one's time? A sharp contrast to the seemingly innocent lives of my friends back home.

At a street corner, I realized I was still clutching the *Nunca Más* report to my chest. It was a thick book, but I made it fit in my bag. While I was eager to spend the next couple of days going through the testimonies, I was also upset with myself for not accepting Franco's invitation. Maybe some of them would have shared their personal stories with me. Franco might have shared his story with me too. At once, I felt I had let an opportunity slip away. I hadn't even actually declined to join him. A bit overwhelmed by what I had experienced, I had run off without properly saying goodbye or thanking him. During the meeting, so much had been going on around me—new faces, new ideas—but walking along the busy Avenida Callao, the air colder in the weakening late-afternoon sun, I became conscious of one particular sensation blooming inside of me. It was surprising but undeniable. I was attracted to Franco.

My phone rang. Who could it be? Juan. I had forgotten about our plans for the evening. It was my second night in Buenos Aires, and we hadn't seen each other in over a month. The idea of going out with Juan was suddenly unappealing. I wanted time alone. I flipped open the phone, glanced at his name on the tiny screen, and proceeded to cancel our date.

CHAPTER 14

January–February 1974

DRIVING THROUGH CÓRDOBA'S ROLLING GREEN countryside, Santiago would only release Valentina's hand when he had to change gears. She was glad to be out of the house. Her mother had tried to keep her from going to the music festival, but her father had told her to let their daughter live her life. Valentina wore cutoff jean shorts and her feet were up on the dashboard. Her hair was in a ponytail and strands of sun-lightened curls had come loose. It was summer. No homework, no being cooped up in her mother's seamstress shop. And the man she loved had come to get her. Smiling, she stuck her arm out the window, making waving motions in the warm wind. Abruptly, she yelled, "Turn here!"

Santiago didn't see where he could possibly turn, but he obeyed and swerved the car off the road. A dirt path appeared among the tall grass.

"There's a river down there. My friends and I used to come here to swim. It's magical. You'll see."

They hiked downhill through the high grasses and trees. At the riverbank, they draped their clothes on big rocks. Hand in hand, they ventured into the cold water that flowed down from the mountains. Valentina let go, ran farther in, and dived into the dark water. When she didn't come back up, Santiago called out her name. Just when he was beginning to worry, her head resurfaced. A long arc of water squirted from her mouth like a fountain.

"Impressive."

"You haven't come in yet!" she chided him, her arms cutting swiftly through the water to him.

Her slicked-back wet hair and smooth swim strokes made Santiago think of a mermaid. "My body needs to adjust to the water temperature," he explained.

"Let me help you," she said, splashing him instead. He jumped back and turned to the shore. But then he swiveled around and started splashing her too until, laughing, they fell into the icy water together.

They had forgotten the towels in her duffel bag, so they dried off on the hot rocks, their faces turned to the sun. Lying beside the woman he loved in these pristine surroundings awakened in Santiago a sense of peace he had never experienced. He thought this could very well be his own little patch of paradise on earth.

Using her hand to shield the sun from her eyes, Valentina grinned at him as if reading his thoughts. "I knew you'd like it here."

"What do you say we grow old in this place?" Santiago asked. "You could build us a cabin."

"In this unspoiled beautiful spot?"

"Mm-hmm. Far from the chaos of the world."

"You sound like an old man," she said teasingly. "I'm not ready to settle down. Not yet. There's so much to see and do, Santiago."

He loved how she pronounced his name with that enchanting Córdoba lilt. "I guess we can wait," he said, and reclined again on the rock.

When they were dry, they put on their clothes and started back to the car. Valentina walked ahead, looking for the dirt path. They used their arms to brush the tall vegetation out of the way. Out of the corner of his eye, Santiago spotted something large, made of metal.

"Valentina."

She came up behind to find him staring at a car on its side. It was a four-door Renault, the color red in the parts that had not been burned. They peered inside. Half expecting to find a charred body, they sighed with relief when they didn't.

"Look at this." Valentina crouched and pointed to holes that had shattered one of the windows. "These were made by bullets, right?"

Santiago inspected them with his finger. Not sure how he would react if his instinct was correct, he walked around to the trunk. The lock had melted, making it impossible to pry open. If he only had a crowbar, he thought—but a part of him didn't want to know what might be in the trunk.

"We should report this," he said, returning to her side.

"To who? The police? No way. What if they had something to do with it? You have no idea how corrupt the Córdoba police are." She took his hand. "Let's go. We're late to Cosquín as it is." As they hiked up the hill to their car, she said, "There are no corpses, so they must have escaped."

"Or they might have even jumped out before the car rolled down the hill."

Trying to find comfort in these unlikely scenarios, they got into Santiago's car and drove on.

They found Máximo, Grace, and Enrique later that afternoon at a campground a few miles from the festival grounds. Enrique had his guitar out and was strumming the chords to a song by Mercedes Sosa.

Grace kissed them hello but was instantly drawn back to Enrique's playing. It took Santiago one glance to guess correctly that the two of them had become a couple. He considered Enrique a bit of a rabble-rouser, but Grace must have seen in him a sexy revolutionary, a close-enough version of Che Guevara.

"So glad to see you both." Máximo hugged them. "How was your trip?"

They had decided not to mention their encounter with the burned-out car. Valentina told the group that there seemed to be more police checkpoints than usual as they approached Cosquín.

Enrique looked up from his guitar. "The cops are all over the place."

"Why?"

"The government doesn't like the idea of thousands traveling to listen to communist songs performed by communists," Máximo explained, and then he shook his head. "And we call ourselves a democracy."

Without interrupting his strumming, Enrique added, "The government is not in favor of music for the people." And then his voice broke into a ditty: "Perón has abandoned el pueblo Argentino...Santa Evita would never have done so."

The mountain air cooled as the sun grew lower, and sweaters, blankets, and ponchos were retrieved from backpacks. Grace served mate to the group while Enrique fetched wood for a fire.

Santiago, struggling to figure out how to set up the tent Valentina had brought, admired the ease with which Máximo had already finished pitching his own tent. With a bit of envy in his voice, he said, "You got that up quickly."

"That's how we Cassinis travel, my friend."

"I grew up camping with my family too! We've visited a lot of the country that way," Valentina told Máximo.

It turned out the Quinteros and the Cassinis had stayed at the same camping grounds in Río Negro and Neuquén. In their enthusiasm, calculating dates to see if they had overlapped while remembering some of their camping adventures and fiascoes, they forgot about Santiago and left him wrestling with the poles, tarp, and stakes.

"Can I help?" Máximo offered when they remembered him again.

"I got it," Santiago said. He had finally managed to keep the tent upright, and the group applauded. Sheepishly, Santiago accepted a mate from Grace.

That night, Enrique's uncle, Augusto Medina, visited them at the campsite. A guitarist and composer of Latin American folk music, he was lined up to play at the festival the following day. As the group gathered around, Augusto began strumming some of his compositions. Enrique brought out his guitar too, and an impromptu peña was born under the darkening skies. Valentina's voice harmonized beautifully with Enrique's, and Augusto said they should join him onstage the next time he performed in Buenos Aires.

Valentina's body tingled from singing and from the offer. "I would love to sing with you again. Would you also consider coming one day to perform for the kids I work with at a day care outside Buenos Aires? The kids would be thrilled, as would the nuns that run the place."

Augusto Medina agreed, saying he would be in touch. After the musician left the campsite, Valentina returned to Santiago's side.

"You sounded amazing, Valentina," he said, with evident pride in his voice.

"I wish I had learned to play the guitar," she replied. "The kids would enjoy having music be one of their activities."

"We should get you a guitar," he said.

She was excited, but her brow furrowed slightly as she contemplated the daunting task of learning an instrument. She had little free time as it was, and after the summer, in addition to her regular classwork and hours at Casa de los Niños, she would start working as a teacher's assistant. It was a prestigious position awarded only to the top students in her program.

"Or I could learn to play the guitar and you sing," Santiago said, sensing her ambivalence.

"You'd learn the guitar for me?"

"For you? Anything." He wasn't serious about learning, but he also didn't want Valentina getting any ideas about Enrique Medina playing guitar for her charges at the day care.

As the evening wound down, Valentina noticed that Enrique's arm was around Grace. "That's a new development," she remarked in a low voice to Máximo and Santiago.

"They hit it off on our bus trip together," Máximo said. "The three of us were going to share the tent, but it looks like they might want some privacy." He got up. "I'm going to stretch my legs."

As he wandered away, Valentina whispered to Santiago, "Where will he sleep? I feel bad for him. Can't he share our tent? There's enough room."

Near them, a woman had been sitting quietly, smoking cigarette after cigarette. She also rose and walked off in Máximo's direction, her straight hair swinging across the back of her poncho.

"Don't worry about Máximo," Santiago said. "He can fend for himself just fine."

They were the last two sitting around the bonfire, and they laid their heads on her backpack.

"Are you comfortable?" he asked.

"Yes."

It was their first time alone since arriving in Cosquín. They turned to each other and kissed for a long time, almost forgetting where they were.

"Can I tell you a secret?" he asked in a soft voice.

"What is it?" she said.

"I've never been happier than I am right here, right now."

"Can I tell *you* a secret?"

"Yes."

"I feel the exact same way."

He kissed the top of her head. Her hair retained the scent of the fresh lake water from their swim earlier that day. "You're shivering. Come closer."

Folding her petite frame into him, he wondered if his arms would always keep her warm and safe. Thoughts of dread and menace had been bubbling just below the surface of his mind. Was it the death of her family friend? Was it the sit-in, where they had been violently separated and she had gotten cut and scraped? The country was in turmoil, true, but he sensed it was more than that. His love made him protective of her in a way he had never experienced with anyone else. Sheltering her with his body, he wondered, would his adoration always be enough?

His gaze drifted upward. The night sky had turned into a dazzling dome of infinite stars.

Pointing up, Santiago said, "See how the stars have formed into the shape of a cupola?"

"It's like a cathedral," Valentina whispered.

"That's right. Every time I see a sky like this one, I feel like it's the universe's way of showing us its sanctuary," he whispered back. "I don't know. Does what I'm saying make sense?"

"I see what you mean, Santi."

He shifted his gaze from the stars to her face. He kissed her on the mouth and said, "I love you so much. I want us to never be apart."

It was nearing the end of February. Summer was drawing to a close. Perón's government stepped up its censorship of media outlets, and soon there would be no room for dissent, political humor, or criticism of the state. As a result, it was hard to come by accurate news. Yet the one news item that reached Constanza Larrea's ears was, in her opinion, true, because it came from a reliable source. Over a cup of tea, her girlfriend, whose husband was a higher-up in the Ministry of Education, had described the UBA School of Law, with its Marxist tendencies and infiltrators, as "getting out of hand." Her husband, she said, wouldn't be surprised if there were some arrests in the near future. The news gave Constanza an idea, and she found herself practically grinning as she kissed her friend goodbye, thanking her for a lovely afternoon.

Constanza's scheme made use of her oldest son Bautista's proposal to have Santiago travel with him on the European spring and summer polo circuit. A Saudi prince had recently poached one of Bautista's teammates, and the team was now short a man. Constanza had objected at first. Having one son away from home was hard enough. Having two sons on another continent was unimaginable. However, returning home from the tea, she realized it might be just the way to remove Santiago from the political influences of the law school. She also hoped that an ocean between her son and that girl he was dating would help cool off the relationship.

"We still need a player, Santi," Bautista said that night at dinner, after his mother had told him in private that he had her blessing to bring up the trip again. The Larreas were dining on filet mignon, roasted potatoes, and a green salad. The team's patron, an amateur polo player from Madrid, wanted someone with Santiago's skills, Bautista added.

"By the time you return to Buenos Aires, things will have settled down at the law school," Constanza said. "With all the strikes and teacher absences, how can anyone study or pass an exam? Besides, your father can place a call to one of his friends at the university if necessary to facilitate the leave. You'll be representing Argentina at world class tournaments, after all."

Santiago looked at his parents. "Really? I can take a few months off from school to go to Europe?" he asked, not quite believing what he was hearing. The new academic year would begin in early March, merely a week or two away.

"Yes, really," Alfonso said. "You can get a seat on Bautista's flight next weekend. Your mother and I would meet you there at some point. It would be nice to have the family together in Paris."

Bautista clapped Santiago's back. "It'll be the tour of a lifetime, baby brother."

Santiago ran his fingers through his hair, wondering about Valentina, when, all of a sudden, he knew what to do. He smiled at his parents and brother. "Sounds good. Sure. I'll go with Bautista."

Excited to share his plan with Valentina, Santiago hurried to Café de las Artes the next day to meet her. She wanted to travel the world. This would be her opportunity. On his way, he made a stop, and when he walked through the café doors, he immediately spotted the back of her head. She was at their usual table.

After kissing her hello, he rested a slim package atop the table. The elegant wrapping paper was secured with a strip of scotch tape and a sticker with a seal from Casa López, an upscale leather goods store.

"What is it?"

"Open it."

He was barely able to contain his excitement. Santiago figured that if she agreed to go on this trip with him, she would be ready to settle down when they returned. Her wanderlust would be appeased. They could get married and have children. He might even propose marriage in Paris, he thought.

"It's not my birthday, and Christmas was months ago," Valentina said, picking up the package and feeling the weight of it in her hands. Santiago liked giving her presents, and though she protested, they were always exactly what she wanted. He knew her. He had never been able to come up to her room in the student residence, but he could picture it, with a few plants and the fresh flowers in a vase he gave to her every time he picked her up. There was also the record player he had bought her so she could listen to the music of the Argentine rock groups they both liked, like Sui Generis and Luis Alberto Spinetta, as well as the folk music she loved so much.

Valentina held up what appeared to be an oversize wallet. Her fingers ran over the tan, handcrafted leather that, when opened, revealed various pockets, some transparent.

"It's a passport holder," Santiago said eagerly.

"I don't have a passport. Not yet. I'm planning to get one, but…"

"Then we need to take care of that as soon as possible, because you and I are going to Europe."

"Are you crazy?" Valentina exclaimed after he told her about the tour and his idea for them to go together. "I can't afford that kind of luxury. I don't have the time or the money."

"I'll pay for everything," he said, not yet having worked out those details.

His parents would give him travel money, but it wouldn't cover both his and Valentina's expenses. He would receive a basic salary, but there would be no prize money, only prestige, if they won any tournaments. While he tried to work out how to finance their trip in his head, Valentina spoke.

"My parents wouldn't allow it. It's tough enough for them having to support me. Remember that my mother wanted me to live at home and go to the National University of Córdoba."

He reached for her across the table. She had a point. Maybe it was too much to ask her to take all this time off, to fall behind on her studies, just so she could travel with him. "All right. You'll come visit me wherever I am during the winter break."

"You'll be gone that long?" Valentina's voice squeaked. She hadn't realized what kind of time commitment Santiago was talking about.

"Until September, yes. Around the time when the season ends."

Valentina thought of the life she had created for herself in Buenos Aires. "I have the kids at the day care. And now that I'm a teacher's assistant, I'm sure I'll be working through the break, grading papers."

Santiago looked crushed. "I thought you wanted to travel."

"I do. And I will. After I graduate and when I've earned some money."

"I'll stay then. I won't go."

"Don't be silly. I can see on your face how excited you are, Santiago."

An ache began to form in her chest even as she encouraged him to go. Busy as she was, they didn't necessarily see each other every day. But he was always nearby, and knowing that kept her heart humming with happiness. This would be different. They wouldn't be able to be at each other's side within minutes. He would be thousands of miles away.

"Not anymore, I'm not," he said, but canceling, telling his brother he couldn't go because of his girlfriend, didn't seem like the right answer either.

"We'll write each other letters. It'll be very romantic," she said, feeling the ache spread across her chest.

Grace entered the café and, seeing them, came to their table.

"Where's Enrique?" Valentina asked after they kissed hello.

"He's at the airport saying goodbye to his uncle Augusto," Grace said, taking an empty chair. "He's moving with his family to Barcelona. Musicians have been getting death threats from the Triple A."

Perón's minister of social welfare, José López Rega, nicknamed "the Sorcerer" for his fascination with the occult, was the shadowy mastermind behind the creation of the Argentine Anticommunist Alliance, or Triple A. The paramilitary group was composed of former police and military men tasked with eliminating artists, intellectuals, politicians, students, historians, unionists, and members of the clergy with left-leaning ideas.

"After we saw him in Cosquín, Augusto continued to play at small clubs around the country. He was arrested at a show in Tucumán," said Grace.

"They let him go, so that's good," Santiago said.

"Only after they brought him in for questioning and tortured him in jail."

The lovers momentarily set aside their troubles as they listened to their friend.

"He was released with the understanding that he wouldn't play or write another 'Marxist song' again. To make sure, they beat his hands to a pulp."

"That's awful!" Valentina cried out. She remembered their night around the bonfire listening to Augusto play and singing with him. Her stomach twisted. "How's Enrique?"

"He says the government won't win. They can't silence the voice of the people."

"And you?" asked Santiago.

"Me?" Grace asked, waving down a waiter. "I'll be better once I have a drink."

Santiago's mind was seized with an image of the musician's hand strumming the guitar while it slowly became a bloody mass of swollen flesh. Horrified, he searched for Valentina's hand and interlaced her fingers with his.

CHAPTER 15

August 1998

THE MORNING AFTER MY VISIT to the Human Rights Center, I went over my notes from Valentina Quintero's file. The desaparecida from Córdoba was a young architect. I pictured her at work on a new design for a home, an office building, or a school. She had been born in September of 1952 and had gone missing in April of 1976. Exact date uncertain. About a month after the military coup. At the time of her disappearance, she would have been twenty-three years old. Just two years older than me.

Right before Franco surprised me in the archives room, I had scribbled down the address of Valentina's studio. I had also written the name of the building's superintendent, José Rivera, the last person to see Valentina alive.

At a newspaper stand, I purchased a city guide and took a table at a café. I unfolded the map and studied the different-colored segments of the capital city while drinking a steaming cup of café con leche. The address was in Almagro, a neighborhood west of the city center. I consulted the transportation options in the guide and, after paying for my coffee, I set out to see what else I could learn about Valentina Quintero.

A bus got me to the neighborhood in about twenty minutes. After asking several people for directions, I located the building and rang the super's bell next to the splintered wooden door. The report had been filed in 1976. Twenty-two years ago. It was a long shot, I knew, but one I would regret not pursuing. Anxiously, I chewed on the inside of my cheek until the door opened a crack.

"Yes?" asked a plump young woman.

"Hi. Is José Rivera in?"

"Who wants to know?" The woman's hair was in a ponytail and she wore leggings underneath an oversize black sweatshirt.

"I'm a student from the United States, and I'm doing research about Argentina in the 1970s."

The woman gave me a wary look. "And what does that have to do with him?"

"I thought Mr. Rivera might be able to talk to me about someone who kept an office here many years ago." I tried to look in but the woman blocked my view. "Is he here?"

The woman hesitated and said, "José Rivera's my father."

"Really?" My enthusiasm was met with silence. "Let me introduce myself. My name's Paloma Larrea."

"Marcela," the woman offered reluctantly.

"Very nice to meet you, Marcela." Silence again. "I'm working on a project about a woman who was a tenant in this building, and I understand that your father was the last person to see her alive before she went missing. So if he's here, I would love to talk to him."

"He died two months ago," Marcela said flatly.

"Oh. I'm so sorry for your loss."

The woman lowered her eyelids, accepting my condolences.

"I'm sure this is a very difficult time for you and your family, but if it's not too much trouble, would you mind if I asked *you* a few questions?" The sounds of a wailing baby came from inside. Marcela turned back her head. "Is the baby yours?" I asked, hoping to draw her into a happier topic.

"I'm sorry but I have to go," said Marcela, and abruptly shut the door.

Disappointed, I walked away. My failure to get any new information on Valentina left me feeling off-balance. I passed a flower stand and a kiosk that advertised international calling cards. Without any real direction or plan, I asked a kid locking his bike to a tree to point me back toward downtown.

Avenida Santa Fe, one of the main city arteries known for its fashionable boutiques, was starkly different from the quiet residential street where Valentina had once kept her studio. Black-and-yellow cabs zipped in and out of traffic. Motorcycles whizzed by, at times so close that I could envision one of them jumping suddenly onto the sidewalk to skirt the traffic. Not a single rider wore a helmet.

I waited at a red light next to an elderly couple. When the light changed, they leaned on each other and warily crossed the intersection. Children in school uniform ran by me in a swirl of shouts and laughter toward a small plaza with swings, slides, and monkey bars. Their mothers or nannies followed behind, chatting, one eye on their kids.

As I got closer to the intersection of Santa Fe and Callao, another wide and popular avenue in the heart of the city, sidewalk cafés began to pop up. In spite of the chill in the air, the cafés brimmed with clients in warm coats and furs. A waiter in a red smoking jacket carried a tray with espressos, tiny croissants, and tea sandwiches above his head. He skillfully navigated the busy sidewalk and entered a clothing store. I stopped to admire the window display. The saleswomen, who looked like they'd walked out of the pages of Italian *Vogue*, flirted with the waiter while he handed each one of them their order.

A dog walker wearing a red bandanna as a headscarf led a pack of dogs of all types and sizes on multiple leashes. One of them, a terrier, stopped and rubbed up against my leg. I let the dog lick my hand and then watched the procession cross the avenue. On the other side, a few people were pasting large posters on a bus stop and billboard.

I recognized a few faces from the HIJOS meeting: Mateo, Sofía, Alejandro. And Franco.

As I approached, I saw that they were putting up the flyer denouncing the priest, Father Aznar. The revisions had turned out well. It was an arresting image. They were busy, working quickly. Nobody noticed me. Franco was using his hands to flatten down one of the posters on a lamppost.

Feeling somewhat nervous, I called out: "Hello."

Franco turned with a surprised look. "Hey, it's La Yanqui." He was in a dark-blue peacoat, the kind a French sailor might have worn.

"Paloma," I said. "Not that there's any reason why you should remember…"

"Oh, I remember your name, all right," he replied, adjusting his eyeglasses. In the natural sunlight, Franco's blue eyes were more pronounced. "It's just that I like to think of you as La Yanqui."

The fact that Franco hadn't forgotten my name almost gave him a pass on the bothersome nickname.

"The flyer looks good," I said.

We admired the poster. Not fully satisfied with the result, Franco reached up to smooth out a wrinkle running across the priest's face. Alejandro snapped photos of the group with his Nikon.

"I'm sorry I left the other day without saying goodbye. I felt that I was getting in the way. I also needed to go."

"Don't worry. Americans are always in a hurry, aren't they?" Franco asked with what seemed like a trace of condescension until he gave me a disarming smile.

"We Americans pride ourselves on being on time. If it seems like we're in a rush, it's because we don't want to be late to our next appointment," I replied in my best diplomatic voice, all the while asking myself how it was that some Argentine men could be charismatic *and* infuriating, all at the same time.

Mateo came to say they were going to go down Avenida Callao

toward Recoleta. Franco picked up his satchel and slipped the strap over his head. Watching them collect their materials, I felt a twinge in my heart. Would I look back on this moment as another lost opportunity?

"Franco?" In my mind I clammed up, but my lips kept moving. "Would you want to go out sometime? Get a coffee or a beer, maybe? I'm in Buenos Aires for a few more days...I mean, only if you're free?" When he didn't respond right away, I offered him a way out. "You're probably busy. It's no big deal if you can't."

"No, no. A drink sounds nice. Why don't you write down your number for me?"

Suppressing a smile, I rooted around my purse for a pen and wrote my name and number on a blank page I ripped out of my notebook.

Franco read my name out loud and then, with a deadpan expression, said, "The name's Bonetti. Franco Bonetti."

Had he just pulled a James Bond move on me? He was grinning. *I believe he might be flirting with me*, I thought, returning his grin.

Before Franco caught up to his friends, he looked back over his shoulder and waved the paper. He mouthed the words, "I'll call you."

Amazed by my boldness—I'd never asked a guy out before—I mouthed back, "Okay." And, resuming my walk down Avenida Santa Fe, I was filled with a lightness I hadn't felt since setting foot in Buenos Aires.

CHAPTER 16

May 1974

Valentina kept herself occupied in the weeks following Santiago's departure. Classes had grown more challenging as she advanced toward her degree, her teaching assistant position was more demanding than she had expected, and the number of children in need of a meal appeared to have grown exponentially. It didn't leave her much time to think about Santiago. Until one night, while correcting papers, her bones began to ache. She crawled into bed and was unable to get up the next morning. Her throat burned, and it hurt to swallow the tea she heated on her hot plate. Lying in bed, she felt a hollow in her chest. One that only Santiago could fill.

Argentina's postal system was notoriously unreliable, and, worried his letters would get lost within the student residence, Santiago had said he would try to mail them to her through his father's connections at some of the Argentine embassies. The letters would then be left with the doorman. Valentina could also stop by his family's apartment for a cup of tea with his mother once in a while if she liked, he had told her, hoping the two most important women in his life would become closer.

Writing him daily made her feel better. She imagined him ripping open the envelope and sitting down immediately to answer her. Yet one month had passed since his last letter. Upset, she had decided to keep writing him but to deliver the letters through his mother until she heard from him next. "It's our awful postal service!" Constanza would tell her during their short visits.

One afternoon, while drinking a coffee at Café de las Artes, Valentina felt her chest hollow out a little more. Rereading one of his three letters would provide some comfort, and she reached into her bag to pull them out. She chose the longest letter of the three and sat back in her chair. She had arrived late to the café for her study group to find several of her classmates at the table where she and Santiago had always sat. It was *their* table. The table where they had spent so many evenings. The table where he'd told her he was leaving for Europe. Whenever she came to the café, she intentionally avoided it. But after her classmates left, she remained seated there. The waiter brought her another café con leche and she half-heartedly stirred a packet of sugar into the milky coffee. Staring at his empty chair, she placed her hand on the pendant around her neck and remembered how he told her he loved her.

When she looked up next, Máximo was standing over her table, holding a beer.

"Hola, Valentina."

"Hey!" He leaned down to kiss her cheek. "Why didn't you say something?" she asked.

"I didn't want to interrupt. You looked like you were deep in concentration."

"I was just reading a letter from Santiago," she said, slipping the sheet of paper into a book.

He sat across from her. "How is he? Conquering the old continent with his horse and mallet?"

"He's great." No point in telling him or their friends that the last time she heard from him had been before autumn arrived to strip the trees bare of their leaves. "I thought you would be at the Plaza de Mayo."

"I'm coming from there," he said, lighting a cigarette.

It was May 1, International Workers' Day, and thousands had gathered at the square for Perón's address.

In his seven months as president, Perón had failed to control the radicalized factions of his party. In a speech from the balcony of the Casa Rosada, Perón had publicly taken sides by calling the far left "stupid" and "unmanly." In response, hundreds of the Young Peronistas abandoned the square. To the extent that anyone on the left still believed that Perón might pivot back toward their agenda, his May 1 speech shattered that illusion. The walkout would mark the definitive rupture between Perón's ascendant right-wing supporters and the left-leaning elements he had rejected.

Enrique came to their table. "We're going to the *villa*. Father Óscar is going to give a talk."

"Do you want to come?" Máximo asked Valentina.

"Sure." Valentina picked up her cup and took quick sips.

"We'll catch up with you," Máximo told Enrique.

Enrique left, and she asked, "Is Grace coming?"

"You didn't hear? They're no longer together." Máximo frowned slightly as if he didn't like being the one to tell her, wondering why she didn't know.

"Oh. That's too bad." Valentina had been so completely submerged in her sadness that she had neglected her friend.

The *villa*, or shantytown, located by the central Retiro train station, was made up of structures built from a mishmash of brick, cement, and corrugated tin. Two men waved to Enrique, and he told Máximo and

Valentina he would meet them at the chapel. The afternoon breeze carried the scent of carbon and grilled meats as they moved farther into the slum. Their sneakers squished in the mud. It had rained that morning, and some residents were still bailing out the water that had rushed into their homes.

Valentina noticed that most buildings were painted in various colors. She supposed that, having run out of one color, the workers grabbed a can of whatever was available to continue painting. Some buildings were unfinished, exposing loose cables and rooms without walls, as if they had been bombed.

"Dolores!" Valentina called out to a girl in a doorway. "What are you doing here?"

"Visiting my cousin," the girl said, waving back.

"How do you know her?" Máximo asked.

"I volunteer at a day care. We get lots of little ones, but school-age kids like Dolores come after school."

Máximo studied her and then said, "I'm going to show you something." He steered her toward a small building that looked deserted. "Enrique and I took this unoccupied place and transformed it into a space where kids can hang out to read, play, and think," he explained while they climbed a flight of stairs. "We also tutor, help kids with their homework."

They entered a dimly lit room brightened by painted murals on the walls. A family holding hands in a circle. The Argentine flag. Children playing soccer. A freshly painted gigantic rose celebrating Mother's Day.

"They're lovely. Who painted them?" Valentina asked.

"The kids, with a bit of my help," he said, as a few children ran up to them. The smallest one held his arms out for Máximo to pick him up. Tugging on Máximo's long, wavy hair, he asked, "Did you bring me balloons?"

"Next week, buddy," he said, and patted the boy's small head.

"What's with the balloons?" she asked him when the kids returned to their game of cards.

"We combine all the birthdays that fall in the same month and throw a party. Enrique plays the guitar, and I'm the balloon man. Give me four balloons and I can twist and bend them into any animal you like," Máximo said, his smile softening his serious expression. He seemed more at ease in this room with these kids than just about anywhere else.

There was a bookshelf with some books and board games. A rug to sit on and read or play. A portable chalkboard, several desks and chairs. He went to a desk and tested it for wobbliness. Finding it sturdy, he nodded to himself, satisfied.

"Did you build the desks?"

"And the chairs. They still need to be painted."

Valentina looked admiringly about the room, and then they said goodbye to the children.

Outside, she said, "I love building things too." Giving him a quick smile, she added, "You probably know that, since I'm studying architecture. But what I love most is when what one builds fulfills more than one purpose. That's what you and Enrique have accomplished. You've built a space where kids can get away from their cramped living quarters to study and learn. But it's also a place where they can play and relax and be themselves. It's as if you've given them a room of their own." Putting her arm on his shoulder, she said, "I like what you've done, Máximo. Very much."

He shook his head as if he were not deserving of the compliment. "There's so much more to be done, and yet we now know that nothing will change, the way things are going with this government," Máximo said.

They reached the chapel at the same time as Father Óscar, who was in the company of another priest and three men, including Enrique. Enrique had been a teenager on a Catholic mission in one of the poorer provinces when he first met Father Óscar, and they often worked together in slums around the city. News of the impromptu Mass had reached all corners of the shantytown. With no space left inside the one-room church, Valentina and Máximo stayed outside. Through the open doors, they heard the sermon. The priest reassured the parishioners that while they might feel like Perón had abandoned them, God never would. He talked about the importance of relying on each other and of remembering that a unified people could never be defeated. Everyone listened with somber faces. Even the local mutts had stopped barking, as if they too had been mesmerized by the priest's voice.

Valentina and Máximo waited for Enrique in a small square by the chapel. The square glowed with colored bulbs resembling Christmas lights, but there were no trees here. The lights had been strung from the buildings, lending a festive air as people streamed out of the chapel.

Enrique brought Father Óscar over to his friends. The priest had a handsome, open face, light brown hair, and eyes that conveyed empathy and compassion. If not for his cassock, one might have taken him for a doctor or therapist. The priests of Valentina's childhood had been old-fashioned and conservative. If Father Óscar had been her priest, she might not have stopped going to Mass, she thought as they chatted.

After thanking the priest for his sermon, Valentina prepared to leave. Máximo offered to walk her back to Retiro station.

"Thanks for inviting me," Valentina said as her bus pulled up. "I found the priest's words so inspiring. I wish there was more I could do."

"We have the kids' monthly birthday party next Thursday. We could always use an extra pair of hands," he said.

"I'd love that. And I'll help you paint those chairs too!" she said as she boarded the bus. He gave a small wave when he saw her in a window seat. Waving back, she realized that Máximo asking for her help at the slum, his attentiveness, made her feel good. For the first time in a long time, the hole in her chest didn't ache.

CHAPTER 17

August 1998

THE ART GALLERY ON ARROYO Street was ready to close. The owner, however, had returned to the reception area to allow my father and me more time to take in the exhibit undisturbed. Dad had a press conference later, but he had come in to Buenos Aires a few hours early to see me. Mom had stayed behind at the ranch with what she thought might be the onset of a migraine.

The artist, whose work had been recommended to my father by his friends in the art world, was from the city of Mendoza. He became an overnight sensation when he was selected by an international committee as one of thirty up-and-coming artists under the age of thirty. We walked on to another piece, but my mind was not on the art. It was on Dad, whom I had not seen since my most recent findings.

It had been five days since Sánchez advised me to leave the past in the past, but how could I? The idea of my father as part of a resistance movement had exploded my preconceptions of him and captured my imagination. I tugged on Dad's sleeve.

"Papá, I need to talk to you about something."

"What is it? Have you seen Juan? You haven't mentioned him since I arrived."

"Juan's fine." Before he could ask anything else and, more importantly, before I lost my courage, I said, "I know about the safe house."

He moved away from me to the next painting, but I could tell by his stiffening pose I had struck a nerve.

"Please don't be upset, Papá. When we were at the campo, I visited Sánchez at his house our first night. And I don't remember exactly why it came up, but I told him I had met Grace and he said he remembered her. And then he told me what you did."

Dad shook his head.

"It's not his fault. I made him tell me. Please don't be mad at him." He looked straight ahead at the painting. "And then, when I came to the city, I met the professor."

"What professor?"

"The writer. Martín Torres. He teaches at UBA. You didn't know?" I hoped that this new piece of information might cause him to open up.

"And this whole time I thought you had come to Buenos Aires to be with Juan," he remarked with an ironic smile.

Dad proceeded to the next painting. More jagged black slashes on a smooth white canvas, although this one was a smaller version.

"Papá!" I followed him. "I can't believe you never told me."

For several moments, he didn't speak. When he looked at me, he said, "Don't take this the wrong way, my love. I'm sure you want to know everything. However, there are some things about my life that are mine and that I don't have to share with you or anyone else."

"But what you did was incredibly brave."

"I'm not so sure," he replied.

"What about the note?"

"What note?"

"The one in your coat pocket."

His face darkened.

"I found it when I was looking for your wallet. I'm sorry. I didn't mean to snoop. It fell out of your pocket."

He touched my arm. "It's okay. I'm the one who is sorry. This is all so unexpected. Forgive me."

He retrieved the artist's catalogue and turned the pages until he found the photo and description of the work before him.

"An old friend who wants to meet at your usual café and won't take no for an answer. I'm pretty sure that's what the note said." My hand rested on his arm. "Papá? What's that about? Who wrote it?"

My father lifted his gaze from the catalogue. "Come. Let's sit down for a minute," he said, indicating a bench nearby. Once we were seated, he spoke again.

"Paloma. When it comes to politics, in this country or in any other country, there are people who are on your side and people who aren't. That's the way it's always been. And when you have power, people hope to get something from you. They want your time or your gratitude if they think that you owe them something. Some demand it from you." He put his hand under my chin and raised it so our eyes met. "Sweetheart…I don't want you to worry about me or anything else that has to do with my new position, all right?"

"All right," I replied. Dad had dodged my question, but I didn't insist. I had more to find out.

"Is that a promise?"

"It's a promise."

"Good." He kissed my forehead. "As for your other question, no one knew, and to this day, no one knows about the safe house, except for the few that we helped out."

"I understand. I haven't said anything to anyone." We sat in silence, and then I asked, "Why did you do it?"

"Any number of reasons, I suppose."

"Professor Torres told me there was a rumor around that time that you built it because of a woman. An architect. He said that she had been important to you."

"He said that?" He was unable to hide his surprise.

"Yes. Who was she?"

He was visibly distracted and didn't answer.

"Papá? Who was the architect?"

"You mean Valentina?" He gave me a nervous glance. "You really want to know?"

"Yes. Please," I said, smiling inwardly at having figured out the woman's name on my own.

For a moment he was quiet. "She was someone I knew. Many years ago." He let out a low exhale. "Before I started seeing your mother. We dated when we were students."

"I thought so," I said.

"We broke up before we graduated. I met your mother not long after." While he spoke, he folded and refolded the catalog.

"Go on."

"A few months after your mother and I were married, the military overthrew the government. Many knew it was coming, and honestly, to most people it came as a relief. The country was a violent mess, and the junta was promising law and order. But we did not know that the new government would escalate the persecution that started under Perón. We were ignorant. Or maybe we didn't want to know, or couldn't find out because the media was censored." He tapped the rolled-up catalogue against his thigh. "I saw Valentina a few times right after the coup. We still knew people in common. I thought we could be friends, but when I understood she wanted us to get back together, I had to stop seeing her. One day I heard she had gone missing." He unfurled the catalog and stared at the cover. "Afterward, I found out that others were disappearing too. I built a safe house at the campo thinking that maybe I could help a few people. It wasn't much."

"Torres says you managed to get a lot of people out of the country." Pointing this out didn't seem to console my father, who looked crestfallen. "Do you think Valentina might have escaped through some other channel? Maybe she's living elsewhere under a different name and identity."

He shook his head once. "She would have come forward after the dictatorship collapsed. At the very least, she would have contacted her parents. There would have been no reason for her to continue hiding."

Dad seemed so despondent that I took his hand and said, "Grace said you were a brave man and that lives were saved thanks to you."

"I don't know about that," he said quietly. "I never told your mother about the safe house. I wanted to protect her. And I was never able to bring myself to tell her I had been in touch with Valentina after we were married. Your mother didn't really get along with her, understandably." He smiled feebly. "Once we moved to the United States, I made a decision to leave it all behind, to start fresh."

His phone rang then. It was one of his new aides. The press conference was starting. Where was he? the aide was anxious to know.

As we left the gallery, I said, "Thanks, Papá."

"For what?"

"For telling me. For trusting me with this."

A block from Plaza San Martín, home to General San Martín's statue and a meeting point for young and old alike, stood the historic Plaza Hotel. Bellboys bustled about, hailing taxis and ushering well-heeled guests through the doors.

A member of my father's staff was waiting. He escorted us through the sumptuous lobby and up a marble staircase to the first floor. The press conference for the new UN ambassador had been scheduled in one of the rooms in the hotel's conference center. After a quick review of his notes, Dad was led to a podium in front of a group of a dozen or so waiting journalists and photographers.

When Dad had delivered his remarks and was ready to take questions, my father's aide stepped forward to address the press. "Please give us your full name and affiliation before presenting your question."

"Eduardo Pérez, *La Nación*. Ambassador Larrea, my question is the following: Will you make the reopening of beef exports one of your top priorities?"

"This is more of a question for my colleagues in the Trade Ministry, but I am confident that once the Americans have tasted our beef, they will soon be replacing their barbecues with our asados."

"Even with a president who is famous for loving spare ribs with barbecue sauce?" asked another journalist, drawing laughter from the room.

"Absolutely."

I could tell Dad was enjoying himself.

"Ambassador Larrea, why don't you tell us a little bit about your family?"

My father's eyes swept the room in search of the reporter who had asked the question, winking at me when he spotted me. He was about to take another question when a man stepped out from behind a column and said, "Over here."

Dad looked at the pleasant-looking, blond-haired man pointedly.

"Are they here with you?" the man called out from the back of the room. "In the city, I mean."

"Please, you must state your publication and full name," the aide insisted.

"You have a grown daughter, isn't that right?"

The aide moved to reprimand the unruly reporter, but my father stopped him. He took a drink of water and then calmly regarded the man. "I'm married to the most wonderful woman I know, and yes, we have one daughter, whom we love very much." I thought he would point to me in the audience but he didn't. His eyes briefly darkened before he gestured to a woman near the front for the next question.

Out of the corner of my eye, I caught the man at the back flashing an odd smile at my father before exiting the hall. The press conference resumed without anyone taking much notice.

CHAPTER 18

June–September 1974

GRACE'S APARTMENT WAS WITHIN WALKING distance of the law school. It was also near Santiago's home. The last time Valentina stopped by the Larrea residence had been a few weeks earlier, to drop off a letter for him. The concierge told her that Mr. and Mrs. Larrea were in Europe. Valentina had returned home, deflated. Why hadn't Mrs. Larrea told her they would be traveling? She would have asked her to take a letter, guaranteeing that Santiago would receive it. A messenger had dropped off a package for her at the residence recently. Inside was a pink silk Hermès scarf, the kind one tied around one's neck and wore to fancy gatherings. The only message was a notecard in Santiago's handwriting that read, "Give to Valentina." His instructions, presumably, to his parents. Why hadn't he included a letter to her? Why had she heard from him so few times in the nearly four months he had been gone? She was determined not to let herself get upset again. Not now.

She glanced at Grace walking beside her. She had sought out Grace to see how she was doing, and somehow her friend had convinced her to come with her to a tea party her mother was hosting at her house.

"But I'm not dressed for a tea," Valentina had told Grace at the foot of the law school stairs, thinking of the pink scarf still in its pretty wrapping in her dorm room. She was wearing an old sweater and sneakers, having come straight from the monthly birthday party she helped host with Enrique and Máximo. She had spent all day at the slum, painting the new bookshelves Máximo had built, which they planned to fill with books, kids' magazines, and comic books collected from friends and from used bookstores on Avenida Corrientes. Valentina showed Grace the specks of yellow paint on her hands.

"Don't worry. You can wash up in my bathroom."

"I was sorry to hear about you and Enrique," Valentina said as they cut through a plaza, their footsteps sending the pigeons into the gray sky.

"I'm better," Grace said with a brief smile.

"It's his loss."

Consulates and embassies had taken over some of the old family palaces in Grace's neighborhood, but her building was on a quiet street that sloped down to Libertador Avenue. When they exited the elevator on the Díazes' floor, Grace showed Valentina the powder room and told her to meet her in the dining room.

After Valentina freshened up, she headed back toward the front hall. In the antechamber, she paused to study the silver-framed family photos atop a black grand piano. Grace was the youngest child and only girl in the Díaz family. In a high school graduation photo, Valentina made out Bautista Larrea with Grace's brother, Sebastián. In another photo, she studied a young Mr. and Mrs. Larrea with Mr. and Mrs. Díaz, the four in tennis whites. The families had been friends for at least two generations.

The dining room was filled with paintings. Some were on the wall, while others were propped up on the mantelpiece, on a side table, and on the floor. A chandelier hung over a long mahogany table decorated with calla lilies as centerpieces. The women sat chatting while passing tiered trays with petit fours and crustless sandwiches. Valentina spotted Grace seated next to her mother. Her eyes then moved to the woman on the other side of Grace. It was Constanza Larrea, back from Europe. For some reason, she hadn't expected to see Santiago's mother there, and she momentarily forgot to breathe.

Grace's mother, Julia Díaz, greeted her. "Valentina, so glad you came! Come, sit with us."

Julia was as energetic and appealing in personality as her daughter. She stood up and added a chair. Valentina noticed Julia's feet were bare under a long caftan dress she'd purchased on a recent tour of Morocco. Her skin, darkened by the African sun, made most of the other women look sickly.

"Meet Grace's friend. Her name is Valentina," Julia announced to the group.

Constanza Larrea looked up from her tea and locked eyes with Valentina before telling Julia, "I know Valentina. She's a classmate of Santiago's. How are you, my dear?" Constanza's eyes narrowed slightly, displeased with the unexpected guest.

"Nice to see you, Mrs. Larrea," Valentina said.

"How is Santiago, Constanza?" a woman asked.

"He's fantastic. He and Bautista were just in West Germany for the FIFA World Cup. They're having a ball," Constanza said.

"I know! Did you see last week's issue of *Gente*?" Julia said, taking one of the magazines from a side table.

Valentina gave her friend a quizzical look. Grace's eyes opened wide. "Mother!"

It was too late. Julia had opened the magazine and flipped to the article she wanted. Smiling, she showed it to the guests. "Constanza, you've seen this, right?"

Valentina's eyes fastened on the photo that took up three quarters of the page. There he was. Her Santiago. And Bautista. They were with two women at what appeared to be a nightclub. The headline read:

THE LARREA BROTHERS CONQUER EUROPE'S POLO CIRCUIT
AND MONACO ROYALTY

"Is that Princess Caroline?" A guest pointed to the woman seated next to Bautista, smoking a cigarette. "Who's the one with Santiago?" someone else asked. Everyone's gaze went to Santiago and the woman beside him. It was plain to see that under the woman's bangs, her eyes were fixed on Santiago's face while he smiled for the camera. The woman was in a halter top that accentuated a man's hand on one of her broad shoulders. *He has his arm around her*, Valentina observed in disbelief.

"Santiago's date looks like a member of the Dutch monarchy!" the woman next to Constanza exclaimed.

Without looking at Valentina, Constanza said, "I have no idea who she is. I can't keep track of the women Santiago sees while he's traveling." Although Constanza knew perfectly well who the young woman was, having read the article at home, she liked to portray herself as a mother who did not meddle in her sons' lives. "What I do know is that he's having fun and that their team is doing so well that Santiago has extended his time abroad. The team has been invited to play in India at the end of the season in Europe. You all know that India is the birthplace of polo."

Valentina listened to Constanza, her mouth frozen into a smile.

"But the headline says Monaco. She must be a cousin of Caroline," someone suggested.

Grace jumped in, saying, "It's just a photo. Santiago is a gentleman and would never let a woman appear bored in a photo." She invented an excuse to get her friend out of the room. "Valentina, would you help me bring in another pot of tea?"

Valentina's body had gone numb until she felt Grace's hand in hers, leading her out of the room.

"I'm so sorry," Grace said, once the door to her bedroom was shut behind them. "I totally forgot about the article. It's a silly gossip magazine. I wouldn't pay any attention to the photo."

Valentina sat on the queen-size bed with green-and-blue-striped covers. "How can I not? He looked so happy with her."

"You would too if, for example, you were dancing with Robert Redford in a nightclub in Monaco," Grace said, glancing at the movie poster of *The Great Gatsby* on her wall displaying Robert Redford and Mia Farrow in fetching white attire. "But it doesn't mean anything."

"So you think she's as beautiful as Robert Redford?" Valentina asked. She buried her face in one of the silk pillows. When she lifted it again, she said, "I knew something was up. I haven't heard from him in at least two months."

"That's not Santiago's fault. You know how it can take an eternity for a letter to arrive, if at all."

"That's what I kept telling myself. But not now. Not anymore," Valentina said, shaking her head. "I'm glad your mom showed us the magazine. And I think Constanza was glad too."

Grace lit a cigarette and raised her window to blow out the smoke. When she turned to Valentina again, she was smiling. "Hey, I have an idea. Why don't we go dancing tonight? Who needs men anyway?"

There was a knock on her door. "Grace, you have a call."

"I'll be right back."

Valentina nodded. It hurt her to breathe. Wiping her tears with the back of her hand, she decided she needed to leave. Imagining the smug look on Constanza Larrea's face, she knew she couldn't walk past the dining room. There must be a service entrance. *These large apartments always have another way out*, she thought. She then remembered her bag was by the front door.

When she stepped out into the hall, Grace was coming toward her.

"That was Enrique on the phone," Grace said nervously, steering Valentina back inside the bedroom.

"What happened?"

"His friend, the priest."

"You mean Father Óscar?"

"Yes. He's been shot. He's dead."

"Oh my God. Where's Enrique now?"

"He's with Máximo. He called me from Café de las Artes," Grace said, dropping into a beanbag chair.

"They must be devastated. We must go to them," Valentina said, opening the bedroom door again. "Get up. Aren't you coming?"

"I don't think I can see him just yet," Grace said, revealing a rare vulnerability that Valentina had not previously seen.

"But if he called you, he must want to see you. He was probably too proud to ask."

"I can't. My mom's tea party, you know. Tell him to call me whenever he wants."

Valentina retraced her steps through the plaza to the café. Máximo and Enrique were at the bar. The men, when they saw her, rose from their stools, their grieving faces showing gratitude. They moved to a table, and Enrique described how his friend was gunned down outside a church in plain daylight. He was shaking, and Máximo, smoking a cigarette, kept biting his bottom lip as if trying not to cry. She had never seen Máximo so upset, and she hoped her hand on his arm gave him some comfort. As she listened, Valentina's anger at Santiago grew. Where was he when his friends needed him, when she needed him? Dancing the nights away in European nightclubs, while their country spiraled out of control.

On a cold morning on the first day of July of 1974, the divided people of Argentina briefly came together to mourn Juan Domingo Perón. Less than a year had passed since he had been elected president again. The cause of death was a heart attack. Overnight, Isabel Perón, his third wife and vice president of the nation, had assumed the presidency. In effect, this meant that her close friend José López Rega was the one actually in charge.

A former policeman who used his self-published book on esoteric astrology to navigate matters of state, López Rega had met Isabel almost a decade earlier, in 1965, while Perón was still in exile. Bewitched by the odd man, Isabel hired him as a personal assistant, and he soon moved into the Peróns' villa in Madrid as their live-in butler.

After Perón's death, the right-wing thugs in López Rega's Triple A grew more brazen, their operations frequently conducted in public and in broad daylight. A congressman investigating illegal arms sales from Libya to Argentina that would incriminate López Rega was shot in the head and chest as he descended from a taxi. The Triple A was also responsible for shooting and killing Father Óscar in front of a church where, minutes before, he had celebrated a Mass.

In the weeks after the priest's assassination, Valentina saw little of Enrique, but Máximo often stopped by Café de las Artes after class. They studied, read, and drank coffee together, at times not talking at all, simply content to be in each other's company.

Except for Grace, Valentina had not told any of her friends about Santiago's betrayal. Telling them would make it real, and she was still protective of their history together. When she was in the company of others, she pushed her sorrow aside. Gradually she grew dependent on Máximo's presence, spontaneously searching for him when she entered the café.

When Máximo began showing up with Paula, a student he was dating, Valentina would sit at an empty table. But if Paula had to leave early for a class, Máximo would pick up his books and move over to Valentina's table. Whenever Máximo was elsewhere in the café with Paula, Valentina became distracted, stealing glances at their table. This frustrated and confused her. Paula was perfectly nice, and Valentina knew she shouldn't interfere or monopolize Máximo's friendship. But when, one afternoon, he casually mentioned that he and Paula were not seeing each other anymore, she found she was glad. Outwardly, her behavior toward Máximo remained the same. After exchanging greetings and banal pleasantries over coffee, they would turn to their homework. But while they sat together studying for exams, a growing excitement rippled inside her.

Lately, however, Máximo had not been showing up regularly. She missed him, but what worried her more was what he might be up to. López Rega's new security law considered any type of social or political militancy illegal. She told him as much when she saw him next.

"I'm not going to stop working for what I believe in. The more people get involved, the more we understand what social injustice means, and the sooner we'll turn this country around," Máximo said, lighting a cigarette. "I can't just sit and watch my brothers and sisters suffer." He let out a ribbon of smoke from his mouth. "But don't worry, I'm not doing anything crazy."

She nodded, his answer placating her for the moment. He puffed on his cigarette, and she was quiet. "This might sound like a crazy idea," she said, putting down a pencil she had been chewing. "I've been fantasizing about building a playground for the kids at the day care."

"That's not crazy at all. It's a brilliant idea," he said.

"So you think it'd be doable?" she asked, her face lighting up in a way Máximo hadn't seen in a while. He had stopped asking her about Santiago after her responses had become short and vague. There was a melancholy in her expression at the mention of his friend's name, and he didn't want to make her sad.

"If you draw up the plans, I'll help you build it," he replied.

A few days later, Valentina invited Máximo to Casa de los Niños. They took the train and then walked through a working-class neighborhood where the paved roads ended abruptly, leaving drivers to negotiate dirt roads with large potholes. Sidewalks, where there were any, were broken, and the stench from piled-up garbage made Valentina bring her wool scarf up to her nose.

At the day care center, the nuns offered them tea and then showed them the half-acre that belonged to the Society of Saint Margaret. The sisters were excited by the idea but fretted over the expenses.

"My dad's garage is practically a carpentry shop. We can build the equipment if we have to," Máximo offered.

Sister Alice said she was good with a hammer, having built homes in one of the Indigenous communities in the north when she first arrived from France. Carmen, the social worker in residence, knew of a playground near her home that was being torn down. Perhaps they could rescue some of the equipment? Her boyfriend had a pickup truck at his disposal.

The nuns, reassured, listened and smiled benevolently, perhaps seeing something of themselves in these young people's desire to improve the world, if only with small actions.

The playground would include a sandbox, a seesaw, a slide, and a swing set. Benches and a picnic table. Additional trees would be planted. Máximo suggested a vegetable garden, saying they could use seeds from his parents' garden. The goal was to have the playground ready by spring. A week later, the sisters blessed Valentina's designs, and Máximo rounded up some of his neighborhood friends.

While the students got to work on the playground, the government got to work on the Universidad de Buenos Aires. López Rega blamed the president of the university for "general internal disorder." On the same day that a bomb exploded in the university president's home, killing his four-month-old son, the late winter sun had come out and softened the earth, making it easier for Valentina and Carmen to plant seeds in the new garden. On the same day that the Ministry of Education installed an appointee to take over the university administration and oversee the "cleanup of guerrillas and Marxist teachers," Máximo and his friends assembled a swing set to the gleeful cries of the children.

Máximo's home was a short drive from the day care center. It resembled all the other small, two-story brick homes on his block. He invited over the playground crew to drink mate. The table was dressed with his mother's embroidered tablecloth, washed and ironed, and the wooden cabinets, designed and built by his father, Enzo Cassini, gleamed from a fresh coating of polish, a homemade concoction using lemon oil. Enzo gave Valentina and Carmen a tour of the vegetable garden. Winter was in its final stretch, and Máximo's father was preparing the soil to plant new bulbs. Valentina talked to him about her mother's garden, and they compared notes and suggestions on how to organize the planting at the day care center's garden.

Nora Cassini was at her happiest when her son brought friends home, and she insisted they come back soon and often for dinner. Over the next month, Valentina, for whom food had become an afterthought since the tea party, ate copious amounts of homemade ravioli, lasagna, gnocchi, breaded veal cutlets. The playground project and crew, her friendship with Máximo, Nora Cassini's cooking, all had a healing effect on her broken heart. Not only was her appetite restored, she also slept better and smiled more.

During dinner one night, two friends from the neighborhood who worked at an underground paper mentioned they needed illustrations. Later, while Valentina helped Máximo wash the dishes, she asked him if he was thinking of contributing any of his drawings. Máximo had shown her some of his work, cartoonish faces and funny political scenes.

"I'm thinking about it," he said.

A breeze from the garden caused the window curtain to flutter. Enzo Cassini's vegetable patch was invisible in the dark.

"Well, if you decide to do it, please be careful."

He contemplated her as she rinsed a wineglass and then said, "If I were Santiago, I wouldn't let you out of my sight for one minute."

"I'm not the one who needs someone watching over them," she replied, annoyed he wasn't taking her advice seriously.

"That's not what I meant," he said, his brown eyes crinkling.

His smiles were rare, but when they materialized, the melancholy expression on his face vanished. Tonight, in this particular smile and in his words, she detected something more. She had been suppressing feelings that were surfacing more and more since they began working on the playground project together. At the same time, she was coming around to accepting that Santiago had forgotten her. There had been no more letters, and the image of him with his arm around another woman in a gossip magazine had finally started fading from her mind. It was Santiago and Máximo's friendship that kept her feelings in check. But had Máximo just admitted his attraction to her? Grabbing a dirty dish, she hoped he hadn't noticed her cheeks flushing with pleasure.

"When is he coming back, anyway? He's been gone forever."

"Soon, I guess. We haven't really been in touch," she said, surprised at how easy it was to speak those words out loud and not cry.

"Hey," he said, taking the plate she was washing and putting it back into the sudsy water. He turned her so he could see her face. "I'm sorry." His voice was soothing and his hands on her arms produced a warm and disorienting effect.

"Me too."

A few weeks later, on an early spring afternoon, the Casa de Los Niños playground was inaugurated. Everyone in the neighborhood came. The sun shone and the kids ran around, trying out the new equipment until it grew too dark to see. When the families left, the celebration continued at a bar. After the waiter poured red wine for the group, Sister Alice tapped a knife a few times against her glass before raising it. In her studied Spanish, she said, "To Valentina and our new dear friend Máximo. We're very thankful to you for bringing this idea to us and for all you have done for the families of our community."

Máximo and Valentina, surprised to have the spotlight on them, smiled shyly. When Valentina went to clink his glass, she saw in his eyes that he wanted to kiss her. But he would not. Not without her permission. They were seated together, and she became aware of his thigh against hers, his arm brushing her shoulder as he reached for the ashtray. His hair was pulled back in a ponytail, making the dark stubble on his jaw more pronounced. If they were alone, she would release his ponytail and run her fingers through his wavy hair. If they were alone, she would touch his lips with her index finger. He would kiss her finger and then her mouth. And she would kiss him back. This she told him with her gaze, and the joy on his face made her want to kiss him right then and there.

Feeling alive like she hadn't felt in a long time, Valentina looked around the table and said, "We couldn't have done it without all of you. Here's to the playground crew!"

The group laughed, raising their glasses to each other and to their ideals, which, on that warm September evening, burned brightly.

CHAPTER 19

August 1998

THE COBBLESTONE STREETS OF San Telmo, a bohemian enclave in the city, were deserted save for a few late-night revelers basking in the aftermath of San Lorenzo's victory over Boca Juniors earlier that night. The cast-iron streetlamps flung golden beams across the fans' faces, high on happiness and drink, as they launched into a rendition of their soccer club's anthem.

Franco, also in a San Lorenzo jersey, chanted heartily along. He had initially entertained the idea of taking me to the match, but when he pictured my slight frame, wide-eyed face, and American aspect, he had thought better of it. The aggressive passion of the most dedicated fans—the *barra brava*, as they were known—was not for the faint of heart. Complicating matters further, the match was being played on rival turf, in La Boca, a working-class neighborhood on the Riachuelo river, where ramshackle multicolor homes had been built from cast-off shipyard materials. We would have had to leave our seats before the end of the match to avoid potential confrontations among rowdy fans outside La Bombonera, Boca Juniors' famous soccer stadium.

Instead, he invited me to a bar that featured large photographs of tango greats Carlos Gardel, Aníbal Troilo, and Astor Piazzolla on its wood-paneled walls. We watched the match on an ancient television set perched above rows of colorful bottles that multiplied against the back wall's gilded mirror. Franco missed being in the stadium for his team's win with a glorious bicycle-kick goal in the final minutes, but I sensed he was enjoying my company. He appreciated my questions and quick enthusiasm for San Lorenzo, although when I high-fived one of the revelers later on the street, he looked bemused by my friendliness with complete strangers—an American trait he had only seen in the movies.

We cut through Plaza Dorrego, a city square that transformed into an artisanal market on Sundays, and turned down a narrow street known for its antique stores.

Franco pointed ahead. "There it is. Only a few like this are left in the city."

We crossed the street and stopped in front of a small building. A wooden sign showed the silhouette of a man and a woman in a traditional tango pose. The couple had been painted in lively colors, and underneath, the letters in *Bar Tanguero* had been drawn in a flamboyant script.

"You'll see this style of writing on some storefronts, especially in this neighborhood. It's also used on some of the older city buses. It's called *fileteado*. Beautiful, don't you think?"

"Yes."

"Sadly, it's a dying art form," he said, bringing me inside.

We were shown to a small round table next to the stage. A slim, gray-haired man in a coat and tie asked what we would like to drink. Franco turned to me, and I said I would have whatever he was having. He ordered two whiskeys. After the waiter left, Franco's eyes darted about the bar. He excused himself, and I watched him talk to the waiter and then walk toward what I thought would be the bathroom, until I saw the sign for the bathroom on the opposite side. Where was he going? I tipped my chair back. He was standing in front of a side entrance. He opened the door with some difficulty and, after peering out, closed it. He hesitated, then opened and closed it again.

The singing drew my attention back to the small stage. A singer with brittle bleached hair was dressed in a black pencil skirt, red-sequined tank top, fishnet stockings, and stilettos. She crooned the tragic lines of a tango. When she finished, she bowed and accepted a single rose from the bartender as if she were a *grande dame* before a full house at the Teatro Colón.

"She's incredible. What a voice!" I applauded. Franco had returned to our table. The singer left the stage and the orchestra broke into a *milonga*. "I've never been to a live tango performance before. What a great idea this was," I told him, glad I had ditched my parents to meet him.

Mom had unexpectedly shown up after the press conference. When I saw her in the hotel lobby, seated on a plush velvet chair between twin marble columns, I recalled how, as a self-doubting and anxious teen, I had tried and failed to model myself after my beautiful, poised mother. From my naive perspective, her life seemed perfect. But as I watched her looking up at the frescoes of angels dancing around robust ladies in flowing gowns, I thought of my father's secret. I walked over and hugged her like I hadn't since the day I moved into my freshman dorm.

"Sweetie," Mom said, surprised by my embrace. "I'm feeling much better if that's what's worrying you. I took one of the strong pain-killers."

"I'm just happy to see you, Mamá."

How would my mother feel if she found out about the safe house? At the art gallery, Dad said he built it because of his ex-girlfriend—an ex-girlfriend he had gotten together with after marrying my mother. The more I thought about it, he had seemed to imply he was unfaithful to her with Valentina. Did a part of her know her husband harbored secrets? And if so, was it manifesting in her headaches? I glanced over at Dad, who was concluding a conversation with a couple of journalists. I hadn't told him I'd found the stone pendant and the photos. One photo showed Mom and Valentina at the campo, which meant Lila and Valentina *had* met after they were married, contrary to what Dad had told me. Why had my parents invited Valentina to El Pinar if she was his former love? As I observed him chatting amiably with the reporters, I suspected he had not been entirely forthcoming with me.

"Are you sure you're all right?" Mom asked again, seeming to read my troubled mind.

"I missed you," I told her.

Her eyes misted. She tended to get sentimental after one of her headaches. Taking my hand, she said, "Let's grab your father before he gets pulled into another long discussion. I've been dreaming about a glass of champagne at the Jockey Club." It was the private men's club where my parents had held their wedding reception.

It was during drinks with members of Dad's staff that Franco had left a message on my phone, asking if I was free. Under normal circumstances I might have been put off by this last-minute invitation, but my time in Buenos Aires was limited, and I wanted to see him. I told my parents I was meeting Juan and kissed them hurriedly, not giving them time to suggest he join our group instead.

"Now it's our turn." Franco reached for my hand, bringing me and my thoughts back to the tango bar.

After drinking the whiskey, I was a bit wobbly on my feet, and he placed his hand on my back to steady me. No one else was on the dance floor.

"You're only supposed to dance the tango to an instrumental piece," he said, pulling me in closer.

"I never knew that, Mr. Bonetti."

He twirled me and I easily followed his lead.

"I have to admit I'm impressed, for a Yanqui."

Did he call me a Yanqui to see if he could get a rise out of me? "Thanks, Argie," I responded in kind, using the derogatory British term for the Argentines.

He accepted my comeback with a lighthearted wince, saying, "Where did you learn to dance?"

"Oh, here and there. But mostly from my dad in New York."

"So you're not a real gringa, are you?" he asked, grinning.

"I'm not one to reveal much on a first date," I answered coyly.

"So you see this as a date?"

"Check with me in an hour," I replied.

A couple in their seventies stepped out onto the floor, and we paused to watch their fluid dance moves.

"I don't know much about you except that you're a good dancer and a loyal San Lorenzo fan," I said when we started dancing again.

"Ask me anything you like, Ms. Larrea. Tonight is your lucky night. Whatever you want to know."

"That's too good an offer to pass up." I pretended to be in deep thought and then looked at him. "Okay. Here's how it goes. I'll give you two words, and you have to choose one or the other. But you have to do it fast. Without thinking. First thing that comes to mind. Ready?"

"Yes."

"Okay. First one. Rock and roll or tango."

"Easy. Tango."

"You're a romantic, Mr. Bonetti," I asserted. After a pause, I presented him with a new pair of words. "Black or white?"

"Gray."

"That doesn't count."

"All right. I'll go with white, then."

"You're an optimist at heart. What else? Let's see…airplanes or trains?"

"Trains."

"Hmm, interesting," I remarked, tapping my chin in jest. "That probably means that you like to take your time in everything you do. Ocean or river?"

"River, especially if I'm camping by one."

"I've never been camping. Haven't even slept in a tent."

"You don't know what you're missing."

"With all those mosquitoes? No thank you, not for me," I said. "All right, here's another one. Moonlight or sunlight?"

"Auuuuhh," he howled, and I tossed my head back in laughter.

"Pajamas or boxers?"

"Neither," he replied with an irresistible smile.

"I shouldn't have asked," I said, blushing, a warm and very pleasant current running through me.

We bumped into the older couple and we all bowed our heads slightly in acknowledgment.

"My turn?" he asked.

"Yes."

"Chance or fate?" He looked at me intently, and I shifted my gaze away.

When I looked into his eyes again, I answered quietly, "Fate."

The tango was still playing, but he stopped dancing. His arms fell and, with a resigned voice, he said, "Yeah. That's what I think too."

After leaving the bar, we walked to the nearby apartment of one of Franco's friends from HIJOS. The host, Nahuel, wearing his straight black hair loose around his shoulders, patted Franco on the back and kissed me hello before showing us into the living room. Colorful textiles were draped over worn sofas and Indigenous masks were displayed in a row on one wall. Nahuel's mother's side of the family was from the Mapuche tribe whose homelands extended the length of Patagonia and across both sides of the Andes.

Franco kept his hand on my back as he introduced me to his friends. While guests danced free-form to a song by the Argentine rock group Soda Stereo, he led me about as if we were still in the tango bar. He invented moments to bring me toward him before spinning me away. Each time, he pulled me in a little bit closer so that, as the song ended, our faces were only an inch apart. I held my breath, seeing only his smiling white teeth, wondering if he might kiss me, hoping he would. A couple dancing next to us accidentally nudged me toward him, and my lips were suddenly on his.

"Oh. I can't believe I just kissed you," I said. *The whiskey made me do it*, I thought to tell him, but I knew I would have kissed him sober too. "Was I wrong?"

By his expression I could tell he was pleasantly surprised.

"No," he said, and brought his palm to my cheek. We were jostled again. The dance floor had become crowded. He clasped my hand, and with our eyes on one another, we moved out of the way. A friend appeared with beers. The apartment was hot and I took several swigs. And then, stupidly, I accepted a cigarette. I was not a smoker, and when I inhaled, I felt a rush that left me dizzy. I stepped out onto the balcony for fresh air. A couple said hello and returned to their make-out session. When the dizziness stopped, I went back inside. The party seemed to have doubled in size. Everyone was jumping, arms waving in the air, singing to a popular song by an Argentine ska band, Los Fabulosos Cadillacs. In search of a bathroom, I bumped into Franco having what seemed to be an intimate conversation with a woman I hadn't seen before. I apologized, and then I remembered little else except climbing into a taxi and stumbling alone into Abuelo's apartment.

CHAPTER 20

November–December 1974

As the year wound down, the number of arrests accelerated around the country. The government's hit list had expanded to include not only leaders of leftist organizations but also anyone believed to have expressed left-leaning ideas. Paramilitary death squads roamed freely in unmarked Ford Falcon cars with the sole mission to hunt down, kidnap, torture, and kill people on the list. Individuals were taken into custody for questioning, later turning up dead in ditches and empty lots.

In the midst of this violence, hidden in plain sight, ordinary Argentinians went on about their daily lives. University students worried about end-of-year exams, papers, and presentations, many clocking extra hours at the library. Valentina was one such student. One evening in late November, she returned to her residence, fatigued after a full day of classes and a bite to eat with some classmates at an Italian restaurant on Avenida Corrientes. She absentmindedly wished a good evening to the building's porter, who was outside smoking a cigarette.

"Hey, miss, that guy you used to go out with is in the lounge," the porter said. "I told him you were out, but he said he'd wait until you came back. I didn't have the heart to tell him that it's against the rules. He seems eager to see you."

Santiago. Eight months later, and he was finally back. Valentina had almost come to believe he would never return. She felt weak and considered not going inside. She thanked the porter as he opened the door.

She found him asleep on the grubby sofa in the residence lounge. The overhead light was on, and the small black-and-white television hummed with a static image of stripes. Television programming had finished for the evening. She observed him, not wanting to wake him yet, trying to gather her thoughts. What would she say? His lanky frame was sprawled out on the sofa, his hands tucked in his underarms. It was hard not to touch him, and after a few moments, she leaned over and gently brushed away the wisps of hair from his forehead.

Santiago startled awake. Valentina appeared dreamlike before him. It had taken him almost two days to fly back from India. His excitement to see her had kept him fully awake on both flights, from Calcutta to Paris and from Paris to Buenos Aires. Disappointed to hear she wasn't in, he had slipped the porter a large bill and was able to wait for her in the lounge. Knowing he would soon be holding her, he had been lulled by the dim lighting and the soothing background noise from the television set.

"Valentina." He propped himself up. "You're here."

"I live here," she said. As nervous as she was, his remark, nevertheless, made her smile.

Santiago thought they would immediately be in each other's arms but she remained standing and he sitting, unsure of himself. He swung his legs off the sofa and when he embraced her, her body stiffened slightly.

"I'm so happy to see you," he said, perplexed by her cold welcome.

"When did you get back?" Valentina asked as she dropped her school bag on an adjacent chair.

"A few hours ago. I left my suitcases at home and came straight to see you."

"How was your flight?"

"Long." Why this formal back and forth? he wondered. "I missed you."

"You did?"

"Yes, of course."

Her voice. Her face. Something wasn't right. Santiago had the sensation that the floor between them might cave in, forming a crater he needed to jump over before she left him on the other side. He stepped toward her.

"Valentina, I'm sorry I was gone for so long. I didn't think it would be eight months. But our team was doing well and we were getting amazing sponsors, and I couldn't abandon the team. I wrote to tell you that I was staying longer."

"In the few letters you sent, not a single one of them mentioned it. In those letters you wrote that you were dying to return to me. You couldn't wait for August. That was three months ago."

"But I wrote to you, often."

"If you did, I didn't get them."

"I'm sorry to hear that," he said, coming a little closer. "My mother told me how sometimes you would come and stay for tea. She enjoyed those visits."

"The last time I saw your mother was at Grace's. Did she tell you about that tea?"

As he heard her question, Santiago couldn't quite believe they weren't kissing.

"No. My mother and Grace's mother Julia have been friends forever. They get together all the time. Was there something special about that particular tea party?"

"You. You were the man of the hour."

He groaned, jokingly. "Don't tell me my mother was going on about Bautista and me. Sometimes she just can't help herself."

"It wasn't your mom. It was Grace's mother who brought out a magazine and showed us the photo of you and Bautista in Monaco."

Santiago tilted his head, puzzled, until he figured out what she meant.

"Is that why you're mad? My sweet Valentina. That was nothing. They're Bautista's friends. We were having fun. It was summer," he explained, moving to kiss her.

"Don't, please."

Santiago's arms dropped. "It was a night out. The damn paparazzi…"

"Go ahead. Blame it on the paparazzi, Santiago."

"I do. And Julia Díaz. What a fool."

"You're the fool for staying away for so long."

"But you encouraged me to go. Now I wish I hadn't. Next time, I won't go without you."

"You should've come back sooner," she said.

"But here I am, standing right in front of you." Saying these words with her in such close proximity, he thought he would burst if he had to wait one more minute to take her in his arms. At once, she was kissing him. He lost himself in her embrace, in how she devoured his mouth with her kisses. A quick sharp pain broke his desire. She had bit his bottom lip, hard.

She pushed him and walked away. "You have no idea how lonely I was."

Had her teeth pierced through? His tongue explored the little bit of blood inside his mouth. "I feel terrible. Please, let me make it up to you."

"If only you had come back when you said you would," Valentina said, turning to look at him. "Maybe things would be different. Maybe we'd still be together."

"But we are. Aren't we?" he said, uncertainty creeping up on him.

"This country's a mess and I waited for you, needed you. It was agonizing. I missed you so much. And then when I saw your picture in the magazine, I thought I had lost you. But when I recovered, I found ways to distract myself…"

"I'm glad to hear it."

"I'm not sure how glad you'll be when I tell you what I have to tell you." She paused. "Máximo and I are together."

It took him a moment to react, and when he did, it was with a question. "Máximo Cassini?" He needed to clarify as if there were more than one Máximo in their lives. Because, he thought, she couldn't possibly be talking about his friend.

Valentina nodded, her eyes downcast. "We became close friends and then it happened."

"What are you talking about? What happened exactly?"

"You were gone most of the year, and Máximo and I spent a lot of that time together. I helped him and Enrique a few times at the villa by Retiro.

"And then when Father Óscar was murdered…did you hear about that while partying in Europe? Probably not. We were very upset. Enrique stopped coming around. I have no idea what he's up to. No one hears much from him. And Máximo. He wasn't doing well. He seemed vulnerable, almost fragile. He grew to rely on our coffees at the café. I think that having a place for him to keep coming back to, knowing that I would be there, helped. You know?"

"But he's my friend," he murmured, not really listening to her.

"He needs to engage in causes he feels will make a difference. He gets sad about the state of the world. But he's compassionate and talented, and you know what? We built an entire playground for the kids at Casa de Los Niños. And doing that project together, we became close, and eventually it grew into something else," Valentina said without looking at him.

"Are you in love with him?"

She took a deep breath. "I know that I enjoy spending all my free time with him. He's gotten more involved in social activism and it's hard not to worry. I feel like I'm an anchor for him, that I can keep him from doing something crazy. He's not practical, not like me at all." She glanced at him and smiled nervously. "His head is always in the clouds when he's deeply committed to working for a good cause."

"I asked you if you're in love with him." Santiago's voice came out strangled.

She finally spoke, her words above a whisper. "Yes. I'm in love with him."

He nodded repeatedly as if this motion would help sink the words into his head and heart.

"Santiago?"

He had closed his eyes, and when he opened them again, his voice was flat. "I guess there's nothing left for me to say then. Have a good night."

"Wait."

He pushed past the porter and stumbled out. His lungs needed to take in deep gulps of air, but it had not cooled off that evening. The air remained dense and hot, and Santiago, unable to fulfill his lungs' demands, became dizzy and had to lean against a storefront window. An older man approached, asking if he needed help. Embarrassed by his public display of weakness, he straightened himself. Finding his breath again, he turned off her street onto Avenida Corrientes and flung himself into the crush of the theater crowds.

Valentina decided not to go after him. Santiago was right. What else was there to say? She had not lied. She loved Máximo. Standing paralyzed in the middle of the lounge, she asked herself if it was possible to love two men, even though she already knew the answer.

She began pacing about the room, a part of her wishing Santiago were still there. She retrieved her backpack from the chair and noticed a bag on the floor next to the sofa where he had waited for her.

It was a large embroidered bag. It was heavy and, upon opening it, she found a silk pouch near the top. A gold bangle was inside. The label on the pouch read *Made in India*. There was more. She tipped the contents onto the sofa to find an array of small gifts, each with a card from the country where he had purchased them. Belgian chocolates, lingerie from Paris, an antique hand mirror from England, a Spanish shawl, a crocheted bikini from Milan. He had been thinking of her all along, she thought, and as she returned everything back into the bag, she silently wept.

Three weeks after Santiago's return and just days before Christmas, Valentina was in the residence lounge, drinking mate, when a student from her floor stopped by and mentioned that she had seen Máximo at the law school. He was joining a group of students at a protest outside the Sheraton Hotel. Two years earlier, before Perón's return, the American chain had opened its first hotel in Buenos Aires. Seen as a symbol of American imperialism, it was promptly bombed by leftist Peronist militants. Ever since, the hotel had remained a target of protests.

Valentina put her mate down and quickly went to her room to grab her purse. Hurrying down Avenida Corrientes to catch a bus, Valentina wondered why Máximo hadn't said anything to her about it. They had an agreement that they wouldn't engage in any sort of protest unless they did it together.

The old bus, colorfully hand-painted with drawings of its number and destination, circled around the Obelisk, the national monument that stood at the intersection of Avenida Corrientes and the central artery of Buenos Aires, Avenida 9 de Julio. Valentina looked out the window at the revolving billboard around the pencil-shaped landmark: *Silence*

Is Health. Ostensibly a national campaign to keep cars from honking and to reduce urban noise in general, its true purpose was something else entirely. It was a warning to journalists, workers, politicians, artists, and intellectuals to refrain from speaking out against the state.

Valentina arrived at the law school out of breath and found Máximo outside the front entrance talking to students. When he saw her, he broke away from the group.

"What are you doing here?" he asked, his face softening at the sight of her.

Valentina hugged him, asking if he was fine.

"More than fine," he replied. "Now that you're here." Under his new mustache, his lips formed a sweet smile.

"My neighbor told me you're going to a protest at the Sheraton Hotel. Are you?"

"They need numbers, and I said I'd help. They think it should be turned into a children's hospital. It makes sense, being so close to the shantytown by Retiro. There are no medical facilities anywhere nearby."

In their time together, as friends and now as lovers, Valentina had never known Máximo to say no to anybody who needed help. His eyes shone, and in them she saw his purity and selflessness. Had Santiago seen the same in Máximo's eyes? Did he know that Máximo would never intentionally hurt anyone, especially a friend? It had been Valentina who had made the first move. She had told Máximo it was over between her and Santiago. She encouraged him to kiss her the night after the playground celebration gathering. She had hoped to talk to Santiago again to make that clear. Thinking he might come back to take the gifts, she waited for him, but he never returned. She knew Máximo and Santiago had spoken. As soon as she told him that Santiago was back, Máximo went looking for him. She never found out what was said between the two of them. Máximo didn't tell her when he showed up the following day at her house with a bruised, partially shut right eye. And she didn't ask. Later, she heard from Grace that Santiago had gone to his family's ranch until the New Year.

"Well, I'm glad you're still here," Valentina told Máximo, still a bit breathless from running from the bus stop to the law school.

"I'm meeting up with them now."

They walked to the pedestrian bridge connecting the law school to Figueroa Alcorta Avenue. The bridge, normally plastered with symbols or messages with an academic, political, or social tenor, had been freshly painted a drab gray by the administration. Thousands of students crossed that bridge on a daily basis. It wouldn't remain sign-free for long.

"Why didn't you tell me about the protest?" she asked as they paused at the highest point of the bridge. It was a clear day, and the hotel could be discerned in the distance.

"They asked me this morning."

"But we have a pact," she said, not able to keep the frustration from her voice.

"I know," he said, looping his arms around her waist and kissing her tenderly. "I wasn't breaking it. I didn't want to bother you. You have finals too. Do you want to come?"

"Can we get a sandwich on the way? I'm starving."

As they came out of a bakery close to the Sheraton Hotel holding *medialunas* stuffed with ham and cheese, a series of patrol cars raced by them and down the hill alongside the Plaza de San Martín.

"I bet they're on their way to bust up the protest," Máximo said. Grabbing her hand, they followed the patrol cars.

The sun, after days of rain, had brought the Porteños outdoors. The playground was lively with children, couples embraced on benches under massive ombú trees, and men with loosened ties rested on the red granite steps at the base of the monument to General San Martín. Valentina and Máximo hastened across the square's lawn, which sloped down the hill toward Torre de los Ingleses, Buenos Aires's Big Ben, a clock tower given as a gift by the British upon the completion of the Retiro train station.

To get to the hotel they had to cross San Martín Avenue, but they were held up by the red light. In spite of the traffic in both directions, they had a good view of the scene. Twenty or so students were marching outside the hotel entrance when, without warning, they were corralled by thuggish-looking officers. Some were in plain clothes. A couple of students attempted to talk with the police, but they were not in the mood for dialogue. The banners were confiscated. Officers shoved students into patrol cars. Those who resisted were knocked to the ground and then dragged. It was awful to watch, but Valentina was secretly relieved they had arrived too late.

"Stay here," Máximo instructed her.

"What are you going to do?" she asked.

"I'm going to try to reason with the cops. They cannot strip us of our right to protest, our right to free speech. We are still, God help us, a democratic society."

"But they'll arrest you too," she said as the light changed.

He stepped off the curb.

"Máximo. If you go, don't expect me to be waiting for you," she warned in an imploring tone.

His body seemed to sway between the violent scene unfolding across the street and Valentina's pleas. When her eyes filled with tears, he returned to the sidewalk and put his arms around her. "All right, I won't go. I may be able to help them get released by staying outside."

With terror in their hearts, Valentina and Máximo helplessly watched the police drive away with their peers in the backs of the patrol cars. Pedestrians brushed by them, unaware of or uninterested in what the young couple had just witnessed. Feeling very much alone, the two did not let go of each other. Outside the hotel entrance, activity returned to normal but for the broken banners on the ground, the only remaining signs of the protest.

CHAPTER 21

August 1998

THE DAY AFTER DAD'S PRESS conference and my night out with Franco, I had breakfast with my parents at La Biela, the café in Recoleta where Dad had proposed to Mom. Clad in black pants, white shirts, and neckties folded impeccably under their aprons, the waiters treated the well-turned-out morning patrons with a courteous familiarity—without introducing themselves or smiling like American waiters—that made me think they were regulars.

"You're a quiet one today," my mother remarked after we had been served medialunas, coffees with steamed milk, freshly squeezed orange juice, and little glasses of fizzy water. Dad had picked up several dailies from a press kiosk on our way to breakfast, including the *Buenos Aires Herald*, which now rested on the table.

It was early, I was a little hungover, and I worried that if I spoke, I would slip up and talk about what was most on my mind—Franco and the people my age he had introduced me to, whose parents had been disappeared or murdered by the military. I worried I might inadvertently mention Dad's safe house. In my mother's presence, my father's secret weighed on me. But I was also honored he had taken

me into his confidence, and I knew I would carry his secret forever. Still, in my foggy state, staying quiet felt like the best course
of action.

Dad spoke: "Did you have a good time last night? How's Juan?"

"Yes. Juan's good." I swirled water around my dry mouth, swallowed,
and when they waited for me to say something else, I added, "We had
a great night."

Mother nodded, pleased, and asked for a few more details. I made up
a story about going out to dinner, just the two of us. I didn't like lying
but it wasn't hard. Later, when they wanted to know if I was going back
to the ranch with them, I was relieved to tell them the truth, which was
that Juan had invited me to a polo match in Hurlingham.

After they left for the campo, I fell asleep on the sofa and woke up
again only when my cell phone rang. It was Juan. As he went over logistics, explaining whom I would be meeting at the Hurlingham Club,
I rose and looked out the living room window. The sun was at its peak
and the river glimmered with hints of silver. I silently scolded myself
for having ordered that last whiskey at Bar Tanguero. All had been fine
with Franco, even wonderful, right up until the moment I downed the
beer at Nahuel's. Why had I had so much to drink? I was sure I had
made a fool of myself. Porteños didn't drink like college students did
in the US. Franco must have thought I was a drunken idiot. Oh well. I
wouldn't be in Buenos Aires much longer, and it was highly unlikely I
would see him again. This last thought was making me feel even worse
when I heard Juan's voice: "Paloma?"

I apologized, asked him to repeat the question, and then answered,
"No. No need to come up. I'll meet you downstairs."

My jacket was nowhere to be found, so I grabbed a sweater from my
room and took the elevator down.

"Oh! Hi!" I had been sure I would never set eyes on Franco Bonetti
again. And yet there he was, standing outside my building, causing my
heart to flutter. "What are you doing here?"

"I was about to ring your apartment." He was holding a jacket. It was mine. "You left this at Nahuel's."

"So *that's* where it was," I said with a small laugh. "Thank you. I'd been wondering where I left it…" My voice trailed off, wondering how to explain and apologize for my sudden departure from the party. I couldn't admit that I was drunk *and* jealous when I saw him talking with the other woman. He rightly would have thought I was crazy.

I could tell Franco was waiting for me to say something more when a BMW squealed to a stop in front of us. Juan climbed out of the driver's seat.

"Hey, beautiful." Juan kissed me lightly while eyeing Franco.

"Juan. This is Franco."

They evaluated one other as they exchanged hellos.

Juan put his arm around my shoulders. "Ready to go, babe?" His phone rang and he flipped it open. "Yes?"

My purse slipped off my shoulder and fell to the ground. I wriggled free of Juan's hold and bent down to pick it up. Franco beat me to it. "Thank you," I said softly. "I'm sorry I left last night without telling you…"

Franco didn't let me finish. He stood back up as Juan snapped his phone shut. "I should be going." Franco turned to Juan and said, "Nice meeting you." He handed me the jacket.

I watched him leave as Juan went around the car to open the passenger door for me.

"So, who was that guy?" he asked as we drove down Figueroa Alcorta.

"Franco."

"I know his *name*. You introduced us. But how do you know him?"

"He's a student. We met the other day when…"

He cut me off. "So what was he doing with your jacket?"

"I left it at a party. He was returning it to me."

"A *party*?" Juan shot me a look. "You went to a party without me?

You cancel our date the other night, and now I hear you went out anyway with this other guy. What's going on, Paloma?"

"I don't know." We stopped at a red light. "I'm sorry, Juan, but I don't think I want to go to Hurlingham anymore." I opened the car door and got out.

As I ran across the lanes, Juan yelled at me. "What are you doing? You'll get run over!"

The light turned green and I could hear the other drivers honking their horns aggressively. When I was safely across, I turned onto a side street, losing myself in the sidewalk crowd.

The next morning, waiting for the water to boil for my cup of instant coffee, I walked into the entrance hall and sat in a tattered gray settee by a narrow marble side table. The answering machine flashed red with missed calls. The first one was from my mother, wanting to know when I would return to El Pinar. The second one was from Juan, wanting to talk before going to his family's ranch south of the city. I knew it was over between us, and I was thinking about why I had dated him in the first place when the next message began to play. Silence. I was about to delete it when, listening more closely, I heard the sound of someone taking deep measured breaths into the receiver. Could it be Juan calling again? I waited for his voice, but the recording ended with a click.

I prepared a cup of coffee, padded barefoot into the living room, and let my body sag into a sofa. If things had turned out differently, I would have thanked Franco for returning my jacket by inviting him out for a coffee. Maybe we would have browsed some of the city's numerous bookstores. I would have asked for recommendations of Argentine authors, and I would have perhaps shared with him a few of my own favorites. Maybe we would have grabbed a bite to eat afterward. Picturing us together, I felt a pang of regret for what might have been. But as I drank my coffee and began to feel fully awake, I decided that, after having spent almost a week in Buenos Aires, it was time to leave. I would call the campo and let my parents know. Nothing was keeping me here anymore.

I was searching for the train schedule when the apartment intercom rang.

"Who is it?" I asked into the speaker, and then pressed the buzzer.

A sweaty and panting Franco was at my door a few moments later. "You're okay," he said, sounding relieved.

"Yes. I am. I just woke up." Self-conscious, I wrapped my robe tightly around me. "What's going on?" I asked, noting Franco's worried expression.

"I called you this morning and when nobody picked up, I thought, maybe...well, nothing. I see now that you're fine," he mumbled more to himself than to me. "I probably shouldn't have come."

A draft came in from the hallway.

"Won't you come in?"

"No, thank you. I'm sorry for bothering you."

"Don't be ridiculous. You haven't even told me why you came." When he didn't move, it dawned on me. "Juan isn't here," I said. "It's just me."

"All right, but just for a minute."

"Can I at least get you a cup of coffee?"

"That'd be great."

He followed me into the kitchen. "I'll make it," Franco offered. He put two small spoons of Nescafé and sugar into the cup and poured hot water over it. Back in the living room, he drank the coffee in two gulps. He said, "I got a call last night."

"From whom?"

"I'm not totally sure, but he was most likely undercover intelligence. It's been a long time since I've heard from them."

"Why did they call you?"

"They like to keep tabs, make their presence known whenever they think we're stepping over the line."

"But who are 'they'?"

"Former military guys, torturers, hired thugs. They view us, both HIJOS and the Madres and Abuelas de Plaza de Mayo, as a threat."

"So why now?"

"Unclear. At first I thought it was because of the *escrache* against Father Aznar, but then he said your name."

"My name? Why on earth would he mention me?"

"I've been asking myself the same question."

Shaken by what he had just told me, I sank into a chair. "I need to tell you something," I began, my eyes staring at my feet. "I'm not really writing a paper on Martín Torres. The real reason I went to the center the other day was to look up someone my father had known. A woman named Valentina. After she was kidnapped, my father built a safe house to help others in danger. I recently found out about all this, and I had to make up a story to protect my father. He's been given a political appointment as ambassador to the UN. The official ceremony is happening in just over a week." I looked at him but he didn't respond. "I hope you'll understand that I had to be discreet. I'm sorry I didn't tell you the truth. Now that I know you, I wish I had."

Franco picked up the copy of *Nunca Más*. He thumbed through the pages in a manner suggesting he was familiar with its contents.

"Do you think this call might have anything to do with my father?"

"You've been reading this?" he asked, momentarily ignoring my question.

"Yes. There's no mention of my dad that I can find in the report, but I did find a couple of witnesses who talk about Valentina Quintero in their testimonies."

He stopped at the earmarked pages. "We should try to locate them."

"Why do you want to help me?"

"I don't think you got the full picture of HIJOS at the meeting. When we first came together, we were mainly a source of support for each other. A bunch of us had grown up hiding our stories, unable to talk about our families. Although most of our parents had been forcibly disappeared, exiled, or assassinated, many of us grew up not knowing, still not knowing, what actually happened to them. We felt different, at times ashamed, but more often than not, marginalized. So when we found one another, we had a lot to discuss, not just about ourselves but about what was happening currently, politically and socially. All these years later, there's still no justice for all the crimes committed. The torturers have been pardoned." His tone rose in anger. "The only course of action was for us to become activists. And that's how HIJOS was born. Our mission is to reveal the truth. We won't remain silent and let our country continue to bury its past," he ended in an impassioned voice.

Listening to Franco, I understood he was still suffering the repercussions from this awful period in Argentina's history. "You're right," I said. "I didn't really grasp the scope of what you are confronting."

"I understand why you had to lie at the Human Rights Center. It's actually good you've been cautious. Then, after you and I went out, a man called me and brought up your name. Paloma Larrea. Now that you've told me about your dad, I'm sure the call was related to him. And you're somehow tied up in your father's story."

"You're not worried they'll come after you?"

"You're going back to New York soon, right?" he asked, shutting the book.

"Yeah."

"Then we don't have much time."

CHAPTER 22

March–April 1975

From the living room Santiago could hear his mother instructing Celeste, the new maid, on how to set the table properly. His father, standing next to him, prepared a tall glass of Fernet-Branca with club soda, no ice. His daily holy medicine, Alfonso liked to call it. Santiago helped himself to a few olives and cheese cubes from a tray beside the liquor trolley. He popped them into his mouth as he strolled into the dining room.

"Are you sure I can't convince you to stay for dinner, Santi? Antonia is preparing your favorite, roast beef with potatoes." His mother brought her hand up to his cheek.

"I've made plans."

Ever since Bautista decided to stay indefinitely in Europe, his mother doted tirelessly on her younger son. Santiago missed his older brother and also resented him for leaving him alone to contend with their parents.

"I hope you're not planning to go to the movies."

A downtown theater had been bombed the day before. There had been no deaths, and the police suspected the Montoneros, an urban guerrilla movement within the left wing of the Peronist party. In 1970, in a show of devotion to Perón, the organization had kidnapped and assassinated General Pedro Eugenio Aramburu for his role in ousting Perón in 1955. But upon his return to Argentina, Perón turned against them, siding with the right wing of his party, whom Montoneros blamed for the Ezeiza massacre.

The massacre had occurred almost two years ago. Yet, from time to time, Santiago dreamed he was near the airport waiting for Perón's arrival. In the dream, Grace wasn't with him. He was alone in the sea of people. And when the shots rang out, he found he couldn't run. His legs wouldn't move and he would wake with a start, his chest heaving.

"Not a bad idea, now that you mention it. Chances are they won't attack a theater again anytime soon," he replied dryly.

"That's not funny, Santiago," she said, correcting Celeste's botched attempt at folding a white linen napkin.

"The Williamses are coming tonight and they're bringing their daughter, Lila. She's been studying in London. You remember her, no?"

"She must have been ten years old the last time I saw her," Santiago said, knowing where this was heading. "I'm not interested in meeting anyone right now, Mamá, but when I'm ready, I promise you'll be the first to know." To put an end to the conversation, he kissed his mother's cheek.

Alfonso, who had been listening, called out from the living room. "What about that hippie woman, the one with the curly wild hair. Are you still dating her?"

His father had never bothered to remember Valentina's name. Neither parent realized to what extent Santiago had fallen for her.

Santiago took a deep breath and replied loudly, "We never dated seriously. We were just friends."

He had spent days and sleepless nights re-creating in his mind his last conversation with Valentina in the lounge of her student residence, the day he returned from the travels in Europe and India that he now regretted. In the refuge of the campo, he concluded that Máximo had seduced Valentina with his intellectual talk of the common man's struggle, inequality in education, political reform, and so on. How could she not have seen through Máximo's intentions? Yet deep inside, Santiago understood how they might be a natural fit. Same middle-class socioeconomic background. Her work in the children's shelter. His legal aid in the slums. All the same, he had made a mistake by staying away from her so long and allowing this to happen.

Santiago found relief when a side of him returned to the man he had been before Valentina. A man who dedicated much of his free time to picking up women at nightclubs, bars, parties, and polo matches without much effort and without much else on his mind but to have fun, no strings attached.

It was March, the start of the new school year, and almost four months since Valentina had broken his heart. An emptiness remained inside of him, yet in some ways he was starting to feel like his old self again. He kissed his mother once more before leaving, then grabbed a jacket from the hall closet and opened the front door. A young woman stood outside, her hand poised to ring the bell. Both startled. He spoke first.

"So, you must be…"

Her honey-blond hair fell straight past her shoulders. A few bangs fell over her forehead. Her eyes were a mesmerizing green.

"Lila," she said. She was tall compared to most women he knew but came across as almost fragile. "I'm early. My parents will be here shortly. I hope that's all right. I was already in the neighborhood, you see," she explained in a melodious voice.

"Please come in. I'm Santiago."

"I know who you are. We met a couple of times, many years ago, but we never really spoke."

"If I ignored you back then, I apologize. That was very foolish of me."

Her pink lips formed a shy smile, revealing the tiniest dimples. "You were a senior in high school when I was only a freshman at Corazón Sagrado." It was the sister school to Santiago's all-boys prep school.

Alfonso appeared around the corner. "Well, if it isn't the lovely Lila."

"How do you do?" she said, and Alfonso kissed her cheek.

"Very well," Alfonso said, and turned to Santiago. "Weren't you leaving?"

Lila raised her right eyebrow at Santiago as if already entitled to an explanation for his comings and goings.

"I was going downstairs to buy a pack of cigarettes"—he patted his jacket—"but I see that I still have some."

Alfonso helped her with her coat. And when Lila faced Santiago again, she caught him admiring her.

Shortly after he started dating Lila, her parents invited Santiago to the Farmers' Ball held each winter at the embassy of the United Kingdom. The annual event celebrated the thousand plus Anglo-Argentines who owned a healthy swath of Argentina's vast farmland. The men wore white tie, and the women were clad in evening gowns. Santiago ate a canapé and watched Lila dance with the British deputy consul, Conrad Robertson, a slim, ginger-haired, slightly balding man in his early forties. A friend of the Williamses, Conrad appeared enchanted with Lila and, in the older man's arms, she looked even younger than her nineteen years. The couple twirled, and Lila's straight blond hair seemed to twirl too. When Lila smiled at him over the British man's shoulder, Santiago raised his glass of champagne. She was everything a man could hope for in a wife, and he could see himself falling in love with her. He also knew he could never love Lila, or any other woman, with the intensity he loved—*had* loved—Valentina.

Queen Elizabeth's portrait hung behind Santiago, and almost

everyone was speaking the Queen's English. One couldn't discern the locals from the British until a guest would slip in an Argentinian idiomatic phrase. Guests skirted around topics of a sensitive nature. If, however, one paid close enough attention, tones dropped when a remark was made about the country's turbulent political climate or the ongoing diplomatic impasse over the Falklands. The contested islands were under the control of the British Empire, but the Argentine government claimed them too, giving the desolate South Atlantic archipelago another name: las Malvinas.

Santiago tugged at his tie and glanced at his watch.

"Order me a drink?" Lila had materialized at his side.

"Another gin and tonic?"

"Mm-hmm," she replied gaily.

Lila had spent a year studying abroad in England, where she had learned how to hold her liquor. The trip had been cut short, however, when her father made a surprise visit and found her spending too much time with a fashion photographer.

Santiago went to the bar, but he didn't get a drink for himself. He was ready to leave. His parents had left for the ranch, and he hoped to take Lila back to the apartment.

"Your British friend's looking our way," Santiago said, handing her the glass. "I think he'd like to be the one getting you this drink."

"Conrad is a friend of my parents. He's practically their age!"

"He likes you."

"No, he doesn't," Lila answered, but after a thoughtful pause she admitted that he had called her an "English rose" when complimenting her floor-length pink dress. She embodied innocent qualities like many Argentinian women her age who had grown up in sheltered households, but she returned from London possessing the right dose of sophistication and glamour that attracted men of all ages.

"Are you trying to make me jealous?" he asked.

"I only danced with him because you won't ask me."

Santiago leaned in so only she could hear him. "Forget dancing. I'd like to ask you back to my apartment."

"But my parents are here. They like you. They won't like you very much if they know you're taking me to your apartment."

"We can tell them something else. Or nothing at all," he said with a mischievous smile. "I live around the corner. They'll think we stepped out onto the balcony to gaze at the moon."

The night Santiago met Lila, he'd viewed her as a temporary diversion, an escape from the lingering pain of having lost Valentina, not only to another man but to a friend. Lila, however, didn't make herself easily available, and he had to chase her in the old-fashioned way of their parents' generation. Whereas he only wanted a fling, everything about her demeanor and the situation told him she had no interest in a casual relationship. Normally he wouldn't have bothered, but Lila's beauty had ensnared him, and he wouldn't be at peace until he made love to her.

The Williamses were talking with the British ambassador and Conrad Robertson, and didn't notice their daughter leave the building. The embassy, built in the Edwardian style and thus less ornate than buildings of the preceding Victorian era, had recently beefed up security, employing a number of uniformed armed guards. The brothers Juan and Jorge Born, ages forty and thirty-nine, had been kidnapped by the Montoneros a few months earlier and were being held for ransom. Their crime was being the scions of one of the largest land-holding families in the Argentine oligarchy—and their multinational company's close ties to international capitalism. On the night of the Farmers' Ball, where many of the invited were in the agriculture and export businesses, security was understandably tighter than usual.

The young pair walked the two blocks to the Larreas' apartment without saying much, both in their own thoughts and nervously antici-pating what might happen next. Santiago's desire for Lila had created such a level of excitement in him that he had not registered that the lights were on in the apartment. He was removing his jacket and bow tie and Lila was folding her shawl to leave in the coat closet when the housekeeper entered the foyer.

"Antonia. What are you still doing here?" Santiago asked. She usually went with her family on weekends. Santiago had wanted total command of the house and saw his plans potentially spoiled.

"It's your father. They were going to El Pinar when he began having chest pains. An ambulance took him to the hospital."

"Which one?" he asked, his ears ringing faintly from a sudden pressure in his head. As Antonia told him, he put his jacket back on.

Lila grabbed her shawl. "I'm going with you," she said in a tone that indicated there was no disagreeing with her.

One of the leading cardiologists in the world was an Argentine who happened to be the head of cardiology at the private clinic where Alfonso Larrea was hospitalized. In an emergency procedure, the doctor performed bypass surgery on one of Alfonso's arteries. When they wheeled him back to the intensive care unit, Santiago and his mother were allowed to visit. Santiago covered his father's cold hand with his own until the nurse told him and his mother they would have to leave. It was after four a.m., and Santiago was surprised to find Lila in the chilly waiting room, her shawl wrapped twice around her shoulders, an empty glass bottle of Sprite on the end table.

She rose and went to him. "Will he be all right?"

"It's too soon to tell." Shaken by his father's ashen face, he held Lila for a long time, feeling her narrow frame in his arms. "Thank you for staying," he whispered hoarsely.

The three left the clinic, and Santiago dropped his mother off first. He drove the ten minutes to Lila's home in silence. When he shifted gears to turn onto her street, she put her hand on his arm.

"Stay on this street, drive a little farther."

"Why?"

"You'll see."

When they reached the dead end, he put his car into neutral. There was nothing to see. It was dark. The only light came from the car's headlights. She told him to turn them off. He did as he was told. He couldn't think. He was exhausted and frightened for his father's life. Lila lifted herself out of the passenger seat and, bunching up her chiffon dress around her bony hips, clambered onto his lap.

He whispered, "What are you doing?"

Her fingers unzipped his pants and, with her mouth, she silenced him.

CHAPTER 23

August 1998

A DIRTY RED-AND-BLUE bus, with *Olivos-Boca* and *152* painted in flamboyant italics, spewed black fumes as it screeched to a stop. Franco and I got on. The burly driver in the white short-sleeved shirt bellowed out that everyone had to pay the exact fare as he would not, under any circumstances, make change. Franco dug the right coins out of his pocket and deposited them in the slot. It was the middle of the day, but the bus was full and we had to stand. Earlier that morning, I had decided to return to the campo, yet here I was a few hours later, still in Buenos Aires, hanging on to an overhead strap as the bus traveled farther away from the city center. A few seats emptied out, and Franco and I sat, shoulder to shoulder, both aware of each other's nearness. We reached our destination, and, as if he'd been waiting for a reason, Franco grabbed my hand to get off the bus.

He asked for directions at a kiosk, and we soon arrived at the gate of a low-rise building with a shabby-looking exterior. Franco rang various buttons on the intercom. No one answered. He pushed hard several times against the gate. The old bolt finally unlatched, and we entered an enclosed patio.

Domestic life could be heard from behind closed doors: a man singing in Italian, a whistling kettle, a child being chastised, a soccer game on the radio, audience laughter from a TV show. We walked up a flight of stairs and along a balcony. Franco stopped in front of apartment number 15. The moment he knocked, the door was flung open.

A woman in tight black leather pants and a faded black tank top eyed Franco. When she looked my way, she squinted as if confused by the sight of me. "I wasn't expecting *two* of you."

She turned back inside and Franco was right behind her. I hesitated before following him into the sparsely furnished room. Two chairs, a desk, a futon, and a tall bureau combined to give the room an impersonal and temporary feel.

"You're early. El Chino's guys are never early." The woman opened the top drawer of the bureau and took out a few crumpled pesos. When she saw our empty hands, her eyes flashed with impatient disappointment. "Where is it?"

"I think you've mistaken us for someone else," Franco said.

"You mean El Chino didn't send you?"

"No."

"So why the hell are you in my house?" she asked through gritted teeth.

"Can we get you something from the store? What is it you need?"

"That will be the day, when we can buy it at the corner kiosk," she replied with a dry laugh.

"I might be able to tide you over until El Chino arrives." Franco produced a pack of cigarettes and offered her one. She took it and he lit it for her. Scars ran up and down her skinny arms.

"Now go," the woman said, exhaling smoke in Franco's face.

He didn't flinch. Irked, she motioned her hands toward us and the door as if we were a pair of pesky fruit flies.

"We may have the wrong person. She seems a bit unhinged," I whispered to Franco. I made to leave, but he stood firmly in his place.

"Your name is Soledad Goldberg, correct?" he asked.

The woman, visibly agitated, did not confirm or deny. "Who sent you here?" she asked, instead.

"Horacio told me where we could find you. He says it's been a while since he's seen you."

A psychologist and escapee of a clandestine detention center in the province of Tucumán, Horacio Lynch ran a weekly support group at the Human Rights Center for survivors of the secret detention centers. When Franco had called him from my apartment, Horacio said that he knew Soledad but that she had stopped attending the meetings.

"So *that's* why you're here?" said Soledad. "Doing some vigilante work for him, are you?"

"No. That's not why." He pointed to me, back by the door. "That's my friend Paloma, and I'm Franco. Son of Mónica and Giancarlo Bonetti."

"And? What's it to me?"

"My mother, Mónica Bonetti, worked for a newspaper before she was disappeared by the military in 1976. She wrote about the exploitation of steel factory workers in Santa Fe. My dad made documentaries. His last film was about sugarcane workers in Tucumán."

"So?" Soledad asked, her tone less combative.

Franco produced the copy of the report *Nunca Más*. "In your testimony, you mention someone we're interested in. You were both at ESMA."

ESMA stood for Escuela de Mecánica de la Armada: the Higher School of Mechanics of the Navy. It had housed one of the largest and most active clandestine torture centers in the country. Throughout the dictatorship, ESMA successfully shielded its clandestine operations from countless members of the public who passed through its doors during office hours. More than five thousand people were tortured there. Few had come out alive.

He held the book out to Soledad, but she didn't take it. "I remember perfectly well what I said. I don't need to read it."

From the book, I had learned that Soledad Goldberg was a high school senior when she was abducted on the eve of her older sister Marina's birthday. They had come for Marina, an outspoken Peronist at the School of Economics, but she had just left the house with her boyfriend, Pablo. After they took Soledad instead, Mr. and Mrs. Goldberg sent Marina to live with a cousin in Mexico. The boyfriend was eventually kidnapped when Soledad "sang" his name to her captors. Pablo remained a desaparecido.

"How about Valentina Quintero. Do you remember her?" I asked, back at Franco's side. Soledad tilted her head slightly, scrutinizing me. "My father knew her," I added. "They were friends. Anything you can tell us about her would be helpful."

Soledad gnawed on her thumb.

"Please," Franco quietly urged.

She took a deep drag of her cigarette. "Where were your parents held captive?" she asked him.

"They killed my dad on the spot. My mom was held in El Vesubio. We haven't found her remains." El Vesubio had been a detention/torture center on the outskirts of Buenos Aires.

"I'm so sorry, Franco," I murmured.

There was a rap at the front door. "Come in!" Soledad shouted. A boy appeared in the doorway. "About time." Soledad stubbed out her cigarette in a cheap ceramic ashtray with the word *México* carved in black around the rim. The boy entered, closing the door behind him. He handed Soledad a small brown paper bag. Her face relaxed when she peeked inside. She gave the boy the pesos. He counted them and shook his head. "It's all I have. El Chino knows I'm good for it."

Franco pulled out his wallet from his back pocket. "How much more do you need?"

The boy, who appeared to be mute, raised and flashed his hands twice.

"Fucking racket," Soledad muttered.

Franco gave him a few more pesos. The boy bowed his head and left.

Soledad tipped the bag, and a few brightly colored pills spilled out into her palm. She chased them down with a glass of water. Her body rested against the kitchen counter in anticipation of the pills' effects. When she walked back toward us, she mumbled a thank-you and clarified, "It's my pain medication. An old dance injury." Soledad signaled to the book, and Franco handed it to her. Turning it a few times in her hands, she examined it as if for the first time. But then, without opening it, she gave it back. "Spare another?" He lit a cigarette for her, and after she inhaled, she spoke, the smoke escaping through her mouth and nose. "You're not going to leave me alone, are you?"

"We could really use your help," I said, pulling out the photo of Valentina and my father at the beach. "Do you recognize her?"

"That's her, all right." Soledad tapped once on the woman's face and then pointed to the man. "Who's he?"

"My father. Did she ever talk about him?"

"What's his name?"

"Santiago."

"Yeah. I remember him. We rarely talked much among ourselves. Tried not to bring up our personal lives. And we definitely avoided using anyone's real name." She paused. "Yet Valentina mentioned him. She was so excited, she couldn't help herself. She definitely said his name when she came back from one of her outings."

"I don't understand. She was free to go *out*?" I asked.

"Yes, though never alone. It was one of their sick pleasures. One of the torturers had taken a special interest in her. With that angelic face of his, everyone referred to him as El Angelito." She sat down and puffed at her cigarette. "He liked her. A lot."

"El Angelito," Franco repeated the name in recognition.

"They had met with her friend Santiago one night, and apparently he promised he would get her out. She told me he would get the two of us out." While Soledad talked, her dancer's frame became slack in

the chair as the pills worked their way into her bloodstream. "I got…,"
she began to say, then stopped, her eyelids coming down.

"You got out and she didn't," I finished the sentence for her.

"I had successfully completed their treatment plan," she said with
a quiet cackle. "Help me up?" We assisted in getting her to the futon.
"These pills sometimes make me a little dizzy," Soledad explained
once she was lying down.

"Why didn't they release Valentina?" I asked.

"I don't know. The last time I saw her she was going into labor."

"She was pregnant? Was it El Angelito's baby?" I asked.

Soledad shut her eyes. Was it possible that the drugs had made her
pass out so quickly? I looked at Franco. He leaned gently over her
and said, "We'll let you sleep, Soledad, but just one last thing. Do you
remember when Valentina would have had the baby?"

Soledad's eyes remained closed. Her mouth twitched and then she
spoke. "Valentina thought her baby might be born on her own birthday
and it was close. I can't tell you the exact date, but it was sometime in
September of 1976."

CHAPTER 24

May–June 1975

ALFONSO LARREA REMAINED IN THE clinic for two weeks. Bautista flew back from Europe, and Constanza, who took to going to Mass every morning before visiting her husband, leaned on both her sons. The family kept Alfonso's condition quiet, only informing those in their innermost circle so that business matters wouldn't be affected. Lila never left Santiago's side, and he came to rely on her presence. The other members of the Larrea family also appreciated her thoughtfulness, her words of comfort.

A few days after Bautista's arrival, when their father was no longer in critical condition, their elder son made it clear that he would stay only until his father was better. His life was in Europe. Constanza didn't have her usual strength to argue and looked to her younger son for support. Santiago promised to help with the family business as needed. He drove periodically to the ranch to check in with the administrator and returned to discuss with his father any concerns or decisions to be made.

Back at the Larrea apartment, where he convalesced for a few more weeks, Alfonso's mood improved whenever Lila came around,

She often stayed for dinner, and Alfonso made every effort to charm her. Without consciously choosing to do so, Santiago stopped seeing other women, dating Lila exclusively. His father's scare had made him rethink his life.

The one time he bumped into Máximo and Valentina with a few other students, they were handing out pamphlets on education reform, and he accepted one, asking a few questions to appear interested. Noticing that Valentina was wearing his necklace, his heart swelled with hope and pain, until Máximo put his arm around her shoulders. He had really lost her, Santiago realized.

So the day Lila arrived all jittery to their date at Café La Biela by the Recoleta cemetery, nearly three months after they began dating, and told him she was pregnant, he almost took the news in stride. It was as if he had been expecting this next and final step into full adulthood. They were at an outdoor table. It was a typically cool evening in May, late autumn. The ombú trees were shedding leaves, and the crisp air sharpened Santiago's senses. Did he love her? His family loved her, and he would too, he told himself. He didn't need more time. It was the right thing to do. When he dropped down to one knee, Lila returned his gaze with her brilliant green eyes.

"Will you marry me?" he asked, knowing her answer would be yes.

Mr. and Mrs. Williams were informed by their daughter that time was of the essence, and arrangements were swiftly made. It was decided that, following the civil ceremony before a judge at the city courthouse, a lunch would be held at the exclusive Jockey Club on Avenida Alvear, where both families were members. Bautista flew in from Madrid, and Lila's cousins from England made the trip too.

On his wedding day, Thursday, June 19, as Santiago put on his morning coat while smoking a cigar with his brother, as he slipped a wedding band on Lila's finger, as he danced the first waltz with his new bride, dazzling in her pearly white silk blouse and frilly midlength skirt, and as they were whisked to the airport in a chauffeured car to catch their plane to Paris, not once did he think of Valentina. This, he believed, was a good sign.

That same month, Máximo and Valentina traveled north to a village in Misiones, a province that bordered Paraguay and Brazil, to volunteer in an Indigenous community. The province, named for the Jesuit missionary settlements of the seventeenth century, had experienced extreme seasonal flooding that autumn, and houses were damaged, many beyond repair.

Valentina was happy to get out of Buenos Aires and to be staying in a tent pitched on a wooden platform above the muddy ground, surrounded by dense forest. It had been several months since the students were arrested outside the Sheraton Hotel, but the images of the violent acts she had witnessed often resurfaced when she was going to bed. Would the protesters ever be released? Or had they been released and sent abroad by their families to avoid further trouble? Or had they been forcibly disappeared? Or were they home and afraid to return to the university? Máximo didn't have answers either.

The Silence Is Health campaign had hooked itself into the Argentine consciousness, and no one was talking. The parents were relentless in their search, going from police station to police station, hoping their children would turn up behind bars in some jailhouse. They were only met with stonewalling and lies at every level. Censored newspapers wouldn't or couldn't report on missing students, even as their numbers continued to grow.

Valentina had never exerted herself as hard as she did working on restoring the houses in Misiones. The recent devastation and general poverty in the community were heartbreaking. It motivated her and all the other volunteers. Except for the first night, when she and Máximo made love and talked quietly about wanting to travel to other parts of the country, they crawled into their sleeping bags at the end of each day, barely kissing before sleep overtook them.

Their last night was spent at the main square, drinking mate with the other volunteers and villagers. The only remaining colonial structures from the Spaniards' presence two hundred years earlier were the town hall and the Catholic church, facing each other across the plaza. Máximo was expressing to a local leader how he wished they could stay longer, when the news came on someone's portable radio.

The kidnapping of the Born brothers was the lead story. Everyone fell silent to listen. One brother had been released in March, and the other one would be freed shortly. The DJ announced that the Montoneros had received a ransom in the tens of millions of dollars—the highest ransom ever paid in the history of the world. The family's company, Bunge & Born, would have to install busts of Juan Domingo and Eva Perón in every one of its factories and to distribute clothing and food to sixty of the most impoverished regions in Argentina, Misiones among them.

Valentina looked at Máximo. He had returned to sipping his mate, his face arranged into a neutral expression. She remembered Máximo saying before they went to Misiones that it wasn't necessary to do a food and clothing collection because Enrique had told him Misiones would be taken care of.

She took him aside and asked, "How did Enrique know that Misiones would be receiving aid?"

"I have no idea," Máximo said, averting his eyes.

She waited for him to say more, but he remained silent.

"I see," she said. "You understand that the food is coming to the villagers because two brothers were kidnapped and held in captivity for months. You get how horribly wrong it was to kidnap those men, right?"

"I do. Of course I do." He had never raised his voice at her before. "I don't condone it. But I also know it's a crime to let our people starve in this land of plenty." His voice dropped to its normal tone, but she could see the tension in his jaw. "Landowners exploit their workers for their own gain and export their grains for profit, letting people in their own hometowns go hungry. The rest of us, you and I, go to sleep every night with our stomachs full. We were born fortunate enough not to know what hunger is, but if we were starving, don't think for a minute that we would question the provenance of any food we were given. We would take it and feed our children and ourselves."

"And Enrique? What would he say?"

"Don't bring Enrique into this. He's following his own path," Máximo replied with impatience. "The government has instilled terror in our society with its violent repression." His hands gripped the mate gourd. "The people are getting desperate. The Born brothers were kidnapped, and yes, that was wrong, but how many innocent people go missing every day somewhere in this country?" He drew a deep breath and said, "I'm studying to be a lawyer because I still believe in our laws." Both of them were aware that lawyer activists were also being detained, but this had not stopped Máximo from pursuing his ideals. "I believe in our country. Look at how beautiful it is." His hands gestured to the jungle beyond the village. He was smiling again. "I love Argentina." And then he kissed the top of her head. "And I love you, Valentina."

"I love you too," she answered, but a knot had formed in her stomach. It was fear for Máximo, fear for all of them.

Gas shortages around the country kept the young couple waiting in a long queue at a gas station on the outskirts of Buenos Aires. By the time they were inside the capital, they were hungry for dinner. They stopped at Café de las Artes, where other students from the community service trip were eating. They ran into Grace and her brother Sebastián, who were getting up from the bar, both in cocktail attire.

"Where have you been?" Grace asked, examining Valentina's man-size sweater and overalls. Máximo was also a sight, with unkempt hair and a frayed button-down shirt under his black leather jacket.

"We were on the road all day, coming back from Misiones," Máximo said. He smiled at Grace and nodded at her brother. "Why are you two so dressed up?"

Sebastián did not catch the look of alarm on his sister's face and answered without hesitation: "We were at Santiago's wedding."

"His *wedding*?" Valentina asked, confused.

"Yes. He married Lila Williams after a whirlwind courtship. It was a small ceremony, followed by a lunch at the Jockey Club. They're on a midnight flight to Paris for their honeymoon."

Valentina looked away, worried Grace would read her mind. She had heard Santiago was seeing numerous women. How did he get to dating only one and then marrying her so quickly? She thought she had finally extinguished any lasting feelings for Santiago. She was mistaken. Sebastián and Grace were waiting for her to respond, but her throat had closed and no sound came forth.

Máximo spoke. "So wonderful to hear. Will you tell him and his bride how happy Valentina and I are for them? Give them our congratulations."

Valentina smiled and nodded, hoping she looked sincere. Later that night, alone in her dorm room, she cried herself to sleep.

CHAPTER 25

August 1998

By the time we arrived back in downtown Buenos Aires from our visit with Soledad Goldberg, the sun had set and we were ready for a drink. As the bus slowed to a crawl entering the permanent traffic jam around the Obelisk roundabout, we hopped off the bus and ducked into a café just off Corrientes Avenue. Franco ordered two beers. I quickly downed mine and ordered another one. The encounter with Soledad had left me feeling odd.

"She was just a teenager when they took her," I said to Franco. "She survived, but at what cost?"

He nodded knowingly but said nothing.

"You must know a hundred stories like this one."

"I do. But this story is peculiar. Very few victims made it out alive from the ESMA. And those who did get out were treated for the most part like lepers—the thought being that they must have collaborated with the military or that they betrayed their companions by giving names, locations, hideouts."

"How old were you when your parents were taken?"

"Six."

"Do you remember any of it?"

"I have gaps in my memory, but it all began in August of 1976. I was at school. So was my older sister, Catalina. My little brother, Luis, was at day care. Our mom was late picking us up that day. The principal let us sit in her office while she tried contacting our parents by phone. She gave us a plate of cookies and a few books to read. I already wore glasses, and one of the lenses had cracked while I was playing soccer at recess, so I couldn't really read anything. Catalina read to me. I was mad at my mother for not coming on time. I wanted to get my glasses fixed before the shop closed.

"Claudia, my dad's sister, showed up a couple of hours later. I remember her eyes were watery and she kept blowing her nose, like she had a pretty bad cold. She said our mom was away, but she wouldn't tell us where she had gone or when she would be back. She put us in the car and drove us to her apartment. Our father came for us that night. He had gone to get Luis at the day care center. His friend Héctor was with him. Héctor was like an uncle to us. We thought of him as Tío Héctor.

"I remember hearing my aunt and my dad fighting in the kitchen. Tía Claudia kept insisting on sticking to our bedtimes and other routines, you know, like we shouldn't miss school the next day. But he must have won the argument, because next thing I knew we were in Tío Héctor's car with Dad in the passenger seat and the three of us crammed in the back along with Héctor's girlfriend." Franco lit a cigarette. "We arrived at a house we had never been to before. In the morning, my dad sat us down and told us that Mom was not going to be with us for a while, but in the meantime, until she came back, we were going to play a game. We were going to pretend that we were all acting in a play or, even better, in a movie. We loved going to the movies as a family. One of our favorite movies was *The Three Musketeers*, and my siblings and I would reenact scenes all the time, so my parents began calling us their Three Musketeers. In this game, my father explained, we would get to choose new names for ourselves. Naturally we told him we wanted to be called Aramis, Porthos, and Athos, but he said no one would believe those were our real names.

"I remember how excited my sister was. She loved to put on costumes, wear our mother's dresses and shoes. Another couple was already living in the house, and they took on the roles of our aunt and uncle. We never did learn who they actually were. They were really nice to us. Our new 'aunt' baked a cake for Luis's fourth birthday, but after we sang to him, he refused to blow out the candles. We had to wait for our mom, he kept saying. Luis was sure she wouldn't miss his birthday. He fell asleep by the front door. He wanted to be the first one she saw when she walked in.

"When he woke up the next morning and realized she hadn't come, he took the cake and dropped it on the floor. That cake had looked so good, the chocolate icing sprinkled with little candies. I wanted to punch him for ruining it. But my sister tackled me before I could get to him." Franco took a long swallow from his beer and then looked at me. "Are you hungry? There's a classic old place a few blocks up on Corrientes I think you'll like."

"Not yet. Please. Go on."

"We went into hiding. Every time we moved, we changed our identities. For a while I got to be Lucas," he said, grinning.

"Who?"

"You don't know?"

I gave him a blank stare.

"Lucas Skywalker?"

"Oh, yes, of course!" I loved Star Wars and had even had a crush on Luke Skywalker, but I had never heard the Spanish version of his name.

"One night we were playing in our bedroom when I heard a car pull up. We were living in a suburb of La Plata, a city an hour south of here. I crawled down the corridor and stopped right where I could look into the living room without being seen." He finished the last of the beer. "My father put up a fight before they pinned him against a wall and began to interrogate him. Then, when he tried again to wrest himself free, they shot him."

My hand covered my mouth. I knew he had lost both parents, but it had never occurred to me that he might have witnessed his own father's murder.

"Franco," I said softly.

He shrugged as if to suggest it had been so long ago it didn't affect him, but his gaze was somewhere beyond me, and I sensed that, in his mind, he had returned to that horrible day. After a slight movement of his head, he looked at me and continued.

"Every place we moved to, our dad had us memorize an escape plan. We had a backpack ready with enough money for three bus tickets and instructions to get to my grandparents' house in Rosario. After we got there, my grandmother wanted us to get back to 'normal' as quickly as possible. Like having us use our real names again and going back to school. That's where I lived until university."

"Where are your siblings now?" I asked.

"Catalina's in Córdoba studying to be a dentist. Luis and I live together. Our grandparents bought us an apartment when we finished high school and moved here for university."

"What about your aunt? The one who picked you up at school that day?"

"Claudia's okay, but she never forgave my mother for getting her brother involved with the Montoneros. My mother had joined the organization before she met my dad, but she distanced herself from the group when their tactics became more violent. She was a journalist and believed the written word was the more powerful way to fight back." He puffed at his cigarette. "The truth is that even if they hadn't been linked to the Montoneros, their fate had already been sealed for being social activists."

In my research those past few days, I had read about the Montoneros. Originally a group of Catholics, university students, and leftists who advocated for Peronism, they turned to violent insurgency in the early 1970s. Their tactics included abductions, assassinations, and bombings of symbolic locations identified with the oligarchy and international capitalism. Their strategy was to destabilize the Argentine government until Perón was able to return from exile. Alas, their faith in the old general proved to be misplaced. Soon after assuming the presidency, Perón gave López Rega and his Triple A free rein to hunt them down along with the other terrorist groups.

"Franco, I'm at a loss for words."

"At least I know what happened to one of them. It's better to know," he said with a melancholy smile.

We left the bar and strolled up Corrientes Avenue toward Pizzería Güerrín, a pizza and empanadas restaurant that had been around at least since the 1930s. A boy stopped me on the sidewalk and offered me a card of Eva Perón portrayed as Santa Evita, who remained a symbol of hope for the poor. I gave him a coin and looked into the impenetrable image of the First Lady of the Argentines. I tucked the card away in my coat.

"What about you? I'd like to know more about Paloma," Franco said as we continued to walk. We hadn't kissed since dancing at Nahuel's party. The embrace had seemed almost accidental, and despite what I felt, I had come to doubt whether he was interested in me romantically. But the way he said my name and the way he looked at me while saying it made me reconsider this conclusion.

"Me?" I said. I looked at the theatergoers lining up for various shows, the bookstores that remained open all night, and the record stores playing music from sidewalk speakers. It was a Saturday night, but it could have been any night—the area had a pulsating energy that reminded me of Times Square in New York. "I love all of this. This street, the people, this city."

He smiled and said, "But what's your story? The story of Paloma Larrea."

We arrived at the pizzeria and he opened the door for me.

"I don't know what my story is. Like most people my age, I'm still trying to figure it out," I answered pensively. We were seated at a table near the back of the narrow, checker-tiled dining hall, under an old fluorescent light. When I faced him, his blue eyes were steady on mine, waiting for me to elaborate. "I know that I feel more at home here than in New York. I was born and raised there, but if my story is about belonging, I feel like maybe I belong here in Argentina. Isn't that funny?"

"Your parents are from here. Right?"

I nodded.

"Your heritage is in you. You can't change who you are just by being born somewhere else."

"I guess that's true." After we ordered a mozzarella pizza with red sauce and fainá, a fried chickpea dough, I looked at him. "Why did you ask Soledad when Valentina's baby was born?" The words came out strongly, and I realized how much the question had been nagging at me.

He noticed my tone and answered cautiously. "I don't know if you're aware of this, but babies born in captivity were often handed over to families in the military or the police force. Or people who couldn't have their own children."

"I see."

"There were more than just a few cases," he continued. "In fact, there were hundreds."

The next moments passed in silence. We sipped our wine.

"My father did date Valentina," I admitted. "But he told me their relationship happened before my parents met."

Franco nodded but I could sense he was skeptical. To preempt any queries on his part, I continued. "Besides, Valentina's baby was born in September. My birthday's in December."

Looking at me over his glasses, Franco measured his words. "Babies were given false birth certificates. Birth dates were made up all the time."

"Why are you telling me all this?"

"Given what was going on at that time, anything is possible."

Except for the tears that began to well, my face was expressionless.

Franco extracted a pressed handkerchief from his back pocket. "May I?" He reached across the table and, gently, wiped away my tears. "If you want to learn more, I know someone we can talk to."

CHAPTER 26

September 1975

On a Friday in early September, Máximo stood for hours under a driving rain outside Luna Park, Argentina's largest indoor stadium, mainly known for boxing matches. He was in line to buy concert tickets for Argentina's most popular folk-rock band, Sui Generis, as an early birthday surprise for Valentina. But on the day of the concert he also surprised her by telling her he would not be able to go. The law school had changed the date for one of his assessments to the following day, and he would need every possible hour to study.

"I'll stay in then. Make us dinner. I have papers to correct," Valentina said, going to the kitchen to see what meal she could rustle up.

Valentina's parents didn't know she had unofficially moved into Máximo's one-bedroom apartment in the neighborhood of Congreso. They thought she was still living in the studio they rented for her in Almagro. They had driven in from Córdoba a month earlier to cosign the lease. It was their graduation present to her. Valentina turned the studio into her workspace instead. As she took out a can of tomatoes to make a sauce for pasta, she told Máximo she could quiz him. Make him a gourd of mate. Whatever she could do to help him pass the exam. She didn't tell him that she saw this as a rare opportunity for them to be together. He was often out late and came back when she was already asleep.

"Go. Don't let me spoil your birthday present. Take Grace," he insisted, looking up only for a moment from the textbooks and hand-outs sprawled across the sofa and low coffee table they had purchased at a flea market in La Boca.

Valentina gave in. She loved Sui Generis, and the concert was billed as the group's last. She invited Grace, and by the time they arrived at the indoor stadium, the band was already on the stage. The lead singer was welcoming the audience, mostly students and young people, who had come in from the cool winter night dressed in wide-collared shirts, flared pants, V-neck sweaters, jean jackets. By the final song, the fans were out of their seats, singing and dancing. The police were outside, powerless to stamp out their joy. In retrospect, the concert would be seen as the beginning of a resistance movement through the arts—in particular, music in the form of *rock nacional*—that would sustain those who survived the government's brutal rule over the next few years.

The women hugged and walked out of the stadium, arm in arm. The man whose shoulders Grace had climbed up on during the encore ran up and asked if they wanted to join him and some friends at a bar.

Grace looked at Valentina and said, "Why not? The night is young."

"You go ahead. I need to get back home to Máximo."

Most buses weren't running due to a public transportation slow-down, but every now and again one would appear, bursting at the seams with passengers. Valentina waited with the other hopefuls, but when the next bus pulled up, she was still unable to get on.

"Valentina!"

She turned. It was Santiago. Her heart leaped in surprise. He was waving to her from inside a car, a Peugeot 504. She didn't recognize it, but then again, it had been at least a year and a half since she had been in a car with him.

He opened the passenger door. "Get in!"

He was smiling, as happy to see her as she was to see him. Without hesitating, she slid into the passenger seat.

"Were you at the concert?" he asked as they left behind the dozens jostling to get a better spot in the bus line.

"Yes, with Grace. You just missed her. Did you go too?" she asked, still feeling a euphoric high from the concert. And now, having run into Santiago, the night had taken on a magical quality.

"Yeah, with some friends."

Santiago didn't mention Lila. Why bring his wife into this unexpected moment with Valentina? He had tried to coax Lila into coming, but she had been feeling melancholy ever since her miscarriage after they returned from their honeymoon. Lila's doctor assured her she would be pregnant again, and Santiago told her there was no rush. She was nineteen. He was twenty-three. They were young. They had time.

Valentina wondered if "friends" included Lila. The idea of Santiago being married was, unexpectedly, still upsetting. Looking out the car window as the mass of concertgoers poured onto the sidewalks, she said, "Weren't they incredible?"

"They were. Charly García's a genius," he said, referring to the rock group's composer, pianist, and singer.

Valentina had forgotten how impossibly handsome Santiago was. As he drove, she took in his profile, his pronounced jawline, his thick eyebrows, his narrow lips. She watched him effortlessly shift gears and maneuver the vehicle. These ordinary movements reflected an innate elegance she had loved.

"Where are you going?" he asked her, taking his eyes off the road for a moment to look at her. His eyes were tender and he was smiling again.

At once, she was conscious of the fact that they were alone in a confined space, and sat up stiffly. "Home. I was ready to walk. Just drop me off wherever is convenient. There's so much traffic tonight."

"I'll drive you," he said, and took a side street, hoping to find fewer cars. "How have you been?"

"Good. Busy. I graduated a couple of months ago, and I'm now working for a professor," she answered, hoping her voice didn't betray the emotions that this chance encounter had awakened. The feelings were welling up inside of her, ready to spill over. Yet he seemed composed, acting as if he were driving an old friend.

"That's wonderful, Valentina."

"How about you?" she managed to ask in a tone matching his.

"I have two more classes to go and I'll be finished. I know Máximo's almost done too. We occasionally bump into each other at school."

"Yes. He has some important exam tomorrow."

An uncomfortable silence filled the car at the mention of Máximo. To break it, Santiago switched on the radio. One of Sui Generis's songs came on. Listening, they couldn't hold back and began to sing along. When the song ended, they were at ease with one another again.

The last time Valentina had been alone with Santiago had been the night he returned from Europe, not quite a year ago. She studied his strong hands firmly on the wheel. His long fingers with their perfectly trimmed nails would have been the envy of any pianist. She recalled how his fingers used to explore all of her with urgency.

When Santiago saw how she was gazing at him, his heart swelled. He asked himself how he had survived all these months without her.

After he had proposed to Lila, he had thrown himself fully into the relationship, getting swept up in the idea of marriage and his role as a husband and soon-to-be father. Lila was, as he had suspected, all that a husband could want in a wife, and in the weeks following their engagement, he had fallen in love with her. But seeing Valentina again, having her seated so close to him, suddenly made the last few months seem inconsequential. It was as if he had been playing at this other life all that time.

No longer able to maintain his casual air, he blurted out, "I can't listen to one of their songs without thinking of us."

You should not be in his car, a voice within Valentina told her. She was silent for a moment. "I heard you got married." She stated it as a fact, not as a question, and not in an accusatory sort of way. After all, she had been the one to give him up. But she needed to say it out loud, to caution him, the two of them, that he was a married man and she was in a serious relationship.

"I did. A couple of months ago. But I find that it doesn't keep me from thinking of us whenever one of their songs comes on."

She looked at him, not knowing how to answer. *I think of you too?* What good would that do? What they were both feeling, she should say to him, was a memory from the past. It would be the right thing to say, but it wasn't true. At least not for her.

As she struggled to find an appropriate response, the car ahead slowed down. A roadblock had been set up and the police, holding machine guns across their chests, directed traffic.

"I can hop out here," Valentina told him. She wasn't ready to say goodbye to him. A part of her wanted to stay and savor this impossible encounter a little longer. But these police checkpoints, materializing everywhere, frightened her. She had witnessed people being patted down and then, without any visible reason, taken away.

A police officer walked in front of them, making Santiago fully apply the brakes. The officer evaluated them through the windshield and signaled to his companion, who came up to the driver's side and commanded, "Step out of the car. Hands up in the air."

A wave of anxiety rushed through her.

He whispered, "Don't worry."

They got out as instructed.

"Face the car. Hands on the roof!"

Two officers held guns to the back of their heads, while the other two patted them down until they located their documents. A flashlight swept the inside of the car, the trunk.

The squat man in charge told the others, "We'll take the woman in for questioning."

Valentina stared, alarmed, at Santiago.

"But why? What's going on, Officer?" Santiago asked in a reasonable voice.

"We're looking for a dark-haired female student suspected of placing a bomb in a police captain's home," explained the younger-looking officer.

"You'll see on my ID card that my name is Santiago Larrea. My father is Alfonso Larrea. General Delgado is an old family friend."

General Delgado was a rank below Jorge Rafael Videla, the new head of the armed forces. President Isabel Perón, under pressure from the military establishment, had appointed Videla, even though he was a staunch anti-Peronist. Videla's influence had grown, and he had begun to remove military officers and other government officials sympathetic to Perón. The purge included the minister of social welfare, José López Rega, whom a newspaper link had exposed as the man behind the state-sponsored terrorist outfit Triple A.

The police officers consulted quietly, examining again both documents.

"She's not your suspect. I can vouch for her. She's been with me all day," Santiago said evenly, unblinking in the flashlight directly on his face.

Valentina's breathing had grown ragged and her knuckles were white from gripping the car roof.

After a few more tense moments, the officer in charge announced, "You're free to go." The younger one returned their ID cards. As soon as they were past the roadblock, Valentina let out a loud sob. Santiago remained calm and reached for her.

"It's over," he reassured her as he drove away as quickly as he could.

They drove a few blocks in silence, reeling from the shock of the encounter. He pulled onto the dark street and parked in front of her building. Valentina had planned not to say anything about her change of address but, rattled by the incident, she couldn't lie. "I'm not at the dorm anymore."

He squinted at her and, with a shake of his head, said, "Of course not. You're not a student anymore. So where to?"

"You don't have to take me any farther. I can walk from here."

"I'm not going to let you walk alone, Valentina. Not at this hour. Not after what happened."

She considered his reasons, thinking there was no longer any point in hiding anything from him. "I don't want you to drop me off. I'm living with Máximo."

"Ah."

Dabbing at her eyes with the sleeve of her jean jacket, she said, "Thank you, Santiago. They would've taken me in if it hadn't been for you."

"But they didn't. You're here."

"You lied for me. You didn't have to. You could've gotten yourself into trouble."

"Valentina," he said, staring through the windshield at the empty street. "Can't you tell? I would do anything for you."

He heard her softly call his name. "Look at me." He did. She was pulling out something from under her turtleneck. In wonder, he gazed at the pendant he had given her when their love was the only thing that mattered.

"You still wear it?" he asked, puzzled but deeply pleased by the revelation.

He held the blue lapis stone with its diamond chips, then flipped it and studied her carved initials. The night he gave it to her came rushing back. And now she was so close to him her scent was making his heart gallop. He looked up from the stone. Her eyes, brimming with tears, met his. She closed her eyes as he pressed his cheek against hers, waiting for a sign from her. She turned her face slightly so that his mouth was on her cheek. He began kissing her face until his lips found her mouth.

CHAPTER 27

August 1998

THE DAY AFTER TALKING TO Soledad Goldberg, I met Juan for a coffee, and, to my relief, he amicably agreed that our fling had run its course. Walking back to the apartment, I felt my mood lift. Rays of sunlight breached the low-hanging morning clouds. It felt as if the sun had melted away my uncertainties, making way for a clearer sense of myself.

As I turned the corner onto my block, I slowed and retrieved my phone to check my messages. My father had left a voicemail wondering if I was coming back to the ranch that day. I wasn't ready to see my parents and decided to tell them that Juan had invited me out. I was starting to tap the number for El Pinar into my phone when my right shoulder grazed against a man who was studying our building directory. Mumbling an apology, I began to pass, but the man moved, standing in my way. When I attempted to go around him again, he shifted, blocking my path.

"Excuse me, señorita. Do you know which apartment number belongs to Mr. Santiago Larrea? I'm an old friend, and I heard he's in town. I tried getting in touch with him, but we keep missing each other.

He left me a message to come visit, but, stupid me, I can't remember the apartment number."

"He's not here," I answered.

"Ah, you know him?"

"I'm his daughter."

"*You're* Paloma?"

"Yes."

"How lucky of me to run into his daughter!" He smiled. "My, you've grown into a beautiful young woman. Santiago and Lila must be proud."

His eyes on me were making me uncomfortable, and then I realized I had seen him before. At the press conference, he had been the one who asked my father about our family. He had heard my father was in town? He was an old friend? Clearly, he was lying. How had he gotten this address? It dawned on me that he might be the person who wrote the unsigned note I found in Dad's wallet, demanding a meeting. I signaled to the doorman through the glass. "Well, as I said, he's not here," I replied, coolly.

"Would you give him a message then? Please tell him Pedro García offers his warmest congratulations on his political appointment."

"Sure."

The doorman let me inside. Waiting for the elevator, I glanced back. The man hadn't left. He was staring at me, a disquieting smile on his face. He bowed his head before walking away.

After taking a hot shower, I called the ranch to tell my parents that I was having a lot of fun in Buenos Aires and planned to stay a few more days. They were out, but I spoke to Abuelo, who was disappointed. I promised that when I returned, I would devote myself entirely to him for the remainder of my trip. Back on the street, I walked quickly.

After we left Güerrín the night before, Franco mentioned again that he knew someone we could talk to about clandestine births. I rationalized that, at this point, we should follow Valentina Quintero's story wherever it might lead and, if possible, find out what happened to her baby. Linking this woman's story to my own birth was a crazy theory, but I decided it was best to put any speculation to rest. I agreed to meet him the next day at Plaza de Mayo, where a protest was going to take place. His contact would be there.

When I rounded the corner onto Avenida de Mayo and saw the square, I came to a full stop. Was it possible that my parents and I had driven through Plaza de Mayo not even a week ago? The square was as crowded as on the day we arrived. It was another protest against Colonel Aldo Rico's appointment as head of the federal police force.

As people of all ages marched by, my heart sped up. How had I ended up in such a mess? This was not my world. I should turn around and leave, I thought. Put what had become a sinister investigation behind me and return to New York. Emily had emailed me that two jewelry stores on the Lower East Side had expressed interest in carrying some of my pieces. I missed Emily, my friends, my old life. I was resolving to leave when a hand grabbed my elbow.

"I was beginning to think you had changed your mind about coming here."

It was Franco. His fingers were firm around my arm. Had he sensed that I was thinking of leaving? He kissed my cheek. "But I'm here now," I said, understanding at that moment that there would be no turning back.

Police officers stood around the periphery of the march. Some tapped their clubs against their hand. Franco didn't let go of my arm, but I found his grip strangely reassuring, the gentle squeeze of his strong hand suppressing my mounting anxiety. I was not alone. We were in this together.

A group of old women walked in unison. Franco hollered to one of them. "Viviana!"

A woman of petite stature looked over, and a smile formed on her aged face.

She kissed his cheek. "Franco, my dear boy. How long has it been? How are you? And your sister and brother? Everyone doing well?" the old woman affectionately rattled off her questions.

Franco smiled, saying, "Everyone's good."

The woman's navy wool coat fell to just below her knees, and she wore thick beige stockings and sensible black shoes. Wiry gray hairs escaped from under her white headscarf with embroidered writing that read:

Robertino Espósito, Desaparecido, 23rd February, 1977
Stella Maris Espósito, Desaparecida, 23rd February, 1977,
Five Months Pregnant

Franco explained that Viviana Espósito was a member of the Abuelas de Plaza de Mayo, dedicating her life to finding the remains of her missing son, daughter-in-law, and unborn grandchild.

"Viviana, I want to introduce you to my friend Paloma."

"Hello," I said, bending down to kiss her cheek.

We fell into step with Viviana and the other Madres, proceeding behind a large banner with the words *Nunca Más*—Never Again— stretching across the length of a row of twelve mothers and grand- mothers walking with locked arms.

"We need to talk to you," Franco told Viviana after circling the square a few times.

We found an empty bench, and Viviana rested her protest sign next to her. Removing one of her gloves, she rubbed her right knee, quite swollen compared to the other one.

"Arthritis," she explained, and then turned to Franco. "Talk to me. How can I help?"

"We need to ID someone who thinks she may be the daughter of a desaparecida."

Nodding, she said, "The most effective method is a new type of test where they sample your DNA."

"But don't you need the mother's body?" I asked.

"A member of the immediate family will do, and all that's needed is a blood or a hair sample, thank God. If not, we would never get anywhere. Any living relatives?"

"No. The desaparecida's parents are dead. No siblings either," Franco told her.

"So what do you have?"

"The mother was held at ESMA. Baby was born in captivity, possibly in September of '76."

"That's specific enough. If she didn't give birth in her cell, then there's a good chance she may have had the baby at San Rafael Hospital. The military destroyed most of the documents, but your friend could still go and inquire. She might be able to get some information."

"Thanks, Viviana. This is helpful."

Viviana placed her hands on the bench to hoist herself up. While rearranging her headscarf, she explained, "Many babies stolen during the dictatorship grow up with a sense that something's not right. Sometimes that discord is felt within the dynamics of their family but almost always within themselves. As they get older, the feeling of displacement becomes obvious and, sooner or later, has to be acknowledged." Her eyes found mine. "It's important to pay attention to that instinct."

Unable to hold the old woman's gaze, I looked away.

Franco handed Viviana her sign. They kissed goodbye. She started back but then turned and said, "Come by the office anytime you want. We're ready to help."

We wandered away from the square and the crowds into the downtown district, which, on that Sunday, was deserted in comparison. After a few blocks, we turned right and crossed the wide avenue separating downtown from the waterfront. We passed through the trendy Puerto Madero district, whose old port buildings had been repurposed into luxury condos and upscale cafés and restaurants. From there, we headed farther toward the river, past the Costanera Sur park to a network of walking paths near the Río de la Plata.

We walked by a man who was reeling in a fishing rod, and Franco paused to ask, "Catch anything?"

The man held up his wrist. From it dangled an antique-looking watch on a rusty metal strap. "Just this old thing. Doesn't even work."

A family was picnicking beneath some nearby trees. The children gathered their toys while the mother wrapped up the leftover food and the father doused the coals still smoldering in the grill. Franco asked if I was hungry. This time I said yes.

We stopped at a street vendor's food stand and Franco ordered two choripanes. The vendor opened two buns and stuffed them with the chorizo sausages, which he then sliced in half. He spooned a generous helping of chimichurri onto the butterflied sausages and swiftly wrapped each choripan in a wax napkin. As soon as we were seated on a bench, I took a hearty bite of the sandwich, and the green sauce splattered on my jeans.

Franco shook his head. "Rookie move." He stood, facing me. "You have to hold it out in front of you, see?" His body leaned forward, legs spread apart, so that when he took a bite the juice spilled onto the boardwalk and not on his clothes. "Ta-da!" he exclaimed like a magician might.

"You're quite the pro!" I smiled, clapping one hand on my thigh. He sat back down beside me. "Did you know that chimichurri has become a trendy sauce in New York? Chefs are serving it on all sorts of grilled meat these days."

"What?" Franco pretended to choke on his bread. "Sacrilege! Don't your fellow Americans know that it only ever goes on a chorizo? A steak, perfectly prepared, does not need any sort of condiment." With a somber look and one hand on my shoulder, he said, "You have your work cut out for you when you return to New York."

"You're right, Mr. Bonetti, and I promise to do my best," I replied in a serious voice, and burst out laughing.

"Chimichurri is no laughing matter," he lectured me as his face lightened into a playful smile.

As the sun fell below the horizon, the waterways of the riverfront district went from a murky brown to an impenetrable black. When the temperature dropped, Franco offered me his coat and suggested we head back. I would have been content to remain seated on the bench beside him for the rest of the night, but I agreed.

When we arrived at my building, we made a plan to meet up again in the morning to go to San Rafael Hospital. He gave me a peck on the cheek and turned to leave.

"Franco. Wait." I moved toward him until I was close enough to see that his glasses were a little smudged. He must have noticed, because he removed them, brought them up to his mouth, and breathed hard, once on each lens, before wiping them clean with a handkerchief. When he put them back on, he regarded me thoughtfully.

"Are you sure?"

I nodded and closed my eyes in expectation.

"What about your friend?"

I opened my eyes. "What friend?" Juan was the last thing on my mind.

Franco smiled his beautiful smile. He cupped my face in his hands. Our lips almost touched and he hesitated before he kissed me once and then twice and then again.

CHAPTER 28

November 1975

Surprisingly nimble for his height, Santiago scrambled up a bare palo rosa tree to the second floor of the building. He took in the view of the darkened and quiet street, and then searched for a bare branch to rap on the window.

Hunched over her drawing table, Valentina jumped at the sound. When she saw Santiago's face against the glass, she let out a gasp.

She raised the window and cried out, "Are you crazy?"

He pulled himself through and, like a cat, dropped down onto the floor on all fours.

"I'm sorry, *mi amor.*"

Santiago had been so excited to see her he hadn't considered how she might react. He continued toward her but she stepped back.

"What are you doing here? We're not supposed to see each other tonight. I have a deadline tomorrow."

"I was in the neighborhood…"

As he spoke, he took a few more steps toward her until she ended up against the wall. His arms stretched out on either side of her with no way out. Smiling victoriously, he leaned in to kiss her.

"I thought you'd appreciate my Romeo-esque entrance."

"Hard to appreciate it when you've just scared the hell out of me."

"I didn't mean to. I'm sorry, my love. But you want to know why I did it? Your superintendent. He's starting to be suspicious of me. All these repeat visits from one of your 'clients'? He's not buying it. You should've seen the look he gave me when I left the other day."

"José?" Valentina wrinkled her nose. "Don't worry about him. I'll tell him you're one of those typical pain-in-the-ass clients who constantly changes his mind about the layout of his house."

Santiago kissed her again, and this time she responded.

"Has he been here yet?" The question slipped out before he could catch himself. They usually tiptoed around any mention of their partners. "I mean your super, José. Has he been inside?"

"Why do you ask, Santiago?" She gazed at him. "Jealous?"

"No, no. That's not why." Loosening his hold on her, he grew serious. "You should be careful with who you let in." He looked around the mostly empty space. "Sooner or later, you're going to have to get proper furniture. Buy whatever it is that an architect needs to get her work done," he said, changing the subject.

Her eyes followed his arms gesturing around the room. "I know, but I need to save up."

Valentina had yet to start making any real money. A former professor had recently hired her to draw perspectives for a residence in the affluent neighborhood of San Isidro. She was feeling optimistic that this job would lead to other opportunities.

"I told you I'd help you."

"If I let you start to pay for my things, I'll feel like your mistress," she said, and smiled up at him, no longer mad.

"But I want to take care of you. Please let me."

The first time he showed up at her studio, not counting the night of the concert two months ago now, he had come bearing gifts, useful ones he knew she would not be able to turn down. They were professionally wrapped in brown construction paper, and as she opened them, her eyes widened with delight at each new tool: a parallel straightedge bar, vellum and tracing paper, an architectural scale, triangles, a lead holder and lead pointer, an eraser shield.

Santiago hadn't known if there would be a second time when she brought him to her studio after the concert. But after they made love, they couldn't let go of each other. They understood their love had never truly gone away.

Raking her fingers through his hair, she murmured, "I don't need you to take care of me. What I need you to do is make love to me. Right now."

Drawing his face to hers, she brought him down to the floor with her. His efforts to undress her were useless. Valentina was in command. When she finished removing his clothes, she pulled up her wool skirt and straddled him. Lying beneath her as she rocked back and forth, his body told her, "I am yours, I am yours," until she moaned in his ear and he rushed himself into her.

Later, stretched out face to face on his overcoat, he shook his head in wonder.

"What?" she asked.

"I was just thinking that it's been forever since I climbed a tree."

"You could've gotten yourself killed. And for no good reason," she softly scolded him.

"To visit the girl of my dreams? That's a pretty good reason, I'd say."

He reached for her, and, giggling, she rolled over a lump in his coat. From underneath her back, she pulled out a rolled-up newspaper inside his coat pocket. It was the evening edition.

"Bad boy!" She hit him with the paper. "You broke one of our rules. Remember?" The paper struck his arms a few more times. "No. News. From. The. Outside. World."

"You're right. Sorry." Santiago held up his hands in surrender, trying not to grin. "I wasn't sure I would find you still here, and I hadn't read the paper yet…"

When he reached to take it back, she turned away from him and unfurled it. She was quiet as she read.

"What is it?"

"Nothing," she said, but she was biting her lower lip and wouldn't take her eyes off the front page.

He sat up on one elbow and, over her shoulder, glimpsed the headline in bold print:

> URBAN GUERRILLAS DIE IN STANDOFF IN CITY CENTER
> Four urban leftist guerrillas, believed to be members of the People's Revolutionary Army (ERP), were shot dead after a failed attempt to bomb a restaurant frequented by off-duty police officers. The ambush took place at...

The week before, another newspaper had reported a suspicious fire in the neighborhood of Flores, where three bodies had been found in a pile of refuse in an abandoned lot. The authorities had identified the victims as subversives involved in a counteroffensive. But there were rumors these "standoffs" were staged by the Triple A. Another rumor was that political dissidents held in clandestine jails would be released in the middle of the night. Told to run, they were then shot and killed, and later reported as subversives who had escaped from jail.

The news upset Valentina. Máximo's unexplained absences upset her. The Friday after she ran into Santiago at the concert, Máximo had disappeared for three days without an explanation or phone call. Too worried to work or sleep, thinking he had been killed, she had almost killed him herself when, on the fourth day, he finally walked through the front door.

The rush of relief at the sight of him quickly turned into anger. His militancy had become more important than their relationship. She resented him putting his life in danger. He tried to justify himself but she didn't give him a chance. The uneasiness she felt cheating on him was mixed in with her reaction. Unbeknownst to Máximo, his absence had given her the extra push she needed to break it off. Moving into the studio would bring her peace, she thought, but she remained divided by her feelings for both men.

The separation lasted ten days. Máximo pleaded with her. His activism was losing meaning, he told her. He was fighting for a better world, but his life was nothing without her. If she didn't come back to their home, he wouldn't care what became of him. Valentina listened while she studied him. He looked like he was coming apart, like he might be losing his mind. Her resolve weakened. She moved back in with him, but soon he returned to his secret activities. He was needed, he said, apologizing. The cause couldn't wait, and she understood. She did. The repression, the violence was affecting them all. It had to stop, and Máximo was sure the work he and others were doing would bring about the necessary change.

Now Valentina folded the newspaper and gave it back to Santiago. "Take it. Put it away," she said flatly.

They dressed in silence. Santiago bent down to retrieve his shirt and sweater.

"Santi."

"Hmm."

Santiago's mind was elsewhere. On Lila. Before leaving that morning—she believed he was spending the day in class or at the library—Lila had made him promise that he wouldn't be late to dinner again. Her parents were coming. He was to pick up some bread rolls on the way home. She had wanted something else. What was it? Wine? He would buy a bottle or two at the wine store around the corner from their apartment.

"Santiago?" Valentina's voice brought him back.

"Sorry. What were you saying?"

"I was asking if you would ever leave the city and settle in the campo?"

Conversations that involved future hypotheticals were another no-no in Valentina's rulebook. He glanced at her before pulling the sweater over his head.

"Would you?" she asked again, rising to her feet.

It had been a long time since he had entertained such a notion. What would his life look like if he moved out to El Pinar for good? It would mean working full-time with his father and leaving behind the opportunity to work at a law firm after he graduated at the end of the year.

Adjusting his shirt collar, he casually said, "Haven't really thought about it."

"What if I were to tell you that I'm thinking about leaving? Going back to my parents' home in Córdoba."

"But you just rented this place." He picked up his coat from the floor.

"I know. And this might sound silly, but I miss my mother's garden. Lately, I've been daydreaming a lot about lying in my old hammock among her flowers."

He frowned, unsure how to respond. Was she testing him? What about Máximo? From Valentina's few vague remarks since their affair began, Santiago had drawn, in his mind, an outline of his friend's present life. He gathered that Máximo was not going to follow the traditional route of joining a law practice. Instead, he had been using his degree to do pro bono work for residents at shantytowns in and outside the city. He was also planning to defend political prisoners. However, for the moment, Máximo's only source of income seemed to come from freelance gigs as a comic book illustrator.

"Would you?" She found his hand and pressed it to her cheek. "Leave the city?" Kissing his palm, she asked, "Come with me?"

During these past few weeks of furtively seeing each other, Santiago had not dared think of such a possibility and had grown used to the unconventional rhythms of his life. Valentina had begged him a few times to end the affair, saying she was too weak to do it. What they were doing was wrong, she would say. But he wouldn't. He didn't want to. He was only truly alive when he was with her.

Santiago hated deceiving Lila, but he didn't have a choice, not for the moment. It would be insensitive, cruel even, to leave Lila so soon after marrying her and losing the baby. More time needed to pass. Since Valentina had reentered his life, he had felt himself involuntarily stiffen around Lila, although he thought he didn't show it. But he must have been acting differently, because at times she was clingy, as if she sensed he was reserving a part of himself. Guilt engulfed him whenever he remembered everything he had come to love about Lila. How she had been by his side when his father had suffered his heart attack. How easily she had bonded with his mother, fit in with his family. How she went along with whatever Santiago wanted. She was lovely, beautiful, and his heart had broken for the two of them when she miscarried their child. But at the bottom of his soul, he knew he would never stop loving Valentina. He could only ever be half the man Lila deserved.

Santiago rolled the newspaper and tucked it into his coat pocket. When he looked at Valentina again, it was with searching eyes.

"Are you being serious?" he finally asked.

"I've never been more serious in my life."

CHAPTER 29

August 1998

SAN RAFAEL HOSPITAL WAS LOCATED in the north section of Buenos Aires in a sprawling neighborhood called Palermo. We arrived early, hoping to beat the crowd, but the waiting area was already full. After standing for a while, Franco said he'd be back in a moment. When two plastic chairs became available, I sat down in one and put my purse on the other one to save it for Franco. The walls were a ghastly green, and the fluorescent lights emitted a low hum, flickering intermittently. No one else seemed bothered by either the drab surroundings or the interminable waiting. It was as if they had all been forewarned that any inquiry in the administrative offices would be an all-day affair.

My mind returned to the night before. After kissing outside my building, I invited Franco up to my grandfather's apartment. Franco dropped onto my favorite sofa, pulling me down with him so that I ended up sitting on his lap. My arms went around his slim neck. His lips were warm and plump, and his mouth tasted slightly of Coca-Cola. But, after a moment, his lips grew rigid. When I opened my eyes, I saw he was looking elsewhere.

"What's wrong?" I asked, convinced it had to do with me.

"Nothing." Franco gently moved me off his lap. "Would you mind, um, telling me, um, is there a service entrance?"

I wanted to laugh. At least it wasn't about me! But his curiosity about another possible door was affecting him. He clenched his jaw and anxiously fidgeted with his fingers. I pointed to the right, explaining that the back door was through the kitchen, next to the maid's quarters. Franco got up. I remained in the living room. I fixed my shirt and gathered my tangled hair into a ponytail. When Franco came back, he said it was late. He needed to go home. It was an awkward goodbye, even as we finalized plans to meet up again the next day. Today. Emily probably would have advised me not to see Franco again, but there I was, seated in an uncomfortable chair in a cold and unpleasant room, waiting for him.

He returned with two coffees in small, brown plastic cups. He added a packet of sugar to each, stirring them with a flimsy plastic stick, then handed one to me. The coffee had a filmy layer on top. It tasted watery and too sugary, but I sipped it until it was gone.

"Number 45. Number 45. Please come forward."

A woman with frosted auburn hair pulled back into a knot with a large hair clip sat behind the glass partition. The nametag pinned to her white lab coat read *Carla Rivas*. She took our ticket and, with a glance, confirmed the number.

"Good morning," she greeted us through the glass opening.

"Good morning to you," Franco began with a friendly smile. Our request was pretty straightforward, he told her. We needed access to the hospital birth records for 1976.

"You have to be a direct relative of the baby in question, and we need to see two pieces of identification before we can commence the process," she responded.

He leaned forward. "But I'm sure you can find a way to make an exception for us, Carla. Yes?"

"I'm sorry, but there's nothing I can do."

"We should go," I suggested.

"Carla, come on. Help me out here," he pressed on, with what he and I both hoped was a winning smile.

"Bring the proper documents next time," she said with more authority.

"All right, then. Thanks for your time," he replied courteously, but before moving off to the side, his fist came down firmly on the counter.

We walked through the hospital courtyard, Franco's hands shoved deep in his pockets.

"We tried, Franco. It's okay. Besides..." I paused, knowing he wouldn't like what I was about to say. "I'm not sure I want to continue with this."

When Franco had offered to help me, I was certain I would stop at nothing to find out more about my father's role in the resistance against the dictatorship and the disappearance of Valentina Quintero. But I never imagined it would lead to questions about what happened to her baby and about my own birth. My mind was having a hard time keeping up, and I wanted to slow the investigation down. He looked askance at me and reached inside his coat pocket for his cigarettes.

"Okay. Fine. Let's go," he said.

A woman in a white lab coat walked up to us. "Here." She extended her lit cigarette. He brought his cigarette to hers and puffed until the tip glowed red.

"Thanks"—he read her nametag—"Bettina Paulsen."

"I work in the front office," Bettina said, waving back to some coworkers across the hospital courtyard. In a hushed voice, she said to Franco, "I overheard your request in the office. What exactly are you looking for?"

Franco glanced at her and nodded warily before answering. "We need to confirm the identity of a baby's parents, and the only way to do that is by locating the original birth record." He paused. Clearly, experience had taught him to be cautious about trusting people in his country, but sometimes there was no choice. "We're pretty certain the baby was born at this hospital during the dictatorship, in 1976."

Bettina waited until a hospital worker walked by. She then leaned toward his ear, muttering something I could not make out; I could, however, tell from Franco's face that our visit to the hospital might not have been in vain.

CHAPTER 30

December 1975

WHILE THE SUN SLOWLY DROPPED behind the low-rise buildings, leaving hues of pink and purple in the sky, Santiago watched commuters scurrying toward the train terminal. *Is she going to come this time?* He was waiting on one of the benches in a plaza in the Constitución neighborhood. Valentina had asked to see him someplace where the chances of running into someone they knew were slim. And not at her studio. She had been firm on that point. The first time she had asked to meet him in a public place, she hadn't shown up. When they spoke again by phone, she barely apologized, only saying she hadn't been able to get away. He hadn't seen her since she had proposed that he leave the city with her, almost three weeks ago. Why was she avoiding him? Did Máximo suspect something?

People sat on nearby benches, enjoying an unusually cool late spring evening. Santiago zipped his jacket as he glanced again at the street, hoping to spot her. Two policemen were headed toward him, but then they changed direction, approaching a group of students instead.

"IDs, please."

The students nervously reached into their back pockets and purses.

One long-haired young man took out his identification card from his wallet, but when he went to hand it to the officer, it slipped out of his hand onto the ground. The police officer's boot covered the card, nearly stepping on the student's hand as he bent down to pick it up. A young woman politely asked the officer to remove his boot so her boyfriend could retrieve his ID card.

"Of course, miss." The officer spoke these words while undressing her with his eyes. She, in turn, gave him a look of loathing. He lifted his boot, uncovering the now soiled card. The boyfriend quickly picked it up, wiped it on his jeans, and handed it over. The other officer studied the identification cards, matching the photos to the students. Everyone appeared to be in the clear, and the students became less tense.

"You." The officer pointed to the long-haired man. "You're coming with us."

The girlfriend turned to the officer. He gave her a malicious smile. She tugged at her boyfriend's arm, a silent plea for him not to go.

"The rest of you, get moving."

As the students gathered their things, Santiago heard one of them complain to the others, "But they can't take him just like that!"

"Shhh! Stop talking or we'll be next."

One of the women put her arms around the girlfriend, whose earlier show of bravado had dissolved into despair. The students hurried through the plaza, passing Valentina on their way out.

The sight of her made Santiago's pulse race with excitement. He took her behind one of the tall palm trees. He went to kiss her, but she only gave him her cheek.

"I've called you at your studio a few times." He wanted to sound casual but it came out more like a whine.

"I'm sorry."

"Are you okay? I've been worried."

"I'm fine."

"I've missed you. We need to discuss our plan. Córdoba…"

The tree trunk didn't hide them from the public eye, but he didn't care. He held out his hand. She wouldn't take it.

"Santiago, I…"

Valentina's expression told him what was coming next, but he was prepared.

"Everything's going to be great for us. I needed some time, but I've worked it all out," he said with more confidence in his voice than he actually felt.

"Please. Don't make this any harder. We both know we shouldn't have…it was wrong. Even if they never find out, and I hope they don't, we hurt them both."

He wasn't listening. "I'm leaving Lila. It's decided. I couldn't break it off with her sooner, but now I can. Lila and Máximo will understand that we haven't stopped loving each other. Lila is young, we don't have children, and I'm confident she'll find someone new soon. Someone who'll really make her happy. You and I can finally start our life together."

"I've been thinking a lot, and it's too late, Santiago," Valentina replied with a weary tone.

"It's not too late. And I don't love Lila. Not like I love you." Santiago took her hands. "I have a present for you, for us. I was going to surprise you. I bought a small plot of land." He pinned her to the tree trunk. "Near where you took me swimming that day we drove to the music festival in Cosquín. It's not too far from your parents'," he added with a smile.

Christmas was three weeks away, and he pictured them spending it in Córdoba with her family. They would drive to the property by the river, and Valentina would begin to envision the type of home she might design for the two of them. It could be a simple cabin. He didn't have an opinion, as long as they were together.

"You did?"

"Yes." His forehead touched hers. "You can have your own garden.

I didn't get you a hammock. Not yet. I thought we could pick out two hammocks together. One for you, one for me. I'm also thinking of looking into the vet school in Córdoba City."

"Santiago. I don't know what to say."

"Say yes."

"I can't. I can't leave Máximo. I tried once already. It won't work. He needs me. He's been contributing illustrations to this underground paper, and he's involved in other things he doesn't talk to me about. He's told me I'm the only reason he comes home at night. I wouldn't forgive myself if something happened to him because I wasn't there." Valentina had been looking down, but now she raised her face, imploring him with her eyes to let her go one more time. She thought back to the day she asked herself if she could love two men at the same time. The answer remained the same. She loved them both. "We're too different, you and I. It would never work in the end. Lila's good for you. You shouldn't leave her."

"Stop." He put two fingers on her lips. "Stop thinking with your head." Santiago then put his hand on her chest. "Listen. Do you hear? I'm talking to your heart now." He searched for her mouth but she turned her cheek. His lips landed on her jaw. His head motioned toward the train station. "We can leave on the next train."

"I can't." Valentina slowly disengaged from his embrace. "This is goodbye, Santiago."

He swallowed hard. "You need time. I can see that. And that's fine. I'll wait for you."

"Please. Don't," she said. In her smile he saw sadness, regret. She gave him the briefest of kisses and turned, leaving as quickly as she arrived.

CHAPTER 31

August 1998

AFTER WE LEFT SAN RAFAEL Hospital and walked a block or two, Franco said, "Tomorrow morning I'm going to follow up on something Bettina said. She asked me to meet her alone if that's okay with you." I said it was fine. Then he checked his watch and smiled, his mood improved by this new lead. He asked, "I have a class later, but do you want to come over for a coffee?"

He lived in a different section of Palermo, referred to as Palermo Viejo. It was a neighborhood of tree-lined cobblestone streets, outdoor cafés, and Spanish-style homes, some with beautifully carved oak doors dating back to the nineteenth century. Upon entering his apartment, I noticed there wasn't much furniture. Rows of books and VHS tapes filled the shelves of one wall, and I walked over for a closer inspection. Evidently, one or both Bonetti brothers were cinephiles. Framed posters of Fellini's *La Dolce Vita* and Truffaut's *The 400 Blows* hung on either side of the television set. The small kitchen had an island with barstools dividing it from the living area. Doors on opposite ends of the living room led to the bedrooms and a bathroom. Bare treetops reached the wide living room windows, which were slightly open and let in a cool breeze.

No male college friend of mine had an apartment that didn't look like it had been hit by a tornado. Even if Franco's place was not totally neat, everything was in its place. It felt like it had been put together with loving care.

I sat on the sofa and watched Franco raise and lower the living room window a couple of times. He leaned his head out, looking down two flights to the street. He then backed away from the window and walked past me toward the kitchen. Curious, I tracked him with my eyes. He went to a small alcove, opened the service door, and stepped out. I heard him move something heavy. When he was done, he returned to the kitchen and began whistling softly while pouring us both glasses of sparkling water.

He sat beside me, and after we drank from our glasses, he took my hands in his.

A young man padded barefoot into the living room, rubbing his eyes.

"Hey," he said, looking as if he had slept in his clothes.

"What's up?" Franco left my side. The men hugged.

"Paloma, this is my younger brother. Luis, meet Paloma."

Luis reacted like he hadn't heard my name before. We exchanged greetings and he sat down across from us.

"Coffee?" Franco asked, and went to one of the cabinets to get some cups.

"Are you also studying?" I asked Luis after we sat in silence for a few moments while Franco prepared the coffee.

He nodded. "Film."

"Like your father," I remarked.

Luis shot a sideways glance at Franco, and I wondered if I was one of the few outside of the HIJOS circle who knew the Bonettis' history.

"Are you interested in being a director or writer?" I asked.

"Not sure yet."

"He just won a screenwriting competition," Franco said, bringing the hot drinks over to us. "Isn't that right, little brother?"

"That's great," I said. "Congratulations."

"And he's getting gigs all the time now as a freelance cameraman. He's been on a shoot and we haven't seen each other in days."

Franco tried to pat his brother's head but Luis ducked out from under his hand. Luis's hair was cut so short that his scalp was visible in spots. Unlike Franco, whose build was small and wiry, Luis had a stocky frame.

"And you?"

"I'm from New York. I study at a college not far from there," I answered.

"So you don't live here?"

"No. Just visiting."

"New York, eh? Nice," Luis replied, but his tone let me know he was not impressed.

"It's home," I said with a forced smile. I drank the coffee as the brothers talked, and when I finished, I stood up. Grabbing my coat off the back of one of the chairs, I said, "I should get going. Nice meeting you, Luis."

"Likewise," Luis answered. He stood and gave me the customary kiss on the cheek.

Franco walked me to the door and said in a low voice, "Hey, sorry about Luis. I should have said something to you before. I forget that he's reserved around people he doesn't know, and, well, he can be kind of a grouch sometimes. But once you get to know him, he's a real softy."

"No problem. Maybe he doesn't like the idea of his brother spending time with a Yanqui."

Franco smiled at this. "Luis knows better than to meddle in my affairs, especially if they're of the romantic variety." He brushed the bangs away from my eyes. "I'll see you tomorrow? I'll let you know what I find out, yes?"

I nodded. He rounded my waist with his arms and softly kissed me goodbye.

A damp chill was in the air, the sky a ceiling of dark clouds, but I wanted to walk back to my grandfather's apartment. It would take me about an hour, and I had no other plans. My cell phone rang. It was Mom.

"Paloma?"

"Mamá. Hi."

"Where are you? I hear traffic in the background."

"I'm outside."

"Are you on your way to the campo?"

"No, I'm not. Abuelo told you I called, right?"

"Yes, but he couldn't remember when you were coming back. We miss you." It had been three days since I last saw my parents.

I bit my cheek. "Juan invited me to visit his family's farm, and I said I would go."

"Okay," Mom responded, her voice disappointed if not frustrated. "I was calling you because we've all been invited to stay with friends for their annual cattle auction. They're throwing a big party. We'll spend a couple of nights." In the campo life, going to visit a neighbor's ranch could easily mean a few hours' drive. Guests usually stayed overnight. "But I understand if you want to be with Juan. I'll tell your father."

"Thanks, Mamá. I'll see you at the ceremony then?"

"Yes."

I heard something in her tone when we were saying our goodbyes. Did she suspect I was actively avoiding them? I didn't like deceiving them, and I reassured myself it wouldn't be for much longer. I was curious to hear what Franco would find out from the woman we met at the hospital, but it was also true that the more time we spent together, the more I was drawn to him and his world.

I was caught up in these thoughts when it started to rain. Should I take a bus? What line would get me back? Buenos Aires had a subway system, but I had no idea if there was a stop nearby. A car sprayed my ankles with rainwater. A few cabs went by, all occupied. I cursed under my breath. As the rain began to come down hard, I finally hailed one. The driver reached back to open the door and I climbed in. I looked down at my soaked pants and thought that as soon as I was home, I would pour myself a glass of wine and indulge in a long, hot bath. The cab sped through an intersection as the light turned red, and I realized that I was not holding on to the door handle like I had when I first arrived in Buenos Aires. As we raced down the avenue toward the apartment, the city was one big wet blur.

The rain subsided by the time the cab pulled up in front of Abuelo's building. I rummaged through my purse for my wallet.

"Miss, are you in some sort of trouble?"

"No. Why do you ask?"

The driver looked at me in the rearview mirror. "A car without license plates has been following us."

"What?" I glanced out the back window.

"They're not behind us anymore." He flicked his hand toward the passenger side. "Over there. In the Ford Falcon."

I made out three people. Two in the front, one in the back. "They must be picking someone up," I suggested uncertainly.

The cabbie, nevertheless, waited until I was inside. I kept myself out of view until I had enough courage to look through the lobby's glass door. The car was still across the street. The driver, a bald man, was staring at my building and caught my eye. And then he, too, moved on.

CHAPTER 32

February 1976

THE WEDDING FOR GENERAL DELGADO's daughter Mercedes was celebrated in the lavish ballroom of the Alvear Palace, a hotel built in the 1930s by a socialite who had wanted to import Parisian Belle Époque grandeur to the Paris of the Americas. Guests clustered around the bride and groom, congratulating them on their union. Santiago placed his hand absently on his wife's back. Lila's emerald gown accentuated the deep green of her eyes, and her blond hair shimmered under the chandelier. She would be a vision if not for her pout. When, earlier that evening, Lila had examined herself in their bedroom mirror, he had reassured her that she was at her most beautiful. But now he had little patience for her sulking.

"I love the flowers," Santiago's mother gushed to General Delgado's wife. "And your dress. Everything is divine."

"Not so long ago, it was you standing here in my shoes, Constanza," the mother of the bride replied, gesturing to Santiago and Lila. When Valentina had been in the picture, Constanza had tried to steer Santiago toward Mercedes Delgado. *Everything worked out fine,* she thought, glancing at her son and daughter-in-law. Lila was a perfect wife for her son. The whole family adored her.

Alfonso Larrea shook the general's hand warmly. The military's first attempt to remove Isabel Perón from office in December had failed, but it was a new year and whispers about another impending coup swirled about the ballroom. The weeks seemed to be numbered for the president.

"Your men are doing a great job. The longer Isabelita stays in power, the worse off this country will be," Alfonso said.

"Between you and me, it's all lining up. We have a lot of work ahead of us to put this country back on track," the general told him in a confidential tone.

After wishing the couple many years of wedded bliss, Lila turned to Santiago and told him that she had to use the ladies' room. Glad to have an unexpected moment alone, Santiago's eyes swept the room, projecting a smile to the crowd. Grace was by the piano, where a small semicircle of people had formed. He joined the group, nodding amiably at a couple of guests. Once he was face to face with Grace, however, he dropped his smile just long enough for her to notice.

"Are you all right?" Grace asked.

He leaned over her ear. By his facial expression, a guest would assume he was relaying a humorous wedding day anecdote, but his voice, largely drowned out by the piano music, was more serious.

"It's Valentina. She won't see me. She ended it two months ago."

A waiter approached with a tray of champagne flutes and Grace took two.

"Drink," she recommended, handing one to Santiago.

"I don't get it, Grace. Why does she keep breaking my heart?"

In his rush to toss back the champagne, Santiago bumped a nearby guest and spilled the bubbly, mostly on himself but also on the floor. The pianist glanced over without missing a note.

"Pull yourself together," Grace said. She raised her glass toward a few surrounding onlookers who noticed the commotion. "You're married. Don't forget that." She whispered in his ear. "What you had with Valentina was an affair. And affairs always come to an end. Always. Besides, I could have told you she wouldn't leave Máximo."

He winced. "Do you have to bring *him* up?"

"You really are still a child," she said, finishing her champagne.

"You know him, Grace. He's not the kind of man you spend the rest of your life with."

She frowned. "Santiago, he's still your friend."

"I'm getting another drink. Can I get you one?" he asked, not waiting for her reply.

As Santiago made his way to the bar, a young man in full dress naval uniform wished him a pleasant evening. Santiago didn't stop, only nodded in passing.

"Hello," Grace said, smiling widely at the officer in an attempt to make up for Santiago's rudeness.

It was Pedro García, the bride's cousin and the high school classmate of Bautista Larrea and Grace's older brother, Sebastián. When they were all younger, it seemed to Grace that Pedro was sometimes left behind by his peers, as if he wasn't quite quick enough to be in on their jokes or adopt the casual ease Bautista and Sebastián used when talking to girls or walking them home from school. However, the few times she had seen Pedro since he entered the naval academy, he appeared changed, more grown up, coming across now as self-possessed.

"Always a delight to see you, Grace," Pedro said, returning the smile.

Lila returned to Santiago's side at the bar. She was less adept at maintaining her smile, and he could tell by her eyes that she was upset.

"What's wrong, my darling?" he asked. *What now?* is what he thought.

"I got my period, again," she murmured, dismayed.

He encircled her with his arms. "Don't worry, Lila. It will all be fine. I promise you."

Santiago kissed her. When he looked over her head, he found Grace watching them thoughtfully.

A few weeks later, in a loud, brightly lit restaurant, similar to any Parisian brasserie along Boulevard du Montparnasse, Santiago and Lila were tucked into a corner booth, eating dinner. Lila chewed on child-size bites of steak while Santiago swirled the wine in his glass, the meat on his plate untouched. He smoked a cigarette out of pure boredom. Lila didn't comment when the smoke floated over her way. They weren't speaking much to each other lately, which was perfectly fine with Santiago.

When Santiago saw the maître d' escort Valentina and Máximo to a table near the front, his chest tightened. Lila picked at her food, unaware.

He stubbed out his cigarette and said, "I have to make a call."

He went toward them, without a plan or strategy. Valentina's head turned in his direction, and he ducked behind a column. A waiter asked if he needed anything. Feeling like he had been caught spying, a red-faced Santiago shook his head and switched directions. He walked toward the men's room, lighting another cigarette to calm himself down. It wasn't like Máximo to come to this type of restaurant. He glanced back at their table. They must be celebrating something. Their exchange was loose and intimate, very much like a couple in love.

CHAPTER 33

August 1998

"Señor Darío Zubieta?" Franco politely addressed the eye staring at him through a peephole. The information provided by the hospital worker Bettina the morning after our visit to San Rafael Hospital had brought us to Mataderos, a neighborhood on the outer reaches of the city. The eye blinked in response and the peephole cover dropped back down. Bolts slid, chains unlatched, and the apartment door slowly opened.

"Come in, please," said Darío, a man whose face I could not fully see because of his stooped posture. A yellow Labrador barked excitedly, plopping his front paws on Franco's thighs. Franco smiled and grabbed at the fold of flesh on the dog's scruff.

"Pipo! Down! Down!" ordered the hunched man with a stern tone. The dog dropped his paws and sniffed our feet.

"Hey, Pipo!" Franco kneeled and rubbed the dog behind its ears. "You're a good doggy, aren't you?"

"I've been waiting for you, eh? Bettina told me you were going to come at six o'clock. It's after seven."

"I know. My apologies. My class ran late," Franco explained.

"We brought some baked goods for tea," I said, holding out a white cardboard box tied with a string. The name of Panadería El Norte, the bakery across the street from Franco's building, was stamped in blue ink across the top.

Darío lifted his head long enough to catch my eye. "Will you prepare us a pot of tea then, señorita?"

He pointed to where the kitchen was, and I left the men.

Earlier, when we went to Franco's local bakery to buy pastries for our visit to Mr. Zubieta, Franco had insisted I sample some of his favorites.

"The best in Buenos Aires," he claimed enthusiastically.

As we were waiting to be served, Franco told me about the Italian bakers who had migrated to Argentina at the beginning of the twentieth century, many of them bringing along their anarchist ideas. A few popular pastries soon came to be known as sacramentos, vigilantes, cañoncitos—names intended to ridicule the church, the government, and the military.

Between the two of us, we must have eaten a dozen pastries. A few of them were sugary or filled with dulce de leche, and Franco used his handkerchief to brush off the sugary crumbs from around my mouth. When he realized we were going to be late, the cashier sent us on our way with a "Pay me tomorrow, Franco!" As we ran to catch the bus, he took my hand in his, sending a warm sensual current through me. I marveled at how, even as my world was flipping upside down, I had had the good fortune of meeting Franco Bonetti.

A box of matches sat on the counter, and I lit the burner under the full kettle. After rinsing the cups and small plates, I arranged everything on a tray I had wiped with a dishtowel. When the tea was ready, I joined them in the living room.

The furniture was wrapped in clear plastic sheets, and a light film of furry gray dust covered the coffee and side tables. A potted plant in serious need of sunlight drooped in a corner. The room could have benefited from some fresh air too, and I wondered when the curtains and windows had last been opened.

Once Darío had a cup of milky tea and a sweet or two, he began to talk. "Bettina is a good woman. Hard to believe that, after all these years, she's still working at San Rafael Hospital." Pipo was curled around the man's feet, and the dog's mouth opened instinctively just before his master would break off a piece of a cocktail-size sandwich for him. "After my daughter was abducted, Bettina visited us every couple of weeks, to check in, you see, to find out if we had received any news. She went grocery shopping for us a few times. My poor wife, it was tough on her."

The old man sneezed and Franco answered, "Bless you!"

"Thank you. These damn allergies." Darío pulled out a handkerchief and wiped his nose. "As I was saying, Bettina was good to us after our Elena went to a better place. You know, she still comes over from the hospital once in a while, but I tell her that I'm managing just fine. I've got Pipo here."

"Did your daughter work with Bettina?" Franco asked.

"They were in the same department, but Elena was a nurse. Obstetrics, you see. She loved babies."

Darío gestured toward the mantelpiece. On it was a photo of a young woman with a bright smile, crouched down, her arms around a Labrador retriever. A few small objects, including a bunch of pressed brown flowers, had been placed around the framed photo. From the fringed suede jacket and oversize yellow-tinted glasses she was wearing, I guessed the picture had to be at least twenty years old.

"She was a hardworking girl, our Elena. Didn't mind the hours. Not her. Her Basque genes, you see." The dog stretched its legs and meandered over to Franco. "He likes you, young man," Darío observed. "Where was I? Oh, yes! So she was working at San Rafael Hospital, and one day they switched her schedule to the night shift. She didn't complain, not my daughter. She loved what she did. Her colleagues were like family to her. She was a happy girl." He paused. "That was how it was, you see, until she started noticing that pregnant women were being brought in at night, alone, without their husbands or parents or siblings or even friends. They were always alone. In the morning, the mothers and babies would be gone. When she asked about it, she was hushed by one of her colleagues. She was told not to ask their superiors. She would only cause trouble, might possibly lose her job. No one at the hospital asked any questions. Everyone looked the other way. But she continued to hear and see things." He signaled to the photo. "Will you bring it down for me?"

I picked up the frame, wiped off the dust with my sleeve, and handed it to him. He gazed at his daughter's image while he continued his story. "One night, a young lady came in. She was in labor. When the doctor left the room to scrub up, the pregnant woman started crying, but not from pain, no sir. She was crying from fear. My daughter could hear the difference, you see. The woman motioned for Elena to come in closer. She needed to tell her something. The woman whispered into her ear that she had been kidnapped. My daughter's suspicions, all those months, were finally explained. She asked if Elena could contact her family. She gave Elena her parents' phone number and then the doctor came back. When Elena went on her break at dawn, she called the woman's parents. She had memorized the number. Smart girl. The parents came as fast as they could, but the young lady was already gone. The baby too."

Darío paused to look us in the eye, but his hunched back allowed him to raise his head only high enough to view our chins.

"Elena was visibly upset when she came home from that shift," he continued. "She didn't tell us why at first, but we knew things weren't right. My wife was worried sick. She kept telling me something was very wrong, convinced it had something to do with Elena's job. It was killing our daughter, my wife said. So I made a decision. I told Elena I would force her to quit if she didn't tell us what was going on. And she did. One morning." He kissed the photo of his daughter's face. "A few days later, they came for her."

Pipo left Franco's side and nestled at his master's feet.

Darío pulled out an old shoebox from under his armchair. "They killed my little girl. But they never knew about this."

He placed the box on the coffee table, lifted the lid, and proceeded to pull out various items: a rusty barrette, a tarnished wedding band, a stained espadrille, a pair of glasses, rosary beads. An ink pad. And then he retrieved a small stack of surgical masks. He took the top one and unfolded it to show the tiniest footprint imaginable.

"After these poor women delivered their babies, Elena would take the little ones to be cleaned. When she was sure that she was alone with the baby, she would take a print of the foot with a small ink pad she had bought and kept hidden in her uniform."

We gaped at the mask, amazed by the perfect dark outline of the tiny foot and the toes, mere black dots.

"What a remarkable daughter you had. You must be proud of her," Franco exclaimed. "May I?" Darío handed him the stack. After examining a few of them, Franco asked, "Have you shown these to anyone?"

Darío shook his head. "I was afraid they would come for my wife next, so I hid the box. But it's been a few years since she's passed. When you said Bettina suggested I talk to you, I figured it might be time."

"Would it be all right if we borrowed them?"

"Would you be so kind as to pour me more tea, young lady?" I prepared Darío another cup, adding milk and sugar. With a slight tremor in his hand, he drank, then eyed the items laid out on the coffee table. "I'm an old man. What good is this shoebox going to do me if it lives forever under a chair?"

CHAPTER 34

March 1976

SANTIAGO STOOD AT A WINDOW and peered into a room full of children seated at long tables, eating soup from colorful plastic bowls. Two little girls sat on either side of Valentina while she read to them. His knuckles rapped softly on the glass. When she lifted her head and saw him, she waved to one of the nuns and handed her the book. Then she looked at Santiago, pointing at the door.

He waited for her by the main entrance, his body vibrating with anticipation. After kissing his cheek, Valentina steered him to the back. They sat underneath a large lemon tree that offered respite from the late summer sun. Valentina folded her hands on her lap as if in prayer. *Those nuns have too much influence over her*, Santiago thought. He hadn't seen her in three months, and her face had thinned. Dark circles under her eyes suggested she had not slept in days.

"Thanks for coming."

"Have you been thinking about us? Is that why you called?" he asked, hopeful she had changed her mind and was returning to him. Strands of hair, moist from the heat, clung to her throat. Santiago resisted the urge to peel them away.

Valentina covered his hand with hers. "No, this isn't about us. I contacted you because of Máximo. If I had told you that over the phone, you might not have come. I'm worried about him."

"Oh."

"He's out most nights, late, even until early morning. Sometimes he doesn't come home. Or he'll go away for a couple of days, God knows where. I don't think he realizes how dangerous it's become."

To keep his emotions under control, Santiago told himself that it was reasonable for Valentina to come to him. She knew of his family's connections to the military and other spheres of power and influence. "Have you talked to him about this?" he asked.

"We don't say that much to each other. He doesn't want to tell me anything. To protect me, he says."

A nun shuffled past them, acknowledging Santiago with a curt nod.

Valentina lowered her voice. "Remember Enrique?"

"Yes. I never thought much of him. Acted as if he was going to be the next Che Guevara. What a buffoon. Still can't believe Grace dated him."

"He's missing."

"What do you mean?"

"We think he's been kidnapped by the government. Máximo and Enrique used to spend time together, so I'm afraid Máximo will be next," she said, her voice down to a whisper. "Would you talk to him? He trusts you."

Santiago couldn't decide if he was disappointed or relieved that Máximo had never suspected their affair. He stood up and took a few steps. "I don't know, Valentina…"

"I need him at home. I can't do this alone."

"You can't do what alone?" He stopped pacing, waiting for her to go on.

"I'm not as strong as I used to be. That's why I was hoping you could talk to him." She briefly looked away. "We're getting married, and I want us to have a normal life."

"I don't understand," he whispered, his heart twisting inside.

Valentina rose. Her hands stretched out toward him as if to soften the blow.

"I'm so sorry, Santiago. I hope you realize I never wanted to hurt you. You know that, right? I need your help. Please."

Never had he seen her this vulnerable. He touched her forehead with his lips. He loved her, but what he needed to do, he finally understood, was forgive Valentina, forgive Máximo.

"Don't worry," he said into her anguished eyes. "I'll talk to him."

A giant wooden board, its surface entirely covered with meats, stood next to the outdoor grill. Santiago sipped a scotch and watched Sánchez season both sides of the various cuts of beef with rough salt crystals. The gaucho hovered over the enormous grill and monitored the glowing charcoal, wiping the sweat from his brow with a large cotton napkin tucked into his wide belt. Once the flames were tamed, Sánchez expertly draped the chorizos and morcillas—blood sausages—across the blackened grates.

Splashing sounds drew Santiago's attention away from the grill. Lila was coming out of the swimming pool, adjusting her bikini bottom as she walked toward the house. Josefina, carrying a tray with empanadas, had informed Lila that guests had arrived. "You stay. I'll see to them, darling," Santiago said.

Máximo and Valentina were waiting inside the front entrance hall. Santiago had invited them to the ranch for the day. Grace and her new boyfriend, Isidoro, were coming out too. The pretext was to enjoy one of the final summer weekends in the company of old friends. Santiago's real intention was to speak to Máximo in private.

"Thank you for inviting us," Valentina said. "It's so kind of you to do this."

"Not at all. It's great to see you both," he said with a polite smile.

"Yes, thank you," Máximo said. "It's wonderful out here, so nice to escape Buenos Aires in this heat."

From Máximo's open and trusting face, Santiago knew he had no idea that this invitation had come from his visit with Valentina two weeks earlier. She was good at keeping secrets from the man she claimed to love, Santiago thought, not feeling one bit sorry for Máximo.

"Join Lila by the pool. I'll be right out," he told them.

When Santiago returned to the picnic table, he put on a smile. Holding up a transistor radio, he said, "The Boca–River soccer match is about to start, but we're out of batteries."

"I keep a radio in the car," Máximo said, setting down the book he was reading, *Rayuela* by Julio Cortázar.

"Fantastic," Santiago said, waving him off. "You stay. I'll get it."

He walked around the side of the house. Máximo's white Dodge Polara was unlocked. He opened the glove compartment, when something sticking out from under the driver's seat caught his eye.

"You won't know where to look." Máximo was standing behind him.

"What the hell are you doing with this?"

Santiago climbed back out of the car, holding a small Beretta pistol in his hand.

"It doesn't concern you," Máximo said, unfazed. "I keep it just in case."

"What about Valentina?"

"What about her?"

"Damn it, Máximo! Who the hell do you think you are?" He grabbed Máximo by the arm and spoke to him in a slow growl, waving the heel of the gun in his left hand. "You idiot. If she ever gets hurt because of you, I'll…I'll kill you with my bare hands."

Máximo slipped out of his grasp and backed away. Santiago looked down and steadied himself. He placed the gun on the ground and kicked it toward Máximo.

"Look at what happened to Enrique," Santiago said, clenching his jaw to keep from yelling.

"How did you hear?" Máximo asked, upset, looking away. But then he turned to Santiago with scorn. "I'm surprised you, of all people, would be concerned about him." He calmly put the handgun back in the car, hiding it under the passenger seat this time. "Don't worry about Valentina. I'm not exposing her to anything. She's not in danger," he said, walking around the back of the car. A small radio lay next to a canvas bag with beach towels and swimsuits. He put the radio inside the bag.

"We forgot to grab our swim things," Máximo said, and with one firm push, closed the trunk. "Che, Santi, don't look so serious!" Máximo offered him a conciliatory smile. "So unlike the Santiago I know and love. Come on, let's go, the match is about to start. I have a strong feeling Boca is going to win this time." And, without waiting for his host, Máximo headed back to the pool.

CHAPTER 35

August 1998

ARE YOU SURE WE WON'T get into trouble?"

"Positive," Franco reassured me, and with a flick of the switch, the forensics lab flooded with light.

In the center of the lab was a long table with two large desktop computers. Although the screens were turned off, they still cast an eerie green pallor. File cabinets had been stored underneath. Numerous shelves held small boxes of bones, each one labeled with a name, a date, and a place.

"Franco. Only for you would I come in to work after hours," said a man as he walked into the room. The round wall clock showed it was ten past midnight.

"Hey, Mariano. How's it going?"

"You really want to know? I would be much happier if I were at home cozying up with someone I love," Mariano said as he placed his keys on a nearby shelf. He gave Franco a kiss on each cheek.

"I appreciate the favor. As I told you, we need to keep this to ourselves for now," Franco reminded him.

"Of course. So you must be the one we're trying to match." Mariano, who looked to be in his early thirties, gave me the once-over.

Franco waved me closer. "Paloma, this is Mariano Menéndez."

"Pleased to meet you," I said.

"Pleasure's all mine." His dark eyes radiated warmth under his bushy eyebrows.

"All right then, let's have a look, shall we? What have you got for me?"

I extracted a thick manila envelope from my bag. I opened it and pulled out the surgical masks. The moment we left Darío's apartment, Franco had wasted no time in arranging this covert meeting in the forensics lab where he apprenticed.

Mariano scrutinized them. "Whoever did these knew what they were doing. They've stood the test of time."

He walked to the computers and flipped on several switches. After washing his hands at the sink, he retrieved latex gloves from a drawer. He pulled out a chair for me and positioned it next to the computer desk. I hesitated. What would Emily say if she could see me now, in this lab, surrounded by human bones and strange machines, about to run tests to see if some other woman was my biological mother? I took a deep breath and sat down.

"Okay, now take off one of your shoes. Whichever one you prefer first. It doesn't matter. We're doing both," he instructed me, fully immersed in his lab technician role.

I bent down to remove one shoe, but a wave of dizziness made me sit up again. Bringing a hand to my forehead, I asked myself why I had let myself get talked into participating in this insane experiment. "Sorry," I murmured.

"That's all right. Take your time."

I looked over to Franco. He gave me an encouraging nod, and a few deep breaths later, I was slipping out of my right sneaker and sock. Mariano placed his chair in front of mine. A large sheet of white paper was laid on the floor by my feet. He pressed a small roller onto a black inkpad and rolled it across the bottom of my foot. It felt cool and wet.

"Stand up but don't put your right foot down." His fingers closed around my right ankle and guided my inked foot to the sheet of paper. "Put your weight down on it now."

His cheery disposition irked me, but I did as I was told.

"Well done. Let's do the left foot now."

I was slow taking off my other shoe and sock. Mariano waited patiently, and when I was ready, we went through the same steps again.

"That should do it." Mariano returned from the sink with a damp cloth. "Use this to remove the ink, and then you can put your shoes back on."

During the next half hour, Mariano took the surgical masks with the baby footprints and scanned them on a large Xerox machine. He then began to upload them to the computer. Biting firmly on the inside of my cheek, I watched with apprehension.

When the upload was complete, the screen split in two. My right footprint was on the left side. On the right, the first infant print began to materialize. When the comparison was complete, the computer indicated that it was not a match. My left footprint appeared for a comparison with the left print of the infant. It was not a match either. Then the computer produced the next infant print.

My throat was suddenly parched. I went to the water cooler, pulled out a cone-shaped paper cup from the dispenser, filled it, and downed the water in two gulps.

I glanced at Franco, who was staring at the computer screen over Mariano's shoulder. A result showing a match would upend my life in ways I couldn't even begin to fathom. My hands were clammy, and I wiped them on my jeans. *There won't be a match.* I knew my parents. They wouldn't have concealed it from me. My father wouldn't. Not him. And then I caught myself. I had recently learned that my father had been keeping a secret about his past. What if this was another secret? A secret of the worst kind. A secret that would reveal my life, as I understood it, to have been a lie. Frightened by this possibility,

I found myself breathless with the urgent need to know, one way or the other.

To calm myself down, I turned my attention to a large map of Argentina hanging on the far wall. Each province was shaded in a different color. The map was peppered with red- and blue-colored pins. "What do these pins represent?" I asked.

"The red ones indicate excavated mass graves, the blue ones are probable sites," Mariano replied.

"There are hardly any red pins at all," I noted.

"The forensic archaeologists in charge haven't been able to get much funding for the exhumations," Mariano explained.

The computer made a slight pinging sound each time a new print materialized on the screen. My eyes went to the pins dotting the province of Buenos Aires. Most were clustered around the capital city. I began to count them and, in doing so, kept my anxiety at bay.

"Paloma, you need to see this," Franco called out.

His voice distracted me and I lost track of the last number. *I'll have to start all over*, I thought. My index finger was on a pin in the northern province of Salta when Franco was at my side, taking my hand and guiding me to the computer.

The screen showed two baby prints. A tingling sensation spread across my arms and legs as if a thousand bees were darting through my veins. The flashing letters swam before my eyes: *MATCH POSITIVE.*

"It could be some kind of mistake, right?" I said.

My eyes flitted between Franco and Mariano. I waited for both to agree, for one or the other to explain that errors happened all the time with this program, to suggest that they throw out the results and redo the test. They both looked at me and said nothing.

CHAPTER 36

March–April 1976

"THE ARMED FORCES HAVE TAKEN control of the republic. With the help of God, we will achieve full national recovery."

Santiago sat at the counter of the Florida Garden Café with the other morning clientele. Everyone was listening to the radio broadcast on repeat with General Videla's speech to the nation.

Shortly after one a.m. on March 24, the armed forces detained President Isabel Perón. She had lasted in office for less than two years. Following her arrest, she was flown to a remote estate in the Patagonian Andes where she would remain in custody for an indeterminate period of time. Argentinians had thus woken up on a bright warm weekday morning to find themselves under military rule. General Jorge Rafael Videla had led the military coup, along with Admiral Emilio Eduardo Massera and Brigadier General Orlando Ramón Agosti. The three made up the military junta that replaced Isabel. In two days, General Videla would officially become the nation's president.

Even as Santiago digested the news, scanning the papers he had bought at the corner newsstand, he was thinking of the day ahead. If he hoped to get to the Tribunales courthouse for a scheduled hearing, he would have to hurry.

Weaving through the mass of pedestrians down Florida Street, Santiago made good time until he reached Avenida de Mayo. A military mobilization was in progress. Tanks churned down the avenue along with armored combat vehicles flanked by hundreds of soldiers clacking their boots in unison.

People stood transfixed, making it impossible for Santiago to continue walking with any speed. He cursed under his breath, even though it occurred to him that it would hardly matter if he arrived on time. As he elbowed his way through the crowd, he caught sight of her from behind. As if she could feel his presence, Valentina turned her head. Their eyes locked. The ground shook as the marching band played a blaring national anthem. The noise was too much for him. He couldn't make out what she was saying, but by the look on her face, he knew she was scared. When he reached her, she clutched his arm. "I'm dizzy. Get me out of here, please."

Santiago led her away from the crowds and into a café on a side street. Inside, it was as if the coup had never happened. They were enveloped in the aroma of coffee, the sounds of milk being frothed and waiters calling out orders to the barista.

He sat her at the first empty table he found.

"Waiter, bring her some water. Quickly."

Santiago had not expected their paths to cross again after she and Máximo had come to El Pinar. When she had ended the affair at the plaza in Constitución, she had asked him to not seek her out anymore, and he had respected her wishes. But here they were, meeting for the third time in four weeks. He studied her as she sipped from her glass. With each encounter, he observed, she seemed to change, to grow a little more unwell. When the waiter returned to take their order, he suggested she have some breakfast.

"I'm not hungry," she said.

They sat in silence. He finished his espresso in two sips and began rolling the sugar cube wrapper back and forth into a little tube.

"Go, Santiago. I'm feeling better, but I'm going to stay here a little longer."

"Where's Máximo?"

"He's away, but he'll be back soon," she answered vaguely.

Santiago felt torn about leaving her until his rational voice reminded him he didn't have a place in her life anymore. "Are you sure? I do need to get to the courthouse."

"Yes. Thank you."

His lips briefly brushed her cheek. And when he walked through the café doors, he did not look back.

The Perón years, defined by the chaos of widespread terror, kidnappings, bombings, and dead bodies, were over. The image projected by the military junta was one of discipline, and the country seemed to let out a collective sigh of relief. Order, at last, would be restored.

Valentina sat on the floor in front of an architectural model of a house. Her thick, curly locks fell over her eyes as she delicately placed a finger on the model to adjust one of the walls. Beside her lay some plastic trees. She took one, glued the bottom, and added it to the row of trees in the miniature courtyard.

The phone rang. She stood and wiped her hands on her hips, leaving traces of dust clinging to her white cotton dress. Feeling a cramp in her lower back, she applied pressure with her hand. She guessed she wouldn't be able to sit on the floor leaning over models for much longer. Moving her hair away from her face, she brought the receiver to her ear.

"Hello?"

"It's me."

"Hi!" she said, sudden joy in her voice. It was Máximo. "I'm so glad you called. I'm leaving soon for the day care. You might have missed me."

"I can't talk long, but I wanted to check in. See how you are. How are you feeling?"

"Okay," she said, adjusting the hand on her lower back. This sort of discomfort was normal, the doctor had told her. No need to tell Máximo. She would buy a more comfortable chair as soon as she could afford one.

"Are you eating?" he asked.

"Yes. I'm taking care of myself. Are you?"

She heard his soft laughter. "I am."

"I'll see you tonight, right?"

"That's what I'm calling you about. I can't."

"Why not? You said you'd only be gone for a day. It's been three days already."

A night, not long ago, after they made love, they found it hard to fall asleep. The sounds of a helicopter flying slowly in circles over their neighborhood disturbed the quiet of their bedroom, big enough to fit only the bed and an armoire that they shared. Valentina curled herself into his body, and he wrapped his arms around her. They lay like that for a while, and then she asked him to reconsider whatever it was that he was doing. Since the coup, he was spending even more time away than before.

"It's dangerous. Too dangerous," she whispered, her head on his chest.

Enrique's disappearance in February had upset them both terribly. He was still missing, and Valentina had hoped it would bring an end to Máximo's activism. Máximo. Her fiancé. Getting married had not been in her plans. The night she met Santiago, when he boldly announced to her that she would marry him, she had laughed at the idea. She had been only twenty-one at the time, still relatively new to the city, with her whole life ahead of her. Three years later, she was marrying Máximo instead. She loved Máximo, but how had she ended up here?

She knew, of course. It was just that she could not quite believe this was how their lives had turned out. Santiago with Lila. Valentina with Máximo.

Máximo drew her head back to look at her. "It's more dangerous to sit around and do nothing," he said.

She admired his courage, but the danger was palpable and it was closing in on them. And yet Máximo had been clear in his intentions. He would not resign himself to what was happening in their country. It was not their first argument on this topic, but detecting a higher note of anxiety in her voice that night, he assured her that everything would soon return to normal. They could marry in Córdoba and stay there indefinitely, if she preferred.

He had thinned, and the lines on his forehead had deepened. His energy, however, had doubled, and the moment she fell asleep, he would get up and move to the living room to smoke and think. He would sketch out ideas for a leaflet denouncing the dictatorship and the illegal detention of Argentine citizens. When ready and printed, the leaflet would be secretly disseminated throughout the city and country. It was the only way to work around the government's censorship and raise awareness.

Valentina switched the phone to her other ear and asked, "Where are you?"

"You know I can't tell you," he reminded her gently.

"Why not?" She was tired of his evasiveness, the nights alone without him. Most of all, she was tired of living in a constant state of dread.

"I'm sorry, my dear." They no longer called each other by their names on the phone. Máximo said more caution and care in all things were needed. "I know this has been hard on you."

"When will you be back?"

"Soon."

He told her he loved her and waited for her to say the same, but she wouldn't. Holding back was the only leverage she had left to shake some sense into him. Valentina replaced the receiver. Immediately regretting how the conversation had ended, she picked it back up again. More than once, he had told her she was the only reason he came home. She would tell him she loved him and would not be at rest until he returned. But the line was dead and she had no way to reach him. Máximo had called from a pay phone. Fiddling with her stone pendant, she stared absentmindedly at the model. It was impossible to concentrate now. She sighed and rolled up the blueprints.

The elevator had broken down again. She would have to take the stairs. When she reached the lobby, José, the building superintendent, met her outside his apartment door.

"Good afternoon, Ms. Quintero. How are you?"

"Very well. And you?"

"Fine, thanks."

A little girl peeked from behind José's back. His daughter, Marcela.

"Marcelita! Come here. I have something for you." Valentina opened her satchel and pulled out a doll-size bed, complete with a painted headboard and a little pillow and quilt. "Look what I made for you." She placed the bed in Marcela's plump hands.

The girl opened her eyes wide with amazement and hugged Valentina.

The street was deserted. The black pavement glistened from the afternoon heat. She glanced at her watch. It was 3:00 p.m. If she caught the 3:30 train, she would make it just in time for her shift at Casa de Los Niños. She gathered her hair with both hands and twisted it into a bun.

A green Ford Falcon without license plates squealed to a stop beside her at an intersection. Valentina turned her head to glimpse the driver, who was staring straight ahead, when she felt a presence behind her. All of a sudden, she was pitched forward into blackness. In a brief moment of confusion, she believed it was someone she knew who had put their hands over her eyes and would soon lift them, exclaiming, "Surprise!"

But then she felt the roughness of the fabric against her eyes and nose. Suffocating, she thrashed her arms, but there were two of them, and they easily forced her into the back of the car.

The driver shifted gears, and with a rev of the engine, the car screeched away, creating a sound that might have alerted other pedestrians except that no one was outside but the old flower woman, who was, for the most part, deaf. Had the woman looked down the street at that precise moment, she would have seen the Ford Falcon speeding through a red light.

CHAPTER 37

August 1998

IT WAS IMPOSSIBLE TO SLEEP the night I found out Valentina was my mother. In shock and unable to think, I had Franco accompany me back to Abuelo's apartment from the forensics lab. Only after I reassured him that I was fine did he agree to leave. It was when he shut the door behind him and I found myself alone in the apartment that I began to shake uncontrollably. The news had turned me inside out.

Later, when the sky began to slowly lighten with the approaching dawn, I remember picking up the phone to confront my parents, but each time I did, my stomach would twist with fear and nausea. Part of me hoped they would say the lab report was absurd, a hoax. A memory came rushing back: I was twelve years old, and I asked why there were no pictures of Mom pregnant with me. She told me she had looked so big that she hadn't let anyone photograph her. Apologizing for her foolish vanity, my mother hugged me, but I felt awful, responsible for her misshapen body. Now that I knew the truth, I couldn't bear them lying to me—as they had been doing, I realized at that moment, my whole life. I would need to recover my strength before speaking to them.

After a fitful sleep, I called Franco. He didn't pick up, and I assumed he was in class. I calculated that by the time I walked to his apartment, he would be back from school. An hour or so later, I was on his block and when I looked up to his apartment, I saw a figure move past his window.

"Hope I'm not interrupting anything," I said when Franco opened the door.

"Not at all. I was looking for an excuse to take a break." He was wearing an old black turtleneck and jeans. A pen was tucked behind his ear and he held a textbook in his hand. "Come in."

I stepped inside and he kissed my cheek. "I called your cell phone a little while ago, wanted to make sure you're okay. Are you?"

"I'm fine." Afraid my parents might call, I had turned my phone off. I wasn't ready to talk to either one of them.

"Really? I know it can't be easy." His brow knitted with worry. "I wish you had let me stay with you a little longer last night."

"I needed time by myself."

He put the kettle on. "Can I make you a coffee or a tea?"

"A tea would be great. Thanks."

I wandered over to his sofa, and he quietly went about the kitchen preparing our tea. He brought our cups to the sofa and sat beside me. We sipped in silence.

"Do you want to talk?" Franco asked.

"I'd like to just sit here for a while if that's okay. I didn't really sleep last night."

"*Claro.* I've got just the thing." He sprang up and soon returned with a blanket and pillow from his bedroom. "It can get drafty in here with those old windows." He pointed across the apartment. "I'll be studying over there." Open books and loose-leaf papers covered the dining room table. "Let me know if you need anything."

"Thank you."

He went to his desk, but after a moment, I called his name. He turned, his kind eyes resting on my face. Surely he'd understand how hard the past eighteen hours had been. How I no longer felt attached to the world I once belonged to. And maybe he'd relate to the grief that had seemed to carve out my stomach.

"I wanted to tell you that…" My throat constricted and I couldn't go on. If I did, I would start crying and not be able to stop.

"What is it, Paloma? You can tell me."

To calm myself, I let out a slow exhale. "I was just going to thank you. You've been a good friend. Ever since I arrived in Buenos Aires, it's like I've been living outside myself. As if everything that's been going on is happening to someone else and not me. In my mind, I had been playing a game, thinking that in the end, it wouldn't affect me. I feel so stupid. I hate myself for not knowing." I pressed my eyes with my wrists. "I always felt ambivalent, you know? About who I was. I would tell myself that all kids go through the painful teen years. But I never imagined this," I said with a brittle laugh. "I feel like I'm in free fall."

Franco had returned to my side, and he caressed my cheek. He told me, just above a whisper, "You can fall into me, if you want. I'll catch you." He dried my tear-streaked face with his handkerchief. "I feel terrible. I probably pushed you too hard. I wasn't thinking about how the results would affect you personally. I'm sorry."

"God, no, Franco. You have nothing to apologize for. I'm so glad you've been with me. Otherwise, I might not have been able to do it on my own. And as upset as I am, you were right. It's better to know."

He held my hand, and right when I thought he might kiss me, he stood up, glancing at the books on the table. He asked, "Can I get you anything else? Are you comfortable?"

"Very. Are you sure I'm not going to be a bother? It looks like you have a lot to study."

"No bother at all. I'm happy you're here."

I watched him flip back and forth between the pages of various textbooks spread out before him. As he read and took notes, it was clear that Franco had a love of learning. I wanted to get up and do something easy and normal—offer to prepare another pot of tea, run out to get something for us to eat. But my body ached and the cozy blanket was making me drowsy. My eyelids grew heavy. Amid the sounds of rustling papers and the faint scent of Franco from the pillow behind my head, I fell asleep.

"Where did you find these?" Franco asked.

We were on a park bench in the Japanese Gardens in front of a lake surrounded by Asian flora interspersed with South American greenery. Across my lap I had fanned out the photos that had fallen out of Martín Torres's book.

I had spent the better part of the day sleeping on Franco's sofa and was waking up when Luis returned from work with a bag full of churros. We ate and drank mate while Luis talked about his day on the movie set. I noticed he was more engaged, making small talk with me, and I guessed Franco had filled him in on my predicament. After we'd cleaned up, Franco suggested we go out for a walk and had brought me to this garden in the middle of the city.

"They were in my father's old bedroom. They were tucked in Torres's first book, *Death by Exile*." I handed him the picture of my dad and Valentina at the beach. "See? She's wearing this stone pendant." I lifted the necklace from under my shirt, having put it on for the first time that morning. It had belonged to Valentina. My mother. A wave of anxiety gripped my chest, but the necklace felt strangely soothing and the stone was warm in my fingers.

Franco examined each photograph carefully. When he flipped over the picture of Valentina standing between my father and Máximo in front of the law school, he read the inscription out loud.

Dear Santiago,
    All's fair in love and war.
    Your friend,
    Máximo

"Grace, the woman in New York I told you about, mentioned Máximo. Apparently he was a close friend of theirs," I explained.

He held the photo out at eye level. "See how they're standing?"

I had looked at the photo countless times, but now it was plain to see that Valentina's body was against Máximo's.

"From the way they're positioned and from the inscription on the back," Franco continued, "I would bet that your father and Máximo were fighting over her. And for once in his life, I don't think your father won."

He gave me back the photo. I scrutinized it. Might Valentina have also been with Máximo? I gnawed on my cheek, disturbed by this possibility.

A man sat on the bench across from us. He had a newspaper open, but his head seemed tilted in our direction.

"Is it possible that Valentina dated Máximo after she and my dad broke up?" I showed him the photo taken at the ranch. "Máximo is also in this one with my parents. He's sitting next to Valentina. See?" After a pause, I continued my train of thought. "But what I don't get is why my father would keep the photo of the three of them. Wouldn't that memory be unwelcome if he did lose her to Máximo, as the inscription seems to imply? And what was my mother's role in this? Presumably she doesn't know my father continued seeing Valentina after they got married." During my sleepless night I had come to the conclusion that I was his love child with Valentina. Why else would he have raised me? I could sense myself unraveling under the enormity of this revelation, and I had to will my mind to brush emotions aside, to hang in there for a little longer.

"All good questions," Franco said.

The man across the path lowered and began to fold up his newspaper.

"And we should find the answers to them," I declared with new resolve.

Franco abruptly collected the photographs. He grabbed my bag and lifted me up by the elbow.

"What's going on?" I asked as he rushed me through the gardens. "Why are we going so fast? You're hurting my arm, Franco."

He only relaxed his hold when we exited the garden onto the bustling avenue. We hurried across the crosswalk as the pedestrian traffic light was flashing red, then walked a couple of blocks farther until Franco stopped and looked behind us.

"Franco, talk to me. You're freaking me out."

"The man on the bench with the newspaper. I recognize his face. He's one of their goons. I've seen him at a few demonstrations. He's been following us."

I looked around, but all I saw were families out for a leisurely Sunday stroll.

"We lost him…for now. But it's obvious they're keeping an eye on you—on us." He placed his hands on my shoulders. "Paloma, what do you want to do? It could get a lot worse."

His words frightened me. Not knowing what to do or say, I looked at Franco. He had been through so much in his life, and yet he was willing to help me, even as my circumstances seemed to have taken a dangerous turn. A strange calm descended on me.

"I haven't conducted a thorough search of my father's bedroom," I said, taking his hand and pulling him along. "I think it's time."

CHAPTER 38

April 1976

"Q*UE LOS CUMPLAS, C*ONSTANZA, *¡QUE los cumplas feliz!*"

The Larrea family and friends sang "Happy Birthday" as Lila brought out a meringue cake for her mother-in-law, who was turning sixty. Bautista had surprised everyone by flying in at the last minute. Constanza was radiant, her husband and her firstborn by her side. Santiago snapped photos. It was warm for a fall night in the Southern Hemisphere. Street noise rarely reached the Larreas' penthouse, and the large sliding windows in the living room had been opened onto the balcony for guests to smoke and take in the views.

As Constanza leaned forward to blow out the candles, Santiago saw Máximo over her right shoulder, across the dining room and in the front hall. He was talking to Antonia. What was he doing in the Larreas' home?

Máximo spun his head toward the dining room, wild-eyed. Santiago felt the hairs on his neck rise. *Máximo has come to kill me*, he thought. *Valentina told him about the affair.* He put down the camera and made his way around the crowded table. He would intercept him before the others saw him. The housekeeper and Máximo turned to him as he entered the hall.

"Thanks, Antonia," Santiago said, and she returned to the kitchen.

He studied Máximo's face, trying to get a better read on the situation. "Che, how are you?" Santiago asked with a strained smile.

"I'm sorry to bother you here at your parents'. I didn't know where else to find you."

"How did you know I was here?"

"I've been watching the front building entrance for the last two nights."

"What's going on?" He pivoted his body to block Máximo's view of the gathering.

"Can we talk somewhere private?"

"Sure. This way."

When he took his friend by the arm, Máximo showed no resistance, following him to the back of the apartment by the maid's quarters.

"Has Valentina been in touch with you?"

"No. Why?" Santiago asked.

"I've been away, and when I came back, she was gone."

"Did you call her parents? She's probably with them in Córdoba."

Santiago remembered her plan to return home. How she asked if he would come with her, leave everything behind. That had been six months ago.

"I did. I didn't want to worry them at first, but I finally had to talk to them. She's not there. She's been gone more than a week now. They're coming to Buenos Aires to file a missing person's report with the police."

"You mean you haven't done that yet?" Santiago looked at him incredulously.

Máximo looked down, despondent. "I'm the one they're after. Can you help me?" Santiago was shaking his head in disbelief when Máximo said, "Please. I need your help. She's pregnant. We're having a baby."

Santiago heard footsteps behind him. Without thinking it through, he said, "Can you get yourself to El Pinar? I'll tell Sánchez you're coming. He'll hide you until I figure something out. Take this money." He opened the service door.

Máximo, folding the pesos into his pocket, stepped into the dimmed back stairwell. "*Gracias, hermano.*"

"I'm not your brother," Santiago hissed, and shut the door.

"Honey?" Lila's sweet voice jolted him back.

When he turned around, his expression was serene.

"Was that Máximo?"

"Mm-hmm."

"Why didn't you invite him in for a slice of cake?"

"He got himself into a difficult situation. Needed to borrow some money. He wasn't in the mood to be social."

"Is he going to be all right?"

Santiago thought to put his arm around Lila as they returned to the dining room but realized she might feel his jittery nerves beneath the skin. "I told him he could count on me."

"You've always been so kind to Máximo and Valentina."

"I'm not kind," he said, beginning to lose his composure. Valentina was missing. He must find her. She was in trouble and she needed him. He had to tell Lila, someone, anyone. But when he opened his mouth to speak or scream, Lila reached for his face and kissed him.

"Yes, you are, Santiago."

A woman's voice was barking at Valentina to get out of the car. As she was yanked out by her arm, she thought her shoulder would come out of its socket. A hand shoved her down a staircase. Her hood was removed, and she was left to drop on a cold cement floor. A dank chill hung in the room. When her shaking subsided, she squinted into the faintly lit corridor. She made out a sign: *Silence Is Health*. Opposite her, another wooden sign read: *Avenue of Happiness*.

A guard motioned toward a closed door at the end of the corridor. "Get up. They're waiting for you."

She was handcuffed, making it difficult to stand up on her own. After a few feeble attempts, the guard grabbed her under the armpits and jerked her up. He tied a blindfold around her eyes, plunging her once more into darkness.

Valentina's body moved an inch to the right and then an inch to the left. Both times she hit something cold and metallic. When she lifted her chest, she pressed up against the same cold surface. And then she heard the others. The moans and cries came from above, below, and either side of her. A bit of artificial light penetrated her blindfold. She was not fully entombed. At least her head stuck out, she thought with stupid relief. A whimper escaped from her lips.

"Shh, it's okay. It's going to be all right. Shh." The consoling sounds came from her right. "There, there, now. Are you badly hurt?"

Valentina turned toward the voice. "I…I don't think so."

"Take some deep breaths."

Valentina tried, but her chest hurt too much. Someone had punched her repeatedly between her breasts.

"Try again," the woman's soft voice urged her.

She managed one full noisy intake.

"That's better," the voice said. "Looks like we'll be neighbors. Tell me. Did they bring you in alone?"

"Yes."

"So no one knows you're here."

"No. I was picked up off the street. I had just left my studio." She began to cry.

"Shh, shh, we don't want them to hear us. Breathe deeply. Again."

Valentina soon grew drowsy and fell asleep, dreaming of her home in Córdoba. She was lying in her favorite hammock among her mother's flowers. But construction noise and the ratatat of the jackhammer disrupted her peaceful afternoon. She was falling to the ground when she woke up.

"What is that?" she asked in a loud whisper.

"It's nothing," her neighbor told her. "The guards sometimes like to play their music real loud. It's fine. Go back to sleep."

The heavy beat gave way to a popular song that Valentina recognized from the radio. *Is this the real life? Is this just fantasy?* But then she became aware of another sound. It was emanating from somewhere out there in the dark. It was a scream. A woman's scream.

CHAPTER 39

August 1998

Franco had barely spoken a word since arriving at Abuelo's apartment. After opening and closing the window in my father's bedroom a couple of times, he ended up leaving it partially open. Pacing about, inspecting the room, he pulled out a storage box from underneath the bed and brought down an old chest from the top of my father's closet. Kneeling in front of the box, he took out each object as if he were a curator handling rare artifacts. Some pieces he held up to the light to better examine. With others, he looked to me for an explanation. He pulled out a few report cards written in blue fountain pen on pink paper, school essays, a polo ball signed illegibly. He showed me an old photo of my dad and Prince Charles after a polo match at Cambridge University. I remember hearing that the prince had invited my father to England after they met at a friend's campo in Pergamino. I shrugged in response. What was there to say? My father had always lived a charmed existence.

Unlike Franco, I had been reckless in my methods, emptying drawers, pulling most of the books off the shelves, leafing through them, and turning them upside down. A trail of items had been carelessly strewn across the bed and floor. I had been bursting with manic energy, certain we would find another piece of information connecting my father to Valentina or Máximo. Tired and hungry, I plopped myself down on my father's bed. I felt foolish for having raised my hopes.

"Franco?"

"Hmm." He was lost in a stack of papers.

"This was a stupid idea. We're probably not going to find anything here if we haven't already. Aren't you hungry? Should we go somewhere to eat?"

"I'd rather stay in, if you don't mind. There's a lot more to go through," he said, clearly absorbed by the task.

I slid off the bed, leaving the room and Franco to his research. In the kitchen, I opened the fridge and checked its contents. A tray of empanadas prepared by Abuelo's housekeeper was on the top shelf. Lifting the foil, I found a note card with instructions on heating and a list of the turnovers' fillings: creamed corn, ham and cheese, spicy beef. I turned on the oven and arranged an assortment of eight empanadas on a flat aluminum sheet. Franco was tidying up when I returned to the bedroom.

"Thanks for cleaning up my mess. I'm not much of a detective, am I?" I said.

He smiled and nodded before picking up some books off the bed.

"Come up with anything else?"

"No," he said, fitting another book back onto the shelf.

"I put some empanadas in the oven."

"I'll be right there."

Back in the kitchen I took a corkscrew from one of the drawers. A glass of wine would calm my nerves. I returned with a bottle of malbec from the wine rack when Franco walked up behind me.

"Can I help?" he asked.

"Grab a couple of wineglasses? They're in the glass cabinet in the dining room."

"Are we celebrating something?" he asked. "I saw lighted candles on the table."

I poured us each a glass. "My mind keeps going around in circles and I'm not getting anywhere. It's exhausting."

"It is a lot, Paloma."

Feeling like I might cry, I took a deep breath. "So tonight we celebrate *you*," I said, raising my glass. "Here's to you. For all you've done for me." I tipped my glass toward him and drank long and deep. "I could be facing this all alone. Or I might not have ever learned the truth. But I'm not alone. You're with me. And I'm grateful to you for that. I'll never forget what you did for me, Franco."

"Okay…you're welcome, my pleasure." He frowned a little. "But I'm a bit confused. Is this some sort of a goodbye speech?"

"It's not meant to be one," I said, taking in a mouthful of wine. The liquid went down warm and smooth. "On the contrary, I was going to see if you wanted to stay here tonight."

"That's what I'll always remember about you."

"What?"

"You were the first woman to ever ask me out and now you're the first woman to ask me to spend the night."

Is *that* how he saw me? His grin told me he was teasing.

"Let the record show, Mr. Bonetti, that you're the first guy I've asked out for a drink *and* also the first guy I've asked to spend the night." I emptied my glass. "Lately I've been doing things I never imagined in a million years. But the truth is I don't want to be alone tonight."

"I don't want you to spend the night alone either," he said, taking my glass and setting it down.

"So you'll stay?" I asked, recalling the last time he was in my apartment and his abrupt departure.

"There's nothing I'd like more," he murmured as his lips gently kissed mine.

He wrapped his arms around me, and the warmth of his body

traveled straight to my splintered heart. I closed my eyes, filled my nose with his scent. "All night?"

"If you want me to."

"I do."

He found my mouth again. His kiss made me quiver with pleasure and I leaned into him. His hands moved down to my hips and I slowly began to lose sense of my surroundings. Suddenly, my stomach made a funny sound, and with our lips still pressed together, we both grinned.

"Not a very delicate sound from a not-so-delicate lady," I said, laughing, a little embarrassed. The only food I had eaten all day was Luis's churros. "Hungry?"

"Starved. I'll finish setting the table."

"You should find everything you need in the dining room."

He left and I brought my attention back to the empanadas. The oven released a delicious aroma, and I pulled out the tray with a pair of oven mitts. I poked open one of the empanadas, letting steam escape. They were ready. It was my first time "cooking" in the apartment, and this ordinary activity was a welcome distraction.

Franco returned to the kitchen, holding a white tablecloth. "I found this folded away in one of the drawers."

We laid it out across the table. Its borders were yellow from age. The words *Café de las Artes* were embroidered in red along the bottom edge of the tablecloth. In the center, in bold script, someone had written, *Universidad de Buenos Aires, Class of 1975*. Franco brought over our glasses of wine, and together we analyzed the old tablecloth. Names were written all over the fabric.

"What's up with all the signatures?"

"It's a university tradition. Classmates meet on the last day of classes to drink, eat, and sign their names on a tablecloth." Franco examined the tablecloth until he found what he was looking for. His finger landed on a slanted signature. "See? Your father got to keep this one."

"Ah, yes. That's his."

We drank and ate while scanning the various signatures. There were easily twenty to thirty names. My eyes were drawn to one with a first name that began with a G and a last name that began with a D. Those initials…it had to be Grace Díaz. Excitedly, I showed Franco. "I bet that signature belongs to my father's friend. She's the one who first mentioned Máximo to me. Her maiden name is Grace Díaz—GD."

Tying to decipher the scribbled names proved to be a challenging task. Many of the signatures may as well have been chicken scratch. I was about to suggest we take a break and eat when Franco pointed to a name near the bottom right-hand corner. Unlike most, this signature was easy to read. It was beautifully written, as if penned by a calligrapher. I read out loud: "Máximo Cassini."

CHAPTER 40

May 1976

By the standards of Argentina's vast geography, Conrad Robertson's land was reasonably close to the Larreas' ranch, and when invited for an afternoon tea with Alfonso and Constanza, the British gentleman who had danced with Lila at the Farmers' Ball flew over in his single-engine plane. So when Santiago phoned him on a Sunday, inviting him for tea at El Pinar, he was sure that Conrad made nothing of it. The opportunities to socialize were relatively few in the Pampas, a stark contrast to Conrad's former life as an embassy attaché, which he had abandoned after marrying an Anglo-Argentine with a sizable estate that needed tending to.

"Santiago. Lovely to be here. And your parents? Are they resting?" Conrad asked him, after being shown to the library.

Spines of leather-bound books sat on built-in shelves along two adjoining walls. It was a large but cozy corner with two reclining chairs and reading lights. On the other side of the room were a stone fireplace and a long brown leather sofa with tartan throw blankets. Faded Persian rugs covered sections of the parquet floor. Prints of landscapes of the Scottish Highlands and an antique map of the United Kingdom, belonging to the former owner, decorated the remaining walls. His guest was smiling, and Santiago knew these touches made his British friend feel more at home.

Conrad's thinning red hair was combed to the side. He wore an olive-green Barbour jacket, a pair of dark jeans, and brown loafers. His Ray-Ban aviator glasses were tucked into his V-neck sweater.

Santiago turned from the fire he had lit for the visit. "My parents are traveling. I'm on my own," he said.

It was a half lie. The part about his parents traveling was true. A couple of days after his mother's sixtieth birthday celebration, Alfonso Larrea had, as a birthday present, taken his wife for a three-week trip to Italy. What wasn't true was the part about Santiago being on his own at the ranch. Máximo was hiding in Sánchez's home, a mere 1,500 feet from the main house.

"Please," Santiago said, gesturing to one of the chairs. Taking a small key from a dulled silver tray on his father's writing desk, he unlocked the top drawer and gave Conrad a compliant wink as he extracted a bottle of whiskey. "A shot in the arm?" he asked, and poured them each a splash into their teacups.

While Conrad drank his tea, Santiago first sat, then stood, and then sat again while discussing in great detail the South American soccer tournament Copa Libertadores, and his team River Plate's chances of winning. Conrad listened and offered his opinion when asked. It was only when Santiago began to dissect his soccer club's biggest rival, a Brazilian team, fidgeting all the while with his napkin and teaspoon, that Conrad finally spoke up.

"Santiago," Conrad said, picking up the bottle for another round. "There is nothing I would enjoy more than to sit here, drinking tea and enjoying your father's fine spirits whilst discussing football. But am I correct in sensing there's something else on your mind?"

Santiago was quiet and then said, "Where to begin?"

"Is everything all right? Does it concern Lila?" Conrad asked.

"No. God, no." Santiago walked to the door, closed it, and turned back to Conrad. "I know that you're no longer officially employed by the British government, but I imagine you still have your contacts?"

"Most of my contemporaries have moved on, but there are a few of us who check in every now and again."

"Right, right. But in this case, I'm thinking it might be preferable if your contacts weren't official."

"I'm not sure I follow you," Conrad said. "It would be better if you were straightforward with me."

Santiago sat back down. "I need a passport, a foreign one."

"Are you in some sort of trouble?"

"No. It's not for me. It's for a friend."

"Okay. What kind of situation are we talking about?" Conrad asked. He then instantly instantly raised a hand. "No, no, better not to tell me. Where is your friend now?"

"I can't say."

"Age?"

"Twenty-four."

"To any country in particular?"

"A Spanish-speaking country would be ideal, but frankly he'll go wherever it's safe."

"Understood." Conrad rose from his chair.

"You can help me then?"

"I'm not making any promises."

"Fair enough. But you'll think it over?"

"For the sake of my friendship with your family, yes."

As Conrad slipped on his gloves, Santiago served himself another whiskey. He took a big swallow and slowly placed the glass down.

"There may be one more, maybe two, after this one."

Conrad raised an eyebrow and took a long look at Santiago, the polo player and bon vivant. *How things have changed*, he thought. He said, "I'll see what can be done."

It had been more than a week since Máximo appeared unannounced at Constanza's birthday party, and back in Buenos Aires, Santiago felt like he was being submerged under the weight of Valentina's disappearance. The news of her pregnancy troubled him even more when Máximo told him he did not know her due date. It made Santiago quietly obsess over whether the baby might be his.

However, he needed to keep up appearances. It was a Saturday, and drinks and dinner had been organized at one of the more fashionable restaurants of the Costanera Norte. Lila had already put on makeup and a new outfit. She had recovered emotionally from a second miscarriage after her gynecologist said that her body was ready to try again. She had also started working in a friend's new clothing boutique. For his wife, life was falling nicely into place.

The steakhouse grill was of industrial size, an attractive focal point for the diners, and every table was occupied with boisterous patrons. Santiago nursed a brandy while the men chatted about soccer. Lila and her friends discussed the boutique and her possible trip to Europe to shop next season's collection. Santiago saw Grace entering the restaurant and excused himself.

They kissed hello. Grace had come with her brother Sebastián and another woman, but the two had gone over to the bar to order drinks while they waited for their table.

"Who's the woman with your brother?"

"She's…I don't know. Her name is Natalia, I think?"

"Guessing it's not serious, then." He lit a cigarette she extracted from her purse and placed between her lips. "Where's Isidoro?" he asked, wondering if her red-rimmed eyes had something to do with her latest boyfriend.

"We're not dating anymore," she said.

"I'm sorry, Grace. You deserve someone who'll treat you like a princess."

"I broke it off," she announced briskly. "Come with me a minute?" They went to the outdoor bar, where a breeze passed through them with the heavy scent of the Río de la Plata. "My parents want me to leave."

"What? Why?"

"They're worried. One of my mother's best friends had to leave. You've met her. Silvia Faure."

"The painter? Sure, I know who she is."

"She's in France. After making comments in an interview for a magazine about how an artist must have total freedom of expression, she started getting death threats," she said, nervously glancing about, making sure they were out of earshot.

"But why you?"

"Enrique. His mother called me, desperate. She told me they dragged him out of his bed one night. That was over two months ago, and his parents haven't been able to get any straight answers."

"What does Enrique have to do with you?" Valentina had told Santiago about Enrique's disappearance when he met with her at Casa de los Niños, but he didn't understand why Grace would be at risk.

"We dated. In their twisted thinking, it might be enough to qualify me as a subversive," Grace said.

The armed militants had essentially been wiped out by the time of the coup, so the armed forces had expanded their definition of "subversive" to include anyone opposed to the new dictatorship.

Whirring sounds from the evening sky made them look up. A beam of harsh light swept over them and other guests outdoors. As the curfew hour neared, it had become customary to see helicopters patrolling from above.

When the helicopter moved on, Santiago asked in a low tone, "Have you been threatened?"

"No, but my parents don't want to take any chances."

"Where would you go?"

"Holland. My father's friend is the owner of a beer company where my family also owns shares. If I go, I'd stay with his family."

Santiago closed his eyes briefly. Valentina. Máximo. Could he tell Grace? Of course he could confide in her. They had been friends for years.

"Valentina's missing."

Grace halted, losing her balance. He caught her elbow. "Oh God. When?"

"Two weeks ago. Máximo came to see me. He's hiding at El Pinar."

"What are you going to do?"

"I'm working on getting him out of the country."

"And Valentina?"

"I've been trying to contact General Delgado, but he's been sent as an envoy to Spain and has been impossible to reach. He may have even already…"

Grace wasn't listening. Her eyes had shifted from him to the restaurant entrance. Santiago looked over his shoulder to see who or what had distracted her.

It was Pedro García. The last time Santiago and Grace had seen Pedro was in February at General Delgado's daughter's wedding. At the party, Pedro had been wearing his formal naval officer's uniform. Tonight, like the group of men accompanying him, Pedro was dressed casually, wearing a polo shirt with a V-neck sweater tied around his neck, khakis, and boat shoes. He carried a pair of sailing gloves in one hand. They must have been out on the river, Santiago thought. Grace narrowed her eyes and pursed her lips in distaste as the men approached. Santiago, on the other hand, saw an opportunity, and turned to them with a friendly smile.

Santiago woke up early the next morning. Pedro García had said to meet at the Richmond, a grand old café on Florida Street in the city's financial district. Drinking his second cup of coffee, he wondered if he had gotten the time wrong. He hadn't. Pedro was and always would be late to their meetings, intentionally operating in direct contrast to his military training. The new relationship between the two men would take place outside the realm of Pedro's official duties, giving him freedom to do as he pleased.

After he arrived and the waiter had brought him a coffee, Pedro began: "You said it was important we speak in private."

Santiago appreciated his directness and responded likewise. "A friend of mine is missing. Her parents have filed a report with the police. I was hoping you could help me, ask your contacts within the armed forces."

"What makes you think we have anything to do with her disappearance?"

"I'm only asking if you would check. I'm exploring all avenues."

Pedro added sugar to his coffee, stirred, and then took a long leisurely sip. "What's her name?"

"Valentina Quintero."

"And her war name?"

Santiago drew in his breath. "She's not a member of any guerrilla organization. She's an architect who volunteers at a day care center," he answered in a steady voice.

"Why the interest in her?"

Santiago faltered. "She's someone I used to date."

"Did I meet her at your parents' gathering for Bautista a couple of years ago?"

"Yes. That's her."

"I remember her. That was a fun night." Pedro's expression became distracted, as if his mind was going over the good time he'd had at the party. He returned his attention to Santiago and said, "If she's done nothing wrong, she'll be released."

"She's done nothing wrong, and it's been more than two weeks now since anyone has heard from her."

Pedro had never managed to be invited into the Larrea brothers' innermost circle, and he was clearly savoring his power over Bautista's little brother. After sizing up Santiago for another moment, Pedro's voice took on a more serious tone. "I'll see what I can find out. But let it be clear that I'm doing you this favor at considerable risk to myself and my position. You are not to speak to anyone about this. Is that understood?"

Pedro had quickly risen in the ranks after his graduation. It hadn't hurt that, coming from a long lineage of military men, he had been favored by Emilio Massera, a member of the military junta and the commander in chief of the navy.

"Understood."

Pedro scraped back his chair to stand.

"There's something else. She's in a delicate state. She's pregnant," Santiago said.

Pedro raised an eyebrow. "Is the baby yours?"

"Yes," Santiago answered, feeling in his heart that it must be true.

"Now I understand," Pedro smiled. He added, "Being pregnant is helpful."

"It is?"

"Yes. Pregnant women, mothers, they're treated differently. Better."

Santiago nodded as he processed Pedro's comment. It informed him of several things. First, that Pedro had, in effect, acknowledged the illegal detentions. Second, that he probably knew the locations of the detention centers. And third, that because Valentina was pregnant, she would be given special treatment. His instinct to tell Pedro about her pregnancy had been correct. And claiming to be the father should help his case. They would release her more quickly. When he stood to shake Pedro's hand, he was breathing more easily again.

Later that day, before getting on the highway to go back to El Pinar, Santiago stopped at a pay phone and contacted a number Conrad had given him. A phone number that couldn't be traced. After receiving further instructions, he went to a pharmacy. It was after dusk when he arrived at the ranch, and he immediately went to see Sánchez.

"Is he in?" Santiago asked when Josefina opened the door to let him in. The small house appeared to be empty.

"My husband wants you to meet him at the old barn," she said.

Santiago hurried up the path and past the guesthouse, the stables, the garden shed, a garage for the tractors. On the edge of an interminable stretch of land was the final structure, an abandoned barn where spare parts were stored and out-of-commission tools were left to rust.

He entered to find Máximo and Sánchez walking around the long, narrow, cluttered space.

Máximo's hair had grown past his shoulders, and a beard now covered his gaunt cheeks. His friend would need a makeover before having his passport photo taken by one of Conrad's contacts. They would have to cut and dye his hair. Shave his face. Have him wear a pair of glasses. His appearance had to be altered as much as possible, Conrad had explained. Santiago had brought supplies from the pharmacy and clothes from his own closet.

"Santi. Any news?" Máximo asked, hugging him.

"I'm working on it," Santiago said. "What's going on here?"

"We were evaluating the space. Maybe if we build a false wall, we could use the last quarter of this barn, create a hiding place," Máximo explained.

"But I'm getting you out soon. I have confirmation that your passport is almost ready."

"Thank you. You're a good man, Santiago. And I'm sure you'll want to help others. They'll need a place to hide. This would be ideal."

Santiago had not considered doing this for anyone else, for the simple reason that he hadn't thought beyond Valentina and her baby.

"I'm very good at building. The three of us could get this up in no time," Máximo added while Santiago pondered the proposal.

He remembered Grace and wondered how many others now found themselves on the wrong side of this dictatorship, facing persecution, torture, and worse. His friend was right. He would continue to help and would need to create a place where those who had to escape would not be found. A safe house. He turned to Sánchez, who awaited his instructions.

"Fine," Santiago said to the men. "And as soon as we get this built, we're getting you out of the country."

"I want to go," Máximo agreed. "But not without Valentina."

"You have to. I don't know how long it will take to get her back."

"You're confident you will?" Máximo's eyes came back to life.

"I am."

CHAPTER 41

August 1998

When Franco said he would stay over, I hadn't quite believed him. But then, as we cleared the plates, after finding Máximo's full name on the tablecloth, I kissed him. And when I pulled back, I saw his eyes were still closed, as if he were savoring the sensation my lips left on his. Whispering, he asked where my bedroom was. I led him to the guest room instead.

He took his time. Each article of clothing unveiled a new part of my body that seemed to require quiet contemplation before moving on. When I was fully naked, he removed his glasses and continued the examination with his hands and his mouth. He was so careful and deliberate in his pursuit that I startled when he thrust himself inside of me. As I neared climax, he covered my mouth with his. He inhaled me deeply as if he wanted to take in my pain, not wishing me to bear it alone. Afterward, he got out of bed. I slid under the covers, certain he had left. When I next opened my eyes, my body tingled with an inexplicably sweet sadness. It was Franco caressing me. We made love again. After, in his arms, I drifted into a dreamless sleep.

The following morning, with Franco still asleep in the guest room down the hall, I returned to my father's bedroom. I tackled, more carefully this time, his bookshelves. Nothing. Next, I turned to his university notebooks. These were in a box under his desk. I had barely glanced at them the night before. I would go through every page of every law class notebook if I had to. It was when I was nearing the bottom of the stack that I came across a worn notebook thickened from overuse.

The first pages consisted of class notes—descriptions of archaic-sounding laws, scribbled bullet points. Nothing meaningful. But then drawings began to appear above and below his annotations. Along the sides. As though my father were growing increasingly bored by the lectures. Caricatures of men in military uniform, political leaders. I made out Juan Domingo and Eva Perón, Fidel Castro, Che Guevara. Comic strips not quite finished. I studied them, amazed. I had no idea my father could draw. Why had he stopped?

The second part of the notebook was devoid of any text, as if my father could no longer pretend, even to himself, any interest in the class. Pencil drawings of human anatomy were followed by a series of faces. Men and women, young and old, gauchos on horseback, Indigenous people. And then I saw a face I recognized. It was Valentina. Suddenly, she was everywhere. Several sketches showed her looking right at the artist. Others were of her profile, her thick eyebrow flowing into the outline of her pronounced nose. In one, she was laughing, her mass of dark curls spilled over her bare shoulders, wisps of hair across her generous lips. I flipped the page to a drawing of Valentina in bed, partially covered by a sheet. Her back was to the artist, but her head was turned with a dreamy expression on her face. Feeling like I had walked in on an intimate moment between two lovers, I quickly turned to the end. And when I did, I briefly shut my eyes. After reading again the words inside the back cover, I let out a long exhale.

> Máximo Cassini
>   Calle La Rioja 1280
>   Quilmes, Provincia de Buenos Aires

Once a quaint town after which Argentina's national beer was named, Quilmes had become just another neighborhood in the ring of working- and middle-class suburbs around the capital. We stood in front of one in a row of identical two-story houses. I checked the number against the address from the notebook, then gave Franco a thumbs-up. When he rang the bell, an old woman answered.

I smiled and began, "Good afternoon. My name is—"

"Are you selling something?" interrupted the woman, with a wary eye on Franco and me.

"No, no. We were hoping to talk to a member of the Cassini family. Are you, by any chance, Mrs. Cassini?" I asked.

The woman hesitated. "Yes. That's me."

"You have no idea how happy I am to hear that," I said. "I'm Paloma Larrea."

"Who's he?" the woman asked, gesturing at Franco.

"He's my friend, Franco."

"Are you conducting a survey?"

"No, nothing like that," I clarified, smiling. "But before I tell you why we're here, is Máximo Cassini your son?"

The woman nodded, uncertainly.

Barely able to contain my elation, I said, "My father, Santiago Larrea, was friends with your son in law school."

"Who?"

"Santiago Larrea."

"Name doesn't ring a bell. I'm sorry, young lady." Mrs. Cassini made to close the door.

"Wait!" I widened my smile. *Cheerful people don't have doors shut on their faces twice*, I told myself, recalling my encounter with Marcela at Valentina's old building. I held out the notebook to Mrs. Cassini and opened it to the back cover for her to see. "I found Máximo's address in this old notebook." The photos came out next. "See here?" I pointed to Máximo on the steps of the law school. Mrs. Cassini put on her reading glasses. "And this man is my dad, Santiago. They were friends. And that's their friend Valentina."

The woman gaped at the old photos, her eyes glistening.

"We'd love to talk to you about your son, if you have a moment."

"I'll make some coffee," she said, ushering us inside.

While Nora Cassini prepared coffee, she invited us to wait out on the patio. It was a crisp winter afternoon. Franco brought his chair next to me and laced his fingers with mine. His smile, intimate and conspiratorial, transported me back to the night before. I smiled back. In that moment, during this strange time, I felt something akin to happiness.

"Milk or sugar with your coffee?" Nora asked, setting down the tray. We thanked her, accepting a cup. She told us she hadn't entertained visitors in ages and was pleased to have company. However, our unexpected visit seemed to have the opposite effect on her husband, Enzo. After a handshake, he was off to the other end of the yard. The drop in temperature the night before had left a layer of frost on his garden, Nora explained, excusing her husband's brusque reception. Once she had offered us cookies, Nora sat and picked up the photo with the inscription on the back.

"Poor Valentina, may she rest in peace. A terrible loss," she said. "Such a lovely young woman. We were so happy our son had found her."

I sat forward in my chair. "So they were a couple?"

"Of course," Nora answered and leaned forward. "They were living in sin," she confided in a hushed tone. She glanced at Enzo trimming the shrubs. "He didn't know. Still doesn't."

"So they were serious?"

"Yes, very much so. They were going to be married."

"Oh, I see," I said, trying to conceal my surprise.

Máximo Cassini had been planning to marry Valentina. Yes, that certainly qualified as serious.

"Did Máximo practice law?"

"He did, providing free legal services to the poor. He planned to defend political prisoners, but it didn't work out. He loved doing community service. Always thinking of others," Nora said, with a mother's pride in her voice and on her face. "Thankfully, he was also good at drawing. He was able to make a living as an illustrator."

Máximo was an illustrator? I felt a flutter in my rib cage. I didn't know my father had been an artist because he had never been one. The sketches were not his, they were Máximo's. The notebook belonged to Máximo. Why did my father have it? I was anxious to go through the pages again, but something stopped me from taking it out of my purse and sharing my revelation with the others.

Nora, unaware of the inner turmoil caused by her recounting, ran a hand through her short gray hair and continued. "Valentina told me herself of their plans to marry." She motioned with her head toward the house. "We were in the kitchen preparing lunch. Valentina started off in a roundabout way, saying that Máximo wanted to visit her family in Córdoba. Not that this was unusual for them—they had gone there together in the past to spend the weekend. But then she said that he was going *alone* and that he wished to speak to her father. So I knew instantly what she was trying to tell me. She asked me not to say anything. Máximo would tell Enzo and me when he returned. I remember how we giggled like two schoolgirls sharing a delicious secret."

"What a special moment that must have been for you," Franco said. "I apologize in advance, but we need to ask you a question, señora. Is your son still alive?"

Nora looked at him, perplexed. "Of course. Why in heaven's name would you think he's dead?"

"I'm really sorry. We didn't know and needed to confirm."

"May God keep him safe," Nora answered somberly.

"Does he live in Buenos Aires?" I asked.

"Oh no, no, no," she said, clicking her tongue. "He left long ago. Moved to France in 1976 when things got difficult here. It was very hard on him after she was taken. It was hard on all of us."

Franco and I exchanged a glance at this disappointing piece of information. Our hostess, however, smiled. Even though this conversation must have been difficult for her, she was visibly delighted to have young people in her home again. Nora sat up straight in her chair. "He moved back to Argentina in 1985, after the end of the military government, but never to Buenos Aires. Too many sad memories, you know."

"He should be here with his mother!"

We looked over to Enzo by the back fence. He had been listening the whole time.

"I'm not mad that he didn't settle down somewhere near us. How could I be?" Nora replied. "Máximo needed to take care of himself."

"Where does Máximo live now?" I asked.

"He lives in the middle of nowhere, that's where!" Enzo barked, brandishing the water can our way.

Nora fixed her husband with a stare and turned back to us. "Don't mind him. Our son lives in the south. In San Martín de los Andes."

CHAPTER 42

May–July 1976

WITHOUT WARNING, THE DOOR SWUNG open, surprising both Valentina and the man who, seconds before, had been whistling along to a classical piece on the radio, while holding an electric prod over her chest. Blindfolded and naked, Valentina was lying down, her ankles and wrists strapped to the ends of the examining table. The only way to anticipate the pain from an electric charge to her armpits or her chest was by the man's wheezing. Musty and stale from cigarettes, his breath would suddenly be on her face. This particular torturer liked to toy with her, leaning and then retreating, laughing a little as her body went rigid, bracing itself for the shock.

"You've been relieved from your duties, Officer," came a command from behind her head.

"But I've only just begun my session with prisoner 322," the officer said, waving the prod as though holding a conductor's wand.

"Prisoner 322 has been elevated and reassigned. She's under my direct supervision."

Valentina heard movement, the definitive sound of the door being shut. Moments passed, and then—the feel of warm fingers on her cheeks, under her blindfold. She had been living in darkness since they kidnapped her and had lost track of time. Living without eating or sleeping for what seemed like days at a time. What sustained her through the terror was the hope that they would release her once they understood a mistake had been made. But the hope was diminishing.

The blindfold was gingerly lifted up onto her forehead. The ceiling lights blinded her, and she blinked. Her eyes watered uncontrollably. A man was studying her face. After a minute, he unbound her limbs. Why had he let her see his face? Even as her vision remained blurry, she recognized him—from where?

"Here, use this." The threadbare towel was small, and she barely managed to cover her torso. "I think we can find something for you to wear," he said, giving her a hand to help her off the table.

He led her up the stairs to a room where confiscated items and clothes were stored—the spoils of the "Dirty War," as the campaign of suppression had come to be called. The man let her sit on the floor as he sifted through the pile of women's clothing. He found something he thought suitable.

"Try this on."

She had lost weight, and the dress easily fit over her pregnant body. He escorted her back to her cell. She thanked him. The words of gratitude were so heartfelt that she barely gave them a second thought.

That night Valentina told her neighbor, whose name she eventually learned was Soledad, of the man and his strange behavior.

"What did he look like?" Soledad asked in a whispering voice.

"He's blond. Blue eyes."

"Does he have a round sweet face?"

"I guess so. He looks young."

"A mole above his lip?"

"Yes."

"That's El Angelito," Soledad said, letting out a low whistle. "He must have taken a liking to you."

The next time the officer appeared, he freed her from her tomb-like cell and took her to an office down the hall. He produced from behind the desk another dress. He then handed her a pair of high-heeled shoes.

"Put these on." She did. He had correctly guessed her size. "I hear pregnant women get cravings, so I thought you and I could go out for ice cream."

He left the office to let her get ready in private. On the desk, he had laid out a hand mirror, a comb, lipstick, and blush. She had never worn makeup, but starting that day, she would learn to apply it meticulously every time he asked her to. She looked at herself in the mirror. Since he had taken an interest in her, the torturers had left her face alone. She fumbled with the blush, and the lipstick stung her cracked lips. Running a comb through her tangled curls felt futile. When he returned and saw her hair, he gave her a barrette to hold it back from her eyes.

"And this, this is yours, isn't it?" El Angelito held out his arm in a fist and, as a magician might do, opened his fingers. Her pendant.

"Yes."

The necklace had been ripped off her during a torture session. El Angelito had come across one of the guards dangling it between his fingers, saying he would give it to his girlfriend for her birthday. El Angelito confiscated it back.

He had her turn and lift her hair. He reached his hands through her raised arms, placed the pendant against her throat, and tied the knot at the back. His cool hands remained on her shoulders, causing the hairs on the back of her neck to stand. She was terrified and confused. Why was El Angelito paying her special attention? Valentina thought the pendant had been lost forever. Clutching the blue stone as if it somehow connected her to Santiago, her throat tightened with fresh despair at having lost him too.

She murmured, "Thank you."

They drove far from the city center to the neighborhood of Olivos, near the presidential residence. The slate-colored sky made everything look gray. She had lost count of the days, the number of weeks, since she had last been outdoors, and she missed colors. He parked the car. It was cold. He gave her his jacket. He only ever wore civilian clothes in her presence. El Angelito didn't grip her arm, confident she wouldn't try to escape. Instead, he held her hand. An intimate gesture, as if they were a couple on a date.

The ice cream store was empty. After taking their order, the cashier congratulated them on her pregnancy. El Angelito smiled and, placing his arm around Valentina, explained that they were expecting their first. They were, naturally, a bit nervous. Being a mother herself, the woman offered advice while Valentina kept her eyes fixed on the drips forming along the side of the cone. She was afraid that if she looked up, the woman might realize Valentina was a hostage, putting herself at risk of being kidnapped.

Another time, El Angelito presented her with a new bottle of French perfume. "Spray yourself with this. We're going out."

"Where did he take you this time?" Soledad asked when she returned later that night.

"An amusement park," Valentina whispered back.

"What does he want with you?"

"I don't know. He won't speak more than is absolutely necessary. He hasn't touched me except for the occasional kiss on the mouth if he thinks we're being watched."

El Angelito didn't seem to be in love with her or even overtly attracted to her, but his interest wasn't arbitrary. Of this she was sure. She was also sure she had met him before, though she couldn't pinpoint how or where. If only she could access the part of her brain that stored memories. But her mind was a fog.

After weeks in captivity, any information Valentina would have had on Máximo's whereabouts was obsolete. The men still asked. When they forced her down on the examining table, she held on to one reassuring thought. If they were still torturing her, it must mean that Máximo was somewhere out there, alive and safe.

Sometimes, when she was about to pass out from the pain, the officer would appear over her and, like a guardian angel, tell them to stop.

One night she dreamed of El Angelito. Others were present, but they were outside her field of vision. He was informing the group that communists had spread like vermin throughout the university. *But we poisoned them all*, he said, his eyes on her as if to reassure her. He smiled and then did something odd. He covered the mole on his upper lip with his fingers. The dream jolted her awake. Her breath was shallow and her heart raced. At once, she knew who El Angelito was and where she had met him.

CHAPTER 43

August 1998

THE MORNING FLIGHT FROM BUENOS Aires's Aeroparque Jorge Newbery to San Carlos de Bariloche, a Swiss-style village nestled in the Andes, took three hours. When we landed, I rented a budget car at the airport for the drive to San Martín de los Andes, another three or four hours away. Franco pulled out a map. He had been to Bariloche just once, on his high school graduation trip, and he needed to reacquaint himself with the area. Once he had studied our route, he gave it to me and asked me to familiarize myself with it.

"You'll be my copilot," he said.

After we had decided to track Máximo down, I had been too busy making travel arrangements to think more about his relationship with Valentina. With my father's ceremony scheduled for Monday, August 24, in a mere four days, we'd had little time left. Sitting quietly in the car as we drove through the outskirts of Bariloche, however, I was no longer able to ignore two new facts that had emerged from our visit to Nora and Enzo. First, Valentina had been living with Máximo when she was abducted. Second, they were planning to get married. So when, exactly, had Valentina been involved with my father?

If only I could talk to him. All at once, I yearned for his reassuring and comforting presence. But I soon chided myself. He was not the open and honest father I had believed him to be. When the time came to confront him, I would need to be strong, detached, armed with facts, or else he would work his charm and self-assurance on me and make up some story. I turned on the radio and fiddled with the dial. Franco put his hand on mine when an old recording crackled through the speakers.

"Wait. Leave it," Franco said. "I can't believe my ears. I love this bolero."

"What are we listening to?"

"Bola de Nieve, 1952. Live performance. Havana, Cuba. One of the best from that era." Franco turned up the volume. "Listen to the piano. And his voice. Notice how he talks as he sings?"

I nodded but couldn't enjoy the music like Franco. While he drummed his fingers on the steering wheel, I tried to keep my mind empty by concentrating on the landscape. The majestic snow-capped Andean mountains and sparkling blue lakes soon drew me in.

In the village of San Martín de los Andes, Franco parked the car on the main street. The sleepy town sat on Lácar Lake at the edge of a beautiful national park. It was smaller in size, but like Bariloche, resembled a Swiss village. The buildings were a mixture of wood and stone, uniform in their alpine style.

We entered the nearest hotel. The lobby had comfortable-looking chairs arranged around a fireplace lit with a welcoming fire.

"You are fortunate," the front desk clerk said, handing us a key. "It's a busy time of the year, but we've had a cancellation."

The room was furnished with twin beds, a nightstand, and a blond wood desk with a chair. Framed pictures of mountains and indigenous flowers adorned the walls. Commenting that the room was stuffy with lingering cigarette odor from the last occupant, Franco opened the window. I didn't say anything, keeping my coat on. After unpacking a few things, we headed back out.

The gusts of Patagonian wind were so strong that I held onto Franco, my hair whipping back. In a shop window, advertising ski gear, were photos of smiling families and couples at the nearby ski resort, Chapelco. An old-fashioned female mannequin, her red lips chipping at the corners, was dressed in a T-shirt that read *Patagonia: Viento. Mucho Viento*. Patagonia: Wind, A Lot of Wind. I smiled in silent agreement.

"Let's go in for a minute," I said.

The shopkeeper, a woman in long braids and a magnificent turquoise choker, greeted us with a friendly hello. I sorted through a rack of winter jackets. Franco's peacoat wasn't warm enough for this climate. I held up a puffy one to show him. He shook his head. It had been a battle to get Franco to let me pay our airfare and all the other travel expenses. Even after I explained that I was using my dad's credit card, he would not budge. Franco ultimately gave in when I threatened to cancel the trip and give up on the whole thing. He said he couldn't let me do that.

I picked up a pair of men's alpaca gloves and handed them to the cashier, along with two ski hats and a pair of mittens for myself. When we stepped back out into the icy air, I presented him with the hat and gloves. Franco jammed his hands in his back jean pockets.

"It's a small present," I said, and disregarded his look by stuffing them into his coat pockets. "And in case you didn't know, it's rude to refuse a gift."

"All right. I give up. Thank you."

As he kissed me, I briefly fantasized we were on a romantic weekend getaway and not chasing down my family's secret history.

We passed several other shops—an artisanal chocolatier, a local art gallery, a window display chock-full of handcrafted mate gourds, silver frames, and colorful textiles. At the end of the block, we found a café and went in.

Reggae music was playing from an old stereo behind the bar, and several tourists sat at a table noisily drinking beer. Franco asked for two cafés con leche and ham-and-cheese sandwiches. We settled onto a couple of barstools. Franco glanced toward the back of the café and was about to stand, but then he took a deep breath. He removed his glasses, still fogged up from the cold, and cleaned the lenses with his shirt.

We held the steaming cups of coffee with both hands, blowing on them before taking the first sip. The barman returned with a plate of thinly sliced ham and cheese on buttery brioche buns. We grew silent as we bit into our sandwiches.

"Franco?"

"Hmm?" he said, his mouth full of food. We hadn't eaten since breakfast in Buenos Aires.

"I hope you don't mind my asking, but why do you, ah, constantly check doors? Or, you know, um, how you slide windows up and down and then leave them open? Just now you looked over to the back. Was it to see if there's another door?"

Franco raised his eyebrows quizzically as if to convey that he didn't understand my question. Then, embarrassed, he said, "You weren't supposed to notice."

It was impossible not to notice, I thought. Wherever we went, Franco behaved as if he were following the flight attendant's instructions to look for the nearest exits.

"I don't do it as often as I used to," he said with a nervous laugh.

"But why do you do it?"

He studied his coffee cup. "The night they killed my dad. I think I told you that I was hiding, watching?" He glanced at me and I nodded. "What I didn't tell you was what happened after they shot him." He took out his cigarette pack and laid it on the counter. "I crawled back to our bedroom to warn Luis and Catalina. We had to get out. They would come for us next. I had to pry open the window and, when it finally gave way, my elbow knocked down a lamp. I'll never forget the sound of the breaking glass. It was loud." He slid out a cigarette from the pack and lit it. "My siblings climbed out. I almost didn't make it.

Luckily, the guy was too big to chase me through the window. By the time they ran outside, we had escaped through a hole in the fence."

"Franco..." If we had been back at the hotel, I would have folded myself around him to show him how sorry I was. For now, my hand on his arm would have to do.

"I try to keep myself from checking all the possible escape routes, but it's hard not to do it when I'm in a new place. My compulsion usually wins out." Franco took a drag and went on. "I make every effort not to be obvious. Guess I'm not doing a good job though, am I?" He smiled, but his eyes revealed the sadness inside. "I also can't stay out a whole night. I always have to go home to Luis. Make sure he's okay. I don't know." He shrugged. "Luis gets mad, reminds me we're both adults now. Says he doesn't need his older brother looking after him."

"But you spent the other night with me."

"Because you asked me to." He tapped my shoulder lightly, smiling. "See? I'm helpless against you."

He ground out his cigarette and looked at me intently. "I was also finding that when we weren't together, I couldn't stop thinking about you. Not to mention that I wanted you so badly, I thought I'd go out of my mind." He took my hand, grazed my knuckles with his lips. "And when we made love, I didn't feel the usual urge to get up and leave. That's never happened to me before."

My heart skipped. I tipped my barstool and kissed him long and hard, oblivious to the tourists.

When the bartender brought the bill, Franco pulled out a paper with Máximo's name and address.

"We're looking for this place. Have you heard of it?"

"No, sorry, but from the address I can tell you it's a ways from here. Do you have a map? I'll show you."

Franco took out the map from the car rental agency. The bartender located our destination and traced the route with his index finger. "It's about an hour's drive, maybe more, depending on road conditions. It's in a remote area." He looked out the window. Snowflakes had started to fall. "You should either go in the morning or leave now, before it gets dark."

I held the map open on my lap while Franco drove cautiously on the icy, unpaved road known as the Camino de los Siete Lagos. The waiter hadn't exaggerated; the trip took the better part of two hours. When I thought we might be close, Franco shifted the car into a lower gear. A night fog had rolled across the road, but I was able to make out a large slab of wood nailed to a post.

"Stop for a second." I leaned out the window and read the sign: *Le Petit Savoyard*. "This is it."

A dirt track led toward a large structure made of logs set against a forest of dense overhanging arrayanes, native Andean myrtle trees. A light could be seen through a small window. We pulled into a spot a few yards away from the restaurant, under a tree with snow-covered branches. Franco turned off the ignition. My hat was under the seat, and I brought it down over my ears. I buttoned my coat, turned the collar up, and slipped on my gloves. With nothing else left to do to prepare myself, I climbed out and trudged behind Franco, who had been waiting impatiently.

A tall, dark-haired woman greeted us through the partially open door. "So sorry. The restaurant is closed. We open again tomorrow for lunch. You will come back, please?" the woman suggested with a hospitable smile.

"Actually we're looking for Máximo Cassini. Is he here?" I asked.

She hesitated. "Yes, he's here. Is he expecting you?"

"No," I admitted.

"We're from Buenos Aires. We've been traveling all day," Franco explained.

She opened the door wider, succumbing to our request. "Come in." We followed her inside. "I'll tell him you're here." She showed us to a dining area, illuminated only by the flames in the fireplace. "Please make yourselves comfortable."

Franco warmed his hands by the fire. I sat at a table, and picked up and studied the laminated menu.

"Hello."

I looked up. A lean man had materialized in the doorway. As he came closer, I noticed his tired, puffy eyes and deep grooves around his mouth.

"Hi. I'm Paloma, and this is Franco," I said, standing.

"Máximo." He pointed to the chairs around my table. "Please, have a seat. Can I get you something to drink?"

"No, thank you, we don't want to trouble you," Franco said. "I'm sorry we didn't call ahead. Our trip down here was very last minute."

Máximo shook his dark hair loose out of a ponytail. He held out a pack of cigarettes to us before taking one. He placed the tin ashtray in front of him. "My wife tells me you've come all the way from Buenos Aires?"

"That's right," Franco said. "Thank you for seeing us. We won't waste your time. Do you remember Santiago Larrea?"

He suddenly looked alert. "I've heard the name. Why do you ask?"

"He's my father," I said. "I know you two used to know each other. We were hoping you could tell us a few things."

Máximo tucked his wavy hair behind his ears. His dark eyes narrowed in on me. "Does he know you're here?"

"Yes, he does. He sends his regards."

"Oh, does he now?" he asked dryly. "Years ago I tried getting in touch with him several times, but he never wrote or called me back." An uncomfortable silence descended over the table. "How did you know where to find me?"

"Your mother gave us your address," Franco answered matter-of-factly.

"You went to see my *mother?*"

Unsettled by his piercing look, I fidgeted with the pendant, wishing Franco had answered more delicately. "Yes. It's a long story," I started, my voice thin. Máximo's eyes rested on Valentina's necklace, and I instinctively covered it with my hand. "Your mother wasn't sure if you still lived here."

Máximo crushed his cigarette in the ashtray. "I don't know what you hoped to learn about your father by coming here, but I don't have anything to tell you about Santiago Larrea. This conversation is over," he said, and stood.

The woman entered the room carrying a tray with glasses and drinks. Máximo stopped her with a single shake of his head. He walked to the front door and opened it. Fat snowflakes drifted inside onto his sweater.

"We didn't mean to upset you," Franco said, reaching into his wallet. On a card he wrote our names and his phone number. "If you change your mind and want to talk to us…" He left the card on the table. "Good evening to you both."

As we walked under the light snowfall, I looked back, vaguely expecting Máximo to come after us, but the door had been shut. After a couple of miles on the main road, I said, "Well, that didn't go as expected."

"Something's going on with him," Franco said. "He clearly disapproved of our visit with Nora. Who knows? Never mess with a man's mother, I suppose."

We drove on without saying a word until I produced a hair elastic from my front jean pocket. A few long wavy hairs were caught in it. I switched on the overhead light and held it in front of the rearview mirror. Franco briefly took his eyes off the road to examine it.

"I don't know what came over me. I grabbed it when he left the table."

Franco smiled approvingly. "We'll have Mariano take a look."

CHAPTER 44

July 1976

Not long after their initial meeting, Pedro called Santiago to tell him he had located Valentina. She was safe and in good health, he assured Santiago, whose heart filled with hope until Pedro spoke again.

"Unfortunately, she's a valuable prisoner. There's not much I can do at the moment."

Santiago felt his anger flare but made sure his voice maintained a businesslike tone. Valentina's fate rested with this man. Any misstep could jeopardize her life. Why was she valuable? Because she was Máximo's girlfriend? What other reason could there be? She and Máximo had also been friends with Enrique, who may have been a Montonero. Maybe Valentina was considered guilty by association? He decided not to ask any of these questions.

"You'll have to be patient," Pedro advised before hanging up.

Following this brief phone call, Santiago would discover deep within himself a well of patience.

While waiting for news about Valentina, he focused his attention on his work at the safe house. After helping to build the fake wall and making sure the hideout was secure, Máximo had crossed the border into Brazil, hiding in the back of one of the ranch's flatbed trucks filled with hundred-kilogram burlap bags of grain, in whose crevices he fashioned himself a small cave to ride out the eighteen-hour trip to the border. Three days and several bus rides later, he was on a plane from São Paulo to Paris. Their goodbye in the cold predawn light had been hurried and unsentimental. The night before leaving, Máximo gave Santiago a paper with the names and phone numbers of three friends at the newspaper who would inevitably become targets of the regime if they weren't already captured or dead. Each one of them would require Santiago's help, and each in turn told him of others in the same situation.

And so it came to be that Santiago found himself immersed in a world he'd had little contact with before the coup, even in the most bohemian of his student days. Driving through the small town of Don Torcuato on the northwestern outskirts of the capital, he turned onto a dirt road illuminated only by the orange moon, which hung low in the sky like a pumpkin waiting to be harvested. The small weekend house was situated amid sparsely planted pine trees on a small, dusty plot of land behind a roadside motel called Los Jardines de Babilonia. The front door faced the potholed frontage road. Santiago waited in the car for Raúl Páez—not his real name. Once the escapee, a scrawny figure, was crouched in the back of his Peugeot, Santiago surmised that his passenger most likely hadn't bathed or changed his clothes since going into hiding a week earlier.

During the drive to El Pinar, the young man told Santiago his story. It started as an uneventful day. After dinner, Raúl was scraping scraps off the dishes into a small garbage bag as his roommate ran a soapy dishcloth over the plates as if handling china of the finest quality. Raúl returned to the living area to wipe down the coffee table, which doubled as their dining table. Floor pillows were arranged haphazardly around it. He bent over to blow out the candles. Several of his roommate's watercolors decorated the room, while others were propped against the wall. The bookshelves sagged from the weight of Raúl's books. Dave Brubeck's *Time Out* played on the stereo.

Raúl lifted the stereo needle, removed the record, and slipped it back into the album sleeve. He entered the kitchen with several albums in his arms.

"I'm going upstairs to bring these back to Beto," Raúl told his roommate.

The hallway was dimly lit, and as he climbed the stairwell, he heard footsteps coming up from below. He paused and peered back down through the railing. A man in a gray pinstriped three-piece suit and two other men in street clothes stopped in front of his apartment. One of them knocked loudly on the door. The others stood with their backs to the wall, handguns drawn.

Holding his breath, Raúl heard his roommate call out from the apartment, "Did you forget your keys again?" He opened the door, holding the damp dishcloth, then froze at the sight of the men and the guns. It was a second too long. By the time he tried to pull back the door handle, it was too late. The shortest and burliest of the three men had wedged his foot in the doorframe as the other two leaned their shoulders into the door and forced their way in. The door was left ajar, and Raúl, still watching in a crouch behind the railing, could see the short man grab his roommate by the throat and shove him against the wall. The other men entered the apartment and dropped momentarily out of view.

"Where's your *puto* roommate?" the short man demanded when the others came back empty-handed.

"How should I know? We don't keep tabs on each other."

The short one slugged him in the face, and his head snapped back. The man in the three-piece suit joined in, "Maybe that will jog your memory, you communist piece of shit."

The third man took the dishcloth from his roommate's hand and stuffed it in his mouth. The men snickered as he gagged. The man in the suit pinned him to the ground and handcuffed him before shoving him out of the doorway and closing the door behind them. Raúl could hear picture frames shattering and books being swept off the shelves onto the floor, and he wondered if the books would be used as evidence against them. They should've burned the books, like some of their friends had, he thought. But Raúl was a reader, in love with the written word. It would have been sacrilege to do so.

The kitchen radio shut off. Their apartment was tiny and contained so few valuables that the assault and robbery were over in a matter of minutes. The aggressors threw a hood over his roommate's head and led him down the stairs. His friend stumbled and had to hold on to one of his captors to keep from falling. It had been a raucous affair, but not a single neighbor had opened their door.

When Raúl could no longer hear them inside the building, he rushed up to a landing where a small window looked out onto the street. His roommate was being pushed into the backseat of a green Ford Falcon. He left the records on the doorstep outside his neighbor's door and ran back to the apartment. After throwing a few of his belongings into a bag, he left without locking the door.

"Why my son?" his friend's mother implored when he broke the news to her. He could not answer her, because there were no good reasons. Her son was a gifted painter who enjoyed reading poetry. Raúl was studying literature. These had become crimes against the state. In another era, he could have gone with her to the police station to report the incident. Instead, he went into hiding. He was a pathetic coward, Raúl had told himself over and over during the agonizing nights he'd waited for a lifeline, which turned out to be Santiago.

Raúl finished telling his story as they exited the highway onto the local roads that would eventually lead to El Pinar. Santiago told Raúl how sorry he was to hear about his roommate. Raúl retorted, "My name is not Raúl Páez. I am Martín Torres and always will be."

In a calm voice, Santiago told him he would have to remember his false identity if he hoped to leave the country alive. "You made the decision to get out, *Raúl.* That's why I'm here," Santiago said. "I can take you back to your apartment if you like."

Raúl, chastened, didn't say much else after that, and the rest of the ride was mostly in silence but for the background noise of the radio.

As whispered accounts of disappearances mounted, Grace reluctantly decided to leave the country. On her last day in Buenos Aires, Santiago confided to her about the safe house. Impressed with her friend's bravery, she gave him the names of two students in trouble.

The night after Grace boarded a plane for Amsterdam, Santiago was in his car, headlights and motor turned off, gliding to a halt in El Pinar. He looked up at the inky sky. Not a single star had come out. Perfect. Darkness was good. Still, he worried that the car's wheels had made too much noise on the gravel, and though he was miles away from anywhere, he had to reassure himself that he was not being watched or followed. He had told Lila the usual story—he was spending the weekend with Sánchez to catch up on some ranch matters. But tonight she had given him a look that troubled him. Was she catching on? *No time to think about that now*, he said to himself as he opened the car's back door. A man and a woman emerged. They were former law school classmates of his. When her feet touched the ground, the woman burst into tears.

"It's okay, Cecilia," the man, Fernando, said.

"You're safe now," whispered Santiago.

The two men took her into the barn. Once inside, Santiago went to the far end and reached for the saddles on the wall. He threw them to the ground, revealing a man-size hole.

They crawled into the space. Sánchez was waiting for them. He held Cecilia's hands to keep her from stumbling. The room was bare but for a couple of cots with sheets, blankets, and pillows; a nightstand with a kerosene lamp; a small table; and some basic wooden chairs. Santiago pulled off a blanket from one of the beds and gave it to Fernando.

"This will keep her warm."

"Gracias," Fernando said, draping it around her.

Sánchez poured her a glass of water from a pitcher on the table.

"Did Lautaro get in touch with you?" Cecilia asked Santiago. "I haven't seen him since Monday."

Santiago and Fernando exchanged looks.

"Cecilia. No one has heard from him in the last two days. We think he's been taken," Santiago told her quietly.

Her legs gave way, and Fernando caught her in his arms.

"I'll try to find out whatever I can. Meanwhile, we have to make sure you're going to be all right," Santiago said.

Fernando brought her to the table, and she collapsed into one of the chairs. A bowl with beef stew prepared by Sánchez's wife earlier that evening was placed in front of her.

"Please. Eat something. You'll feel better," the gaucho advised.

"Sánchez, when does the next truck leave for Brazil?" Santiago asked.

Within a few weeks, the safe house had become fully functional, and the transports from the ranch on the agricultural trucks were running like a well-oiled machine. Each time he learned that his charges had arrived safely abroad, Santiago felt almost giddy. He knew it was illogical, but in his mind, each person he helped brought him one step closer to saving Valentina. He had no way of checking in with Pedro. He had been forbidden from contacting him directly. But after every escape, he was convinced Pedro would call him with news that Valentina was being released.

"The next truck is on Tuesday," Sánchez replied.

"Good. That's in three days. Until then, get some rest."

CHAPTER 45

August 1998

Exhausted from the trip to San Martín de los Andes, all I could think about was how I would crawl into bed for the next twelve hours. I retrieved the apartment keys from my purse when I noticed that the front door was not completely shut.

I turned to Franco. "I could've sworn I locked the door when we left for the airport. Maybe the housekeeper was here and forgot to close it properly?"

Franco moved me gently aside. "Let me go in first."

He turned on the light. The apartment was silent. He signaled for me to come in. I did and hung the keys on a hook by the door. On top of the front hall bureau I noticed a long box decorated with a festive red ribbon. Intrigued, I untied the ribbon and removed the lid. Inside was a slim wooden object. It was approximately six inches long with two thin needles jutting out of one end. I recognized the instrument, having seen similar ones at the ranch. An electric cattle prod.

"What the hell?"

Franco took it from my hands. He raised a finger to his lips. Gripping the prod like a weapon, he proceeded further into the apartment.

What would he do if the intruder was still there? After a few moments, he returned to the foyer.

"Whoever left us this little present is gone. But we can't stay here," he told me.

I didn't respond, holding something else I found in the box. It was a Polaroid photo of the two of us at a counter speaking to a clerk. A large sign behind the employee's head read: *Budget Car Rental. Welcome to San Carlos de Bariloche.*

"You can stay here as long as you like," Alejandro said, inviting us into his home.

"Thank you, Ale," Franco said, hugging his friend.

We spoke in low tones. Alejandro's abuela and sister were sleeping. We had shown up unannounced sometime after midnight, but Alejandro had come to the door, wide awake. The last time I had seen him was when he was photographing his friends from HIJOS on Avenida Santa Fe.

Alejandro brought blankets and pillows, and after we improvised a sleeping area in the living room, we filled him in on what happened. Franco told me that the cattle prod, known as a *picana* in Spanish, had been a preferred torture device in concentration camps around the country. *Was someone threatening to use it on me?* I wondered, suddenly feeling queasy.

"Nothing surprises me anymore," Alejandro said. Seeing how my face had paled, he asked, "How are you holding up?"

"I'm okay, but I might turn in soon if that's all right."

"Absolutely. The bathroom's down the hall, but please don't turn the main light on. You should be able to see fine with the darkroom light." The bathroom, he explained, doubled as his photo lab when the rest of the household went to sleep. "I'm a self-professed insomniac." When we gave him a sympathetic look, he clarified, "It's actually a good thing. I get my best work done when the apartment's quiet and dark."

One of the walls along the hallway was covered with his photos. Some shots were of city life, but most of the images showed protests and strikes. I studied various close-ups of the Madres and Abuelas, some members of HIJOS. Through the photographer's lens, I felt like I had been granted permission to enter his subjects' interior worlds, to know where they had been, to discover their most intimate thoughts. A self-portrait of Alejandro, his face freshly bruised and scratched from a run-in with the secret police, hung front and center. I stopped in front of the photos of HIJOS members putting up Father Aznar posters. The day I asked Franco out. It seemed a lifetime ago.

Alejandro came up beside me.

"Did you take all of these?" I asked. "They're so powerful."

"Yes." He signaled to a section further along the wall. "And over there is my very own Hall of Shame."

It was a series of photos of men in military uniform or civilian clothes. "Who are they?"

"They are all, each and every one of them, torturers and murderers."

Fascinated by the subjects' normal appearances, I searched their faces for any signs of monstrosity. Interspersed among the photos of the torturers were pencil drawings of skulls with question marks underneath.

"What about these? What are they there for?"

"Those are holding places for the ones I haven't been able to photograph yet. That's the challenge, you see. I need to personally shoot them on film or it doesn't count. There are also a few blank ones for torturers who have yet to be identified. Once I've got the name and photo, I replace the skull."

I stopped in front of an image of a man in civilian clothes next to a Ford Falcon car. His hand was on the driver's door as if he were about to get in behind the wheel. Although the photo was taken from a distance, Alejandro had used a zoom lens, and the man's face was in focus. "Franco? Can you come here for a second?"

"What's going on?"

"I…I recognize him," I began, my finger on the man. "He was, um, at my father's press conference, and then the other day I found him outside my building…" My words tumbled out. "He was asking for my father. Said he was a friend. He told me his name was Pedro García."

"Your family *knows* García?" Alejandro asked me with a look of disbelief. "What did you say?"

"Well, that's what he told me. I haven't had a chance to talk to my father. It was just the other day. The whole time he acted as if he knew who I was." All at once, I was sure he had penned the unsigned note to my father. A note that I now re-read in my mind as a threatening one. Dread filled my stomach, but I had to ask. "Why is *he* on your wall?"

Alejandro stared at me for a beat and then turned to Franco as he took down the photo for a closer look.

"Do you remember when Soledad Goldberg told us about Valentina and the guard who would occasionally take her out for coffee or dinner?" Franco asked me. "El Angelito?"

Of course I remembered. Soledad had also talked about the torturer's blond and boyish good looks. "Pretty boy" was how she had described him. Franco handed me the photo. I analyzed the man's features. All at once, I found it hard to breathe.

"That's him." Franco's finger circled the face. "Pedro García is El Angelito."

CHAPTER 46

August–September 1976

THE MEETING WAS TO TAKE place at a run-down bar near the edge of the city. Santiago had given himself plenty of time in case he was stopped and frisked at a random military checkpoint. Even though he knew Pedro would be late as usual, he arrived a half hour early and, as instructed, sat at a table in the back, positioned so that his eyes were on the glass entrance. He had been in negotiations with Pedro for months— five months, to be exact. Winter had come and gone. Trees were showing buds, and this was the first time he would finally get to see Valentina.

When they walked through the doors, he forced himself to stay seated until they were at his table.

Placing his hand on her swollen belly, he murmured in her ear, "Thank God you're alive."

Pedro summoned a waiter with a snap of his fingers. "Can we get some beers here?"

"She shouldn't be drinking," Santiago objected.

"It's all right," Valentina said.

Pedro put an arm around her. "As you can see, she's doing very well."

Santiago reached inside his coat and extracted a thick envelope. He handed it to Pedro under the table.

"How's my old classmate Bautista? Still living the life in Europe?"

Santiago caught a hint of—what was it? Resentment. It was resentment in Pedro's voice. It puzzled Santiago. What did he begrudge Bautista? He muttered that his brother was fine as Pedro glanced at the contents of the envelope before slipping it into his inner coat pocket.

"Isn't this your lucky day? I have to take a piss." He wagged a finger at Santiago. "Don't try anything stupid. I have someone outside watching," he warned as he left the table.

"It's good to see you," she said. Her bottom lip was badly cracked.

"My God, Valentina. How are they treating you?"

"I'm surviving for my baby."

She saw him staring at her hands. She tried to hide them, but he grabbed them and turned them over. Cigarette burns on the inside of her wrists.

"Valentina." A wave of helplessness washed over him.

"Please don't ask." She put her hands on her lap, out of sight. "Tell me about Máximo. How is he?"

"I got him out of the country. He's safe." Santiago looked around and wondered if anyone nearby might be eavesdropping. "I've been able to help some people," he said softly.

The waiter appeared with three icy mugs and poured the beer in an agonizingly slow manner. When they were alone again, Valentina spoke hurriedly.

"Santiago. Should anything happen to me, please find Máximo. Make sure the baby's…"

"Don't talk like that. I'm getting you out." He didn't want to hear her say out loud what he had been forced to admit to himself when he saw her pregnant figure walk into the café. He had calculated that if he were the father, the baby would have already been born, about two months ago. The baby was not his, but he could not dwell on this new knowledge. They had precious little time.

"I promised my friend. Yes, I made a friend inside. Soledad. I said you'd help her too."

"Of course, Valentina."

She began to untie the pendant. "It has given me so much comfort inside. It's meant a lot to me." Her voice wobbled. "I've been thinking a lot about us, and I want you to hold on to it to remember me, in case I don't…"

"Did you not hear what I said? You'll be released any day now."

"For safekeeping then. They took it from me once already. Please." Before she could fully untie the knot, Pedro was back at the table.

Pedro took a swig from his beer and then brusquely lifted Valentina out of her seat by the arm. "Time for us to go now. I'll be in touch."

Valentina looked back at Santiago. He intended for his confident smile to reassure her that all would be well, but he was not sure he succeeded.

A shriek drew Valentina's eyes away from the typewriter. A naked woman ran down the short narrow hall of the clandestine detention center operating in the underbelly of ESMA. A smiling guard pursued the woman calmly, holding out a dress, knowing that the "streaker" wouldn't get very far. Valentina recognized the dress as formerly belonging to prisoner 687, the schoolteacher from Liniers. It was light blue with large yellow sunflowers printed along the bottom. The guard and prisoner danced around each other. He finally grabbed her around the waist and forced the dress over her body.

As if she ever stood a chance, Valentina thought to herself, and resumed her work. After El Angelito had singled her out for special treatment, she had moved up the ranks of prisoners. She adjusted the hood hanging loose around her neck. It was a recently gained privilege—not having to constantly wear a blindfold or hood. She turned back to her work, typing a title certificate for a house in Moreno. Blank spaces were left for the false names and dates. These would be filled in later by an officer.

When Valentina stretched her arm to pull out the sheet of paper, she felt a bit of blouse sticking to her chest. She gently peeled the fabric off. This latest sore from last week's interrogation session would not heal. What she would do for a clean soft cloth to wipe the discharge. But it was unwise to draw unnecessary attention with such a request.

There had been a few sessions when the pain had been so extreme that Valentina's sole wish had been to be put out of her misery. Relief, however, only came when she passed out or when they stopped. A doctor was always present in the "operating room" to monitor her heart after each electric shock to her body. He knew her limits. They wanted her alive.

Were her nipples permanently damaged? Would she ever be able to nurse her baby? "Valentina the Valiant," Soledad had called her one night while they lay awake in their neighboring cells. Valentina smiled at the melodious phrase and then corrected her friend. "There's nothing out of the ordinary in what I'm doing," she had whispered back. "Any woman would stay strong and fight to stay alive for the sake of her child." Concerns about how she would deliver the baby she kept to herself. She could not pee without biting her lip to keep from crying in pain.

"Valentina."

She lifted her eyes from the typewriter to find El Angelito smiling down at her. With that baby face of his, he could easily be mistaken for one of the younger naval cadets they rotated in to guard the prisoners. He asked her to follow him to a small room set aside for the very sick or women in labor. A woman was lying on the sole cot.

"She asked for you," he said.

"What happened?" She ran to Soledad's side.

Soledad's right eye was swollen shut. Her upper lip was bloody, twice its normal size. Her words came out slurred and Valentina had to bring her face close to hers to understand.

"Leandro tried to kiss me and I bit his fucking tongue off. Or at least I'd like to think I did."

Valentina used a damp cloth to wipe the blood from Soledad's face, murmuring to her that the nightmare would soon be over. Her friend

Santiago was going to get them out. She said his name. This went against the prisoners' code. One did not utter the names of friends or family, for fear that the military would go after them too. But Valentina was whispering and she needed to pronounce his name, to make their meeting and his promise real. Santiago would save them both and they would get their lives back.

She was asking Soledad to be her baby's godmother when she was distracted by a roar followed by the faint but unmistakable sounds of cheering.

A naval student forgot that he was supposed to keep a watchful eye on the detainees and stuck his head into the infirmary, unable to contain his excitement.

"Argentina just scored!"

Fierce whispers spread the news throughout the cells. "They're at River Plate Stadium!" "Those sons of bitches!" "Who's playing?" "Argentina–Brazil!" "We scored! The entire country is watching, and it's happening right outside our fucking window!"

Valentina looked out the small dirty window. She could hear the fans clearly now. They were singing the national soccer anthem.

Vamos, vamos Argentina
Vamos, vamos a ganar
Que esta barra quilombera
No te deja, no te deja de alentar

It was a rousing chorus, and Valentina almost felt she might sing with them—her freedom was that palpable. When she turned around, she noticed that Soledad's one good eye was moving from her face to the floor and back to her face again.

"What? What is it?"

All at once, Valentina became aware of a silky wetness sliding down the inside of her thigh. A small puddle was forming between her legs. With a frightened nod, Soledad confirmed her suspicions. Valentina's water had broken.

CHAPTER 47

August 1998

Aᴛᴛᴇʀ sᴘᴇɴᴅɪɴɢ ᴛʜᴇ ɴɪɢʜᴛ ᴀᴛ Alejandro's, Franco decided it was safe to return to his apartment. Luis was away for the weekend, so it was just the two of us. I exchanged a few short emails with my parents, who continued to believe I was spending time with Juan and his family at their campo. My last message to them was that I would be back in Buenos Aires tomorrow, Monday, in time for Dad's ceremony. And, yes, I would bring Juan too, I responded, after my mother wrote back, asking. I no longer felt bad lying about Juan and my whereabouts. They would learn the truth soon enough.

We were finishing dinner when the phone rang. It was Mariano, his friend from the lab. One look at Franco told me the outcome, but I still brought the phone to my ear. Mariano read me the lab results, confirming what I was feeling in the pit of my stomach: Máximo was my biological father.

My hands and feet turned ice cold, and I couldn't keep my teeth from chattering. As I lay on the couch, Franco's nurturing hands and words nursed my body until I finally succumbed to a feverish sleep.

When Máximo phoned Franco early the next morning, it had been simply to inform him that he was on the overnight bus from San Martín to Buenos Aires and would be arriving in an hour. I had been listening in on the call and had signaled my consent to Franco.

"Paloma was hoping you would phone…yes, she knows. She wants to see you too. We'll meet you at the station."

We took a cab to the bus terminal in Retiro. The orange-and-white, twin-level intercity bus spewed brown diesel fumes as it parked in its assigned lane. Máximo was the last to descend. When he saw me, he stopped moving. So I was the one who did the walking.

I had woken up feeling different. The fever had left me, perhaps taking with it the last shreds of my former life. Prepared to rewrite my story, I calmly stepped up and kissed Máximo on the cheek. He looked at me silently until Franco came over and shook his hand. We found a café inside the station where a few tables were occupied by backpackers, traveling salesmen in tired-looking suits, a mother with a child on her lap.

"I'm sorry about the other day," Máximo apologized. "I should've been more hospitable."

A waiter brought three coffees with hot milk and a plate of warm medialunas.

I tried hard not to stare at him. "We understand."

He fished around for his cigarettes and smoked while Franco and I drank our coffees. I offered him some water. After I poured him a glass, he took my hand in his.

"You have Valentina's hands. She was always making something. Such graceful fingers." He realized he had been holding my hand for too long and released it. "Sorry. I don't know what I'm doing."

"Please stop apologizing. I'm glad you came." Even if I was not quite able to comprehend the situation or the man sitting across from me, I felt, at least momentarily, like I was the only one in control of the situation. We quietly sized each other up. Then, Máximo lit another cigarette and began talking.

"I'll tell you what I know," Máximo said, sitting straight up in his chair. "Valentina was pregnant when she was kidnapped. We hadn't yet shared the news of her pregnancy, mainly because we didn't want to upset her parents. Her parents were religious, and it was important to Valentina that we respect their beliefs. She agreed to marry me, and we decided that I would ask her father's permission first. I was planning to go visit them in Córdoba, but I had some things I needed to take care of beforehand." He nervously twirled the lit cigarette around his fingers. "I was away the day they kidnapped her." His gaze dropped. "They took her because of me," he said, and paused. "I had to go into hiding, and I couldn't look for her. They were after me. Her parents reported her missing to the police, and Santiago said he would do whatever he could. He helped me get out of the country. It all happened fast. A few weeks later, I was living in France." Máximo stamped out the cigarette. "One day he called and told me that Valentina and the baby had both died during childbirth."

"He did?" Why would my father tell him such a lie?

"I had no reason not to believe him. We were friends." Máximo brushed his hair behind his ears, and when he looked at me again, his eyes were wet. "But when you showed up at my house and said you were Santiago's daughter, something clicked. My instincts shouted at me to pay attention. But if I did, everything I believed in would be thrown into question, and my brain couldn't begin to entertain the possibility that maybe you were Valentina's daughter, my daughter…so I asked you to leave. After you left, my head continued to fill with thoughts and ideas that I would normally dismiss as outlandish." Máximo's anxious smile showed teeth yellowed from years of smoking.

"What do you mean?"

"The necklace you wore when you came to see me. Seeing it around your neck was so unexpected that I initially thought my mind was playing tricks on me. The one you're wearing now." His gaze fell on my throat. "It belonged to Valentina."

"I found it in my father's childhood bedroom." I removed the pendant. "Do you want to look at it?"

Máximo held the necklace, its smooth blue stone gleaming in the palm of his hand. He treated it as if it were a delicate butterfly he was afraid of crushing. "Santiago gave it to her while they were dating. Later, when we were together, she asked if it bothered me that she still wore it. I could tell the pendant meant something to her and I didn't want to impose limits on her that were driven by my own insecurities," he said with a dry laugh. "I told her I was okay with it. I respected her, and whatever she decided was fine with me. So she kept it on. I admired that in her, her independence." He handed me back the pendant and said, "The thing is, as far as I know, she never once took it off. So, you see, there's no doubt in my mind that she was still wearing it the day she was kidnapped."

The implication in Máximo's words lodged itself in my brain like an ice pick, releasing a tremor down the length of my spine. How then, dear God, had my father come to possess the necklace?

CHAPTER 48

September 1976

THE LOBBY OF SAN RAFAEL Hospital was deserted, and the only sounds reverberating through the empty corridors were Santiago's rapid footsteps. When he arrived at the cafeteria, he was met by a couple of men in jeans and bomber jackets. They patted him down and let him through the doors. The lights were dimmed for the night. The cafeteria was quiet but for the humming of a restaurant-size refrigerator. He wondered if he was there alone when Pedro emerged from the shadows.

"Do you have the rest of the money?" Pedro asked, taking a few steps toward him. He carried a small, bulky package.

Santiago pulled out a heavy envelope and handed it over.

"It's a girl. Valentina named her Paloma," Pedro said, and thrust the package into Santiago's arms. He glanced down. A newborn, fast asleep.

"When can I see her?"

"She died in labor."

"You son of a bitch!" Santiago lunged at him. "You killed her!"

Pedro raised his hand, which held a shiny, metallic gun.

"Careful now," Pedro warned with a sneer. He waved the gun toward the exit. "Go on. Get the fuck out of here. You should be thanking me for giving you the baby."

Santiago adjusted his arms around the bundle, and when he looked back up, the gun was pointed at his chest. What was there left for him to do here? Valentina was dead.

With the baby partially tucked inside his jacket, he walked out of the cafeteria, past the thugs, without stopping. He had underestimated Pedro. And now Valentina was dead.

As he was nearing his car, a van with Pedro García at the wheel drove by him to the other end of the parking lot. Santiago instinctively crouched behind a dumpster. The baby started crying and he put a finger in her mouth to quiet her down. A man and a couple of women in hospital gowns appeared from a side entrance of the hospital. Then someone pushed the women roughly into the back of the van. It was dark, and Santiago couldn't see their faces.

He rushed to his car. He held the baby down on the passenger seat and started the engine with his free hand. He would catch up to them and force the van off the road. He turned right and sped down the street, racing through a few red lights. The van was nowhere in sight. He veered onto a boulevard and frantically wove through the night-time traffic. Maybe Pedro had lied to him and Valentina was inside that van. His fists pounded the steering wheel repeatedly. How could he have lost her?

He drove around in a daze, losing all sense of time. When he could no longer ignore the baby's crying, he parked the car. He tried to soothe her by jiggling her a little. The cries subsided. The baby's blanket had opened up, and in one of its folds, his fingers grazed something. It was the pendant. Someone had tucked it into the hospital blanket. He brought it up to his mouth and howled into it. The baby began to whimper again. He swaddled her in the thin blanket and got out of the car. He entered a twenty-four-hour phone center where he could place an international call. He was shown to a private booth and given the signal to pick up the phone when the operator had successfully placed the call to France.

"Hello? Who's this? Is it you, Santiago?" Silence. "Who's there?"

He rested weakly against the pay phone. "Máximo," Santiago cried into the receiver.

"Santi!"

As Máximo's voice ricocheted in his ear a dormant part of Santiago's brain sprang awake. In an instant, he saw everything differently. Clearly. He blamed his friend for Valentina's death, and realized that if Máximo learned about the baby, he would return, putting both himself and the baby in danger. The infant squirmed in his arms.

"What's going on? What's that sound?" Máximo asked.

"She's gone. They're both gone."

CHAPTER 49

August 1998

. . . I CAN PERSONALLY VOUCH FOR Ambassador Larrea's commitment. He is a true hero and a worthy representative of the democratic values of our country."

The audience applauded Professor Torres as he stepped away from the podium.

The foreign minister, a polished man in his late fifties, appeared on the stage. As he introduced Argentina's future ambassador to the United Nations, the minister's aide brought out a Bible. My father rested his left hand on it while holding up his right.

"Do you promise to carry out your duties to uphold the constitution and the laws of the Republic of Argentina, to faithfully represent her interests in your new office?"

"I do," he said. Then he turned to address the audience.

"It is a great honor to be here tonight. Argentina is in my heart…"

He looked to the door at the back of the hall and saw me. I had arrived a moment before the ceremony began at the Casa Rosada and intentionally stayed in the back row of the crowd. Our eyes met, and he managed to maintain his smile. I did not offer him mine in return.

After meeting Máximo that morning, I had returned to Abuelo's apartment to gather the remainder of my belongings. Knowing my parents would stop by before the ceremony that afternoon, I tidied up and packed in a hurry. On the entrance hall table, I placed the photograph of them at the campo with Valentina and Máximo next to a note reading, *We need to talk.*

I held Dad's gaze, and when I turned to leave, I heard his voice falter.

"I…I thank you all for coming tonight…"

A handful of security guards were standing at attention when I walked out into the courtyard.

"Paloma!" My mother was hurrying toward me. I stopped and waited for her under the archway.

"Where are you going? It's your dad's ceremony." She looked around. "Did you come alone? Where's Juan?"

"I'm not with him. We ended it."

"Oh, my sweet baby, I'm sorry. Are you all right?"

"No. I'm not."

"Come back inside with me, we can talk about it after the ceremony, okay?"

"I'm not going inside."

"Why not?" My mother's expression was one of confusion.

"Did you not see the photo I left in the apartment?"

"I…yes, we did. We were surprised. Such an old photo. Where did you find it?" I eyed her skeptically. Was my mother feigning ignorance?

"I wasn't with Juan all this time in Buenos Aires. I was curious about Dad's past, and after digging around, I found out you've both been lying to me," I told her quietly, while my pulse began to quicken.

She tensed. "About what?"

"About me, about who I am. About everything."

"I don't know what you're talking about," she said.

"Our family is one big horrible lie. Were you ever going to tell me? The truth about my parents?"

Her face slowly distorted, and I thought she might turn and leave, but she stayed, immobile. "I was afraid," she finally whispered.

"Of what?"

"I was afraid you'd stop loving me if you knew. I couldn't have babies of my own. You probably wondered at some point why we didn't give you a little brother or sister?" I remained silent. "It was crushing me and my marriage. And then, like a miracle, you came into our lives."

"Don't you realize how selfish it was to hide this from me?" My hands flew up in frustration, but something inside me had already shattered.

"Not ever do I stop thinking about you and loving you. You're my life, Paloma."

I turned to walk away.

"Even if you have learned it on your own, I still want you to hear it from me."

It was my father's commanding voice. He had hurried out of the ceremony after giving his remarks. He led us away from the guards to an empty corner of the courtyard.

His tone was low but firm. "Valentina is your biological mother. She was pregnant with you when she was taken. Lila and I made a decision a long time ago not to tell you. Valentina's death…it was so terrible. As you grew older, we knew we needed to tell you, but it never felt like the right moment. I suppose we were cowards." He waited for a reaction from me, but I wouldn't give him one. "When Valentina was kidnapped, I did everything in my power to save her. I negotiated to get her out. I even made arrangements to see her to make sure she was alive. And I promised her that if anything happened to her, I would give you the best possible life. And I have. Haven't I?"

I shrank away from his touch. "Please stop, Papá. I know about Máximo. I know he's my real father."

He looked at me, baffled.

I paused, letting my words register. "That's right. I met Máximo. You told him I died along with Valentina."

He shuddered. Hearing Máximo's name left him reeling. He held on to my mother for support.

"He's not your father," he whispered.

"He is. I have proof."

My mother struggled to hold him up. His legs gave way, and like a wounded man, he doubled over. She bent down to help him back up.

Neither one spoke, and after a moment, I glared at them and asked, "So you have nothing to say to me?"

"I never saw Valentina again. I did what I could, I swear to you." My father's arms were down, his palms turned out. He was not hiding anything anymore. "I loved her."

"More than Mamá?"

My mother flinched but remained otherwise stone-faced.

"It was different. We were young. Valentina was my first love."

"And what about me?"

"Paloma…Valentina's dead. And I raised you. You're my daughter. Of course I love you."

"If you loved me, you would have told me the truth when I asked you about Valentina the day of the press conference. I gave you a chance to explain."

"You caught me off guard," he said.

"Instead, you tried to present yourself as the good guy saving people from the military by building a safe house."

"What is she talking about, Santiago?" Lila interjected. "A safe house?"

"But you were also lying to your friend so you could keep his baby."

When Dad spoke next, he was on firmer ground, and despite my anger, I was relieved to see his face regain color. "I needed to protect you. We had to leave the country. I was pretty sure time was running out on me. That I, too, would be apprehended. Betrayed by someone, any-one. They were picking people up off the street, from their offices and homes." Turning to my mother, he said, "Lila, I couldn't tell you what I was doing. It was better that way, for your safety. For all our safety."

"But how did I end up with *you*?" I asked, breathless with dismay.

"When they abducted Valentina, I got into contact with someone within the military who was able to help me. I also knew I had to find Máximo before he got arrested and send him somewhere safe. They were after him, and I was able to persuade him to leave. He did. Had I told him about you, he would have returned, and they would've killed him too."

I desperately wanted to follow my father's rationalizations, but I couldn't make any sense of it.

"My thinking was that when Argentina returned to democracy, we would come back. But then life took over. And you blossomed. By then, we didn't think you would benefit from knowing. We were wrong. I see that now. You were our joy, our everything. We didn't want you to suffer."

I let out a bitter laugh. "I think you've got it all backward. You were the ones who benefited from my not knowing. Like you said at the start of this conversation, you've been cowards all along. You couldn't stand the idea of suffering. You were afraid you would lose me. So you took a gamble. A big one. You thought that by keeping me in the dark, I would never find out and leave you. But all that shows me is that you never had any real faith in our family."

"Not true."

"Yeah. Okay. Keep telling yourself that, Papá, if it makes you feel better." His justifications had worn me down. I looked toward the street. "I'm leaving."

"Please don't go. We're your family, Paloma." My mother had found her voice.

"You're our daughter. You always will be. We're the ones who raised you." And when I didn't reply, he asked, "Tell me, what makes a father?"

As I slowly faced him, I felt a combination of pity and contempt. "I don't know what makes a father, but what I do know is that you never gave Máximo the chance to be one."

CHAPTER 50

September 1976

LILA WOKE UP. IT WAS dark outside. She faced the empty half of the bed and extended her hand. The sheet was cold. Another night without Santiago lying beside her. Where was he? Each night that she slept alone, she felt like she was that much closer to losing him. She sighed and turned on her back. She was tired of this stuck-in-the-past country, where everyone wanted to know, the moment you married, when the baby would come. They had been married well over a year, and each time she was asked, Lila was reminded that as far as they were concerned, she had not yet been fully realized as a woman. The pressure. The constant scrutiny. It was unbearable. She also saw the disappointment in Santiago's eyes. They could all go to hell. Except him. Not Santiago.

"Lila. Lila."

She opened one eye and then the other. Early morning light filtered through the curtains from Liberty London that her mother had given her before the wedding. She realized that she'd fallen asleep again.

"Lila."

Her husband leaned over her. He was so attractive. She never tired of gazing at him.

"Wake up, Lila. It's very important."

"What's the matter?"

She stretched her arms out, not quite awake yet. She noticed he was in the same clothes he wore yesterday.

"Come out to the living room. I'll be waiting there for you."

Lila washed her face, threw on her silk kimono, and hurried out of the bedroom. The sun streamed through the blinds, illuminating the room in streaks of pale white light. Her eyes went to the coffee table. A large can of powder sat unopened. A happy baby smiled back from the can's label. It was infant formula. Next to it was a pacifier.

"Santiago?" Her question came out tentatively because her eyes couldn't quite fathom the sight. He stood by the window holding a tiny infant. He was moving it gently up and down in his arms.

"We've been asked to take care of her. I said yes."

Astonished, Lila looked back up at him and saw that he'd been crying. "Give her to me."

Lila smiled as the baby's tiny fist flopped against its red cheek. When the newborn's lips rounded into a perfect circle, she instinctively knew what it meant.

"The poor little thing is hungry. Get the can of formula. We need to boil some water. Hurry."

Santiago told Lila about the kind doctor who had quietly helped an unwed teen find a good family for this baby. Lila didn't understand why he hadn't involved her in the decision, but she didn't question him. The mother had had only one request. She asked that the adoptive parents keep the name she had given the baby: Paloma. They did. Lila also went along with Santiago's plan to leave Argentina. Santiago told her they wouldn't tell their parents about the baby, but as soon as they were out of the country, they would announce Lila's pregnancy. "The baby will be ours, ours completely, because no one will ever know," Santiago said, holding on to Lila as if for dear life. Lila agreed. It would be their secret. It would bind them for life, she thought. Now he would never leave her.

A few days later, on a morning before the sun showed itself, Santiago took a cab to Belgrano, a neighborhood populated by many Anglo-Argentines. Conrad Robertson lived in an old aristocratic mansion on a residential street, free of shops or offices. An English maid escorted Santiago down the long hallway to a bright and spacious study. Conrad was at his desk, waiting.

"Here's everything you need," Conrad said, businesslike, handing him a folder. Santiago leafed through the documents: tickets on Pan Am Airways to JFK, banking information, a lease on an apartment on the Upper East Side of Manhattan, and most importantly, the documents for Paloma. Santiago set these down on a table and inspected them carefully. He had asked Conrad to procure two different sets of passports and birth certificates for Paloma that would be identical except for the place and date of birth. Name: María Paloma Larrea. Mother: María Liliana Williams de Larrea. Father: Santiago Larrea. Weight: 2.8 kilos. One set of documents would record Paloma's date of birth as September 20, 1976, in Buenos Aires. The second set of documents would show December 15, 1976, in New York. The first set of documents would be presented to enter the United States, and then would be destroyed. The second set of documents would be used once they were installed in New York. The birth announcement would tell the world that Paloma was born in New York on December 15, 1976, providing enough time and distance from Buenos Aires to avoid questions.

Santiago nodded to Conrad, indicating everything was in order.

"Does Lila know about Paloma's mother?" Conrad asked.

"Not yet. Now that everything's in order, I'll tell her. Tonight. After dinner." But Santiago would ultimately wait until they were in New York. If he told Lila that Paloma was Valentina's baby before they left Buenos Aires, she would back out of the plan. He could not let that happen.

Conrad asked, "Are you sure that this is what you want to do?"

"I'm not sure of anything anymore," Santiago said, returning the papers to the folder.

"You'll be safe there."

"Why wasn't *she* kept safe? She hadn't done anything wrong. Why didn't they let her go like they said they would?"

"I'm afraid the measures taken by your government are reprehensible. Beyond the pale." Conrad's anger took hold of him for a brief moment before he regained his diplomatic composure. It would take several years before Conrad's suspicions about the detainment and killing of innocent civilians were proved correct. "Santiago, you must move forward. Think of your family, your new baby girl."

Santiago stood to leave.

The men had become close friends, but it would be the last time they would see each other. A year later, Conrad would be transferred by Her Majesty's government to Hong Kong. Had Santiago known, he would have again expressed his gratitude for all Conrad had done for him and for those who passed through the safe house.

Conrad walked around his desk and gave him a firm embrace. He said, "You and Lila will be loving parents."

CHAPTER 51

August 1998

A MOCK-UP POSTER RESTED ON the center of the table in the conference room at the Human Rights Center. Along with other members of HIJOS, Franco and I gathered around the table to study it. It was an image of Pedro García with the word *ASSASSIN* below his face. *PEDRO GARCÍA, A.K.A. El ANGELITO.*

"He was able to keep a low profile all these years," Julián said in his soft manner, shaking his head.

Miriam, who had come in to empty the garbage can, offered to prepare mate for the group.

"Gracias, Miriam. Always taking such good care of us," Mateo said to the cleaning lady as he helped himself to one of the pastries from a plate.

Sofía entered the room and announced, "I just got off the phone. We have the go-ahead for the escrache." She checked her notes. "Looks like the other organizations are also confirmed." She turned to me and her voice took on a warm tone. "As you can imagine, what you and Franco uncovered means a great deal to us."

I smiled reticently. I had moved in with Franco and his brother a couple nights earlier, and it was the first time I had been back with him to a HIJOS meeting.

"I need to get to class." Franco began gathering his books. "But Paloma and I will finish compiling the evidence and putting together the list of victims. Whoever wants to join us, we'll be at my place, tonight, eight p.m."

At Franco's apartment, we scoured through an assortment of documents spread out on the dining room table: journals, handwritten letters, old newspaper clippings, photos, scanned excerpts from the *Nunca Más* report, and various typewritten testimonies. Franco's approach throughout the whole process had been methodical. The phone rang and I heard him murmur, "Thanks for letting us know, Sofía." He hung up and looked at me. "We need to work faster, Paloma."

I plunked down two sturdy cardboard boxes on the table. All the papers had been neatly divided into separate piles, and we began to file the documents into the boxes. When the boxes had been sealed and labeled, Franco turned to me with a satisfied grin.

"I think we're ready."

Heavy clouds loomed low as we carried the boxes into Franco's neighborhood bakery, Panadería El Norte. Right as we settled behind the counter, a Ford Falcon coasted to a stop across from his building. We were spying through the window, and my breath caught in the back of my throat. In the driver's seat was Pedro García.

Sofía's phone call to Franco had confirmed his suspicions about Miriam. Ever since Miriam had started working as a janitor of sorts at the Human Rights Center, HIJOS members had been receiving threatening phone calls or reported being followed. After our meeting earlier that afternoon at the Center, Sofía and Franco's brother, Luis, surreptitiously followed Miriam to a bar where, moments later, Pedro

García showed up and sat at her table. She had been working as an informant for him all along.

Pedro flicked his hand in the air. The man in the passenger seat and the two men in the back climbed out of the car and crossed the street into Franco's building. A few moments later, Pedro got out and glanced up at the windows of the third-floor apartment. He pulled out his cell phone, about to dial a number, when a hard object pressed against the back of his neck.

"Goddamn it," Pedro cursed, dropping his phone.

He wasn't fast enough and failed to reach the front of his jacket. His arms were swiftly pulled behind his back. Handcuffs were deftly placed around his wrists. In a flash, darkness enveloped him. It took Pedro a little time to figure out what was happening. And when he understood, he cursed again. A hood, of all things, had been thrown over his head.

Julián found the gun in Pedro's jacket. He handed it to Alejandro, who then threw to the ground the lead pipe he had held against Pedro's neck. Mateo—his rugby days not far behind him—easily pushed Pedro down onto the floor of the back seat. Alejandro joined Mateo, while Julián got behind the wheel. The keys were still in the ignition. Franco and I came out of the bakery, carrying the boxes. We loaded them in the trunk and I slid onto Franco's lap in the front seat. With a look of unbridled joy, Julián, the timid graphic designer, sat behind the wheel and pointed the car toward the city center. The entire operation had been executed in under four minutes.

The Ford Falcon hurtled down the national highway. After a few miles, Julián exited into one of the poorer neighborhoods on the outskirts of Buenos Aires. We drove down an unpaved road, then veered sharply into a deserted parking lot. Franco twisted around to face the back seat. Mateo's and Alejandro's feet were firmly planted on Pedro's torso.

"So, Angelito. Tell us. What would come next?" Franco asked, his tone deliberately calm.

"Go to hell." Pedro's voice came out muffled through the hood.

"No, really, we want to know. We're new at this. What's the best way to get someone to talk? Cigarette burns on the skin? A good old-fashioned beating? Or better yet, plunge your head in a toilet until you almost drown? Which one's your favorite?"

Mateo pulled Pedro up onto the seat and Alejandro yanked off the hood.

"Do we strip you now, or do we wait until you're in your cell?"

Julián turned off the ignition, climbed into the back seat, and took out a pair of scissors from his jacket. While Mateo held down his legs, Julián began cutting one of Pedro's pant legs.

I spoke from the front seat. "I want you to tell me what happened to my mother."

"I don't think so."

Franco revealed the cattle prod that had been left at my apartment.

"We don't have a doctor on hand, so you'll have to tell us what voltage to use. Never thought you'd get to experience it firsthand, eh?"

Pedro looked out the window and saw just one other car at the end of the lot. The rain was beating down on the car roof. He let out an exasperated sigh as though he were the one in charge of the situation and we, a bunch of twerps, were testing his patience.

"Get your friend to stop cutting off my clothes and I'll tell you."

Franco was the one to break the silence that followed Pedro's account of my mother's final days. "And you've been walking around all these years, a free man," were the only words he managed to say.

Julián, who had stopped cutting Pedro's clothes during the confession, took to the scissors again and snipped off the last of his pant leg.

Alejandro pulled out a small tape recorder and pressed the Stop button. "I think we've got all we need," he told the group.

Pedro looked at the tape recorder and then at Alejandro. "You think that tape will make a difference?" He scoffed. "You have no idea how the system works."

"We'll see about that," Alejandro replied cheerfully.

Mateo lightly slapped Pedro's face several times. "It's been a real pleasure."

We left him half-naked in the back seat. As we began to run to the other car, Pedro called out, "Mónica Bonetti." Franco's mother. Franco stopped running.

When he turned around, I cried, "Don't go back!"

"You go with the others. I need to hear what he has to say."

I stayed and watched him return to the car and open the back door. I was thinking Pedro might attack him until I reminded myself that he was handcuffed.

Moments later, he was back by my side.

"What did he say?"

He shook his head. "Not now." The rain was soaking us both.

The driver's window slid down. Sofía sat behind the wheel, and Luis Bonetti was in the passenger seat. As we all squeezed in, the adrenaline continued to rush through our young bodies, providing levels of elation most of us had never experienced before. Sofía reversed the car out of the parking lot and we returned to the city.

The rain had eased into a drizzle when we parked in front of a building near the city's port. Above the entrance was a sign in gothic letters: *The Buenos Aires Herald.*

The newspaper offices were closed. It was after midnight, and the security guard was fast asleep. On top of the desk we left the two cardboard boxes, labeled:

Documents and Confession of Pedro García, alias EL AN-
GELITO
    August 26, 1998

CHAPTER 52

September 1976

THE VAN CAREENED AWAY FROM San Rafael Hospital. One of the men drove, while another man sat on a bench in the back with the two women. Pedro twisted in the passenger seat to keep an eye on Valentina. She lay in a fetal position on the cold metallic floor, her hospital gown splattered with blood.

Lying about her death had been a last-minute decision. As much as Pedro disliked Santiago and his brother, Bautista, he hadn't wanted a Larrea brother to think any less of him for not keeping up his end of the deal. Strangely, Santiago's opinion of him still mattered. Letting Santiago believe she died in labor had been an act of kindness. Her involvement with a subversive made Valentina complicit. She would remain a prisoner—unless she really was in the process of dying right then and there on the van floor. There was a lot of blood. He stared hard at her inert body until he finally perceived her chest rise and fall. He sighed and directed his mind back to his magnanimity.

Giving the baby to Santiago was another generous gesture. Pedro had pocketed a tidy sum of money in the transaction, but nevertheless, he had taken risks in order to make that happen. Had Santiago not lashed out at Pedro, accusing him of killing Valentina, would he have expressed gratitude for the baby? Pedro had not given him another chance, couldn't allow Santiago to have a fit. A Larrea losing his temper. He had not predicted that. He grimaced. What an ungrateful son of a bitch.

The sight of Valentina on the floor suddenly upset Pedro, and he turned back in his seat, facing forward. His feelings of attraction for her had waned as she entered her final month of pregnancy. In that state, she had reminded him of a malnourished child with a distended belly. Looking out the van window as the city lights flickered by, his thoughts meandered to a fictional time and place where her body regained its shapely curves and her face its sensual appeal. Pleasantly lost in this reverie, he smiled and almost forgot the real Valentina, who remained motionless for the duration of the ride.

The first days after the birth, Valentina remained in a feverish state, delirious at times. She was confined to a small cement cell, called a *cucha*, or dog kennel. There were no windows, and she had no way of knowing if it was day or night.

The blindfolded prisoners' hands were tied behind their backs and their legs were in shackles. One of the women knew how to loosen the rope around her hands and would shuffle into Valentina's cell to cradle her in her arms, stroke her hair, and whisper comforting words. When Valentina emerged from her haze, she realized she was in a different detention center.

"Where am I?"

"El Vesubio," the woman answered. "That's what the guards call it."

El Vesubio was a series of buildings in a military zone outside Buenos Aires. The Triple A had turned the facilities into an illegal detention center in 1975.

Valentina asked for her baby.

"I don't know where your baby is," the woman replied, giving her small spoonfuls of watery soup. When the woman would hear the jingling of keys, she would return to the cell opposite Valentina's.

"You need your strength," the woman answered when Valentina refused the extra piece of bread she had procured for her. "Your baby is somewhere out there waiting for you. I have three of my own, and they're waiting for me too."

One afternoon, after a meager lunch of dry polenta and a glass of tepid water, a guard brought out some of the prisoners into the hall. Stumbling along in a single file, Valentina was oblivious to the milk leaking from her breasts and the painful shivers throughout her body. The numbness that entered her heart when her baby was torn from her had deadened her senses.

Twenty prisoners lined up against the wall. Valentina's legs buckled beneath her. The kind woman was beside her and grabbed her before she hit the floor.

"237. 364. 248. 209."

Each number corresponded to a prisoner who was then instructed to step forward.

"310. 375. 413."

Valentina flinched when she heard her number, 322, unable to bring herself to move. The woman, who still held her arm, whispered to her encouragingly. "I think they're going to release you."

Could it be true? Were they finally letting her out? Valentina felt a surge in her chest. She would be reunited with her baby girl. She told El Angelito she had named her Paloma, and he had smiled and congratulated her. El Angelito had given Santiago the baby. Hadn't he? Santiago would be taking good care of her baby. Like he had taken care of Máximo by getting him out of Argentina. Máximo was now safe, thanks to Santiago.

Santiago. Santiago.

"322. Come forward now. 322."

A tear rolled down her face. Why had she constantly pushed him away? Santiago had never stopped being the love of her life. As soon as she got out of this hell on earth, she would tell him. If he would still have her, she would never again let him go. They would raise Paloma together. It was amid these thoughts that she found the strength to step into the line.

"You'll be transferred to a work camp in Patagonia. Conditions will be better. It's the final stage in your reintegration to society," the guard explained while inspecting the newly formed group of prisoners.

A doctor waited for them in a side room. He proceeded to insert a needle into each prisoner's arm. One jerked his arm away.

"Keep still. It's a mild sedative to help you travel more easily."

Blindfolded, they were loaded onto a truck. Drowsiness soon overtook the majority of them. A couple of prisoners flopped against Valentina as the truck traveled over uneven terrain. When the vehicle came to a stop, the back doors opened and they were ordered out. From the damp smell in the air, she sensed they were near water. Someone stepped on her heel, and she stumbled. Her blindfold slid off. It was dark, and the guards didn't seem to notice that she could now see. They were busy carrying the prisoners who had stumbled under the effects of the sedative.

They were on a tarmac. Ahead was a large military cargo aircraft with a ramp extending down from the rear. Its camouflage exterior distinguished it from other aircraft. The turboprop blades slowly came to life. A prisoner behind Valentina, upon hearing the distinctive whirring sounds, mumbled that a passenger airplane would be better for the long flight to Patagonia. There were no seats on this type of aircraft.

When Valentina felt the plane move and then lift up, above the buildings of Buenos Aires, she opened one eye. It seemed that almost all her fellow passengers had fallen unconscious, but thinking of Paloma delayed her from succumbing to the drug.

"Are they dead?" an air force officer shouted above the noise. It was his first time on one of these missions.

"You idiot!" Pedro, seated in the cockpit, scoffed. "They're sedated, you incompetent dope." He looked out over the prisoners slumped over one another. "We're Christians, for God's sake. We're giving these lucky sons of bitches a merciful way out." He turned to the pilot and asked, "What's our position?"

They had flown southeast over the Río de la Plata. Twinkling lights along the dark Uruguayan coastline could be discerned in the distance. The pilot gave a thumbs-up.

"It's time," Pedro said, signaling to the other officers.

An officer approached the sleeping bodies. He crouched in front of a man picked at random. They stripped the prisoner until his emaciated body was naked. A weight was clipped around the captive's ankles. Hooking his hands under the man's armpits, he waited while the other officer unlatched and lowered the back door. He dragged the body to the opening and, together, the officers pushed the sleeping soul out of the aircraft.

They moved on to the next body and the next, until they reached Valentina. Her eyes were shut. When they lifted her up to remove her clothes, she practically floated out of their hands.

"She can't weigh more than a bird, this one," one of the officers remarked.

"Let's see if she can fly like one," the other one said with a chuckle.

A crosswind gust tipped the aircraft to one side, throwing the officers off balance. Valentina opened her eyes. Stunned to find one of their prisoners still awake, the officers loosened their grip. She broke free but tripped over a body. The plane climbed higher. The men were hurled against the wall and before they could recover, Valentina was at the door. Pedro turned in his seat. The wind whipped her hair about her face. She gripped the sides of the door. She looked below. The water shimmered varying shades of black and silver. Above her, a thousand stars flickered just beyond her reach. A sanctuary in the universe, she thought, suddenly remembering when she lay with Santiago by the campfire, looking up at the stars. Slowly, she released her hold. Pedro called out her name. Her hands smoothed down her flapping hospital gown and, without looking back at her captors, she stepped into the air.

EPILOGUE

September 1998

FRANCO WIPED THE KITCHEN COUNTER and put away the last coffee cup in the cupboard above the stove. He tied the strings of a garbage bag and took it out to the service stairwell. Looking to his right, then his left, he ensured that nothing was blocking the stairwell. Back in the apartment, he paused long enough to address Luis, sprawled out on the sofa. "What are you doing just lying there? We need to get going."

"I'm ready, brother. Only waiting for you to stop running around," Luis answered with a lazy smile.

Franco looked at his watch and called out, "We're going to be late."

Moments later, I came out of the bathroom, combing my wet hair.

"Sorry to keep you waiting."

Franco crossed the room, retrieving a piece of paper from his back pocket. "She phoned again this morning, while you were still sleeping."

It was from my family's housekeeper, Rosa. I read the note:

> *Please tell Miss Paloma her mother has not been able to get out of bed in days. Don Santiago is in Europe on a diplomatic mission.*

Dad had called just once since leaving Argentina, his message direct and to the point: When can we talk?

The last time we spoke was on the day we were supposed to return to New York. I called from Franco's to tell them I was staying in Buenos Aires for a semester, maybe longer. My father accepted my plan, saying he only wanted my happiness. He said he would have my plane ticket changed to an open return. I gave him Franco's phone number, and as he was writing down the address, my mother grabbed the phone.

"Paloma. Don't listen to your Papá. Come home with us tonight. Please."

"Mamá, don't do this. I'm staying."

"I've made so many mistakes. I wasn't the mother to you that I should've been. I now see that we owed you the truth and let you down. I don't expect you to forgive me right away, but if you come home with us…" She choked on her tears. "As wrong as we were, I want you to know that everything we did was for you. We need to be together as a family."

I could still hear my mother, but I wasn't really listening anymore. In my mind, I had already placed my parents back in New York, giving me the distance I desperately needed from them. She refused to say goodbye, and eventually, I hung up the phone.

The first time Rosa called from New York, concerned that my mother wasn't well and my father was hardly around, I responded by writing them a letter.

In it, I sketched a general picture of my life in Buenos Aires. My college agreed to a gap semester, and I had moved in temporarily with Franco and Luis. At Alejandro's suggestion, I enrolled in a photography class. Through my field assignments—the doors of old houses being the only subjects I felt safe tackling at that point—I was getting to know the city while learning about exposure, light, and shadow. I left out the part about how I was slowly piecing together the life of my mother, Valentina Quintero. I had traveled back to San Martín de los

Andes to visit Máximo, his wife, Agathe, and my three half siblings, Valentino, Ernestina, and Guadalupe. Bright-eyed and openhearted, their love for their older sister was immediate and uncomplicated. I also visited Abuelo. My parents had told him everything, and he assured me he had not known. He loved me and asked me to please consider moving in with him. I did not write that, like my mother, I couldn't get out of bed some mornings. Franco carried me through those tough days. I finished by saying I promised to call soon, but that for now, a letter was the best I could do.

As Franco, Luis, and I stepped onto the boardwalk along the Puerto Madero, the frantic sounds of the city receded. By the water, it was a peaceful spring morning. Choripan vendors were setting up their grills and greeted us as we walked by. A portable radio was tuned to a cumbia station.

The song ended and a DJ's slick voice came on: "It's Saturday, September 25, top of the hour, and these are the leading stories of the day. Pedro García, a former high-ranking military officer, is under investigation for his alleged participation in an illegal adoption ring during the last military dictatorship, a crime not covered by the subsequent amnesty laws. In other news…"

The night we dropped off the boxes with Pedro's confession at the *Buenos Aires Herald*, Franco and I returned to his apartment. It had been turned upside down by Pedro García's goons in their failed attempts to find us. To do what? Threaten us? Hurt us? Kidnap us? We did not know. Franco held me. I thought about my mother and all the suffering she had gone through. And about the nameless others who had endured pain, torture, and death during that dark time. And about the simple acts of kindness that some offered to others despite their own suffering. And about people like Franco, who had lost so much and yet remained so generous in spirit.

Later that night, Franco said, "El Angelito knew my mother. She had been at El Vesubio, like your mom. He wanted to tell me how he

had felt a particular pleasure throwing a Montonero out of the plane."
Franco shuddered. I was the one to put my arms around him this time,
and we stayed that way for a long time.

Our mothers had been at the same concentration camp. Had they
been there at the same time? If so, had they talked to one another?
We would never know. The records had been destroyed, so we would
never learn the precise dates. And their remains were still missing.
These agonizing facts filled our conversations in the weeks to come.
Trying to reconstruct an imaginary timeline, we decided not to rule
out the possibility that perhaps our mothers had overlapped at El
Vesubio, and maybe even met. What we did know was that each one of
them had spent her final days at the same concentration camp, and this
certainty, amid so much else that remained unknown, was strangely
comforting.

When we came to a bend in the river where the ecological reserve
began, I looked beyond the reeds and cattails and drew in my breath.
A large group had gathered in a clearing near the water. As we neared,
Máximo was the first one to walk toward us. With him were his parents;
his wife, Agathe; and their children, who rushed over to hug me.
Nora Cassini kissed me several times on both cheeks. I saw Professor
Torres talking to Horacio Lynch, the psychologist and survivor of
a clandestine center in Córdoba. Horacio had been the one to put
Franco in touch with Soledad Goldberg. Soledad was there too. She
held on to Horacio like one might hold on to a tree branch hanging
over a waterfall. Grace Díaz had flown in from Amsterdam. Emily had
flown in the day before as well, and had instantly fallen in love with
Buenos Aires. Viviana Espósito and a few women from the Madres and
Abuelas de Plaza de Mayo were there. Alejandro, Julián, Mateo, Sofía,
and other members of HIJOS surrounded me.

A large photo of Valentina had been set up on an easel on the narrow
shore. Flowers had been placed underneath. Two friends from her
university days began to play and sing folkloric hymns on the guitar.

Today would have been her birthday. She would have been forty-six years old.

Overcome by the unexpected turnout, I sought out Franco, remembering how, before the first morning light, we had clung to one another. Me with my new pain. He with his old. I'd murmured into his ear that his embrace might be the only thing to heal me.

"Then you will stay in my arms until you are fully healed," he commanded in a comical voice.

"Is that an order, Mr. Bonetti?"

"Honestly?" He cupped my jaw, his face suddenly serious. He lowered his mouth onto mine and breathed me in. "I don't know what I'll do with myself if you go back to New York."

Now, wearing that same serious expression, Franco cut through the crowd toward me. He found my hand, and together we watched the attendees, one by one, take a flower and throw it into the river. When it was my turn, I walked to the water's edge. The pendant was in my palm. I brought the stone to my lips, kissed it, and threw it as far out into the water as possible. What I retained from my mother now, intangible yet vibrant, could never again be taken away.

AUTHOR'S NOTE

I grew up in Argentina amid the turmoil of the 1970s until my parents moved our family to North America. We lived in Canada and the United States, and when I completed my graduate studies, I moved back to Buenos Aires. In the late 1990s, I followed with interest the emerging stories of the children of "the disappeared" from Argentina's last military dictatorship. At the time, these children were just coming of age in their teens and early twenties. I attended some of their meetings, and a few of the children let me interview them and document their experiences. Their stories inspired me to write this novel.

The dictatorship lasted from 1976 to 1983. Around that period, between 9,000 and 30,000 people (depending on the source) were forcibly disappeared. It is believed that around 500 babies were born in captivity or kidnapped along with their parents and channeled through the illicit adoption ring run by the regime. According to the Madres and Abuelas de Plaza de Mayo, 130 of those missing babies have been "recovered." It is thought that the others, now in their forties, remain in the dark about their past.

ACKNOWLEDGMENTS

I left Argentina and moved to New York City in the early 2000s. One morning around that time, I woke up to the remnants of a dream about a young woman who uncovers her family's past on a trip back to Buenos Aires. I sensed all those years ago that this story had the potential to become a novel, but none of it would have been possible without the help of numerous people.

First and foremost, I am immensely grateful to the sons and daughters of the *desaparecidos* who shared their stories with me.

Thank you to my agent, Johanna Castillo, who saw the book's potential and guided me with invaluable advice at every stage. Gracias de todo corazón! I am deeply grateful to my editor Karen Kosztolnyik, whose thoughtful reading improved the book immeasurably. Many thanks to Ben Sevier, Brian McClendon, Matthew Ballast, Andy Dodds, Tiffany Porcelli, Rachael Kelly, Alison Lazarus, Ali Cutrone, Karen Torres, Albert Tang, and the rest of the incredible team at Grand Central Publishing. Thank you, also, to Wendolyne Sabrozo and Erin Patterson at Writers House.

I owe special gratitude to Valerie Thomas, who helped craft this story in its earliest iterations, and for her encouragement when I set out to write the novel. I wish to thank my literary godmother Greer Hendricks, as well as Janice Y.K. Lee and Jennifer Egan for their insights and guidance. A big thank-you to Molly Schulman and Elaine Colchie for their editorial suggestions, and to friends and family who took the time to read early drafts or provide other support along the way, including: María Soloeta, Kathryn Murdoch, Brooke Russell, Jhumpa Lahiri, Juana Eggimann, Heather Mitchell, Rachel Horowitz, Lucía López Gaffney, Fabian Spagnoli, Alexandra Milchan, Paula Campos, Milena Alberti, Julie Richardson, Jessie Sheehan, Mark Roybal, Jordanna Freiberg, Nick Kurzon, Deborah Yaryura, Olivia Yaryura, Mackenzie Yaryura, Connor Yaryura, Sheila Clark, Fugen Neziroglu, Soraya Chemaly, Michele Balfour Nathoo, Toland Sherriff, Electra Reed, Beth Forhman, Lisa Immordino Vreeland, Adrienne Wilson, Napua Davoy, and all my book club friends.

Santiago and Valentina's story unfolds in the tumultuous world of Argentina in the1970s, and I could not have navigated this complex period without relying on the accounts of talented journalists, historians, and other observers of the period. Though these are too numerous to name, I am especially indebted to the work of Marcelo Larraquy, Uki Goñi, Jacobo Timmerman, Horacio Verbitsky, Rita Arditti, Federico Lorenz, Robert Cox (former editor of the *Buenos Aires Herald*) and Horacio Mendez Carreras (an attorney for the French families of the disappeared).

Thank you to my siblings Ana María, Ricardo, and Adriana, and to my mother, Roberta, for their love and unflagging support.

In loving memory of my brother Roberto and my father, José Aníbal.

Lastly and, most importantly, all my love and gratitude to Simon and our sons, Cameron and Lucas.

READING GROUP GUIDE

QUESTIONS FOR READERS

1. The novel alternates between the perspectives of Paloma in 1998 and Valentina in 1973. What parallels did you draw between both characters' lives in terms of passion and personality? Did you prefer one timeline to the other?

2. In the first half of the novel, we see the gradual erosion of civil liberties in Argentina, such as the elimination of the free press, the acceleration of arrests, and the state's sponsorship of the Argentine Anticommunist Alliance. How did these changes lay the foundation for the atrocities that were later committed by the dictatorship? Were you familiar with Argentina's "Dirty War" before reading *On a Night of a Thousand Stars*? How did reading about these events affect you?

3. HIJOS, the Sons and Daughters for Identity and Justice Against Oblivion and Silence, and the Madres and Abuelas de Plaza de Mayo, Mothers and Grandmothers of the Plaza de Mayo, were formed to expose the human rights violations committed during the dictatorship, and overturn the regime's mandate of Silence Is Health. "The only course of action was for us to become activists," said Franco in Chapter Twenty-One. "Our

mission is to reveal the truth. We won't remain silent and let our country continue to bury its past." What would it mean to dedicate your life to a cause with so few answers and so much pain? How do groups like HIJOS support and protect one another while pursuing such difficult work?

4. In Chapter Nine, Paloma meets Martín Torres, a professor at the University of Buenos Aires. He is one of the many people Paloma's father, Santiago, helped to flee the country in the 1970s. Torres tells Paloma about Argentina's democratic election in 1983, when Raúl Alfonsín was elected president: "Many decided to stay in their adopted countries. Those who came back to Argentina soon understood that living in exile had changed them in ways they hadn't foreseen. They would remain foreigners when they returned to their homeland." In light of this statement, why do you believe Martín Torres called his first book *Death by Exile*? How else does the theme of displacement present itself in the novel?

5. As an architect, Valentina's greatest desire was to provide affordable housing, as she believed everyone had the right to adequate shelter. How else did Valentina's creative and professional aspirations reflect her social and political leanings?

6. In Chapter Eighteen, the nuns look benevolently upon Valentina and Máximo, "seeing something of themselves in these young people's desire to improve the world, if only with small actions." In your own life, how have small actions led to big changes? How have young people in recent generations worked together to bring about a better world?

7. Could you find any similarities between Santiago, Máximo, and Franco's aspirations for Argentina? Where did their dreams for their country overlap—and where did their worldviews diverge? How did Franco's Argentina differ from Santiago and Máximo's?

8. In Chapter Twenty-Two, Valentina decides to commit to her relationship with Máximo and end her affair with Santiago. In his sadness, Santiago concedes that the two are a more "natural fit" for one another because of their passionate desire to help the poor and shared socio-economic background. Do you agree or disagree with Santiago's assessment here? What do you believe is most important when it comes to cultivating and sustaining romantic love?

9. In Chapter Twenty-Five, at the pizzeria with Franco, Paloma admits that she feels more at home in Argentina than she does in New York, despite being born and raised in the city. Franco replies: "Your heritage is in you. You can't change who you are just by being born somewhere else." Discuss the sense of home and homeland in the novel and the benefits and disadvantages of being raised in two cultures. How much does a physical place—or the absence of it—characterize a person?

10. The lives of so many characters in the novel are defined by events that transpired under the dictatorship. Have any world events played a defining role in your life? Are you generally influenced by politics?

11. How did learning of Santiago's revolutionary leanings change Paloma's preconceptions of her father? Have you ever learned

something about a parent that changed your understanding of who they are—and who you are by extension?

12. Family, both biological and chosen, is an important theme in *On a Night of a Thousand Stars*. In your opinion, what is it, exactly, that makes someone family? Is it blood? Marriage? The choice to share your life with someone? How would you cope with the destabilization of your family unit, as Paloma did?

13. In the Epilogue, Franco tells Paloma that their mothers spent their final days at the same concentration camp, a notion that comforts them both. Do you believe in destiny or coincidence? Have you ever felt like a greater force has been at play in your own life?

Q&A WITH
ANDREA YARYURA CLARK

Q: **What kind of research did you do for** *On a Night of a Thousand Stars*, **and how long did the process take? What was your most surprising discovery?**

A: My research dates back to when I was living in Buenos Aires in the late 1990s (the same era as Paloma and Franco's story in the novel). It began when a family friend, a human rights lawyer, told me about a group that was meeting weekly, whose members were children of the Disappeared. The children were now young adults, coming of age about twenty years after the 1976 military coup.

These gatherings, held at a Human Rights Center for Families of the Disappeared/Detained for Political Reasons, were under the umbrella of a recently-formed national organization known as HIJOS, which stands for "*Hijos por la Identidad y la Justicia contra el Olvido y el Silencio*" (Sons and Daughters for Identity and Justice Against Oblivion and Silence). I attended a few HIJOS meetings and, after gaining their trust, asked certain members of the group if I could document their stories. I initially envisioned making a documentary and filmed several of the subjects, both in interview settings and going about their daily lives. I also wrote a few drafts of creative nonfiction and even took a stab at a screenplay based around these narratives. Although this material never evolved into a viable product, the stories stayed with me. Years later, they would serve as the inspiration for the novel.

The book in its current form took about seven years to write. Originally, it focused more on Paloma's journey, but after some excellent feedback, I realized I needed to spend more time with Valentina and Santiago in the 1970s. Before delving deeply into their story, I did more research. Books that were helpful included: Marcelo Larraquy's *The 70s, A Violent History*; Horacio Verbitsky's *The Flight*; Uki Goñi's *The Real Odessa*; Rita Arditti's *Searching for Life*; Jacobo Timerman's *Prisoner Without a Name, Cell Without a Number*; and *Never Again*, a compilation of survivors' depositions prepared by CONADEP, the Argentine National Commission on the Disappearance of Persons. I also studied old issues of popular magazines, newspaper articles, watched movies, and conversed with family and other contacts who lived through those times.

My most surprising discovery during this process was how much I personally began to recall about those years. Childhood memories of daily life in Buenos Aires, including a few encounters with the security forces, came flooding back. I remembered my friend's older sister, a university student, suddenly leaving Buenos Aires one day. I later found out, as an adult, that one of her classmates had disappeared, and that she had left the city fearing she might also be targeted.

Q: *On a Night of a Thousand Stars* takes place in the context of true events. What license did you give yourself to write imaginatively while re-creating historical persons and events?

A: I'm not a historian, and the era in which Valentina and Santiago's story unfolds—from Perón's return in 1973 to the beginning of the military dictatorship in 1976—was a particularly bewildering and complex time in Argentina's history. I worked hard to grasp the relevant historical figures and timeline of events. At the same time, this is fiction, so mainly I let my characters guide me through the landscape. Valentina and Santiago appear, at first, to be the architects of their own destinies, but eventually larger forces overtake them.

I was living in Buenos Aires during both periods when the novel takes place: the 1970s and the 1990s. My family left the country in 1975, when I was in middle school, and I returned as a young professional in 1992, making Argentina my home again for another eight years. I remember being surprised by the absence of any talk about the dictatorship among my relatives and friends. Simultaneously, I understood how difficult it might be for a country to confront its troubling past.

Salman Rushdie once wrote, "The only people who see the whole picture are the ones who step outside the frame." I would never presume to say I see the whole picture—certainly not a picture as complex as Argentina in this period. That said, I believe that leaving the country as a child gave me a certain distance and perspective that were key to being able to write this novel.

Q: Take us through some of the choices you made while writing in terms of structure, voice, plot, and scene setting.

A: There were two stories I needed to tell: the experiences of young adults in the years leading up to the dictatorship, and the discovery a daughter makes about her family's past. I wanted to alternate chapters between both timelines, and found that the stories developed at a similar pace, which pleased me enormously. Initially, I wrote Paloma in the third person, but then I tried her in the first person and that's when her voice really came through.

I knew from the beginning how the story would end, as it sadly had to follow the fates of the thousands of Disappeared. The mystery for me, therefore, was in crafting how the characters' journeys would unfold, and learning more about them along the way.

Q: Are there any "behind-the-scenes" details that didn't make it into the book?

A: Several! I was deeply engaged with all my characters, including the ones who didn't get much space on the page, like Máximo Cassini, Martín Torres, and Soledad Goldberg. For example, in a very early draft, I wrote about Soledad's family's experience when she disappeared and how their neighbors ostracized her (and her parents) when she returned home. I included passages from Professor Torres's memoir about his years in exile in Spain, and I described Máximo's time as a political refugee in France. I also had more detail about Paloma's life as a privileged teenager in New York, and at one point, even Pedro García had a couple of short chapters devoted to him. Even though these pages didn't make it into the final version, writing them further enriched my understanding of these characters. (And some of these tangents have provided ideas for a future book.)

Q: How did you deal with the emotional impact of writing a story that hinges on such a troubling and heartbreaking period in history?

A: It is difficult knowing that my characters, having only recently embarked on their existence as adults with all their hopes and dreams, would have the course of their lives changed in profound and violent ways. When writing difficult passages, I often found solace in music. I listened to a lot of Argentine artists, everything from tango to folk to *rock nacional.* Listening to music brought me closer to the places and events I was trying to re-create.

There are also elements of fear and menace in the book, and I felt these emotions at a personal level more than I expected, and more than I ever had before. My family left Argentina several months before the coup. Knowing what I now know, I realize how lucky we were to leave when we did. My father was a prominent psychiatrist and a published author, and intellectuals were viewed with suspicion by the security forces at the time. Although the circumstances of my family's departure were multi-layered, my father had experienced and witnessed enough to know it was a good time to leave the country.

Q: What, in your opinion, are the most important elements of good writing?

A: I don't have any formal creative writing training and am tempted to look up what creative writing professors have to say about this!

As a reader, I consider good writing to be any story that transports me, teaching me something along the way. Complicated ideas, emotions, or story lines that are conveyed simply also qualify as good writing for me.

As a writer, I find that writing from the heart usually gives me rich material to work from. Once I have a rough first draft, it's time to revise. This is where structure, logic, and coherence need to be addressed (and where more new ideas may emerge). Relentlessly trimming the "fat" improves my writing too. If a scene doesn't move the story forward, it needs to go. Finally, I try to pick the best possible words to create simple, clear sentences.

Q: Describe your writing space and take us through your process. Any interesting quirks?

A: Given how long it took me to write the book, I have had the pleasure of occupying various writing spaces: cafés, the dining room table while the kids are at school, a friend's borrowed cabin in Maine, a hotel room with a desk. Luckily, I can often tune out whatever is going on around me if I'm wearing headphones, listening to music. I love listening to music, especially during the early stages—it feeds my imagination!

We recently moved into a bigger place in Brooklyn and, for the first time, I have my own office. It's a narrow space, but it has a window that looks out onto a ginkgo tree. I usually light a candle and leave my cell phone outside the room. My plants, my books, and my dog keep me company. I prefer writing in the morning. Sometimes I have to trick myself into sitting at my desk. I tell myself all I have to do is write one page, or review only what I wrote the day before. Or, if researching, I have to look up just that one article, or if revising, go through just one edited chapter. Next thing I know, I have been fooled and am immersed in the project once again.

Q: Which books or authors have most influenced your life? Have you ever read something that made you feel or think differently about fiction? Did a particular story or novel influence the way you wrote *On a Night of a Thousand Stars*?

A: I'm drawn to books that read as if someone is telling me a story out loud. The writing flows in an uncomplicated, conversational (or confessional!) way. Elena Ferrante, Sigrid Nunez, Kazuo Ishiguro, to name a few.

I equally love reading books so beautifully written that after one or two pages I may pause and meditate on what I just read. Toni Morrison, Marilynne Robinson and Tracy K. Smith come to mind.

These powerful books have expanded my thinking on fiction: Anna Burns's *Milkman*, George Saunders's *Lincoln in the Bardo*, and Jennifer Egan's *A Visit from the Goon Squad*.

I grew up reading North American authors like S. E. Hinton, Judy Blume, Kurt Vonnegut, and John Irving, but I also discovered at a young age in my father's library Latin American authors like Gabriel García Márquez, Ernesto Sabato, Julio Cortázar, and Jorge Luis Borges. Reading authors from around the world reminds me time and again how much we have a shared human experience in our joys, suffering, struggles, and love.

Michael Ondaatje's *The English Patient* influenced the way I approached writing a novel with interplay across two different time periods.

Q: What book do you wish everyone would read?

A: I can't think of just one book—I love and carry many within me!—so here are a few suggestions: Isabel Allende's *The House of the Spirits* and her more recent novel, *A Long Petal of the Sea*; Julia Alvarez's *In the Time of the Butterflies* and *How the Garcia Girls Lost Their Accents*; Imbolo Mbue's *How Beautiful We Were*; and Jhumpa Lahiri's *The Lowland*.

Ultimately, I hope young people will, at one point or another, come across a book that ignites a love of reading for the rest of their lives.

Q: What do you hope readers will take away from reading your novel?

A: Readers, even those familiar with the history, will hopefully gain new or further insight into this tragic chapter in Argentina's history. My book is a work of fiction, but it was inspired by real people I have met or read about who suffered unspeakable tragedies at the hands of a cruel regime. I have great admiration for those who survived and for those who seek out truth and a measure of justice. I hope I have honored them through this story.

ABOUT THE AUTHOR

Andrea Yaryura Clark grew up in Argentina amid the political turmoil of the 1970s until her family relocated to North America. After completing her university studies, she returned to Buenos Aires to reconnect with her roots. By the mid-1990s, many sons and daughters of the "disappeared"—the youngest victims of Argentina's military dictatorship in the 1970s—were coming of age and grappling with the fates of their families. She interviewed several of these children, and their experiences, not widely known outside of Argentina, inspired her debut novel. She lives in Brooklyn with her husband, two sons, and a spirited terrier.